Suzanne Wright lives in England with her husband and two children. When she's not spending time with her family, she's writing, reading or doing her version of housework – sweeping the house with a look.

She's worked in a pharmaceutical company, at a Disney store, at a primary school as a voluntary teaching assistant, at the RSCPA, and has a First Class Honours degree in Psychology and Identity Studies.

As to her interests, she enjoys reading, writing, reading, writing (sort of eat, sleep, write, repeat), spending time with her family, movie nights with her sisters and playing with her two Bengal kittens.

To connect with Suzanne online:

Website: http://www.suzannewright.co.uk
Facebook: https://www.facebook.com/suzannewrightfanpage
Twitter: https://twitter.com/suz_wright
Blog: http://www.suzannewrightsblog.blogspot.co.uk

THE DARK IN YOU SERIES

Burn
Blaze
Ashes
Embers
Shadows
Omens

SUZANNE WRIGHT

FALLEN

A *Dark in You* novel

PIATKUS

PIATKUS

First published in Great Britain in 2021 by Piatkus

1 3 5 7 9 10 8 6 4 2

All characters and events in this publication, other than those clearly in the public domain, are fictitious and any resemblance to real persons, living or dead, is purely coincidental.

A CIP catalogue record for this book is available from the British Library.

ISBN 978-0-349-42846-8

Typeset in Goudy by M Rules
Printed and bound in Great Britain by
Clays Ltd, Elcograf S.p.A.

Papers used by Piatkus are from well-managed forests and other responsible sources.

MIX
Paper from responsible sources
FSC® C104740

Piatkus
An imprint of
Little, Brown Book Group
Carmelite House
50 Victoria Embankment
London EC4Y 0DZ

An Hachette UK Company
www.hachette.co.uk

www.littlebrown.co.uk

For everyone in my reader's group. You're an amazing bunch of people who never fail to make me smile—and I'm not much of a smiler.

CHAPTER ONE

Switching off the ignition, Raini Campbell let out a shaky breath. She could hear the thumping music filtering out of the nightclub up ahead. There was a long line of people waiting to enter, just as there had been on the first and only other time she'd come to the Damned.

Raini felt her hands flex around the steering wheel. She'd sworn she'd never come back here. She'd sworn she'd keep her distance from *him*. And she really would have. Probably. But right now, she needed help. Needed intel. And Maddox Quentin, well, he was a man who *knew* things. A powerful Prime who gathered information for a living.

He was also a descendant—a breed of demon that possessed angelic blood, since one of their earliest ancestors had been a fallen angel. She'd once heard that some archangels had fallen, too. Right now, she *desperately* needed the aid of one, but there was no way to contact an archangel, and they had no interest in Earth-related matters anyway. A demon with archangelic blood, though? They might be able and willing to help. If such a being existed, surely Maddox would know about it.

Of course, there was no saying that he'd tell her if he did. He was her anchor—or predestined psychic mate, to be precise—but they hadn't bonded. Which was why her inner demon was perpetually pissed these days. It had initially been excited on finding its anchor. But the longer he'd gone without trying to form the bond, the more the entity felt the urge to rip out his spinal cord.

Demons came in pairs, but it wasn't an emotional pairing like with shifters; it was purely psychic. When a demon fused their psyche with that of their anchor, an unbreakable link formed that enabled them both to have the power, strength, and mental stability to assert dominance over their inner entity. This meant they would never turn rogue—something that could otherwise easily happen, given how difficult it was to share your soul with what was essentially a psychopath.

Anchors were utterly loyal to each other and played a big part in each other's lives. Growing up, Raini had longed to find her own; to have someone who'd support and shield her, who she could trust wholeheartedly. And now she'd found him. Only . . . he wasn't what she'd expected.

Maddox Quentin was cold. Unremorseful. Calculated. Not to be trusted. Possessed few ethics.

Now, to be fair, some would say the latter two qualities could also be applied to not only her father but the majority of her lair—imps specialized in everything from lying and thievery to embezzlement and identity theft. But Maddox was *far* more ruthless than they could ever be. He brokered the kind of deals that others wouldn't touch; the kind that had people *kidnapped*, for Christ's sake.

More, he was a man who knew how to ferret out secrets. That

wasn't good. Because Raini needed hers to stay hidden. Which was largely why she'd been set on keeping her distance from him. If he'd *wanted* to form the bond, it would have been different, because she could have trusted that he'd never betray her confidence. But he had no interest in claiming her as his anchor.

Still, he hadn't turned his back on her. He telepathically reached out to her on a daily basis, even though she never replied. And she suspected he had some of his lair members subtly check on her occasionally. But that didn't mean he'd help her now.

Who would, in his position?

She'd ignored him for *months*. She'd been intent on cutting him out of her life. And now she was appearing at his club to ask something of him. It made her seem like a total bitch, but she wouldn't so unfairly do this if it wasn't an emergency.

Her girls—women she'd grown up with, built up a business with, and who'd always been there for her—were more like her honorary sisters, and she loved them with everything in her. Now, one of them was dying. Khloë was literally on her deathbed, her body ravaged by the death essence that flowed through her. And they were all helpless to save her.

Raini closed her eyes. Dread twisted her stomach, thickened her throat, and made hot tears burn the backs of her eyes. If there was one person who deserved to live—who knew *how* to live—it was Khloë. But only pure life could destroy death essence, and so they needed an archangel. A demon with archangelic blood would be the next best thing.

Maybe such beings existed, maybe they didn't. Maybe they could help, maybe they couldn't. Raini had nothing to lose by trying to find out. So she did another thing she'd sworn she'd never do. She telepathically reached out to Maddox. *I'm outside your club.*

His mind slid against hers, coldly sensual and far too familiar. *I know.*

Raini jerked back in her seat. The fuck? How could he possibly—*cameras*, she remembered. The first time she'd come here, she'd noted the security cameras in the lot. Not out of any interest in them, but because her father had made it instinctive for her to spot them. He'd also taught her how to disable security systems, but that was off-topic.

She licked her lips and reached out to Maddox again. *I need to talk to you. It's important.*

Then why are you out there instead of in here? he asked, cool and airy.

It wasn't exactly a welcoming invitation to enter the club, but it seemed that he was prepared to hear her out. Which, to her shame, was probably more than she would have done if he'd come looking for her.

She slipped out of the car and crossed the lot, her hand clenched tight around her keys. A bulky male stepped out of the shadows—one she recognized as a member of Maddox's lair, though she'd never spoken with him. Descendants were pretty insular and had no time or regard for other breeds of demon.

As the guy's eyes met hers, his pupils dilated, his breath caught, and his skin flushed—like arousal had smacked him right in the gut. Yeah, being a succubus meant she often had that effect on people. Her kind exuded a preternatural allure. They could turn the dial up on that allure; could scramble thoughts, lift inhibitions, and assail "prey" with a terrible lust that drew them in. Succubae could even snare people, making them obsessed.

She was basically a walking, talking sexual pheromone. Raini mostly hated it, because she never knew if a guy was truly drawn to her as a person or merely a "victim" of the succubae package.

Plus, many men assumed that her being a sex demon also meant she'd be happy to jump into bed with just about anyone. And how uber special was that?

Although Maddox didn't *appear* to be affected by her preternatural allure, she suspected he was to some extent. It seemed the likeliest explanation as to why he persisted in contacting her.

She broke eye-contact with the descendant in front of her and cleared her throat. She looked back just as he double-blinked and rolled his shoulders.

"Follow me," he said, gruff but not rude. He didn't take her through the main entrance. He led her around the side of the building and over to a steel door. He punched a code into the keypad on the wall and then opened the door.

She followed him inside and over to an elevator. He held a keycard up to a small, electronic screen. The shiny metal doors then slid open, and she stepped inside. He didn't join her. He reached inside, pressed the "up" button on the panel, and then backed away.

The elevator whirred to life and began to smoothly ascend. Knowing it would be a humungous mistake to let her inner turmoil show, she did her best to wipe every trace of anxiety from her face. Maddox Quentin was an apex predator—showing weakness in front of him would be a bad idea.

He was also an opportunist who wouldn't hesitate to take advantage of this situation for his own gain. If he could and did agree to help her, that help wouldn't come for free. He'd once said that the idea of having Knox Thorne owe him a favor would appeal to him. And since Khloë was both a close cousin of Knox's mate and a member of his lair, Knox would no doubt grant Maddox whatever favor he requested.

When the metal doors opened, Raini stepped out . . . and found herself in a very spacious office. It was swanky with the executive, L-shaped desk, the leather desk chair, the comfy seating area, and the overly large aquarium. Monitors featuring CCTV feeds hung on one wall. The floor-to-ceiling glass window overlooked the club floor below. But none of that held her attention. Because there was really no way *not* to focus on the alarmingly magnetic male who stood a few feet away—tall, still, watchful.

Right on cue, her hormones tripped all over themselves.

Um, had she mentioned that he was hot as holy hell? Probably not. She tended to try to overlook that. But, really, it was impossible. You couldn't overlook a tower of sheer power, solid muscle, blatant danger, and dark sexual energy. Particularly when it was wholly focused on you.

His disturbingly vacant eyes were a very vivid Prussian blue that seemed to hold an element of power—*compelling* you to make eye-contact. His short, stylishly tousled hair was black as the sea at night, and *damn* that mouth was all kinds of sinful. His white, crisp shirt looked perfectly tailored to fit his broad shoulders and hard chest that—

Hell, this wasn't the time to ogle him. She was there for a *reason*. A very, very good one. So her hormones would just have to get their shit together.

He didn't greet her. Didn't ask why she was there. Didn't look all smug and triumphant at the fact that she'd come to him, which surprised her. He simply waited.

Conscious of the time ticking by, she took a single step toward him. "I'll understand if you tell me to fuck off—I wouldn't even blame you for it. I've done nothing that would give me the right to come to you for help, but I don't know who else to ask."

He still didn't speak. He just kept watching her, expectant.

"I realize this is a long shot, but you're the only person I know who might be able to point me in the right direction. I once heard that it wasn't only angels that fell from heaven long ago; that some archangels fell along with them and copulated with demons."

His expression didn't whatsoever change, giving her no hint as to whether the rumor had any substance.

"Do you know of anyone who might have descended from archangels?"

His eyes narrowed *ever* so slightly. "Why?" he asked, his authoritative voice pitched low and deep.

She'd never admit it aloud, but she liked his voice. Liked hearing it in her mind. Still, she'd never replied to any of his mundane, throwaway questions. She *definitely* hadn't replied when he straight up told her he wanted to strip her naked and feast on every inch of her.

"I really need to get in touch with one," she told him.

"And why would that be?"

She opened her mouth to reply, but a ball of emotion clogged her throat. She didn't want to speak the words. Saying it aloud would make it real. Still, she swallowed hard and forced herself to respond, "My friend, Khloë . . . she's dying." The words sounded like crushed rock.

Not even a *flicker* of emotion crossed his face. "She's injured?"

"Yes and no. She was hit by an orb of death essence. Twice. She doesn't have long left." Raini felt tears pool in her eyes, but she didn't bother to wipe them away. There'd be no hiding them from him. "An angel tried to help her but couldn't. I know it's possible that a demon who's descended from an archangel might be just as useless to her, but I can ask."

Maddox stared at her long and hard, much like he had the first night they met. A smile didn't touch his mouth this time, though. His face remained an impassive mask as that vacant stare drank her in for what felt like minutes.

She went to push for an answer, but then finally he moved. Her pulse began to quicken as he started to cross the space between them, each step slow and purposeful.

His eyes flitted over her face, which was no doubt lined with her fear for Khloë. "It wasn't easy for you to come to me," he sensed.

No, it hadn't been. It had meant breaking all sorts of promises she'd made to herself.

His gaze tracked the path of a tear that had dripped down one side of her face. He gently thumbed it away. "She means so much to you?"

Raini swallowed around the hard knot that wouldn't leave her throat. "Yes." And if she had to beg him for help, she would. She wasn't too proud to do it if it meant that Khloë would live.

He twisted his mouth. "I can heal her."

For a moment, Raini could only stare at him, shocked. "You … *you* can heal her?" she asked, embers of hope flickering to life in her belly. At the same time, though, a hint of unease snaked through her, because it meant he possessed the blood of both a demon and an archangel—that could never be a good mix.

"Yes." He dipped his head, his eyes snaring hers. "But you'll owe me."

"Fine," she blurted out, even as it surprised her that he wouldn't seek a favor from Knox.

"You don't know what I want from you yet."

"It doesn't matter. All I care about right now is Khloë."

"Exactly. That's all you care about *right now*. But later," he began, ghosting the tip of his index finger down the side of her face, "when you're no longer feeling so desperate, you might find yourself regretting the deal you made here. Then you'll try to wriggle out of our agreement."

"No, I won't. I keep my word. Just tell me what you want."

"You're sure you want to be indebted to me, Raini?"

Want to be? No. But she'd agree to owe him for Khloë's sake. "I'm sure."

"I have several conditions," he warned.

"Hit me with them."

"All right." He edged into her personal space, swallowing it up, bold as you please. "From now on, you'll respond whenever I telepath you—no more ignoring me."

"No more ignoring you," she agreed.

"You also won't obstruct any of my attempts to make you safe, and you won't allow your friends or lair members to do it either. We might not be bonded, but you still belong to me. It's my right to protect you. I'm claiming that right."

Raini gritted her teeth, battling back the urge to point out he had no business claiming *any* rights, all things considered. "Fine."

"Thirdly, you will telepathically reach for me if you are ever injured, no matter how small that injury is."

She frowned. "You're saying, what, you can heal wounds?"

"Yes. So if you are hurt, no matter how minor the injury, you will reach for me. You will not suffer unnecessarily."

"Okay." It wasn't like she *enjoyed* pain or anything. "Is that all?"

"No. You will come to me once a month. You will spend a few hours here each time so that my demon can see for itself that you're well."

Annoyance flared through her. Essentially, he was picking and choosing what parts of the anchor situation he wanted, wasn't he? He wanted access to her. Wanted her acceptance. Wanted to claim his right to protect her. But he didn't want to bond with her, he didn't want to be the anchor she'd been waiting for, which hurt like hell and made her demon want to throat punch him. This here and now wasn't about Raini or her entity, though. It was about *Khloë.*

A face-to-face meeting once a month wouldn't be so bad. She could still keep him in the dark about a lot of things. Raini shrugged. "Fine. Okay. Deal."

"I'm not done. There's something else I want you to agree to. And you're not going to like it."

He told her his final condition, and her mouth fell open. "You can't be serious."

"I'm perfectly serious."

She frowned, flapping her arms. "But . . . why? Why would you ask this of me? It's not like I'm important to you."

"Just because I don't want the bond doesn't mean you don't matter to me."

"Funny. Because it doesn't *feel* like I do."

"And other than not form the bond, what have I done to suggest that you don't matter?"

She opened her mouth . . . and then realized she had nothing. He truly hadn't done anything that would indicate she was insignificant to him. Quite the opposite, in fact, given that he continued to telepathically reach out to her despite that his efforts came to nothing. He'd never once vilified her for ignoring him. And even now, when he'd have every right and reason to send her on her way, he was agreeing to help. Yes, he had conditions, but it was better than him turning her request down altogether. Still . . . "Can we not scrap this last condition?"

He slowly shook his head. "If it was related to anything other than your safety, I might consider it."

Doubtful. Maddox was a man who'd insist on having his way in all things. She flexed her fingers. "It would give you too much power."

"I don't want power over you, Raini."

"Sure you do. Anyone can sense you're a guy who likes to control his environment, and I suspect you're very skilled at it."

He gave a small shrug, not bothering to deny it. "This wouldn't enable me to control you, though, would it? The only power it will truly give me is the power to pull you out of any form of danger." He toyed with a few locks of her blonde, pink-streaked hair. "I don't intend to hide who you are to me. Few people are aware of it right now because we haven't been seen together. But that will change, and the news will soon spread. I have enemies who may think to strike at me through you. So no, I won't consider dropping this final condition."

Raini bit back a curse. She understood his reasoning, but she didn't want to agree to this. Khloë would have done it for her, though, if the situation were reversed. She would have agreed to just about anything to save Raini.

"I will heal your friend, I will rid her system of every ounce of death essence, but this is my price." His brow inched up. "Are you prepared to pay it?"

Raini didn't hesitate to answer, because there really was only one answer, even if it wasn't one that she liked. "Yes. Whatever. Deal. As long as you heal Khloë first."

His eyes narrowed, but he inclined his head. "I can agree to that. Tomorrow, however, you will come back here to me so I can—"

"I will, I promise. So can we *please* go now? I don't think she has much time left."

His eyes searched hers for long seconds. Finally, he nodded. "We can go."

CHAPTER TWO

Four months later

Khloë slammed down the phone and whirled around, placing her hands on her hips. "That is the fifth cancellation we've had this week. *The fifth.*"

Harper tilted her head. "Be honest, what bothers you more? The number of cancellations, or the fact that it's an uneven number?"

The OCD receptionist sniffed. "I don't see how that's relevant."

Raini rolled her eyes and went back to wiping down the checkered partition that stood between her station and that of her business partner, Harper. Devon, who did both tattoos and piercings, had her own station adjacent to theirs. They were all readying the place to be shut down for the night, which was why the scents of citrus cleaner and disinfectant now almost completely overrode the smells of paint and ink.

"Seriously, this isn't good," Khloë pressed. "It's one thing to know that someone's trying to get people to boycott Urban Ink by sending our clients gift cards for other tattoo studios. It's another to know that it's *working*."

Putting away her equipment, Harper sighed. "I know. I'm still struggling to understand why anyone would bother to make this play. Well, I can see why the owners of the other tattoo shops around here would bother. But Knox confirmed that it wasn't them."

Probably by scanning their minds, Raini thought, adjusting the position of her station's black leather recliner. "Whoever's behind it could be someone that one of us pissed off." She exchanged looks with both Harper and Devon, who each nodded.

Khloë frowned, her head jerking back. "Why are you all staring at me?"

"You fuck with people like it's your job," Devon pointed out.

"It's good for the soul," defended Khloë. "Anyway, *I'm* leaning more toward the theory that it's an indirect attack on our lair." She looked at Harper. "I mean, three of the four people who work here are part of said lair, and you're the co-Prime of it. Moreover, you also own half of Urban Ink."

Raini kind of missed the time when they were all part of the same lair. But after Harper met and mated with her anchor, Knox, she transferred to his lair and now ruled it alongside him. Devon had later mated one of his sentinels, Tanner, and Khloë had mated another of the sentinels, Keenan, so both girls had also switched lairs.

Knowing her girls were so happy with their mates, Raini was thrilled for them all, but she suspected she would have felt somewhat . . . left behind, maybe, if Khloë had moved out of the neighborhood and into Keenan's apartment. Instead, he'd moved into the imp's home, which was very close to Raini's.

"Knox thinks the same," said Harper. "He'll keep looking into it. We'll find out who's playing these games eventually. They seem seriously petty to me." The sphinx's gaze slid to Raini. "Speaking of petty . . . is your sister speaking to you again yet?"

Raini felt her lips thin. "No." But Demi had frozen her out so many times over the years that it no longer stung.

Harper shook her head. "If she's going to be mad at someone, it should be Dwain the Dweeb, who needs to go home *yesterday*."

Oh, Raini couldn't agree more. Her sister's anchor was an irritating asshole at times. "He wants to spend a little more time with his family and my sister so they can get to know his brand spanking new mate."

"Grams said she got the impression that Dwain wants it to bother you that he's now mated," said Harper, whose grandmother—Jolene Wallis—was the Prime of Raini's lair.

"I can't think why he would. It's not like his past feelings for me were real." Raini crossed to the reception area and used the remote control to switch off the wall-mounted TV. "Succubae snares wear off unless the succubae wills them not to, and I didn't snare him on purpose—he just fell into it."

"It happens. Some demons are susceptible to them," said Devon, cleaning her station's large wall-mounted mirror. "If your sister had been a succubus like you and your mom instead of an imp like your dad, Dwain probably would have been enchanted by Demi instead."

"Probably." Raini placed the remote on the coffee table, careful not to knock off the portfolios. "I hate that he doesn't see how much he's hurting Demi right now."

"What *I* hate," began Khloë, "is that your own sister blames *you* for the fact that she's hurting. It is *not* your fault that Demi fell for her anchor. It is *not* your fault that he fell for you. And it is *definitely* not your fault that he's now mated to someone else."

No, it wasn't, but . . . "In Demi's mind, if I hadn't rejected him, he wouldn't have moved away, and she and him would have gotten together eventually."

Harper frowned. "But if you hadn't rejected him, Demi would have hated you for dating the man she loves, so there's really no way you can win here."

"Oh, I know. But she never lets reason or rationality get in the way." Most imps didn't, to be fair.

"Do you think Dwain knows how Demi really feels about him?" asked Devon, idly fiddling with a pen from the reception desk. The hellcat scowled when Khloë snatched it from her and put it on a *very* specific spot on her desk.

"I don't think so," replied Raini. "He cares for her a lot. If he'd known this news would hurt her, he would have told her in private, not sucker-punched her with it by just turning up unannounced and saying, 'Meet Harmony, my mate.'"

"I don't like Demi, never have," Devon said to Raini. "Mostly because she's always been pissy toward *you*. So I'm finding it hard to feel bad for her right now, but I'll keep trying."

Raini snickered. She and Demi were like chalk and cheese, and they'd never gotten along. The whole mess with Dwain only made it worse. "To her credit, she hasn't been rude or unwelcoming toward Harmony. She hasn't tried to taint this for Dwain. Only those who know her well can sense she's hurting."

"Well, let me tell you, Grams is *furious* with him for being so blind to it," said Harper.

"Yeah, I picked up on that easily enough. She often looks at him as though she'd like nothing better than to skewer him with a spear." It really was a pleasant visual.

A cold, familiar psyche touched Raini's, and then Maddox's voice flowed into her mind. *How was work today?*

Coming from anyone else, the mundane out-of-the-blue

question might have seemed like an awkward attempt at small talk. But one thing Raini had learned about Maddox in the past four months was that there was no small talk with him. If he asked you a question, it was because he wanted to know the answer.

He generally didn't bother with hellos. He got straight to the point. Unless, of course, he was toying with someone. He could turn on the charm then, but it was just a mask. He didn't wear it with her. She liked that.

It was fine, she replied. As per their agreement, she always responded now.

Don't forget you're due to come to my club tomorrow.

I won't.

His mind briefly sort of stroked hers, and then he was gone.

She would have thought their little meetings would be awkward and strained, but they weren't. Probably because he only ever asked her simple everyday questions as opposed to anything too personal. She suspected he already knew most of her private business; that he'd already compiled some sort of dossier on her—Maddox provided that service for people for a fee.

Initially, she'd expected him to attempt to seduce her, given his past sexual telepathic whispers. But he'd never once flirted with her or said anything suggestive, although a glitter of heat had occasionally flashed in those usually vacant eyes.

Maybe he'd quite simply decided that introducing sex into the mix would only complicate things. She'd have to agree with him on that. Which both disappointed and relieved her, because she was so very conflicted where he was concerned.

She wanted to dislike him. Wanted to hold that image of him being cruel and malicious in her mind so that she wouldn't lament that he didn't want the bond. But it was hard to truly dislike someone when you couldn't help but feel sorry for them. He was a demon who carried the very potent blood of a powerful archangel. How hard must it be to feel torn on the inside by both dark and light—two such extremes?

You'd exist in the gray.

It explained why his emotions rarely seemed to fluctuate and why very little seemed to touch him. He often made her think of someone walking around an art museum bored out of their mind. He saw everything. Noted everything. Processed it all like it was data. But he didn't really *see* it in a way that allowed him to appreciate it. And that seemed so sad.

Her inner demon wasn't so sympathetic. But then, it wasn't a creature who could feel compassion or empathy. It was too predatory. Too callous. Too dark. And *exceedingly* pissed that their anchor wouldn't just claim them already.

"Hello?" sang Khloë, waving her hand in front of Raini's face. "Raini, this is base, do you copy?"

Snapping back to the present, Raini poked the petite woman's shoulder. "Smartass."

"You had that 'I'm not home right now' look in your eyes that told me you were having a telepathic chat with someone. Was it Maddox?"

"He was just checking in, as usual."

"Hmm." Khloë folded her arms. "Grams said that Demi was smug on hearing that he doesn't want to bond with you."

"Your Grams said it to you, or she said it to someone else and you were eavesdropping?"

"Let's not wander off the subject."

Raini snorted.

"*Is* Demi all smug and shit?" asked Devon, frowning.

"She likes the idea that my anchor rejected me, yes," replied Raini.

Harper's face darkened. "But he hasn't rejected you. He's rejected the bond, which isn't the same thing at all. Doesn't she know he assigned you a guard—one I rarely notice, she's so damn good at subtly watching over you—and had a hi-tech security system installed at your house?"

Both acts had originally annoyed Raini, but he'd ever so kindly reminded her that she'd agreed not to obstruct his attempts to keep her safe. That seemed to be an umbrella term that would let him get away with all kinds of shit. Like when he'd had a protective spell put on her car—it wouldn't stop a crash from happening, but it would keep the vehicle intact, which would mean she'd suffer less injuries.

"Oh, she knows," Raini replied. "But she sees that as him simply giving the impression that he cares."

Harper's brow creased. "Maddox isn't interested in people's impressions of him."

"Well either she hasn't heard about that or just prefers to believe what brings her joy." Raini shrugged. "Whatever the case, she's pleased that he doesn't want to bond with me."

Devon shook her head. "You know, with any luck, she won't come back from her upcoming cruise. Maybe the sea will take her."

"It's more likely to spit her back out." Khloë twisted her mouth, her gaze locked on Raini. "I was sure Maddox wouldn't hold out long; that he'd choose to form the anchor bond at some point. But then you made your little deal with him, so now he's getting the best of both worlds and has *zero* motivation to give in. Don't you know better than to make deals with shady dudes like Maddox Quentin?"

"I wasn't going to let you die." Raini raised a hand. "No, don't start giving me grief again, Wallis. I made a choice, and I don't regret it. You'd have made the same choice if the situation was reversed. You can't say you wouldn't have."

"Actually, I can, because I don't know *exactly* what you

promised him," said Khloë. "Without all the info, I can't make an educated guess as to whether or not I'd truly have agreed to it in your shoes."

"I told you the conditions of the agreement." Mostly.

"No, you told us *some* of them, not all."

Raini had held back the final condition. Why? Because they'd be furious that he'd request such a thing when he wouldn't even bond with her. More, they'd tell Jolene for sure, who'd be equally furious. And when someone was bat-shit crazy right down to the bone and liked to demolish entire buildings when their temper was running high, it was not a good idea for them to be in a fury about anything.

Oh, Jolene would understand Maddox's reasoning. She just wouldn't care. And Raini would really rather not be stuck in the middle of a dispute between her anchor and her Prime.

Besides, what would be the point in bemoaning the situation or having anyone take him to task over exploiting her desperation that night? Raini would never try to renege on a deal, so it wasn't like anything would change.

Khloë sighed. "Look, if you're keeping the rest from me because you worry I'll feel bad that you agreed to this deal to save me from dying, then don't."

Raini rested a hand on the imp's shoulder. "If there's one thing I'll never do, Khloë, it's worry that you'll 'feel bad' about, well, anything. Guilt has never quite been your thing."

"It's a wasteful emotion."

Raini's inner demon happened to agree with that.

Khloë sighed. "I worry about you, that's all. I felt his power flow through me and . . . it was just *so cold*, Raini. Cold, but it burned and prickled. A little like chilblains. And now you . . . Look, don't get me wrong, I'm happy to be alive, I'm grateful he helped. But he's *mega* powerful. Like scary, mega powerful."

"*But*," Harper cut in, "fate wouldn't have paired Raini with him if it didn't feel she could handle him."

Raini inwardly snorted. Maddox wouldn't be easy to deal with unless he was in the mood to be. Which seemed to be never, from what she'd so far observed.

The bell above the door rang as it swung open. Knox entered with three of his sentinels—Tanner, Keenan, and Levi. Naturally, each of the first three males made a beeline for their prospective mate and delivered a few soft, lingering kisses.

"You ready to go home, kitten?" asked Tanner.

Devon smiled at the hellhound. "Almost, pooch."

"I'll just lock the back door," said Harper, who then headed to the rear of the shop.

"I gotta set my desk to rights," Khloë told Keenan, who frowned . . . probably because, to anyone else, the desk looked the epitome of organized.

Watching as Knox and Keenan moved to the side and began talking quietly, Raini felt her mouth tip up. After Khloë almost died, there'd been a short period of time during which the two males hadn't spoken to each other. Raini hadn't understood why. Well, not until she overheard Harper and Keenan talking in the sphinx's office here at Urban Ink a few months ago . . .

"He could have saved her, Harper," Keenan insisted. "He could have stopped her from being hit by the death orb, but he didn't. Aren't you pissed? She's your cousin."

Harper sighed. "Keenan—"

"Hey, I get it, okay. Knox is so good to you and Asher that it can be easy to forget that he's *not good. I know he doesn't have a basic reflex to help others. I know that you and Asher are his priorities and that he'd never help someone—not even himself—if it negatively affected his mate or son. And exposing to everyone that he could call*

on the flames of hell would sure as shit not be good for the family you three have built."

Raini felt her mouth drop open. There'd been rumors that Knox had such an ability, but Raini had hoped they weren't true, because nothing was impervious to the flames of hell—they could destroy the freaking world.

"I do get all that, Harper," Keenan went on, "but—"

"But Khloë's yours, and you love her, and you don't want her to die," Harper finished. "You're wrong in thinking that Knox hesitated that day because he didn't want to expose his ability—he knew he could erase the incident from people's minds."

"Then why did *he hesitate?"*

"I was speaking to him telepathically just before Jolene's shield crumbled. He was so *angry, Keenan. There we all were—tired and injured from a damn battle during which his own son had been fighting alongside us in his astral form . . . and all because someone suspected—simply* suspected*—that Knox possessed the ability to call on the flames.*

"Right then, Knox hated and resented that he had it. The last thing he wanted to do was use it, but he would *have if he'd known that Jolene's shield would fall. He couldn't have known it would. I hadn't. I hadn't thought we'd need the flames. I mean, there was a bunch of us against one man. None of us could have known that Jolene's shield wouldn't survive the final attack. Her shield had cracked a few times during the battle, but it hadn't faltered until then. Knox hates now, with the benefit of hindsight, that he hesitated. You and I both know he wouldn't have held back if he'd thought Khloë would otherwise be hit by that last death orb."*

Keenan said nothing for a few moments. "Why didn't he say any of this to me when I ripped him another asshole?"

"Because he feels that he let you down, so he's not looking for you to forgive him or excuse what decisions he made that night."

Harper paused. "Put yourself in his shoes. If it had been me who Enoch wanted to kill, you'd have been worried for me, but your priority would have still been Khloë. The fact that she was unsafe would have been all you could think about. Fearing for the life of a person you love fucks with your head and makes it hard for you to be rational. You wouldn't have put Khloë's life before mine, would you?"

Keenan exhaled heavily. "No," he admitted, the word seeming torn out of him.

"So you can understand why he didn't put her before me?"

Another heavy exhale from the incubus. "Yeah. And I get why his head was all kinds of messed up after seeing Asher there. I don't think I could have thought straight either, in his shoes."

"So then maybe you could stop hating him."

Keenan softly snorted. "I don't hate Knox. You can't hate someone you walked through fire with for years to come out the other side. He's saved my life more than once."

"And mine. He's almost lost me several times. It plays on his mind that there'll be a 'next time' and I won't survive it."

Keenan sucked in a long breath. "I'll talk to him. I can't say things will get back to normal fast, but I'll talk to him."

"That's all I'm asking."

Raini had walked away after that, so she wasn't sure what else had been said. The conversation between Knox and Keenan must have gone somewhere good, because they'd begun speaking again shortly after Harper spoke with the incubus. Things had seemed a little awkward at first, but not so much now.

She hadn't told anyone what she'd overheard, and she never would. If it was well-known that Knox could truly destroy the world so easily, many demons would band together to kill him. She doubted it would get them anywhere, but they'd still try it. Others would get hurt and potentially die.

Some secrets just couldn't be shared. Raini knew that better than anyone.

Ready to leave, she crossed to the coatrack near the vending machine and slipped on her jacket. "Hey, Levi," she greeted the reaper.

The guy possessed that elusive badass quality that was all kinds of hot. There'd never been any chemistry between him and Raini, though.

He didn't seem affected by her succubae allure, which was part of why she felt comfortable around him. She suspected he was good at treating it as background noise because one of his closest friends was also a sex demon.

He tipped his chin in greeting, his steely eyes sweeping the space. "Where's your bodyguard?"

Raini flicked her hair out from under her collar. "You always ask me that, and you always seem so disappointed in me when I can't give you the answer."

"I'm not disappointed in *you*. I'm disappointed in Maddox. Why put a guard on you if they're not going to do their job?"

"She watches from afar. Kind of like a guardian angel as opposed to personal security. Only she's not an angel. She's a demon. And I don't think she likes me much. When I do see her, she's always frowning at me."

"Who keeps moving my stapler?" Khloë burst out.

Keenan slung one arm around the imp's shoulders. "Maybe it was you."

Khloë frowned and jabbed the desk with her finger. "It goes *there*." She then pointed at a spot a few inches away. "Why would I put it all the way over there?"

The incubus opened and closed his mouth a few times. "Good point."

Soon enough, they'd locked the place up and were beginning

their walk toward the exit of the Las Vegas Underground. The subterranean, demonic paradise had everything from bars and casinos to racing stadiums and rodeos. There were also many small businesses like coffeehouses, bakeries, and delis. It basically had everything that would keep demons—who, by nature, were easily bored thrill-seekers—happy and entertained.

The Underground was owned by Knox . . . as were a lot of things, considering the guy was a billionaire. Being his mate, Harper co-owned most of those things.

Many CEOs were demons. Their kind tended to gravitate toward jobs that provided them with power, respect, and control.

Finally, their group reached the elevator that would take them to the basement of the nightclub that Knox had built above the Underground to conceal its entrance.

After a quick upward trip in the elevator, Levi took the lead as they all filed into the basement, briefly greeting the demons that guarded the elevator.

Heading toward the staircase, Raini looked at Harper. "So how's my little dude, anyway?" she asked, referring to Harper and Knox's son.

"He's just as fine as when you last saw him, which was yesterday," replied Harper. "You always ask as if you haven't seen him in months."

"I like to check. That's what honorary aunts do."

As they reached the staircase, a male shimmered into view on the middle step, a dagger in hand, his eyes filled with intent as he stared at Knox.

The sentinels exploded into action in an instant, surrounding Knox and the girls. Tanner accidentally knocked Raini, who stumbled and crashed into Knox . . . just as the blade hurtled through the air.

She doubled over as white-hot pain thrust into her stomach, shocking the breath out of her lungs and making her heart slam in her chest. Looking down, she frowned at the dagger buried in her stomach. The steel glowed white. *The fuck?*

She heaved in a breath as something . . . God, it was like a magnetic force of some kind was viciously *pulling* at her very being. Pulling and wrenching and *demanding* something from her. The force was so fucking strong, it sent her to her knees.

Orbs of hellfire crashed into the bastard who'd tossed the dagger. He didn't cry out in pain. He just vanished. Mere milliseconds later, he reappeared a few feet away, completely unharmed—no burns, no damage to his clothing, nothing.

Astral projection, she thought. You couldn't kill a projection. Even so, the people around her attacked him.

The power in her belly surged forward, wanting to protect and avenge her. And then that alien magnetic force *pulled* at her power, trying to suck it into the dagger like a fucking hoover. *Oh the hell no.*

She was distantly aware of the mayhem around her—of voices yelling, of hellfire hissing and spitting, of power rippling through the air—but she was mentally caught up in the frightening sensation of her own power leaving her system in small drips.

Raini closed her hand around the hilt of the dagger. Under any other circumstances, removing the blade wouldn't be wise, considering it was currently staunching the flow of blood. But this dagger . . . it had to be removed. First, she wanted what it had fucking *stolen* from her.

Gritting her teeth, Raini fought the magnetic force, wrenching back dreg after dreg of her power. And, God, it *hurt*. She honestly worried the veins in her temples would pop from the strain.

Her head pounded. Her teeth chattered. Her vision began

to blur and dim around the edges. But she didn't stop. She kept fighting. Kept taking back what was hers.

And then she had it.

Raini yanked out the dagger, hissing at the white-hot slash of agony. Warm blood soaked her dress, and her world tilted. Oh, this wasn't good.

Before she'd even thought about it, she reached out to the one demon that could help her. *Maddox*, she managed to say just as someone crouched at her side and grabbed her arm.

What is it? demanded Maddox, a snap in his voice.

Before Raini had the chance to respond, her belly rolled, and her surroundings flashed white. Then, suddenly, she was in his office.

I'm not gonna pass out, I'm not.

It was the last clear thought she had before it all went dark.

CHAPTER THREE

Ending his call, Maddox looked at his sentinel, who'd been waiting patiently on the sofa at the opposite end of the office. "Well?"

"It's true," replied Hector. "Another lair was wiped out earlier today—no survivors."

Maddox swiped his tongue over his front teeth. "It's safe to say that someone seeks to cull the population of descendants. Maybe even to eradicate our kind altogether."

"Do you think maybe that's why Viper has asked to meet with you?" he asked, referring to the president of the Black Saints—an MC club that popped up out of nowhere six months ago. "Think he wants to make it his business?"

"It's possible. But I don't see why he would. Neither he nor any of his 'brothers' are descendants; they don't even have demonic blood."

"But they *are* angels who've fallen, much like our ancestors, so we're one of the closest species they have on Earth to their own." Hector twisted his mouth. "I heard a rumor about the president."

"That some believe he's an archangel? One of the infamous Seven?"

Surprise flickered across the sentinel's face. "Yes. Do you think it could be true?"

"Possibly." Maddox crossed to the sofa opposite Hector and sank into it. "If so, he'll be a force to be reckoned with. All the members of the Seven are dangerous."

"If I remember the ancient stories about them rightly, there's Michael, Raphael, Uriel, Gabriel, Samael, Azrael, and Raguel. Which one do you think Viper could be?"

Maddox shrugged. "It's not as if we can contact someone up above and ask who's missing." He drummed his fingers on the armrest. "I'll find out what Viper wants tomorrow during our meeting. Moving on, did you find out who's trying to cause dissension among our lair?"

"From what I can tell, the whispers originated from Euan and Marcella."

Maddox exhaled heavily. "I thought as much."

"Yeah, that was my guess as well. But I was hoping Euan had nothing to do with it, considering he's your cousin. I don't think he truly cares much that Raini isn't a descendant, but others do. He's capitalizing on how uneasy they are that, for the first time in history, a descendant's anchor is a breed other than our own."

Which was why both Maddox and his demon had been utterly shocked to realize that Raini was theirs. Being far too jaded, Maddox had thought himself impervious to such an emotion, but shock had slammed into him hard that night. When his demon snapped out of its stunned state, all it had wanted was to form the bond and leave the anchor mark on the hollow beneath her ear, declaring she belonged to them.

"They don't know what it means, or if it even means anything," Hector went on. "But they are nervous about having

Raini around, because she could see things she's not supposed to see."

"She only comes here once a month, and she only ever comes through the side door and then up to my office. Although the window overlooks the dance floor, she can't see the VIP area from here. In any case, I always give the lair advanced notice of her arrival. They know to curb their . . . activities until she's gone, just to be on the safe side."

"I know. As do they. But they're still nervous about her coming here. And Euan is claiming that your inability—or refusal, whichever—to stay away from Raini is both a demonstration of weakness and an indication that you don't have the lair's best interests at heart."

Pausing, Hector rolled his eyes. "He simply wants to be Prime—always has. Those of us who've claimed our psi-mates understand it's not so easy for demons to keep a distance from their anchor. Hell, I couldn't have kept my distance from Carmen," he added, referring to a sentinel who was Hector's mate as well as his anchor. "The lair's attitude toward her might change once they're used to her."

"Are Euan and Marcella working together to cause issues?"

"No. Marcella's not implying you're weak. She's simply trying to play on how nervous people are, making them imagine all sorts of scenarios that might occur if Raini learned and leaked our secrets—claiming Knox Thorne would be a problem and that he'd stir up the other Primes. In truth, what Marcella wants is to be your co-Prime, and she's observant enough to sense that you want Raini in your bed. Marcella therefore sees her as a threat. I think she's hoping that you'll walk away from your anchor if enough of our lair pressure you to do so."

"She should know better." Maddox didn't respond to pressure.

"And so should Euan. No one agrees that you're 'weak.' Nor

are they unaware that he's only trying to undermine you because he wants your position. They also know what Marcella's true problem is with the situation. But the lair is still uneasy."

Initially, Maddox had been just as uneasy about Raini. He didn't like the thought of his fate being tied to that of another. More, having an outsider around was *not* wise. So he'd resolved that he'd leave her alone; that he'd go on as if he'd never met her. But avoidance wasn't his thing. Nor was denying himself what he wanted. In spite of everything, he wanted a place in Raini's life; to be able to see her from time to time; to ensure her safety, as was his right.

He also wanted to fuck her until neither of them could move. They'd get to that part eventually.

Making a place for himself in her life hadn't been so simple. He'd never blamed her for being angry on discovering he was her anchor. How could he, when he knew he was not what she needed? But he was a selfish creature, so when he'd seen an opportunity to firmly plant himself in her life, he'd taken it.

Did he feel bad about it? No. Employing dirty tricks to get what he wanted wasn't new for Maddox.

"Your demon has got to be riding you hard, wanting the anchor bond," said Hector.

"Not as much as it once did. It settles for a while if it sees or hears from her." Maddox had originally thought that the strength of the bond's 'call' would dull if he and Raini were apart. Having no contact with her had only made it worse, though.

Being close to her did dull it for a while, just as it soothed his demon. But Maddox suspected the reason the entity was no longer so angry was that—given Raini was now part of their life—it believed Maddox would eventually succumb to the temptation to claim her.

Raini's mind abruptly touched his. *Maddox.*

The pain and weakness in that one word made him tense. *What is it?* he demanded.

And then there she was right in the middle of his office with Carmen, slumping to the floor like a sack of spuds.

Maddox was at Raini's side in an instant, gently rolling her onto her back. She'd passed out, he realized. His demon hissed on seeing the wet crimson stain on her tee. Maddox flipped up the material and cursed at the vicious stab wound. It was ugly. Jagged. *Blistering.*

He joined his palm to her own and *pushed* power inside her. Red as blood, it pumped through her veins, lighting each one as it traveled up her arm, down her chest, and made a beeline for the gut wound.

She arched, her amber eyes snapping open and gleaming with pain. She tried snatching back her hand, but he held it tight.

"Shh, I know it hurts." Because there was nothing soothing about the power inside him, even as it healed her.

"Burns," she bit out.

"I'm almost done." The blisters were shrinking, the blood was clotting, and the skin was knitting back together. He briefly glanced at Carmen. "What happened?" he asked, a hard bite to his voice.

"I didn't see everything," replied the sentinel. "I had to wait for the Underground's elevator to come back down and take me up to the basement—she'd gone ahead of me with her crew. When I got up there, she was on her knees on the floor with a dagger buried in her stomach. It was weird. Glowed white. Her friends had surrounded her, their backs to her. She yanked out the blade just as I teleported to her side. I brought her straight to you."

His demon roared inside his head. Maddox was not what anyone would call emotional. Not much moved him one way or the other. But when triggered, his anger could be a feral thing. It could pound inside him like a heartbeat, driving him to hurt;

avenge; kill. Right then, it did exactly that. And his demon encouraged him to act on it.

Grinding his teeth as he fought to keep a lid on his rage, he examined Raini's wound. Seeing that she was fully healed, he released her hand and scooped her up. "Did you get a good look at the person who threw the dagger?" he asked Carmen.

"Yes, his astral self was popping in and out of view. I didn't recognize him."

His demon hissed again, still pressing Maddox to go search for the fucker who'd hurt their anchor. But there was no way Maddox could leave her right then.

As he carefully laid her on the sofa, she looked up at him, her eyes hooded. "It stripped my power from me."

"What did?"

"The dagger. It took my power from me. Like a magnet."

His inner entity froze. The last thing *any* demon needed to be was vulnerable. Right now, Raini was as good as human. "There'll be a way we can return it to you."

She weakly shook her head. "I already took it back."

Maddox blinked. "You took your power back?"

"It was mine." Her eyes fluttered closed. "Brace yourself. My Prime, my girls, and their guys will be here soon. Good luck with that." And then she was out.

"She's right," said Hector, "they'll come."

Carmen nodded. "And they won't be happy that I took her."

Maddox looked from one sentinel to the other. "Wait for them outside. Bring them up here when they arrive."

Carmen hesitated to leave. "I apologize for failing you. Failing her."

"You didn't fail anyone," said Maddox. "You did exactly as I told you to do. You saw she was in danger, and you brought her to me."

Carmen swallowed and then followed Hector into the elevator. The metal doors slid closed, and Maddox found himself alone with his anchor.

He sat beside her on the sofa and lifted her head to rest it on his thigh. She didn't stir or make a sound. He wasn't surprised. If she'd fought whatever power was in that dagger, she'd have expended a whole lot of psychic energy—that was always draining.

Seeing her this way only increased his demon's fury. It wanted blood. Wanted vengeance. It would get it at some point, but not right then.

Maddox sank his hand into her soft hair and glided his fingertips along her scalp. He allowed himself to touch her occasionally, wanting her to get used to his touch. But he hadn't tried to take it further, because he wanted her to feel comfortable around him; wanted her to trust him. More, he wanted her to realize that his wish to have her in his life wasn't about sex.

He'd done his homework on Raini. Very in-depth homework. He knew a lot about her, including that she didn't particularly like being a succubus. More to the point, she didn't like that so many of the men who pursued her only did so because they were caught up in the succubae spell.

Many coveted her like one would a shiny, expensive car. They sought to claim her. Possess her. Own her. Some had even been so deeply ensnared that they'd become obsessed with her.

If Maddox had guessed correctly, she worried that he only wanted her around because he was caught up in the sexual, compelling allure she radiated. She worried that he didn't truly care about her safety or well-being; that he was simply subconsciously driven to have her in his life, like many others were before him.

He got that. He could understand it. Little did she know, but he was resistant to compulsions—including that of succubae, no matter how powerful they were. That didn't mean he didn't want her in his bed.

A man would have to be dead not to want Raini Campbell. She was beyond beautiful. Bedroom eyes. Long, thick lashes. Plush mouth. Perfectly symmetrical face. Flawless skin. Full, round breasts. Shapely legs. Curves that made a man think of sex and sin.

Maddox would make his move eventually, but not until she trusted that he wasn't under the influence of the allure she radiated.

Hearing the whir of machinery, he lifted his head. Soon enough, Hector stepped out of the elevator. Behind him were Raini's coworkers, Knox Thorne, and three of Knox's sentinels. Their eyes went straight to the woman sleeping on the sofa, her head still resting on Maddox's thigh.

Harper eyed him. "Your sentinel said her wound is healed."

"It is," Maddox confirmed, again stroking his fingertips along Raini's scalp.

"Was it necessary for your demon to take her?"

"She needed healing, so yes. I won't apologize for putting her before what you would have wanted."

"You can't only be her anchor when it suits you."

He didn't credit that statement with a response. He wasn't going to justify himself to Harper Thorne or anyone else.

Devon crossed to the sofa and gave him a small smile. "Thank you for healing her. She's very important to us, you see, so we're a little on edge after seeing her be hurt."

The hellcat settled on the other end of the couch and placed Raini's feet on her lap. Harper perched herself on the armrest while Khloë sat on the floor and put her hand on Raini's leg.

Noting how disapproving the males looked at the sight of the women so close to Maddox, he almost snorted. They were safe from him purely because they meant something to Raini.

He looked at Knox. "I don't suppose you managed to kill the demon who attacked, considering he was astral projecting."

The Prime shook his head. "But we have the dagger." He stepped closer to Maddox and held up the blade. There were no smears of blood, so Knox must have wiped it clean. There were, however, strange runes carved into the steel—some of which Maddox had seen before.

"An incantor either made that dagger or simply inscribed the runes onto it," said Maddox. "That blade wields magick, which explains why Raini said it stripped her power from her."

Devon gasped. "Stripped her power?"

"She took it back, which is probably why she passed out." Maddox noted that none of the women looked surprised to hear that Raini had been strong enough to wrench it back. Knox and his sentinels, however, exchanged a look.

The elevator whirred to life again. Moments later, Carmen walked into the office swiftly followed by Jolene Wallis and two of her sentinels.

Jolene's gaze locked on a pale, unconscious Raini. Like that, her expression hardened, and the walls of the building began to tremor.

"She's okay, Grams," Harper quickly assured her.

Jolene's eyes snapped to Maddox. "Her wound?"

"Healed," Maddox assured her.

The tremors slowly settled. "You're handy to have around," Jolene told him. Her mind then touched his. *Of course, that won't stop me from peeling the flesh from your bones if you hurt her.*

She will never come to any harm while with me, said Maddox.

Jolene turned to Knox. "I want to know *exactly* what happened."

"What happened," began Knox, "was that Raini got caught

in the crossfire. The demon who threw this dagger was aiming for me. He hit her by mistake."

Taking the blade to examine it, Jolene frowned. "Why throw this at you? It's not as if a stab wound is likely to kill you. And what the hell are these marks on the steel?"

"Maddox believes they were made by an incantor," replied Knox. "According to Raini, that dagger stripped her power from her, but she took it back."

"She did?" asked Jolene, looking appropriately surprised, but Maddox wasn't buying it. As a very proficient liar, he knew when he was looking at someone just as skilled at it.

"There are demons who make a living stealing abilities from others and selling them on the black market," Maddox cut in. "Some work alone; some are part of very profitable businesses. It could be that the person who threw that dagger meant to steal and sell your abilities," he said to Knox.

"I know of someone from another lair who was once targeted in such a way," said Jolene.

Her sentinel frowned at the blade. "But how can *that* store power?"

"You would have to ask an incantor how it works," said Maddox. "Allegedly, such weapons suck in a demon's concentration of power. Later, the weapon is emptied. Each of the abilities manifest themselves as orbs of glittering dust. Or so I'm told."

"And how would the orbs be passed onto someone else?" asked Khloë.

"If what I've heard is correct, only the dagger can impart a power into a person," replied Maddox. "The ability is drawn back into the blade, which then pierces the 'buyer's' skin to pass it on. *But* . . . an ability won't integrate itself into a demon's psyche unless that psyche was built to control it, so the effect is usually only temporary. The power can even corrupt and kill a demon if they're too weak to hold it."

Devon's brow furrowed. "Then why would people bother to buy them? Where's the sense in taking the risk?"

Tanner looked at her. "People will risk a lot of things for power." He slid his gaze to Knox. "It's possible that the demon tried stealing your powers simply because he knows you're powerful—he might have even done it on the off-chance that the rumors are true and that you can conjure the flames of hell. But there's also a chance that someone hired him to specifically target you."

Jolene nodded. "If that's the case, they might try again, Knox. You should keep your guard up."

"I always do," said Knox.

"I'll show the dagger to Ella," said Levi. "She may be able to tell us who enchanted it."

"She's an incantor?" Maddox asked him.

Levi only nodded.

Turning to Jolene, Knox held out his hand for the dagger.

Jolene closed her hand tight around the hilt. "Raini is one of mine; this injured her."

"Yes, it did," Knox allowed. "But it wasn't meant for her, it was meant for me. And Tanner's right, whoever used it could make another attempt to target me. I intend to find them before it happens. I don't want anyone else getting caught in any crossfire. I'm happy for us to work together on this, but I need that dagger or Levi can't show it to his friend."

Jolene very reluctantly handed it over, but not before her sentinel took multiple pictures of it with his cell phone. She looked at Maddox. "I suppose you'll do your own investigation."

"I suppose I will," said Maddox. He wasn't surprised that neither Prime proposed the three of them work together on this.

They didn't entirely trust him. *He* wouldn't trust him either. Maddox was loyal to few people. One of them happened to be the woman who was stabbed by that dagger, so he would of course seek to find out who enchanted it.

Knox narrowed his gaze on Maddox. "If you discover who was behind this before we do and you manage to get your hands on them, don't kill them. I'll have questions for them."

"As will I," said Maddox. But would he let them live a while? Only for the purpose of torturing them. Whether or not he called Knox would really depend on his mood.

After they spoke a little more about the dagger, people made moves to leave.

When Harper asked Levi to carry Raini, Maddox shook his head and said, "I'll take her home."

The sphinx's nostrils flared.

Before she could object, he pointed out, "You don't know the code for her house alarm anyway."

"And you do?"

"Yes."

That didn't seem to please Harper at all. "Does Raini know that?"

"Of course."

Harper's lips thinned. She opened her mouth—no doubt to give him shit—but then her eyes turned inward, and he suspected she was having a telepathic conversation. Harper abruptly snapped her mouth shut and slid her grandmother a put-out look. "Fine," she finally bit out.

Maddox wondered why Jolene, of all people, would ask Harper to let it go. But he didn't enquire as to why. He simply stayed where he was.

As the group was too large to fit into the elevator, Hector escorted Knox and his companions out of the office first and then came back for Jolene and her sentinels.

Once the elevator began its descent, Carmen blew out a breath and turned to Maddox. "I think it's safe to say you haven't been welcomed into the fold yet. Which pisses me off, because you healed the little imp."

"But I didn't do it out of kindness or concern for Khloë, I did it for Raini," Maddox pointed out. "And I extracted a fee of sorts from her."

"Do you think they'd prefer to have you out of the picture?"

Maddox shrugged. He really couldn't care less. "I don't see how it matters one way or the other. I'm firmly in the picture now. I'm not going anywhere."

Hector teleported back to the office. "They're gone."

Intent on making enquiries about the dagger, Maddox said, "Let's get her home." He carefully slid both arms under Raini and cradled her against his chest.

They teleported to her house. All descendants possessed the ability to teleport. He suspected that was due to their angelic blood, since angels were also able to teleport—something they referred to as "wavering," since the air itself wavered when they appeared or disappeared.

In her bedroom, Maddox flipped back the coverlet and laid her on the mattress. He tugged off her shoes and, knowing she wouldn't want to wake to find herself still dressed in blood-stained clothes, he took off her tee and jeans. The sight of her in only her underwear went straight to his cock, making it twitch and swell.

With a silent curse, he dragged the coverlet over her, felt the air chill . . . and realized her eyes were now open. But it wasn't Raini looking at him, it was her demon. And he could see the agitation in those obsidian eyes.

He slanted his head. "You're not very happy with me, are you?"

"You think you can control the bond's call if you control her," it said, its tone flat and cold. "You are wrong. You are also wrong if you believe she is truly under your control. She has too much fire for that—she just hasn't let you see it yet. But if you push her too hard, she will push back. Harder. Then you will finally see what you have so far failed to realize."

"And what's that?"

The demon smirked. "She can kill you easier than she can breathe." It then retreated, and those eyelids fell closed once more.

Hector sidled up to him. "What do you think it meant by that?"

Maddox pursed his lips. "I have no idea."

"Do you think it was bluffing?"

"What I think . . . is that my anchor has secrets." But then, so did Maddox.

CHAPTER FOUR

Listening to her father rant the next morning, Raini sighed. She loved the man. She truly did. He was fucking extra. But she really had no idea why he insisted on proclaiming himself "laidback." No imp was laidback. Hell, they didn't know the meaning of the word.

Imps were bold, wild, daring, and delightfully uninhibited. And "in the name of the sanctity of retaliation," which was a phrase her father Lachlan commonly used, they *always* hit back. You often didn't know how or when they'd do it, you just knew it wouldn't be subtle. So the one thing that was always guaranteed to set them off was when they didn't know the identity of the person they needed to strike back at. Hence Lachlan venting his ass off while pacing up and down in front of her fireplace.

It didn't matter to Lachlan or any of her other relatives that Raini hadn't been the intended target of last night's clusterfuck. Nope. They still intended to shit fury on the person responsible. She'd anticipated that, of course, so she hadn't been shocked when she came downstairs to find a bunch of people helping themselves to coffee and food—sadly, Demi had brought Dwain along. Something that seemed to annoy Jolene almost as much as it did Raini.

There was one thing Maddox must have forgotten when he'd had Raini's security system installed—no system was imp-proof. Nu-uh. They could get in and out of pretty much any building, and you'd never even know they'd been there. They left no trace of themselves behind. Though . . . her uncle Bram *had* been known to take a dump in the houses he'd robbed over the years. Usually right on top of a bed. Just because.

The Campbell imps were a small branch within her lair. Unlike Lachlan, who'd mated Raini's succubae mother Evangeline, most of the Campbells were shacked up with Wallis imps. The two lineages had blended well. Probably because neither let little things like *legalities* get in the way of anything they wanted to do. Ethics were no real barrier either.

To be fair, some *did* run official businesses. Lachlan's bank heist days were behind him now, so he ran a mechanic shop with his three brothers. He also sold ill-gotten goods via the shop's back door, but they didn't talk about that.

Maddox's mind touched hers, pulling her out of her thoughts. *How are you feeling?* he asked.

Okay, she replied. *Thanks for healing me.*

Get some rest today. It wasn't advice. It was a firm order. *I'll see you later tonight*.

Raini felt her brow crease. *I thought . . . well, I thought you'd consider last night our monthly meet.*

You thought wrong. His mind slid softly against hers, and then it was gone.

"You're not listening to me, are you?"

Blinking, Raini looked up at her father, who'd finally stopped pacing. "I'll admit, I kind of zoned out partway through your rant. Look, I get that you're upset, but I'm fine."

He glowered at her. "You say that like it makes everything okay. It doesn't. You were stabbed—"

"By accident."

"—had your power stripped from you—"

"Temporarily."

"—and might have bled out if you hadn't been healed."

Raini felt her face scrunch up. "I wouldn't go *that* far. It was a bad injury, but I would have recovered. I just recovered a lot faster because of Maddox."

"At least he's good for something," Lachlan sniped. "Where is he anyway? He should be here. With you."

"He's probably making enquiries about the dagger," Jolene cut in, lounging in an armchair. "Hopefully he's able to unearth information I wasn't able to find."

"Hopefully," said Raini, still disappointed by Jolene's earlier announcement that, according to her sources, the dagger had been wiped of any magickal "fingerprint," so there was no way to tell who enchanted it—something Levi's incantor-friend apparently confirmed.

"Maddox is an expert at gathering intel," said Jolene. "If there's anything more to be found about that dagger, such as where it was purchased and who by, he'll uncover it."

"Assuming he gives a shit," muttered Demi. She widened her eyes when everyone looked at her. "What? It's not like he embraced the psi-bond, is it?"

"But he *does* look out for your sister, in his way," said Evangeline, sitting beside Raini on the sofa. "He's involved in her life to some degree, Demi. Her safety clearly matters to him."

Demi snorted. "Her safety? Really? She'd be safer *anchored*, considering that would prevent her from turning rogue. He isn't exactly bothered by that, is he?"

Well no, no, he wasn't. But Raini would really rather her sister didn't take such joy in pointing that out.

"I heard a lot of bad things about Maddox Quentin," said Dwain, speaking for the first time. "Really bad things. Maybe you're better off without him, Raini."

Jolene sniffed at Dwain, dismissive. "I don't believe there'll be any 'without him.' Maddox is not going to walk away from Raini—I sensed that for myself last night."

"That good ole succubae allure at work, huh," said Dwain, the tiniest edge to his tone. "Doesn't seem fair to either of you," he added, directing a sympathetic smile at Raini. That sympathy wasn't present in his eyes, though. No, his gaze held a hint of something ugly.

See, that was the thing. When a succubae snare lost its hold on a person, they were often left feeling angry and hateful, because who would like that they'd been unnaturally *compelled* to want someone so badly?

Dwain was right on one thing, though. It wasn't fair on Maddox that he was preternaturally driven to keep her close, just as it wasn't fair on Raini, because she couldn't change what she was.

"I don't believe Maddox is ensnared," said Jolene, her brow creased. "He's exhibited no signs of being obsessed with her. If he was, he wouldn't be able to go without seeing her for long periods of time."

Well that was true. He only saw her once a month, and he didn't appear to be struggling with that.

"Wanting a place in her life is just typical anchor behavior," Jolene added.

Evangeline nodded. "I believe he simply needs time to adjust to having someone take up such a big role in his life. Some don't find it easy to let new people into their world—not even if those people are their anchors."

Lachlan licked the edges of his teeth. "Well, if time goes on and he still doesn't 'adjust,' I'll be having a talk with him."

Raini tensed. "Dad . . ."

He raised his hands. "It'll be perfectly civil."

Oh, the man was unreal. "What's civil about you and your brothers setting fire to his club? No, don't tell me that isn't your plan. You're all about burning down people's businesses."

He shrugged. "It's usually effective when you want someone's attention. People tend to listen to you more carefully after that."

"Dad, this isn't some guy who owes you money, screwed you over on a business deal, or snitched to the cops about the warehouse where you keep the shit you steal."

"Many of us prefer the word 'purloin' to 'steal.' It sounds classier. As for that rat, he should've kept his mouth shut. To be fair, he never blabbed to the cops again."

"Probably because you set his business on fire."

He shrugged again. "As I said, it's effective."

"It really is, you know," Bram chimed in, to which her father's other two brothers nodded.

Shaking her head, Raini turned back to Lachlan. "Returning to the point I was trying to make . . . Maddox Quentin isn't some man who wronged you. He's my anchor."

"In theory, not in practice," said Demi.

Ignoring her sister, Raini went on, "I need you to respect that, Dad. *Not* to dig out the gasoline and toss balls of hellfire around."

His brow furrowed. "I don't tend to use gasoline these days. Stinks worse than a rancid ass. I don't use hellfire either. I prefer matches."

"*Dad.*"

"Fine." He rolled his eyes. "I won't set his precious club on fire."

"Or his house, or any other building he may own," she prompted.

"His possessions are safe from me. Unless he hurts you. Then things will change."

"And burn," added Bram.

Nodding, Lachlan pointed at his brother. "What he said."

Raini turned to her mother. "Help me."

Evangeline slid her arm around Raini's shoulders and drew her close. "I already did that by convincing him to give Maddox time—which was not easy." Seeing that Lachlan was now talking with Jolene, Evangeline quietly went on, "He's your father, he loves you, he wants you to have an anchor who appreciates you. It hurts him that both you and your sister have been let down in this area of your lives."

Exhaling heavily, Raini leaned into her mother. They'd always been close, sharing a similar sense as humor as well as a love of shopping, bargains, and spa days. They were very unlike in one respect, though. Evangeline embraced being a succubus and didn't try to tone her appeal down with casual clothing. She'd tried encouraging Raini to do the same but to no avail.

"Why don't you come down to the salon today?" Evangeline proposed, referring to the local hair salon she owned and managed. "You can relax, have a facial, get your hair and nails done. The salon's busy on Saturdays, but I can fit you in. We could even go to the movies later; have some mom and daughter time."

Raini gave her an apologetic look. "I promised I'd meet Maddox at his club tonight."

Evangeline's eyes lit up. "All the more reason for you to come to the salon today. You want to look your best for later. You'll feel better having that 'armor.' More confident. Less nervous. A girl should always look her best anyway."

"A little time with my mom *would* be nice." And highly distracting.

Evangeline beamed. "You know how much I love pampering my girls. Demi rarely lets me nowadays." Evangeline's smile faded. "She used to love it. I don't know why she doesn't anymore."

If what Demi had once said to Raini when totally blitzed was true, it was because she didn't see the point of getting "prettied up" when Raini would always be more beautiful than her. Her sister had then laughed and said, "*Don't feel sorry for me; I don't wish I was a sex demon too. In fact, I pity you, Raini. You effortlessly reel in all these men, but none care who you are. To them, you're just eye candy. A notch on their bedpost. They don't take you seriously or assume you have a brain in your head. All they want is to bang you. None have really loved you, have they?*"

No, they hadn't—the reminder of that had hurt. What had hurt more, though, was the scorn and venom in her sister's voice. It had almost made Raini flinch. Her inner demon had been so pissed it had wanted to toss a ball of hellfire at Demi's crotch.

Bram stood. "We gotta roll if we're gonna open the shop on time, brothers."

Demi also rose to her feet. "Dwain and I need to leave, too."

Raini did a mental fist pump.

Standing, Dwain smiled. "My mate went shopping with my mom and sister, so Demi and I are going to spend the day together." The self-involved asshole didn't even notice how Demi had winced at the word "mate."

People said their goodbyes to Raini and then slowly trickled out of the house, until only Jolene remained. The Prime leaned forward in her seat and said, "Now think hard, Raini. Think very, very hard. Did that demon truly hit you with the dagger accidentally, or do you think he was aiming for you?"

Raini bit her lip. Since waking this morning, she'd replayed the event over and over in her mind, dissecting every little thing that happened. "If Tanner hadn't bumped into me and made me stumble into Knox exactly when I did, I don't believe the dagger would have hit me."

"What about afterward? Did the demon look annoyed that the blade had missed its target?"

"Not from what I saw, no. But that doesn't mean he aimed for me. It only means he either hid his frustration or just figured he'd sell whatever abilities *I* had and then come back for Knox another time."

Jolene's shoulders relaxed. "Then it doesn't seem that your secret is out."

"I don't see how it could be—we've all gone through great pains to keep it. Few people know about it."

"But even one person knowing is one too many, given how our lair would react." Jolene sighed. "It makes more sense that Knox was the intended target. But be careful all the same."

"I will."

Jolene slanted her head. "Have you told Maddox what you can do?"

"No."

"You don't trust him?"

"Not fully, no. He . . . I don't think he's as cruel as he seems. I think his coldness is more of a byproduct of what he is. And I don't think he'd ever physically hurt me. But he's only loyal to the demons within his lair."

"Then it's better if you don't spill your secrets." Jolene lifted a brow. "Be aware that Maddox is a highly perceptive person. If anyone will see through the harmless front you present to the world, it's him."

Oh, Raini knew that well. It worried her a whole lot. Really, it didn't so much matter if the world at large knew about the gift she sought to hide. No, it was her lair who needed to be kept in the dark, because they'd react seriously badly if they ever learned what she could do.

Lachlan had helped her develop a lot of "talents" from an early age, such as how to hotwire a car, pickpocket like a pro, and spot an undercover cop. But when her final preternatural gift developed, his priority changed from—essentially—making her into a petty criminal to ensuring she knew how to blend; how to be someone who didn't draw attention to themselves. Which wasn't easy, considering she was a succubus.

It had meant not involving herself in the "family business." Not becoming a sentinel or a member of the Force, even if she'd have made a damn good one. It had meant going her own way; seeming normal. Easygoing. Relatively innocuous. Even boring—demons never paid attention to anything boring.

Lachlan had instructed her not to flaunt the "life skills" he'd taught her. He'd encouraged her to allow people to underestimate her and to let them believe they had her all figured out.

Raini had put all her father's lessons into practice and, in doing so, she'd become someone who only really made an impact with her appearance. In actual fact, it benefited her that people often only saw the surface and never looked deeper.

"He so far hasn't prodded me with personal questions," said Raini. "Which suggests he's done what he does best and compiled a dossier on me."

Jolene nodded. "If he's not asking questions, it's because he thinks he knows all he needs to know. He'll have been surprised that you were strong enough to wrench your power back out of that dagger, though, so he might be wondering if the picture he has of you in his head is truly accurate."

"Oh, he'll wonder. But even if he suspects I have a gift I haven't revealed—something that isn't uncommon for demons—he'll never suspect I can do what I can do. As long as that doesn't change, all will be fine."

Taking a swig from his whiskey tumbler, Maddox didn't break eye-contact with the man sitting opposite him. There were different angelic breeds—five, if what Maddox had heard was correct. All were powerful, but not all had wings or halos. The weakest was the most common breed; they were quite simply referred to as angels.

Viper was *definitely* not a common angel. Power glimmered in his hard eyes, dripped from his low-pitched voice, and surrounding him like a full-body, invisible halo.

The three "brothers" he'd brought along to the meeting, all of whom stood behind the sofa on which their president sat, weren't common angels either. Maddox couldn't get a handle on what breed they were. But Viper? Oh yeah, he was an archangel all right. A supremely powerful one. Which made Maddox believe that one of the Seven truly had fallen. And he'd brought some friends with him when he fell.

No one really outside the upper realm knew how the process of "falling" truly worked. Some thought it was a *literal* fall. Some thought it was metaphorical. Others believed it was no more than a simple decision to leave.

Why Viper had formed an MC club, Maddox didn't know. Maybe it was merely a cover. Maybe they liked the thought of being free. Or maybe it was an excuse for them to not have to fully blend in with society, which wouldn't be simple for them.

Maddox didn't ask, because he didn't particularly care. He did, however, wonder why a fallen archangel had turned up here. And since Raini would be arriving sometime within the next hour, he saw no need or sense in dancing around pleasantries. He preferred directness in any case.

Balancing his tumbler on the sofa's armrest, Maddox asked, "Why contact me?"

If Viper was offended by the lack of welcome, he didn't show it. "I won't insult your intelligence by asking if you're aware that several lairs of descendants have been killed over the past few months." He stretched his legs out in front of him. "Do you have any idea who's behind it?"

"No. But I'm sensing that you do."

A smile flirted with one corner of the president's mouth. "I'm sure you figured out for yourself that my brothers and I fell only recently."

"It was quite obvious. You all appeared out of nowhere."

"It caused quite a stir among the Earth-bound angels," said Viper, referring to those who were placed on Earth and forced to earn their way back to the upper realm—only then would they be granted their halo.

Maddox didn't know why that happened to some angels while others were halo-bearers from birth. Again, he didn't ask. Because, again, he didn't care. He just listened as Viper continued to speak.

"The Earth-bound tend to avoid us. I think they worry that associating with the Fallen will reflect badly on them. They'd be right in thinking that. The beings up above"—Viper shook his head— "they're never pleased when angelic breeds fall. It rarely happens nowadays, but eons ago? I think about two hundred fell. Possibly more."

Yes, Maddox had heard the stories.

"The beings upstairs didn't like it at all. They really didn't like that the Fallen spread the love and produced children with humans. And they really, *really* didn't like that some of them produced children with demons.

"Most of the Nephilim were hunted and killed by halo-bearers. Any children born from a fallen angel and a demon, however, were generally left alone. Because demons tend to react badly if someone harms their offspring, and they can do a *lot* of damage. No one wanted a war between the light and the dark—there'd be no winners, so the half-bloods were left alone. Which is why *your* breed eventually came into being. And yes, your existence *galls* the people upstairs."

Maddox felt his gaze narrow. "You think someone in the upper realm is no longer so happy to leave us be."

"They were *never* happy to leave you be. They simply knew better than to eradicate you."

"Why would anyone up there suddenly decide it was worth the risk?"

"That I don't know. But it could be because there are so many of you now. You'd give demons a big 'edge' if there was ever a battle between the light and the dark. Angels and demons are well-matched. But demons with angelic blood? They're *more* than a match for angels. And as a descendant with archangelic blood in his veins, you are a threat that the upper realm will definitely want *gone*."

Maddox wasn't surprised that Viper knew he wasn't a typical descendant. "Why would you so freely share all this with us? Why bother to warn me?"

"Descendants are the closest creatures on this Earth to angels," said Viper, echoing what Hector—who was leaning against the wall with Carmen—had said only yesterday. "We're almost relatives, really. Family, even. And families should look out for each other, shouldn't they?"

"You want an alliance," Maddox realized.

"It makes sense. Your kind is a breed of demon, yes, but you've never truly been accepted by the other breeds, have you? They still see you as mutts. You're outsiders. So are we. There's safety in numbers."

All of that was true, but . . . "I don't think you really need an alliance with anyone, Viper. *None* of you are common angels. Your club is more powerful than you want people to believe. I doubt you'll ever need backup from anyone. What is it you really want?"

A slow smile crept onto Viper's face. A smile that said, "perceptive," but he admitted to nothing. Maddox hadn't expected him to.

Viper slanted his head, his grin fading. "Do you know what happens to the entities inside angelic beings when we fall? Most don't. You think the predator that shares its soul with *you* is dark. Our entities? The fall twists them. They lose their light, lose their ability to feel. And they want only one thing. Crave it, even. It's the only thing that makes them feel alive . . . because it *is* life."

"Blood." Maddox knew.

Viper gave a slow nod. "Blood. Vampires aren't the only creatures who crave it." He tilted his head again. "But you already know that, don't you? Your kind inherited that same craving from its ancestors, didn't it? I doubt the craving is as intense for descendants, because you're not wholly angel. You all probably only need to feed once every month or so, depending on how strong you are, but the craving is still there. And *that's* why you have this club, isn't it, Maddox? It's not really simply a business to keep your lair afloat. It's a feeding ground."

CHAPTER FIVE

Maddox sensed more than saw his sentinels stir, losing their deceptively lazy air in an instant.

Viper didn't fail to notice. "You have no need to worry that I'll share with anyone that descendants inherited this curse," he told Maddox. "After all, we're stuck with it, too. We don't want it made public either."

Maddox believed him.

"Your kind was right to keep it to yourselves. There were a few blood-drinking demonic breeds back in the old days. Feeding on blood, on *life*, made them too strong; it made them *the* strongest breeds, in fact. So other types of demon wiped them out."

"Yes, I'm aware of that. We all are."

"And so you keep it quiet, and you've supplied your lair with its personal hunting ground." Viper pointed at him. "I like that. It's smart. You make your prey come to you. You ensure your demons are always fed. You confine the feeding to one place, lessening the chance of your secret getting out."

"You came to me because you want to use the club to feed," Maddox sensed.

Viper nodded. "Unlike descendants, we need weekly access to 'food.' I'm planning to take inspiration from you and build a nightclub, but that won't happen overnight. We need somewhere else we can go in the meantime. This place is open almost every night. It isn't far from my clubhouse. And I'd feel better knowing that my brothers had their backs covered by demons that we're allied with."

Maddox took an unhurried swig of his whiskey. He didn't form alliances easily. But, given how powerful Maddox sensed the Black Saints were, they'd make good allies—especially if angels really *would* come calling soon to wipe out his lair.

"I can agree to an alliance," said Maddox. "But I'll have a condition. I do nothing for free."

Viper grinned. "I knew I was going to like you."

"If, as you anticipate, beings from upstairs *do* come here looking to take out my lair, I may expect backup from you. You might not find it easy to provide that, because you may well personally know the people who are sent here. You'll be expected to fight them, even if they're friends of yours. Can you do that?"

Viper poked the inside of his cheek with his tongue. "It's possible I may know those who're sent after you—I can't be sure either way. What I do know is that you don't have to worry that I'll fail to back you up. My brothers are my priority now. For them, yeah, I can do it."

"Can you guarantee that they will fight at your side?"

One of Viper's brothers straightened and said, "That will never be in question—we go where he goes."

Maddox inclined his head and then met Viper's gaze again. "If I allow your brothers to use my club, I'll also have rules. One, they don't cause fights or draw unnecessary attention to themselves. Two, they only feed in the VIP area, they heal the bite wounds afterward, and they ensure that the humans don't remember the incident. I'm assuming that, as angels, you can all heal minor wounds?"

"We can," Viper confirmed. "As can your kind."

They could. Only Maddox could heal fatal ones. "Three, they only feed from my demons if it's consensual. And lastly, they understand my anchor is completely off-limits—they touch her, they die."

"Ah, yes, I heard you recently discovered your psi-mate. A succubus from Jolene Wallis' lair. The first archangel to ever fall and copulate with a demon chose none other than a succubus, you know." He leaned forward in his seat. "I agree to your terms, and I'll ensure my brothers understand and obey your rules while here. So, do we have an alliance?"

"We have one." Maddox shook the hand that Viper held out.

It wasn't long after that the Black Saints left the office.

Carmen pushed away from the wall. "Do you think they'll keep their word and provide backup if necessary?"

Maddox drained his glass. "Yes. They need us. And I don't just mean because I'm allowing them access to the Damned. We've grown up craving blood. They haven't. It's all new for them. I think Viper wants his brothers to look at our lair and see that they can still have a life; that they're not going through their struggle alone." Maddox stood. "I'll hold a meeting tomorrow and inform the rest of the lair about our new allies."

"Don't be surprised if they're not excited by the news," Carmen advised. "They never react well to change."

Maddox sighed. "So I've noticed." He looked at Hector. "We need to step up the security around here for a while—you know what measures to put in place."

"It'll be done," said Hector.

"Warn everyone to be extremely alert. They're already on their guard due to the number of descendant lairs that have been targeted recently, but that's not enough."

"I'll make sure they all understand the need for vigilance," Hector promised.

"Do you think it might be better if you ask Raini not to come here until all this has blown over?" asked Carmen carefully.

Maddox's demon stiffened. "It's not necessary. She'd be safe within these walls. And if any trouble did break out, one of us can teleport her home. Who's on her right now?"

"Duncan and Hoyt," replied Carmen, referring to the two most experienced members of the lair's Force.

"Good," said Maddox. "After tonight, I'll be teleporting her to and from the club on days she's due to come here. If for some reason I can't personally collect her, I'll ask one of you to do so. There's no point in me doing it tonight, because she'll already be on her way here. Hector, I want *you* to be the one who escorts her from the parking lot to the club and back again tonight. No one from our lair would harm her, but they also wouldn't be mindful of her safety. I would have continued to trust Gunther to escort her if he wasn't . . . indisposed."

Hector grimaced. "That's the third time this year we've had to put him in the mausoleum. I know it's better that he's there, but still."

Maddox nodded. "But still."

The mausoleum was situated in the cemetery of the private land he owned. There was also an old monastery, which he'd updated and modernized so it looked more like a hotel. The entire lair lived there—it was their idea of a private joke, really, given that they were far from holy. There was also a cathedral, which was where they held lair meetings.

He'd considered taking Raini to his land a time or two. He'd thought of showing her around the monastery, and fucking her in his bed. But he couldn't guard the secrets of his kind if he brought her so fully into his world. That his kind drank blood was only one of those secrets, and it wasn't even the worst.

Well this guy's new, Raini thought as she locked her car with the key fob. Maybe her usual escort had a night off. *This* descendant was big and broad and carried an air of authority. Probably a sentinel. His eyes scanned the lot, searching the shadows.

"They're in the Charger near the exit," she told him.

He looked at Raini. "Who?"

"My from-afar-guards."

His eyes narrowed. "You made them?"

"I grew up among imps. One of the first lessons my dad taught me is how to know when I'm being followed. He has that down to a science. It's necessary for imps to learn that kind of thing, considering they often end up under police surveillance at some point. We use a lot of 'code' when speaking over the phone, because we don't always know if the lines are being monitored."

The descendant looked at her for a long moment. "I really don't know what to say to that."

Raini shrugged. "People often don't."

He grunted. "Maddox is waiting for you."

She followed him to the side entrance and into the building. Her demon straightened at the sight of a woman standing near the elevator, clothed in a slinky "fuck me now" dress that beautifully complemented her every curve.

The male descendant's shoulders went stiff. "What the hell, Marcella?"

The woman blinked. "Hector, hi. I wanted to go see . . ." She trailed off as she noticed Raini. "Oh, hello."

Was Raini *really* supposed to buy that overdone look of surprise? Apparently so.

"A succubus," she observed. "You must be Maddox's anchor."

Raini's demon did *not* like the proprietary way in which this heifer had spoken his name. Okay, so maybe she wasn't a heifer. She could be a wonderful, compassionate, kind-hearted person . . . though Raini doubted it. She'd grown up around imps—she knew when someone was trying to fuck with her. Marcella was doing exactly that and so, yeah, the whole "heifer" thing was looking likely.

Hector made a sound of disgust. "You knew Raini was coming. The whole lair knew she was coming. And everyone knows that Maddox doesn't like his time with her to be disturbed. So, I'm assuming there's an emergency, because surely there'd be no other reason that you'd try to go up to his office now."

"Really, Hector, it went right out of my head that she was coming," Marcella swore—well, lied. "I just wanted to see if Maddox was busy and . . . it's fine, I'll come back later." And it was perfectly obvious by the sexually suggestive hint to her voice that she wanted Raini to believe that Maddox and Marcella would do the dirty "later." Ugh.

Hector towered over the woman. "Don't think you can play games, Marcella. He's not happy with you as it is. Don't make it worse for yourself."

Her eyes flickered. "What does that mean?"

"Exactly what you probably fear it means. Now go."

Marcella swallowed and straightened her shoulders. She gave Raini a look filled with so much rancor that Raini's inner demon hissed and prepared to surface, eager to drop-kick this bitch. But then Marcella gracefully swanned off.

Shaking his head, Hector whipped out his keycard and got the elevator ready to roll. Raini walked through the shiny metal doors and gave him a small smile. He only grunted again, and then the doors closed. Soon enough, the elevator came to a smooth stop at Maddox's office.

Entering, she found the demon in question alone, talking with someone on his cell phone. That smooth, low voice . . . it did things to her body that she did *not* like. Things that made her skin heat and tingle and flush.

Her demon was equally affected by him, which made her feel a little better. It meant she wasn't alone in this struggle.

Raini allowed herself a moment to take him in; to admire that far too attractive face and all that hard, lean muscle. It wasn't only his looks that pulled her in. She'd always had a weakness for dominant men. She wasn't sure why, she just dug the alpha male thing. And Maddox? Well, he was certainly that.

He projected a cool certainty that his authority wouldn't be questioned; that what he said went. She'd never before met a man who oozed so much sheer absolute confidence. Honest to God, he was so self-possessed and sure of himself that it was kind of intimidating.

His gaze locked on her, sharp and unflinching. Even as he continued to speak into his phone, he swept that compelling gaze over her, noting every detail—the loose curls in her hair, the soft pink nail polish, the slim-fitting oversized white tee, the skin-tight jeans, and the black strappy shoes. Her mom had been in despair because Raini insisted on dressing casually.

Maddox flicked his fingers, inviting her further inside, and gestured at the small sitting area.

Raini took her usual spot on one of the two sofas. There was a glass of red wine waiting on the black glass table, as per usual. Beside the glass was a bowl of nachos—another constant. Maddox always set the scene, taking control before she'd even walked through the door of the building. Which she supposed was typical of someone like him.

Her demon rolled its eyes at his control-freak ways. Raini, too, found some amusement in the whole thing. That didn't stop her from munching on a few nachos.

Once he'd finished his call, he slowly made his way toward her, a half-full glass in hand. Maddox never rushed—not when he talked, not when he moved. He did everything with a slow deliberation and sense of purpose, always alert yet relaxed . . . as if positive he could handle whatever came his way. He probably could.

His eyes flitted over her face. "You look better."

"I feel better."

He sat directly opposite her, his back straight, his gut sucked in, his thighs spread . . . pretty much claiming the space as his own. "I take it you rested today."

"I didn't rest, but I took it easy. I'm sure your men told you that I went to my mom's salon. She was in the mood to do some pampering." Raini crossed one leg over the other. "Again, thanks for healing me. And for making sure I got home okay."

He shrugged and took a swig of his drink. "Someone had to. And the others didn't know your alarm code."

Raini snorted. "Jolene and Khloë are imps, Maddox. They don't need alarm codes. Nor does Harper. She might be a sphinx, but she's an imp for all intents and purposes."

"She didn't much like that I insisted on taking you home. She even objected."

"You say that as if she *forgot her place* or something. You know, you need to get over this whole issue you have with others watching out for me. I have a big family, and they're all very protective. As are my girls and Jolene. They can't—and won't—switch that off just because you're now around. Maybe you could stop thinking of them as people trespassing on your anchor-rights and instead be glad that I have them."

His brows lifted. "You think I would prefer for you to be alone in the world?"

"No. I think you want to be the main figure in my life. It's totally a psi-mate thing, and it's why so many demons struggle to accept their anchor's mate. They don't want to be second to the aforementioned mate—it's a reflexive psychic response." Raini doubted her demon would react well to Maddox claiming someone, particularly since he wouldn't even give Raini the anchor bond. "Moving onto another subject, Marcella seems nice."

He sighed. "Yes, Hector got word to me telepathically that she made a play downstairs."

"She wants me to think you guys have a thing."

"What she wants is to be my co-Prime. Why does that make you snort?"

"You're too controlling to share the power you have. I'm kind of surprised that hasn't occurred to her."

"I'm sure it has occurred to her. But Marcella's sense of ambition knows no boundaries. She doesn't like to back down or give up. And now I'm done talking about her—she isn't important. What is important is that you and I get one thing clear."

She groaned and picked up her glass. "I hate it when you say that. It always means you're going to tell me there'll be a new thing you want me to do or allow *you* to do that comes under the whole 'me not obstructing your attempts to ensure my safety' condition." And she went along with it without complaint for two reasons. One, she wouldn't go back on a deal. Two, it was sort of fun to let him think he truly held all the control here. "What is it this time?"

"From now on, you won't drive to and from the club. Either

I or one of my sentinels will teleport you here and then later return you home."

Raini narrowed her eyes. "Why?"

"It's simpler and safer."

"Simpler and safer," she echoed. "You're not thinking the dagger was deliberately hurled at me, are you? Because if so, that's just plain paranoia at work. It hit me by accident."

"I like to err on the side of caution."

She sighed. "Fine, then go err."

"You're not going to object?"

"Object to not having to haul my ass all the way here and back home again? No. Teleportation is a much quicker and more convenient way to travel." She sipped at her wine. "Did you find out anything about the dagger?"

"It's too common a model to trace to a particular store or buyer. There was no magickal fingerprint on it, which you don't look surprised by, so I'll assume Jolene's investigation revealed the same. If another attack is made on Knox, we may learn more. If there is a next time, you won't get caught in the crossfire," he said, his voice dark and cold.

"That's the plan." She felt a thoughtful frown furrow her brow. "It's kind of weird that the guy struck when and where he did. He could have waited until Knox was alone. Well, he's rarely alone in public. Still, Mr. Astral could have at least attacked when Knox only had a sentinel or two with him."

Maddox knocked back the last of his drink. "Striking while Knox had a large entourage was a strategic move. As there was a high number of demons there, they arrogantly assumed they could take their attacker, so no one teleported to safety. There were several people, lots of confusion, plenty of chaos . . . and the fact that you were badly hurt got lost in the midst of all that. The attacker kept everyone distracted by astral projecting from one spot to another, giving the dagger time to do its job so he could retrieve the blade once it was done— although Knox was the target, the attack wouldn't have been a *complete* failure so long as the dagger came back full of gifts that could be sold."

Huh. She hadn't thought of it like that.

Maddox drained his glass and then pushed to his feet. She watched his very fine ass as he headed to a high, circular table on which a few bottles were set.

"Pulling your power back . . . that was impressive, Raini." He topped up his glass with more whiskey. "You effectively fought magick and broke a spell. That's no easy thing to do."

"Which was why I passed out." Her demon was still rather aggrieved by that, viewing it as a weakness.

Turning back to her, he pinned her gaze with his as he took a swig from his tumbler. "I sensed the minute I first met you that you were powerful. Still, what you did last night surprised me—and not much does that. It makes me wonder, though, why Jolene never made you a sentinel. She doesn't even have you on her Force."

Ugh, well *of course* his sharp mind would go there. "I don't want to be part of her ranks. She respects that." Close to squirming at being the focus of those steely eyes, Raini casually stood and moved to the wall of glass that overlooked the dance floor.

"No Prime would let an asset go to waste," he went on. "Jolene Wallis is a master manipulator. She knows how to get what she wants. If she truly wanted you in her ranks, that's exactly where you'd be."

He had the right of it there.

"But she's content to let you do your own thing, which makes others assume that you're not strong enough to be of any great use to her. I have to ask myself if she *wants* people to assume that."

Raini gave him a quick glance over her shoulder. "Well, you have fun chewing on that."

"Your demon issued me a warning last night. It basically indicated that you could kill me if necessary."

The fuck? It took everything Raini had not to whirl around in shock. Why the hell had her demon done that? To tweak his curiosity? To communicate that it wasn't weak, hoping to lure in the predator that he was? Right then, her demon only sniffed, not seeing a need to justify its actions.

Slowly turning to face him, Raini pointed out, "Everything can be killed. Except maybe for water bears. Also known as moss piglets. They're eight-legged micro-animals that can survive just about anything. Radiation, extreme temperatures, starvation, dehydration, air deprivation, extreme pressures. You can find them in all kinds of places—volcanoes, Antarctica, rainforests. Some even survived a trip to outer space."

One corner of his mouth quirked. "You don't have to tell me about all the skeletons in your closet, Raini."

"Why? Because you respect my privacy?" she mocked.

"I have no reason not to respect it."

"And yet, you don't. As evidenced by your final 'condition.' And you can't deny that you also dug into my life and found out everything there was to know."

Seeing no reason to deny it, Maddox shrugged and slowly stalked toward her. "I was curious about you. I wanted to find the answer to the puzzle."

"What puzzle?"

Coming to stand in front of her, he replied, "Of why you're my psi-mate. There's never been a descendant whose anchor wasn't a fellow descendant."

Those lips he wanted to bite parted on a soft gasp. "Never?" she asked.

"Never. So discovering that a succubus is my anchor was . . . unexpected. But I haven't yet found anything that would explain the phenomenon." He was beginning to think there was no explanation. Some things just *were*. "As for my final condition . . . that wasn't about invading your privacy."

"But it does traipse all over it."

True. "I don't like that that bothers you, but I won't undo what I've done." And he'd be lying if he said that he had any regrets.

"Oh, I know that. And I'm not going to ask you to. I made a deal with you, and I won't renege on it. But there'll never be a time when what you did *doesn't* bother me."

"Even though you know I only did it because your safety is important to me?"

"I don't believe it was only about my safety. I mean, knowledge is power, right? When a person has power, they can also have control, and that's kind of your thing. Digging up all sorts of info about me and then finding a way to monitor my every move? That's a *whole* lot of knowledge."

It was, yes. And it did soothe his need to be in control. That same need rode his inner entity. "I've told you before, I don't want power over you." Which, of course, was a lie. He wanted to have *some* influence over her. Wanted to have a handle on the anchor situation, just as her demon had sensed.

She gave him a look that called him a liar. "Yes, you do. That's part of the reason why you want to be my go-to person. The one I most rely on. But you can't be that for me, Maddox."

His demon narrowed its eyes and slinked closer to the surface. Maddox hiked up a brow. "I can't?" he asked, sounding dangerous even to him.

"You already have the best of both worlds. Be content with that. Don't push for more. You won't get it. I'll never feel I can fully rely on someone who's singularly focused on their own wants. You do things that incidentally help or benefit me, but you don't do them *for* me. You do them because you want to; because you don't want others stepping on your 'rights.' Like a kid who'll keep a toy they don't much like rather than give it away to someone who'll want it, because they quite simply don't want anyone else to have it."

Maddox felt his jaw harden. There was a whole lot there he did not like. "I don't think of you as a toy."

"You don't think of me at all," she said, sounding somewhat . . . sad, yet resigned. "Everything you do is about you. And I'm not condemning you for that. You are who you are, and I think a lot of it comes from being *what* you are. But that doesn't change the situation." She sighed. "I guess it's a good thing we're not officially anchors. It would never be an equal relationship, would it? You don't fully respect me."

All right, now he was getting pissed off. "Bond or no bond, you *are* officially my anchor," he stated firmly, leaving no room for argument. His demon couldn't agree more. "I have no idea why you'd believe I don't see you as my equal, but that is not true."

"No?"

"No." He tapped her temple. "That psychic tag I put in here that bothers you so much . . . I could have planted that in your brain at any point and then taken away the memory of my doing it afterwards—you'd never have known the tag was there. I could have as easily embedded a compulsion in your mind that would force you to come to me whenever I called you. Kind of like a psychic bell. I'd ring it; you'd come . . . and you'd believe you were doing it because you *wanted* to. You'd believe the decision was yours and yours alone."

Some of the color leached from her face. She stared up at him, her lips parted once more. He wasn't surprised by the unease that flashed in her eyes. She hadn't known until right then how psychically vulnerable she was to him. Most didn't. Because despite the rumors of what he could do, people tended to believe that said rumors were either exaggerated or pure bullshit; that no demon could have that degree of psychic power. If it hadn't been for his archangelic blood, he probably wouldn't have.

She swallowed. "That sure would have made things a lot simpler for you, so why didn't you do it?"

Finding that he didn't like the wariness in her gaze at all, Maddox stroked his hand down her hair and made an effort to soften his voice. "I may be a cold bastard, but I wouldn't turn my anchor into a puppet. So whatever you might think, I don't view you as a toy. I might be mostly focused on my own wants, but not to the extent that yours don't matter to me." Which surprised him, to be truthful.

He edged a little more into her personal space. "You might not like it much, but you belong to me. I wanted a place in your life. I was set on getting it. But I also wanted you to come to me and grant me that place of your own free will. It quickly became apparent that you weren't going to do that. So, yes, I took advantage of how desperate you were to save Khloë. I won't apologize for that, because it would be a lie. I don't regret it; never have, not even for a single moment. You wouldn't have let me in your life any other way."

She stared up at him again, her brow creased. "You outright baffle me at times. You have absolutely no wish to form the bond. At the same time, though, you're so intent on having me around that you'll stoop to wrenching deals out of me if it means getting what you want. I thought you might be firmly in the grip of a snare. But now . . . "

"Now, what?" he prompted, whispering his fingertips along the side of her neck and down to the pulse beating there frantically, a temptation that made his mouth water.

"Now I'm seeing that you're far too strong for one to trap you. Or even to be drawn in by the allure that sex demons exude."

"And that unnerves you," he sensed. "Maybe I'm not the only one here who likes control."

Her frown deepened. "I don't want to control people."

"But you've always had the security of knowing that if you *wanted* to ensnare someone, you could," he pointed out. "You could make them vulnerable to you. It gave you an edge. You don't have it with me, and you don't like it." He half-expected her to go on the defensive and deny it. Instead, she went quiet, pensive.

Finally, she said, "Okay, maybe so. But I wouldn't have tried to ensnare you."

"And I wouldn't have turned you into a puppet." He cupped the side of her face and swept his thumb across her cheekbone. "What we can do and what we're prepared to do aren't always the same, are they?"

"N-no." She licked her lips, making him think of biting them all over again. Maybe even biting hard enough to draw blood, just so he could have a little taste of her. Even the thought made his gut tighten.

He found his thumb brushing along her lower lip, following the path her tongue had taken. "I'm not claiming to be much of an ethical creature. I've done a lot of bad things. I'll continue to do a lot of bad things." He dipped his head, staring into those striking amber eyes. "But never to you. Okay?"

"Okay," she said, her voice whisper-soft, but he wasn't sure if she truly meant it.

"You don't ever need to feel unsafe with me." He lowered his head a little more, his mouth mere inches from hers, not hiding his intent. Satisfaction snaked through him when she didn't push him away. "It doesn't work, you know."

Her brows met. "What?"

"Dressing down doesn't make you blend. It definitely doesn't make me want you any less. The more skin you cover, the more I want to see every inch of you bare." He slid his hand from her cheek into her hair. He fisted the soft curls tight, tugging on her scalp enough to wrench a little gasp out of her. Her pupils swallowed the color of her eyes, and her plump lips parted. That was all the invitation he needed.

Raini gasped as he took her mouth, sweeping his tongue inside. If he hadn't spent the past fifteen minutes or so touching her, stroking her, setting her nerve-endings on fire, priming her body for him, she might have pushed him away. *Might* have. But right then, all she wanted was more.

Kissing him back, she slid her hands up his chest and gripped his broad shoulders. His hand splayed on her throat while the other bunched her hair tighter in his fist as he *fed* on her mouth. That was how it felt. And she let him. More, she reveled in it. On being so wanted. Because for the first time in her life, she could be sure that the person kissing her wasn't whatsoever compelled to do so. He might like what he saw, but he wasn't *bewitched* by it. Wasn't in the grip of a preternaturally triggered lust. He just plain wanted her.

God, he was so . . . sure in the way he touched her, in the way he devoured her mouth with such greed and urgency. Sure and bold and dominant, and *so* out of her fucking league.

A thread of reason moved through her mind, reminding her why this would be a bad idea. She broke the kiss and backed up, only stopping when she hit the window behind her.

He didn't close in on her. He lifted a taunting brow. "What are you doing all the way over there? Scared, Raini?"

She adjusted her top. "I think it's better if we keep things platonic, that's all."

Glittering with heat and need, his eyes narrowed, studying her intently. "Is that what you really want?"

"Yes."

The air chilled as his eyes bled to black. *Shit.* His demon ate up the space between them with two fluid strides. "That was a lie," it whispered, its voice monotone.

Yep. Totally.

"You can try fighting this if you want, but it will not work." The demon tucked her hair behind her ear. "Still, by all means, try. He and I have waited this long to have you. We can do so a little longer. I believe it will be worth the wait." And then the entity withdrew, and Maddox was once more looking down at her. "I'd have to agree with my demon on that."

She shook her head. "This situation is complex enough. Adding sex into the mix doesn't seem wise." It would be insanely fucking satisfying, but not wise.

"That's not why you're backtracking," he softly accused. "You're afraid. You might not have liked that the men in your past were under the influence of some preternatural allure, but it's what you know. And it meant they held no power over you. Any dominance they thought they had in your dynamics was nothing other than an illusion. But me? I'm immune to that allure. You like that. And yet, you don't. It scares you that I might take you over." He lowered his head, putting his face closer to hers. "More, it scares you that you might like it."

Raini balled up her hands. She wanted to deny it. All of it. She wanted to firmly state that he hadn't read her as well as he thought he had thankyouverymuch. But every word of it would have been a damn lie.

He cupped her chin, pinning her with that far-too-intense stare, letting her see the raw need there. "I *will* have you, Raini. Beneath me. Above me. Any way I want you. Any way my demon wants you. Yes, I suspect it will fuck you often. Very often. It won't go easy on you. But then . . . neither will I."

CHAPTER SIX

An elbow nudged Raini, making her pause in chewing her baguette. She gave Devon a "What the hell?" look.

"Spill," said the hellcat. "You've been distracted all morning. We know something's wrong. Tell us what's going on."

Raini looked at the other two women sat at the table of the tattoo studio's break room. Like Devon, they were looking at Raini, expectant. Inwardly sighing, she finished chewing her mouthful of baguette.

Her stomach rolled at the mere thought of the upcoming conversation, leaving her unable to properly enjoy the tastes of roast beef, mayo, crunchy lettuce, red peppers, and the fresh bread that was both crusty and soft. Not that the girls had taken her off-guard. They'd spent the morning sliding her sideways looks, so Raini had suspected that they'd grill her for information at the first given opportunity.

It was unlikely that Raini would be able to blow off their questions, but she could try. "I'm just tired."

Harper softly snorted. "You know we can tell when you're lying, right? Well, not *always*," she quickly amended. "You're pretty proficient at it. But you feel guilty when you lie to us, so it makes you less convincing."

"Which is one of the reasons why I totally recommend the guilt-free lifestyle," said Khloë. "Now come on, what gives?"

Raini shrugged. "I'm just a little conflicted about something. I need to work it out in my head."

"No, you don't," said Devon. "You need to talk it out with *us*. You need to offload all your worries. Let us take this burden from you."

Raini almost crossed her eyes. "You are so nosy."

"Absolutely," Devon admitted, unrepentant. "But I prefer 'curious,' as you know. On a serious note, I'm worried about you."

"This has something to do with Maddox, doesn't it?" Khloë narrowed her eyes. "I know you went to see him last night. Your mom mentioned it."

Devon straightened in her seat. "What did he do? Do we need to pull out the bat?"

Raini gave the hellcat an exasperated look. "No, you don't. He didn't do anything, he just . . . made a few things clear that surprised me."

"Such as?" Khloë pressed.

Raini took another bite of her sandwich. "He isn't affected by the succubae allure."

Harper's brows flew up. "At all?"

"Nope," replied Raini.

Devon pursed her lips. "That's good, right? I mean, you feel more comfortable around people like that."

"I do," Raini confirmed. "And it *is* good. It's just that, well . . . he wants to cross the platonic line."

"That can't surprise you. He eye-fucked you the first time he saw you." Khloë frowned as a pickle slipped out of her sandwich. "I'm actually surprised it took him this long to make a move. You really didn't expect it?"

Shaking her head, Raini rested her half-eaten baguette on the crackly wax paper it had been wrapped in. "He didn't say or do anything over the past four months that would imply he was interested in going there. At first, I thought he'd decided not to complicate the situation. Now I'm thinking that, in truth, he was giving me time to get comfortable around him so that I'd be less likely to turn him down." She folded her arms. "Go on, tell me I'd be stupid for not doing exactly that."

Harper forked up some creamy coleslaw. "Look, I'm not his biggest fan, but it isn't really anything against him as a person—I don't know him. I simply don't like that he won't claim you as his anchor. Not just because the bond would stop you from going rogue, but because I don't like that he doesn't appreciate how insanely lucky he is to have you. If it wasn't for the fact that Khloë's alive because of him, I would have ripped him another asshole by now. But what me, Devon, or Khloë think of him isn't what matters."

Khloë's brow creased. "It's not?"

Harper scowled at her cousin. "No, it's not."

"Speak for yourself," the imp uttered before taking another bite of her sandwich.

Harper slid her gaze back to Raini. "What matters here is what *you* think of him."

Raini bit her lip. "I know he's not *good* in the typical sense of the word. But I don't believe he's entirely bad either. He's so very alike and in tune with his demon, which I think is because he exists in a kind of emotional purgatory. Because if you're filled with both pure light *and* pure darkness, you're neither one nor the other. So your world would be . . . gray."

Devon's shoulders lowered, and her face softened. "Yeah, that would be a fucker. And now *I'm* feeling sorry for him."

Harper lifted her water bottle. "It's no wonder he wants you in his life, then, Raini. Someone like you—bright and bold and beautiful—would act like a beam of light slashing right through that gray. And I'm finding it hard to begrudge him having that."

Khloë frowned again. "Why?" she asked with a child-like confusion.

Harper sighed at the imp. "I thought you and Keenan were working on your struggle with empathy."

Khloë straightened, affronted. "I can be empathetic. I feel bad for people, like, *all* the time."

"That's *sym*pathetic," Harper pointed out. "Also, you're lying." She cut her gaze back to Raini. "What was your demon's reaction to his declaration?"

Raini drank more of her soda. "I would have thought it'd be *totally* against the idea of me hopping into bed with him, since it isn't exactly happy with him right now. But it hasn't put up any kind of objection."

Pulling open a bag of potato chips, Devon narrowed her eyes. "It's up to something."

Khloë nodded. "That would be my guess, too. Our inner entities often have their own agenda, and they don't always want to share it."

"It's also a little smug," said Raini. "My guess? It views him acting on the sexual chemistry as his resolve weakening, and it thinks that if he and I are sleeping together, he'll eventually give in to the call of the bond."

"That would make sense." Done with her sandwich, Khloë wiped her mouth and fingers with a napkin. "In your shoes—if I didn't have Don Juan, of course—I wouldn't be opposed to playing a game of attacking the pink fortress with Maddox."

Harper's brows snapped together. "A game of what?"

Khloë lifted her shoulders. "You know . . . exploring Punarnia. Stuffin' the muffin. Slaying the vadragon. Shampooing the wookie. Getting one's Twinkie stinky—"

"All right, you're done," Harper declared. "Stop laughing, Devon. You'll only encourage her."

Khloë rolled her eyes. "Raini, I'll put it in less crude terms to appease Mrs. Prim and Proper over there. I personally think it wouldn't be so bad for you to let Maddox go paddling up Coochie Creek."

"Oh, for God's *sake*, Khloë," Harper burst out, shaking her head at Raini for snorting a laugh.

Tearing the wrap of cellophane from her brownie, Khloë eyed the sphinx. "God, you're snippy today. Hasn't Knox done any paddling lately? Is that what it is?"

"I'm done engaging with you." Harper returned her attention to Raini. "What are you planning to do about Maddox?"

Raini puffed out a breath. "I don't know. Honestly, my libido is all for riding him like a pony. But my brain is telling me it would be dumb."

Harper gave a nod of understanding. "It was the same for me when Knox made his move years ago. I fought him—and myself, for that matter—on it for a while, as you know. Obviously, I don't regret giving in. But it could have ended so differently. He could have gotten tired of me and found someone else. That would have hurt. Is that what you're worried will happen?"

Raini felt her brow furrow. "I don't think it would *hurt* to hear Maddox claim he'd had his fill of me, because we already have so many walls between us. He'll never let me close. Ever. So I'm well aware that sex between us wouldn't lead to anything else."

"Not that I'm saying you *shouldn't* be conflicted," Devon cut in, digging another chip out of the bag, "but why are you if you don't think this is a situation where you could potentially get hurt?"

"I just feel like I'm swimming in unfamiliar waters right now." Raini leaned back in her chair. "I've never felt sexual chemistry before. I didn't imagine that it would be so electric and . . . vicious. It truly feels vicious. Like it has teeth and claws and isn't gonna let go. Is that normal? Does it pass on its own?"

"It's normal, but not *common*," said Devon. "I've never felt it so strongly with anyone other than Tanner. And it flared between us for *years*. That's not to say that the chemistry between you and Maddox won't ease up, though." She tossed a chip into her mouth. "What else is in these unfamiliar waters you mentioned?"

"I've never once been with a guy who can't be snared, but I always wished I could find someone like that. Now that I have, you'd think I'd be thrilled, wouldn't you? You'd think I'd be eager to explore this chemistry we have." Raini rubbed her arm. "Although I *like* that I have no preternatural influence over him, it makes me feel vulnerable."

"Because to have no influence over him is almost like he's counteracted your power which, as a succubus, is linked to your sexuality," Harper pointed out.

Raini felt her eyes widen. "Yes. I couldn't put it into words before but, yes, that's it." She exhaled heavily. "It turns out that, like he said, I'm more comfortable with what I know."

"Most are." Harper took another swig from her bottle. "That's not wrong."

"And maybe he's also right in saying I worry that he'll take me over," Raini conceded with a brief tilt of her head.

"Oh, he'll give it his best shot," Harper predicted, setting down her bottle. "You've got an alpha on your hands. That's kind of what they do in the bedroom. And out of it, for that matter. So your worry isn't a senseless one."

"He also accused me of being scared that I'll *like* it if he takes me over."

"You might in the bedroom. That's not wrong either. Submitting isn't a demonstration of weakness."

"I know that, and I wouldn't *feel* weak. I'd just feel . . . It's hard to explain. I've never been with a man who's so . . . so everything. Maddox has this *huge* presence. It's intense and overwhelming and sometimes even a little oppressive. And I don't know how old the dude is, but I get the sense he's been walking this Earth for a lot longer than I have."

"You feel out of your depth."

Raini pointed at the sphinx. "Yes. Exactly. I feel out of my depth. Especially when he says shit like he and his demon will have me any way they want me and that neither of them will take it easy on me."

"He said that?" Khloë fanned her face. "Yowza." Right then, the imp's cell beeped. She tossed the last of her brownie into her mouth and then whipped out her phone.

"Yeah, I'll admit, my hormones were totally yelling 'yowza' when he said that," Raini confessed. "But doesn't he demand enough of me already? It would only get worse if we crossed the platonic line."

Devon put a hand on Raini's arm. "But you're going to do it anyway, aren't you? You're sitting here basically *beating* the message into your brain that you shouldn't sleep with him. But you already know it's a lost cause."

Actually, no, she . . . Okay, yeah, the hellcat had totally called it.

"Let yourself have this, Raini." Devon licked away the salt that dusted her fingers. "What's the worst that could happen? It's not as if your heart is on the line. You don't have any hopes that it will lead anywhere. It'll just be crazy good sex. And that's *always* fun."

"Motherfucking son of a fucker," Khloë spat out.

Raini frowned at the imp, who was glaring at her phone. "What's wrong?"

"Hopefully, *Ciaran* is wrong," replied Khloë, her thumbs tapping on the screen of her cell. "Because if not, the person trying to boycott Urban Ink has stepped up their game."

"In what sense?" asked Harper.

Khloë briefly held up one finger. "Give me a sec. He told me to check out a forum on . . . *That rat bastard*."

"What, what is it?" Raini leaned over to look at the phone screen. "Someone left a review about our studio on there?" Conscious that the other two women had gathered behind them, Raini quickly speed-read the paragraph, and her mouth fell open. "You've got to be fucking *kidding* me."

"Wait, they're saying one of us screwed up that sorry excuse for a neck tattoo?" asked Devon, pointing to a photo that had been uploaded onto the forum.

"They're saying that Raini did it," said Khloë. "They probably got the image from a website that sells royalty-free images or something."

The "reviewer" had also described Urban Ink as dirty and unhygienic, claiming it was only so popular because it was co-run by Knox Thorne's mate.

Harper planted her hands on her hips. "What piece of shit wrote that? Oh, they call themselves 'Anonymous.' Well of course they do."

"Maybe we can somehow trace the review back to the source," said Devon.

"I doubt it'll work," said Raini. "But we can look into it."

Khloë looked at Harper. "We need to find out who's doing this before they pull any more of this fucked-up shit. I still say that this is an indirect attack on you and our lair."

"Knox would agree with you, which is why he's going to *flip*," said Harper.

"I don't like it."

Standing near the altar of the gothic cathedral, Maddox looked at his cousin, barely refraining from rolling his eyes. The man was painfully predictable and seemed utterly oblivious to it. "What don't you like, Euan?" he asked, deceptively patient.

His inner demon wanted Maddox to snap the traitorous asshole's neck. It didn't care that Maddox had promised Euan's now deceased father that he'd look out for him. If Euan fucked up one more time, Maddox would consider that promise null and void. He was done with the man's shit.

"A*nything* about this situation," replied Euan. "Viper told you that angels are looking to wipe out descendants. In the same breath, he's asking you not only for an alliance but for access to our club . . . and you granted him both. He's an angel. An enemy. An enemy who wants rid of us."

Euan skimmed his gaze over the demons lounging on the pews, clearly expecting someone to voice their agreement. No one said a word. That wasn't to say that everyone must *dis*agree with him, only that no one wanted to jump onto Euan's confrontational bandwagon. They didn't need to use him as a voice anyway. Maddox wasn't a Prime who didn't invite questions. He had no problem with people speaking up or expressing their concerns, he only insisted on it being done in a respectful manner.

Maddox lifted a brow at his cousin. "You think Viper plans to double-cross us?"

"I'm surprised you don't," said Euan.

"Why?" asked Maddox, keeping his voice curious, as though Euan were a small child missing the point. "The angels up above don't need the Fallen to do their dirty work. Nor would they need to find a way to infiltrate our lair—they're strong enough to attack from outside it, and there are more of them than there are of us. It makes no sense that the Fallen would agree to work for them anyway."

Euan spluttered. "Okay, so maybe Viper and his group aren't working for angels. That doesn't mean they're not our enemies. Within six months of them falling, several lairs of descendants have been eradicated. You don't think the timing is coincidental?"

"I suspect someone is hoping we'll blame the Black Saints. But the fact is they have nothing to gain from targeting the people who are most likely to grant them alliances. On the contrary, it means they lose out."

"If we're dead, they could have the club."

"They're planning to build their own, like I told you," said Maddox with a patience he didn't feel. "They merely want to use the Damned in the meantime. I know there are people here who like the thought of having another club they could go to where they could be themselves." He'd sensed that when he made the announcement to the lair only minutes before. "An alliance will work well for both sides."

"Yeah, *if* Viper doesn't kill you."

"If he wanted me dead, he'd have attacked in my office. There'd be no need for him to wait for another opportunity or to drag this out. You know that. You know your arguments are weak. You know that the Black Saints have no motivation to kill descendants. But you want the spotlight, and you think that challenging my decisions makes you look strong." Maddox felt his face harden. "It doesn't. It makes you look disrespectful. It shows a blatant disregard for the chain of command, which isn't the mark of a good leader—something you apparently believe you should be."

Euan's cheeks flushed. "I was only asking questions."

"Questions are fine. Implying that my decision-making skills are flawed is not. Nor is attempting to cause dissension among the lair, but you've made it your business to do so recently, haven't you?"

Euan's eyes rounded in an "oh shit" way. "I'm not trying to cause *dissension*. I merely expressed my worry that having an outsider around—"

"I'm well aware of what you've 'expressed.'"

Euan lifted his chin a notch, but he couldn't quite meet Maddox's gaze. "You can't blame me for being nervous about this situation."

"I won't justify my decision to have contact with my anchor. That's what you want me to say out loud, isn't it? You think you can imply to others that it makes me weak. *Weak* would have been refusing to take responsibility for her merely because it would be simpler for me." Maddox swept his gaze over all his demons as he added, "If there is anyone here who can honestly tell me they would consider it a sign of strength for me to ignore my anchor's existence, say so now."

Heads lowered. Shoulders drooped. Bodies squirmed.

"I'm already forsaking the bond to protect our secrets. I will not abandon my anchor altogether. If anyone here doesn't like that, come to me at some point in the next hour and I'll arrange for you to transfer to another lair—there'll be no hard feelings on my part. I'll be in my office at the club." Maddox sliced his gaze to Marcella, who'd slid down in the pew in an attempt to keep a low profile. "First, though . . . Euan isn't the only one who's been trying to stir up trouble, is he, Marcella?"

She only made fleeting eye-contact with Maddox. "I'm allowed to have concerns."

"But you're not allowed to spur people into pressuring me to walk away from my anchor. Nor are you permitted to play the kind of games you played last night. I hope you don't think that Raini bought your act. She saw right through you. Most do, Marcella. I'm not sure if you realize how many people are aware that your efforts to cause problems stem from your determination to be my co-Prime. I've made this clear to you many times, but you've never listened, so I'll say it again now—right here in front of the entire lair. I don't enjoy embarrassing people, but nor do I enjoy anyone trying to fuck with my anchor."

"Maddox," she wheedled, sitting upright.

"You'll never be my co-Prime, Marcella. I have no interest in taking you to my bed, let alone claiming you as my mate. If you want the position so badly, you should really look to joining another lair. There may be other Primes who'll feel differently about you."

Twin flags of red stained her cheeks, and her eyes flared with anger. She clamped her mouth shut, as if not trusting herself to speak.

Maddox looked from her to Euan as he told them, "This is your only warning. Cease trying to manipulate your own lair members into acting against me. It really is a simple order. If either of you fail to follow it, you *will* pay."

Marcella's mouth set into an ugly twist. "If it's so important to you to have your anchor around, you'd better hope she never finds out about the curse of our kind. She was hesitant enough to accept you before. She'll want not one thing to do with you if she finds out the truth about us. About *you*."

"Marcella's right," Euan told him. "I know you could pluck the discovery back out of the succubus's mind so that she'd continue to come here blissfully unaware, but you'd always remember the disgust on her face. You'd always know she never really accepted you for who you are."

Maddox stilled. His inner demon slinked closer to the surface, sensing where this situation might go. "Here's another order that you had both better follow," said Maddox, his voice pitched low, his tone dark and dangerous. "Stay away from Raini. Do not talk to her. Do not approach her. Do not contact her in any way. *Definitely* do not expose our secrets, counting on me to wipe the memory of it afterwards. If either of you disobey me on this, I swear to fucking Christ I will put you through a world of pain. Then I'll heal you. And then I'll do it all over again. The process will probably be repeated several times, so I'd advise you to heed me on this."

Blanching, Euan gaped. "You'd really put an outsider before *me*, a demon from your own lair? Your *cousin*?"

"A cousin who has invested a lot of time into undermining me so that he can take my place as Prime, pissing all over my trust and breaking his loyalty to me in the process. So tell me, Euan, why *wouldn't* I put my anchor before you?"

Euan snapped his mouth shut.

Marcella, too, said nothing—she merely sat there, her face now deathly pale.

Again, Maddox spoke to the entire lair. "As I said, I'll be in my office for the next hour if anyone wishes to request a transfer."

Nobody did.

That evening, Raini opened the kitchen drawer and fished a spoon out of the cutlery organizer. Her father would tell her that having cereal for dinner wasn't "healthy." Her father would also tell her that crime kept the economy going and that, as such, he provided a positive service to society.

The man was a nut.

Which was why she didn't quite trust that he wouldn't turn all pyro on Maddox's club. Sure, Lachlan had promised not to. But he'd also promised he'd stop breaking into fast-food restaurants to cook himself a burger—he didn't always live up to that vow.

She used her hip to bump the drawer closed and then crossed to the fridge. She closed her fingers around the handle, intending to pull open the door and grab the milk jug. Her peripheral vision screamed a warning.

Raini turned to face the stranger standing a few feet away. His eyes were hard, bright, and shimmered slightly like two pure blue jewels. And above his head was a fucking halo. A halo so pretty and distracting that she didn't react fast enough.

Raini's heart jumped as a heavy weight abruptly fell over every inch of her body. No, clamped *around* it. Her bones felt like they would shatter from the sheer *force* of the power pinning her in place. The fuck?

The air wavered, and then two other halo-bearers materialized near him. Well, wasn't she popular tonight? Angels generally didn't fuck with demons, and vice versa. But these guys didn't seem to have come for a simple chat.

"Telepath Maddox," ordered the one who'd "trapped" her, moving closer. "Tell him you need him."

Telepath *Maddox*? So, what, she was being used as bait? Why? And where was her freaking guard when Raini needed her?

She went to ask what he wanted with Maddox, but she couldn't move her mouth. Couldn't move anything—not her arms, not her legs, *hell* she couldn't even flap her damn hands. And that was bad.

Her inner demon went ballistic, and the dark power that dwelled within Raini rushed to her palms, raring to attack and protect her. But since she was pretty much immobilized right now, she couldn't release it.

"Telepath him," the angel insisted.

Lure someone to their death? Nu-uh. Not Raini's style. Of course, she could warn Maddox it was a trap so that he'd bring some of his fellow descendants, but the halo-bearers had to know that. For them to believe that they could handle whoever came, there had to be more of them around—maybe outside the house, maybe inside. She didn't want to take the chance unless she had no other choice.

The halo-bearer in front of her narrowed his eyes. "Do it. Now."

She glared daggers at him, letting him know with a single look that it wouldn't happen.

The force subduing her tightened painfully around her head, putting so much pressure against her skull she was surprised her eyes didn't pop out of their sockets. God it *hurt*. It felt as if her head was trapped in a red-hot vise that sought to crack every bone and burst every blood vessel. She'd have cried out in agony for sure if she could have moved.

"I don't wish to hurt you," he went on. "I simply need your cooperation. Call Maddox here."

She gave him a look that said, "Go fuck yourself."

The force tightened again. Her head pounded, her facial bones throbbed, her jaw ached, and her teeth rattled. Jesus *fuck* her skull was going to pop like a zit if he didn't stop. Tears pooled in her eyes, which pissed her off—she hated that they could reduce her to *this*.

"You can make the pain end by doing what I asked. I hope you're not counting on your bodyguard to come rescue you. She's a little distracted at the moment."

Raini had figured as much, and it confirmed that there were more halo-bearers close by.

"Call. Out. To. Maddox."

Nope, but she *would* call someone. Raini reached out and touched Jolene's mind. *Need a little assistance. I've got three halo-bearers in my kitchen, and there are more hanging around. Don't come alone. Round up some people. Lots and lots of people.* The halo-bearers would be prepared for descendants, not for other breeds of demon. And no one could quite prepare for imps.

Those sons of bitches made a grave mistake coming here, said Jolene, her telepathic voice vibrating with rage. *We'll be there fast.*

The angel's eyes flared with impatience, and the force around her head contracted. Fuck the pain was so excruciating she almost blacked out . . . which gave her an idea. Raini went limp in the hold of his power, feigning unconsciousness.

He let out a sound of disgust. "I was warned she was weak, but I didn't believe she was *this* weak."

"*Now* how do we get Maddox here?" asked another voice.

"Wake the woman he had guarding the house; maybe we can get her to call out to him."

Raini hit the floor hard as the force trapping her vanished. *Fucking ow.* She didn't hesitate to act. She raised her hand and let out a blast of raw, scorching hot power that rippled through the air, shimmering like waves of heat. The halo-bearers had no time to react. The power coming for them was too fast, too deadly. It didn't crash into them, it forcibly *poured* into them—entering their bodies through their mouth, nostrils, and ears.

Their heads jerked. Their eyes rolled back. Their bodies shook. Their knees buckled. Then they dropped like stones, dead, and their halos disappeared.

Moreover, their skulls—shattered by the force of the blast—caved in, leaving their heads gruesomely deformed. Because that was what happened when you were hit by a lethal dose of psychic hellfire. It ate at your brain, devoured it, leaving nothing behind. And that was bad enough. But it was the *other* thing psychic hellfire could do that made people fear it.

She instantly lit up each of the corpses' heads with good ole regular hellfire, intending to burn away the evidence. The fire would soon engulf every inch of them, which would not only leave an ungodly stench but potentially scorch her floor. Better that, though, than exposure.

She almost jumped when Jolene, Ciaran, and Khloë appeared in the doorway.

"Oh good, they're dead," was all Jolene said. "You were right about there being more. I have people outside fighting them." She and Ciaran then left, presumably to join the battle.

Raini pushed to her feet, every bone feeling almost . . . rickety.

Khloë crossed to her. "Damn, girl, what did they do to your eyes?"

Cricking her neck, Raini lifted a brow. "Bloodshot, huh?"

"*Seriously* bloodshot. Maddox is gonna freak."

The man himself materialized a few feet away. Speak of the devil . . .

His gaze locked on Raini, narrowed, and then took in the blazing corpses. Those vacant blue eyes briefly glittered with something . . . malevolent. Fury swept across the room like a tidal wave, so bitterly cold she wouldn't have been surprised if a sheet of ice formed on every surface.

The hairs on the back of her neck stood on end. Her demon pressed close to her, ready to defend, though it doubted he'd ever harm Raini.

"What happened?" he asked, his voice hard and clipped, as and he made a beeline for her.

Raini licked her lips. "They came looking for you. They were halo-bearers."

"The dumbasses either didn't know I was in the bathroom upstairs or didn't consider me a threat," Khloë cut in. "She and I tag-teamed them. In a totally non-sexual way."

Nothing in Khloë's tone or body language gave away the fact that she was lying. Jolene had taught her well.

"It was lucky I was here," the imp tacked on.

Maddox looked at Khloë. "Yes," he agreed. "Lucky."

He put his palm against Raini's, and the familiar cold burn of his healing power shot straight to her eyes, making her flinch and hiss out a breath.

"Your guard telepathed me and said she'd been attacked by halo-bearers who knocked her out with a psychic blow, not thinking she'd recover so fast. She feared they might have targeted you."

And the psychic tag he'd planted in Raini's mind had clearly led him straight to her. "Is she okay?"

"Yes." He glanced at the dead bodies. "You say they came for me?"

"They came for you," she confirmed.

His jaw went hard as granite. "And you didn't think to call out to—" He cut off, and she felt a weird vibration against her psyche; realized he was having a telepathic conversation. He cursed beneath his breath. "I'll be back. Call me if more come here." Then he was gone again.

Khloë frowned. "What was that?"

"I don't know." Raini raked her hand through her hair. "I don't know why halo-bearers would want Maddox."

Khloë twisted her mouth. "I heard Knox tell Keenan that several lairs of descendants have been destroyed recently. I thought one of their own kind had turned on the others or something, but now . . ."

"It could have been halo-bearers. They could want Maddox and his lair dead. Though why they didn't just attack the club, I don't know. There seems no sense in using me as bait to bring him *here* . . ." Her words trailed off as realization hit her.

"Distraction," said Khloë.

Raini nodded. "It was only meant to be a distraction."

CHAPTER SEVEN

Responding to Hector's telepathic warning, Maddox appeared in the shadowed area behind the rear of the monastery. Five halo-bearers were several feet away, attempting to light up the building with holy fire. Those attempts weren't working so well, but the angels didn't seem deterred, too confident in the potency of the power they were wielding.

They had every right to be confident in it. Holy fire could easily destroy buildings. Usually. Fortunately, the angels here hadn't accounted for the many ways in which having archangelic blood made Maddox different—mostly because he kept those "ways" as secret as possible.

Even now, as the halo-bearers hurled balls of holy fire at the monastery, it hadn't occurred to them that their efforts were pointless; that the flames would continue to simply lick at the bricks and then disintegrate. They'd probably sensed that magickal wards protected the building and had no doubt arrogantly assumed that the holy fire would eventually burn them away.

How wrong they were.

Hector's mind touched his. *Do we attack?*

Conscious that the sentinel and several members of the lair's Force stood in the shadows, waiting for direction, Maddox replied, *If we charge at them as a group, they'll simply waver out of here. I'll deal with them alone for now. Keep watch for more of them.*

Maddox stepped into the light. "Normally, I'd ask what would bring five halo-bearers to my home."

The angels whirled around and tensed.

"But you've made your reason quite apparent," Maddox added. "It might have been better if your friends had come here with you instead of going after my anchor, or they'd be alive right now."

The angels instantly began blasting him with holy fire. So very predictable. His demon sniffed, unimpressed by their display of power.

Maddox didn't retaliate. Didn't ask them to stop. Didn't try to counteract the holy fire—he didn't need to. Each fiery orb stopped mere inches from his body, not even singeing his clothes.

Finally realizing that the orbs were having no effect, the halo-bearers ceased attacking. They gaped at him; some frowning, some wide-eyed.

"Impossible," one breathed. He hurled another orb of holy fire.

Maddox sighed, bored. "It won't harm me any more than it would harm an archangel."

"You're not an archangel," he spat.

"Obviously," said Maddox, drawing out the word. "But I have the blood of one, so holy fire isn't going to touch me, let alone wound me. It *would* have destroyed the wards … if I hadn't bolstered them with my blood, making them as immune to the effects of holy fire as I am." He shrugged. "I had to ensure my lair was protected against your kind, just in case you ever came here. Why *did* you?"

"Your kind are abominations," he accused, all superiority. "You have no right to exist. No right to possess holy blood when you are the epitome of darkness."

Maddox pointed a finger at him. "You're chatty. Good. That makes you useful." *Hector, grab him before he can escape,* said Maddox as he glanced at the other angels, subtly conjuring an orb of red, arctic energy in his palm. "The rest of you I don't need." He hurled the orb their way, watching as it split into large splinters that sank into the skin, muscle, and bone of each angel.

They cried out and tried frantically to find and remove the splinters, but they were embedded too deep. Maddox's demon watched with a feral grin as the halo-bearers jerked, flinched, shivered, and sucked in pained breaths.

Some of their forms shimmered as they tried to waver to safety—it was no use. Not when they were dying so rapidly. The cold energy was spreading inside them, icing their blood, fragmenting their bones, rupturing their organs, killing them from the inside out.

It wasn't long before they were sprawled on the ground. Mere moments after their hearts ceased beating, their halos disappeared into thin air.

Secure in Hector's hold, the chatty halo-bearer gawked down at his friends, too deep in shock to struggle or panic.

"Compel him to sleep and take him to the cathedral's cellar," Maddox told the sentinel, who promptly obeyed the order. Maddox tossed balls of hellfire at each corpse and then glanced at the members of his Force. "Patrol the land. Make sure we don't have any additional visitors."

They nodded and quickly dispersed.

Soon enough, Hector teleported to Maddox's side and said, "The halo-bearer's secure. He won't wake until I lift the compulsion."

Maddox nodded in satisfaction, watching as the hellfire consumed the bodies.

"I need to check on Carmen," Hector went on. "She assured me that she's okay now, but . . . "

"What happened to Carmen?" asked a new voice as several lair members came striding out of the rear door.

"Halo-bearers," said Maddox. "She's fine." Feeding on their blood had helped her overcome the after-effects of the psychic blow. She'd been able to then telepath him, but she'd been too weak to teleport to Raini's side. Now, though, Carmen was fully recovered after having consumed more angelic blood. "Some went to Raini's house. They meant to use her to lure me to them."

"They knew you'd take several of us with you to defend her; they thought we'd all be easier to take out if we were divided," Hector said to Maddox, who nodded.

"And she *let* them use her as bait?" asked Euan. He blanched at the hard look Maddox gave him.

"No, she didn't," replied Maddox, somewhat pissed about it, just as his demon was. "Which is why she and I need to talk." He looked at Hector. "You go to Carmen. I'll be with Raini."

Honing on her psychic tag, Maddox teleported straight to her. She was in a living area he didn't recognize, but he was guessing by the number of imps in the room that the house belonged to one of her lair members. Many of the framed pictures featured Jolene, so it could quite possibly be her home.

Raini rose from the sofa and looked him up and down. Checking for injuries, perhaps? He wasn't sure. Her shoulders relaxed, and she gave him a weak smile.

"Ah, you're here," said Jolene before he had a chance to speak. "I'll make the introductions, and then you can tell me why halo-bearers tainted my lair's air. You already know Harper, Devon,

Khloë, and their mates. Over there is my anchor, Beck, and my grandson, Ciaran. Beside them are Raini's uncles and her sister, Demi. The couple standing near Raini are her parents, Evangeline and Lachlan."

"I'd thank you for healing my daughter," said Lachlan, his voice as hard as his expression. "But I strongly suspect that no angels would have showed up at her house if it hadn't been for her association with you. It's a loose association at best, of course, despite that she's your—"

"Dad, you promised," said Raini.

Lachlan's brows lifted. "Am I not being civil?"

"Are you not holding a knife in your hand?" she shot back.

He gave her an exasperated look. "It's not like I'm going to throw it or anything."

"Then why did you conjure it?"

"Sometimes a man likes to feel the weight of a blade in his hand."

"And sometimes he thinks he can bullshit his daughter. Would you please get rid of it?"

Lachlan rolled his eyes, and the knife disappeared from his hand. He turned back to Maddox, and his face went hard once again. "Did you know that angels were looking to wipe out your kind?"

"We were warned that that was the case," replied Maddox.

Lachlan's jaw went tight. "And still you left Raini vulnerable."

"I didn't believe they would target her," said Maddox. "She isn't a descendant or part of my lair. She also isn't bonded to me, so her death wouldn't psychically weaken me. Plus, it didn't seem a wise move on their part to drag others into it. Especially a lair that mostly consists of imps." Which was why Maddox was beginning to question his beliefs about the angels' motivations. "You're quite big on vengeance."

"They came for me to distract you, didn't they?" Raini guessed more than asked.

Maddox nodded. "They tried the whole divide-and-conquer strategy."

She bit her lip. "Were there any fatalities?"

"Not on my lair's side. I didn't expect them to target you, or I would have taken precautions."

"Could it be that this isn't the first time they struck at Raini?" asked Beck. "Maybe the dagger didn't hit her by accident after all."

Maddox pondered that for a moment. "No, I don't believe the incident is related to this. If they wanted to strip someone of power, they would surely have targeted me, not Raini. It is I they want dead, not her. But I doubt they would have made such a move in any case. They generally don't recruit others to do their dirty work—they're too arrogant to think they need help."

Tanner let out a grunt of agreement. "It was that arrogance that brought them here."

Raini nodded. "They must have thought they could leave without anyone knowing that the people responsible for the damage were angels—after all, no one would have suspected they'd do something so stupid and out of character. They told me they didn't *want* to hurt me, but I don't believe that. They wouldn't have left witnesses who could point the finger at them."

"Why would they try to eradicate your kind, Maddox?" asked Jolene, folding her arms. "They consider you abominations, I know. But I doubt they're acting on hate alone."

"Probably not," said Maddox. "I'll know for sure after I've spoken with the angel I'm keeping as my . . . guest."

"I wouldn't have thought the upper realm would give an order to wipe out an *entire* breed," said Devon, rubbing her arm. "I mean, they're risking starting a war."

"No, they're not," said Knox. "If they were to attack succubae or hellcats or another kind of demon then, yes, there'd be a chance of war because all other breeds would unite to fight. But descendants aren't a well-accepted breed."

"It's true that most demons don't consider us anything other than mutts," said Maddox, not particularly bothered by it. It benefited his kind that other breeds didn't get too close. "They wouldn't side with us."

"We will," declared Jolene. "Those bastards attacked both Raini and Khloë. They dragged us into this, and they'll damn well face the consequences."

Raini studied Maddox's face. Nothing there gave away whether he did or didn't believe that Khloë helped her fight the halo-bearers earlier. He had a tip-top bullshit meter, but both Jolene and Khloë were tip-top bullshitters, so there was no knowing what was going through his head.

"It's not necessary for you to involve yourselves," Maddox told them.

Lachlan frowned. "Of course it isn't. But we still will. In the name of the sanctity of retaliation—"

"Oh, God," Raini groaned.

"—we *will* ensure those bastards pay for bringing this fight to my daughter's doorstep."

Bram sidled over to his brother and gave him a supportive back-slap. "She's okay, Lachlan."

"I know, I know. But how can I not want to scorch the fucking Earth when they went after one of my girls, Bram?" Lachlan looked at Maddox. "Usually, I'm a pretty laidback man—"

"Really?" Raini cut in. "Seriously? You're gonna go there again?"

"I don't know why you insist on arguing that point," Lachlan said to her.

"You know what the definition of 'laidback' is, right?"

"Yes. Me."

Evangeline smiled at her. "You walked into that one, sweetheart." Her smile dimmed as she slid her gaze to Maddox. "Do you think more angels will be sent after your lair?"

"Yes, which is why I'll be increasing the security around Raini," said Maddox.

"What security?" Demi snarked, a tremor in her voice that said she wasn't quite as confident challenging Maddox as she'd like others to think. "You had *one woman* watching my sister's home tonight. One. And hey, I get why. There's no sense in wasting resources guarding someone you don't give two fucks about. But why bother with the pretense? Why not just admit that you don't want to be in Raini's life and then walk on right out of it? Because if you *had,* those angels would never have come for her."

"Demi," Jolene drawled.

"You know I'm right," Demi said to the Prime. "They only went after Raini because *he* gave them the mistaken impression that he cared what happened to her."

"It isn't an impression, it's a fact," countered Maddox, a hint of frost in his voice. "And the *one woman* you mentioned is my sentinel. She killed seven halo-bearers single-handedly. Almost died in her attempts to keep Raini safe. She'd do it again."

Demi's eyelids flickered, and she squirmed under the weight of that vacant stare. "Raini could have died, too," she said, her voice quieter, much shakier. "It would have been *your* fault. If it really is a 'fact' that you care, walk away now before you bring any more danger to her life." With that, Demi stormed out of the house, slamming the front door behind her.

Evangeline sighed. "She's just shaken from what happened tonight. She doesn't want to lose her sister."

"She won't," said Maddox. "The angels won't get near Raini again. Which brings me neatly to what I was about to say before." He turned to Raini. "I want to move you to a safer location until all this is over."

"Actually, we've been talking about that," said Raini. On the one hand, she didn't want to be chased out of her home. On the other hand, she didn't want any of her lair members being collateral damage if the halo-bearers returned for her. "When Khloë was dealing with the Enoch business, she moved to the Underground for a while. Harper and Knox have a penthouse suite right across the road from Urban Ink; they said they'll let me use it. It has excellent preternatural security—no halo-bearers could angel-port into there."

Maddox's demon balked at the thought of Raini relocating to the Underground. It wanted her close; wanted her where it could see her. So did Maddox, which was why he was sorely tempted to have her temporarily stay with him at the monastery. But she'd never go for it—like him, she had her secrets; she wouldn't want Maddox getting close enough to sense what they were. That worked both ways, because Euan was right; she'd look at Maddox with disgust if she ever discovered the truth.

Maddox cut his gaze to Knox and Harper. "I will only be able to teleport to her at the penthouse suite if you both agree to allow me entrance." Their blessing alone would be enough for the shield to permit him to pass. He could probably circumvent their preternatural security measures, but it was better that the pair wasn't aware of that.

"We'll allow it," said Knox. "We want Raini safe."

"It might be better if you two have your monthly meetings at the penthouse until all this blows over," Harper told Maddox. "I think even you'd agree that your club isn't a safe place for Raini right now."

On the contrary . . . "It's one of the safest places she could be." No angel could get to her there, because it had the same magickal wards as the monastery.

Harper frowned. "What does that mean?"

"It means that you're not the only people with exceptional security measures." Maddox turned to Raini. "You and I need to talk. In private."

Nobody moved until Raini gave a slow nod.

Once the two of them were alone, Maddox crossed to her. "As I said, I'll be stepping up the security around you. I'd imagine your lair will do the same. Nonetheless, if danger gets close to you again, you call me, like you should have called me earlier."

Raini frowned. "I wasn't going to lure you into a trap, and I won't apologize for the fact that I didn't."

Agitation flared to life in his belly, and his demon locked its back teeth. "Failing to telepath me when you're in danger stops me from aiding you, which obstructs my attempts to keep you safe—you swore you wouldn't do the latter."

"Honestly, I really didn't think of it that way, but you're right, I kind of violated our agreement—I'll own that. I'd be lying if I said I was sorry, though."

"I'm not asking for an apology. I want you to assure me that this won't happen again."

"Would *you* lure *me* into a trap?"

He pushed into her personal space. "This isn't about what I would or wouldn't do. You and I have an agreement. You swore you would stick to it. I believed you. Was I wrong to do so?"

Okay, Raini's demon did not like his tone *at all*. It charged to the surface and said, "Back away. You are testing my patience."

Maddox's nostrils flared. "I get that you're pissed at me, because I know her safety's imperative to you. It's just as imperative to me, so maybe you could work with me on this."

It flicked up a brow. "Why would I do that? She does not need you to protect her."

"Maybe so, but that isn't the point."

"Then, pray tell, what is?"

"I'm *supposed* to protect her. She's my anchor."

"Something you only acknowledge when it suits you. That means *she* does not need to acknowledge it when it does not suit *her*."

Maddox's eyes bled to black as his own entity surfaced. "I do not like that he holds back from the bond," it began, "but I do understand his reasons. Whatever you may think, she is important to him."

Raini's demon sniffed. "I will believe that when he shows it. And now I am done with you both." It subsided, leaving Raini once more in control. But Maddox's entity didn't retreat. It watched her with those black eyes that were like huge voids of nothing.

"Your demon has attitude," it said.

"So do you," Raini pointed out.

It hummed and then pulled back. Maddox's Prussian blue gaze then locked with hers, no longer as hard and cold as it was mere minutes ago.

"I don't think we should let them communicate often just in case they end up at each other's throats," she said.

Maddox was silent for a long moment. "Your demon is wrong if it truly believes I only acknowledge you're my anchor when it suits me. Perhaps my actions don't reflect that, so I don't suppose I can blame the entity for thinking otherwise. But *you* know better."

After the conversation they'd had during their last monthly meet, yes, Raini did know better. She might not be as important to him as she should rightly be, but she mattered to him about as much as he'd ever let anyone matter.

"I know you're not weak, Raini. But you wouldn't survive a fatal hit of holy fire. I'd say it's unlikely that angels will return for you. But I also would have said they would never target you in the first place, so I refuse to take chances here. I don't see any reason why you'd want to take them either. You're smarter than that."

"Which is why I'm going to stay at Harper and Knox's penthouse for a while."

"If halo-bearers are determined to get to you, they'll find a way. Probably by flushing you out to lead *you* into a trap. So I need your assurance that you won't again break your word."

She could take on any halo-bearers who came for her, because they wouldn't take her off-guard a second time; she wouldn't hesitate to act as she'd done earlier. But each time she used psychic hellfire, she risked others finding out about it. So if Maddox wanted to take on the angels, she'd be good with that. As such, she saluted him and said, "Whatever you say."

He narrowed his eyes, suspicious. She wondered if he'd yet worked out that she wasn't anywhere near as cooperative and subdued as she allowed him to believe.

Finally, he gave a satisfied nod. "It's lucky Khloë was with you tonight," he said, a skeptical note in his tone.

"Totally," agreed Raini. "I'm thinking I should send her a thank you card and a fruit basket."

"I'd prefer a box of donuts, if anyone's taking notes," Khloë called out.

Raini sighed and rolled her eyes. The girl was *such* an eavesdropper.

"Do you need help moving your things to the Underground?" asked Maddox.

Raini shook her head. "But thank you for asking."

He gave another nod. "I have an angel to speak with. I'll check in with you later." With that, he teleported away.

People began to trickle back into the room.

Evangeline blew out a breath. "He's . . . intense."

Raini hummed in agreement.

"Whatever Demi or anyone else might think, you do matter to him," her mother claimed. "I don't think he really knows how to handle it yet. He'll learn."

"He'd better," added Harper. "Well, Raini, you up for moving to the penthouse tonight?"

"Now's as good a time as any, I guess," said Raini.

Harper nodded. "Then let's go pack your stuff."

Maddox's inner demon smiled with a twisted sense of satisfaction as the sleeping halo-bearer shivered within the arctic energy forcefield. Maddox had erected it around the angel, sure it would contain him. No one had ever broken out of it before—not demon, not fey, not vampire. He doubted an angel would be an exception.

Maddox looked at Hector and said, "Wake him."

Moments later, the angel's eyelids fluttered, and he squirmed restlessly. The fog of sleep finally seemed to clear, because he opened his eyes. And, of course, he tried wavering away, but his form did no more than wink like a faulty lightbulb. Then he sprung to life and battered the forcefield with holy fire.

Maddox sighed. "I wouldn't bother wasting energy trying to escape. There's no way to take it down or waver out of it."

But the angel continued to fight, refusing to admit defeat. He would eventually, though. And then he could clear up a few things for Maddox.

In ordinary circumstances, Maddox would pluck the information he needed from his captive's mind—few mental shields could keep him out. But it was agonizingly painful for a demon to delve into the psyche of an angel, and vice versa. Maddox might have archangelic blood, but he was still a demon. It would also lead to psychic burnout, and Maddox couldn't afford to be weak—not as a Prime responsible for his lair, and not as a person who was currently marked for death.

There were ways of extracting information from people that didn't include invading minds, though. Ways which his demon found much more enjoyable, since they involved dishing out pain.

Finally, the halo-bearer gave up. He stood still, breathing hard, each exhale fogging the chilly air within the forcefield. "You killed them."

Rolling up one sleeve of his shirt, Maddox said, "Oh, you mean your friends. Yes, I did. They would have killed me and mine. And that's because we're abominations, right?"

"Nothing dark should possess holy blood."

"Why not?" Maddox began to roll up the other sleeve. "Why should only celestial beings be entitled to anything holy?"

The angel's chin lifted, but the defiant gesture was ruined by the shiver that ran down the length of his body. "None outside of the upper realm are worthy."

Maddox's demon rolled its eyes. "You people really do think you're superior to everyone and everything else, don't you? Why? Because you can wield holy fire? It's not much different from hellfire. Just stems from a different source of power."

Another shiver racked the angel from head to toe, and he pulled his limbs closer to his body. "Holy blood is only for the pure."

"Is it? What's pure about executing people who've done you no harm? What's pure about stationing an angel on Earth and forcing them to earn their way back home? The latter can take eons, from what I've heard. You lot are no better or worse than us. You're just different. And more narcissistic."

"Think what you like. The fact is, you should not exist."

"Says who?"

"Angels. Demons. Everyone."

"I don't say it." Maddox looked at Hector. "Do you?"

The sentinel shook his head. "Can't say I do."

Maddox slid his gaze back to the angel. "It can't be that great up above if some choose to fall."

"Only the weak fall," the angel sneered.

"Are the infamous Seven archangels weak? I've heard not. I also heard that one of them fell recently."

The halo-bearer tried not to react, but he betrayed his surprise by the flicker of his eyelids.

"You hadn't expected that we'd hear of such things, I see. I'll bet the archangel's fall caused a stir. A major one, in fact. There must be people clamoring to take his place. But to become the new seventh archangel, they would have to prove themselves, wouldn't they? They might even choose to do something big to make them stand out from the others who seek the position. Even something as big as eradicate the descendants."

Shivering again, the halo-bearer swallowed.

"Archangels generally don't care what occurs on Earth. But everyone upstairs cares that a breed of demon possesses holy blood. That just rankles all of you, doesn't it?"

Hector snickered, clearly enjoying the idea.

Maddox slipped his hands into the pockets of his slacks. "At first, I thought that an order was given from someone much higher up to wipe us all out. But then your friends went after my anchor, thereby bringing her lair into this mess. That was sloppy. Ill-thought out. Definitely not something the upper realm would sanction unless they wanted a war, and I don't believe they do. There'd be no winner. There would only be death and destruction on both sides—neither wants that. Plus, there are much simpler ways to begin a war, if that was really what someone wanted.

"My guess is that an archangel recruited you, your friends, and a bunch of other halo-bearers to do his bidding. He believes that ridding the Earth of my kind will grant him a place among the infamous Seven. I would like his name."

The angel gave him a stubborn look.

"It really isn't wise for you to shut down now. You've lived this long in my company because you like to talk. So talk."

"I will die before I betray him," he said, his teeth chattering so hard he'd be lucky if he didn't bite his tongue.

"You realize that if an angel dies in this realm their soul doesn't return to heaven, yes?"

"Yes. But I will die knowing I played a part in the ascension of—" He cut himself off.

"Don't stop now." Maddox wasn't entirely surprised that the angel stayed silent. His demon wasn't disappointed, because there were ways to make him reconsider being so uncooperative . . . and the entity would enjoy seeing him suffer, given that he'd happily been part of a plot that involved hurting its anchor. "What is your worst memory?"

The angel frowned. "My what?"

"The most painful moment of your life. What is it?" Maddox tipped his head to the side. "Let's find out, shall we?" He held up his hand, conjured the cold red energy that hummed constantly beneath his skin, and sent out a *call* he couldn't quite put into words. Just as angels could *call* on a person's happiest memory—something they usually brought to the surface of someone's mind to help them peacefully pass on to the next life—Maddox could call on their worst.

"What are you doing?" demanded the angel, his eyes wide.

"Ah, there it is," said Maddox as a memory played through his mind like a fast-forward video clip. "You love her, but they won't let you have her, will they? The moment she publicly bound herself to another angel broke something inside you. Not just because she'd never be yours, but because she looked happy. You hate her for that. Still, you don't hate her more than you love her. You wish you did, but you don't."

Pain flashed in the angel's eyes. "Stop," he bit out.

"Have you ever heard of time loops? It's when a person has to continuously re-experience a certain period of time. And me, well, I can place a person in a psychic time loop, forcing them to relive something in their mind over and over again for as long as I please. They know they're caught up in it. They know it can be stopped. But *they* cannot stop it. Only I can free them from it. I think you see where I'm going with this."

The blood drained from the angel's face.

"You can choose to be a martyr if you want, of course. But I won't *kill* you for keeping the archangel's name from me. I will simply torture you. I will force you to relive that moment where you had to officially accept that you'd lost her for good; that she'd never really loved you, not if she was happy without you."

Pausing, Maddox took a step toward him. "If you think it was agonizing the first time, ask yourself how it will feel when you've re-experienced it for the fiftieth. And no, you won't get used to it. Because you'll also relive the pain, not just the moment itself. Whoever the archangel is . . . he's not worth it. And if he's truly so great, he'll get where he's meant to be without your help, so you'd only be suffering unnecessarily. Now . . . what is his name?"

CHAPTER EIGHT

Holding his phone to his ear, Maddox sank into the armchair near his bed. "What do you know about an archangel named Castiel Ozera?"

"Where did you hear that name?" asked Viper.

"From a halo-bearer who tried to kill me. He told me plenty about Castiel, but it was praise, praise, and more praise. Let's just say he's a devout follower of Castiel."

"But not so devout that he refused to tell you what you wanted to know."

"I can be very persuasive."

Viper chuckled. "I'll bet." There was a pause. "Well, Castiel is quite high up in the heavenly host," he said, referring to the upper realm's army. "He's ambitious. Cunning. Arrogant. Seeks positions of authority to compensate for his own weaknesses—you know the kind. They need to be someone in power in order to feel they're worth something, and then they abuse that power. He 'collects' people who are weaker than him yet just as ambitious—feeds them false praise, promises them promotions, and says he 'sees' something special in them."

"In other words, he tells people what they want to hear to manipulate them into doing his bidding."

"Yes. How did he crop up in your conversation with the halo-bearer who tried to kill you? On a side note, I'm surprised only one came for you."

"He had some friends with him. Several went after my anchor."

There was a stunned pause. "They *what?*"

"Yes, it confused me as well. Heaven's higher-ups surely wouldn't sanction dragging non-descendant lairs into this situation."

"No, they wouldn't. Not when it would risk starting a war."

"Which made me wonder if someone was acting alone. Someone who wanted to fill the position that the seventh archangel left open when he fell."

"One of the Seven fell? Interesting."

Ignoring Viper's attempt to play dumb, Maddox went on, "I wondered if said 'someone' sought to ensure he stood out from the rest by coming after my kind. So I had a chat with one of the halo-bearers sent to decimate my lair, and he admitted as much."

Viper hummed. "It's no secret that Castiel wants to be one of the Seven—many do. He'll never get the position. He's high up in the heavenly host, but he doesn't have enough experience to be even *considered* a potential candidate."

"So he cooked up a plan that would make him be considered."

"It might have worked. No one upstairs would have shed a tear over the extinction of your kind. But they won't be happy if they find out he stepped on the toes of other breeds."

"How do I get to him?"

"You don't. He's an archangel, completely out of your reach. You need him to come to you."

Maddox figured he'd say that. "Is there a way to get a message to him?"

"Are any of the halo-bearers he sent after you still alive?"

"No."

"Then no."

Maddox couldn't say he regretted killing Castiel's devout follower, but maybe he'd been a little hasty. Still, it wasn't a lost cause, because . . . "Castiel will send more. He's killed enough descendants via his minions to feel that his plan does have the potential to be a success."

"Castiel isn't an archangel who would call it quits easily—it's an ego thing," said Viper. "Is your anchor all right?"

"She's fine. But Castiel will still pay. It was allegedly his idea to use her as bait. He gave the order to lure me into a trap and then kill her before her lair could realize that angels were behind her death." Which was why Maddox's demon had spent the past ten minutes dreaming up ways to make the archangel suffer.

"I'll bet her Prime wants blood. Jolene Wallis's lair might not be high in number, but I wouldn't want it chasing my ass. Castiel seriously fucked up. If he'd just stuck to picking off your kind, it's doubtful that anyone would have questioned who was actually giving the orders." Viper paused. "I remember overhearing something he once did."

"What?"

"His father planned to fall once upon a time. He'd lost his woman and couldn't bear the pain anymore, so he confided in his sons that he would fall after he'd put his affairs in order. Castiel went to the higher-ups and told them. His father was taken and punished horrifically before being killed. Castiel was rewarded with a promotion. That's the kind of person you're dealing with, Maddox. He'll do *anything* to get ahead. Anything. And he won't care who gets hurt in the process. So don't underestimate him.

People like Castiel? There are no limits as to what shit they'll do to get what they want."

Then it seemed that he and Maddox had something in common.

The next morning, Raini stood in front of the penthouse's floor-to-ceiling window, taking in the view of the Underground, while drinking coffee. People walked along the sidewalks of the busy strip. Cart vendors set up their mobile stalls. Street sweepers cleaned up the empty bottles, cigarette butts, and other litter. A busker was singing his heart out and, if the reactions of the passers-by were any indication, he wasn't all that good at it.

Open 24/7, the Underground was always a hub of activity, no matter the hour. So it was no surprise that a number of the pedestrians were staggering, swaying, and heckling people, clearly plastered. Some also began a singalong with the busker, who appeared to be thoroughly enjoying it.

Maddox's mind brushed against hers. *How did you sleep?* he asked, and damn if that quintessentially male voice didn't get her hormones all wound up.

I wasn't tired, so I just lay in bed and binge-watched a TV series, she replied, sipping her coffee. *What about you?*

I didn't sleep either.

Demons didn't need to sleep as often as humans. They could go days without doing so. Although Raini had been psychically tired after the scuffle with the halo-bearers, she'd been too wired to settle. Maddox's kind had pretty much been marked for extermination. He and Raini might not be as close as most psi-mates were, but he was still her anchor, and she still worried about him. *How did your talk with the angel go? Did you learn anything new?*

He was in a talkative mood. He merely confirmed what I'd already suspected. Maddox relayed the full story. *It's important that you be on your guard, Raini. Castiel clearly has no issue with using you to get to me. He may not do so again, but it always pays to be cautious.*

I'll be careful, she promised because, yeah, going up against an archangel didn't sound fun.

Good. There was a brief pause. *I need to go. I'll check in with you later.* His mind brushed hers one last time before he then broke contact.

Raini sighed, wishing not for the first time that there didn't have to be this . . . gulf between them. Wishing they had the same easy companionship that both Devon and Khloë had with their anchors. Well, at least Raini had found her psi-mate—many demons weren't so fortunate in that respect.

Putting the matter out of her mind, she washed her cup in the kitchen and then took a hot shower. Done, she dressed and dried her hair. She was about to leave for work when her cell phone rang.

Snatching it from the nightstand, she frowned. *Unknown caller.* Huh. "Hello?" she answered absently, grabbing her purse.

"Hi, it's, um, Dwain."

Ugh. Wondering why he could possibly be calling her—and where the hell he got her number—she not-so-brightly greeted, "Hi."

"I heard what happened last night. I just wanted to say I'm glad you're okay."

What, like they were friends or something? She felt her brow furrow. "Thanks." *I guess,* she barely refrained from adding.

"I would have come to see you but, um, I'm pretty sure that the Thornes are particular about who they let into their penthouse," he said with what seemed like a forced chuckle.

"They are pretty particular about it, yeah," Raini confirmed, walking out of the room.

"Figured as much." He cleared his throat. "I drove Demi to the marina this morning and waved her off. I'm surprised she still went on the cruise, given how worried she is about you."

Raini's demon snorted. Sad as it was, Demi wasn't going to lose sleep over the fact that her own sister could be in danger. And nothing would have kept her from going on that cruise in any case, because it was the perfect excuse for Demi to get a break from seeing Dwain with his mate.

Heading toward the foyer, Raini was about to round up what—to her—seemed like a pointless conversation, but then he spoke again.

"So, anyway, me and Harmony are going home tomorrow."

Oh, excellent. It was the best news Raini had heard all week.

"With all the shit that's going down, I'd rather get her away from here, you know? But you and I never got a chance to catch up, so I was thinking maybe we could have lunch today. I'm in the Underground right now. I have plans to meet with some old friends at the hellhorse tracks. You and I could meet up afterward."

Raini scratched the back of her head. "Dwain, I don't understand why you'd want that." She frowned at the whir of machinery. Someone was apparently coming up the elevator to the penthouse. "You're still a little mad at me for what happened years ago. I would think you'd rather not spend any more time with me than you already have."

There was a heavy exhale. "I just think it would be easier on Demi if there wasn't so much awkwardness between her anchor and her sister. And I'm not mad at you, Raini. I'm mad at myself for being so blind to reality for a while back then, but not at you. I'm sorry if I've made you think differently. See, this is why it would be good for us to meet up and talk. We could clear the air and get things back on track. I think it's long past time we did it."

Raini totally disagreed. It wasn't like they'd ever been friends, or that they ever would be. And despite what he seemed to think, Demi *wouldn't* be happy if the awkwardness between him and Raini was gone. So, really, what was the point in rehashing it all when it would be simpler to just move forward? Besides . . . "We kind of *did* clear the air. Look, what happened is in the past. No one's holding grudges. There doesn't seem any need to do anything other than let it lie."

Right then, the elevator doors slid open. Harper, Devon, and Khloë stepped into the foyer.

"Still, I think it would be good for us to talk," he persisted.

Devon frowned at the phone, and her upper lip quivered. Ah, her hellcat hearing had picked up the sound of Dwain's voice.

"Who's that?" Khloë mouthed, nosy as ever.

Knowing the imp would have no compunction with jumping onto Raini's back to be able to listen, Raini put the call on speakerphone and said, "Really, Dwain, it's not necessary. Everything between us is cool as far as I'm concerned. Plus, I agreed to have lunch with Maddox anyway." There, that should nip this shit in the bud.

Harper flicked one brow up in a "Really?" gesture. Raini shook her head.

"I thought he only wanted to see you once a month," said Dwain. "Demi told me you went to his club a few nights ago."

"Well he wants to talk to me a little more about what happened with the halo-bearers."

"And you can't say no, because he now pulls all your strings," said Dwain, a mocking bite to his voice.

Raini felt her brows lift, and every one of her girls bristled. If Dwain really thought someone could make Raini their very own marionette, he didn't know her at all. But she wasn't going to jump to her own defense here—this idiot just wasn't worth it. "Yeah, he calls the shots," she agreed, exchanging an eye roll with Harper.

"Don't you hate it?" he asked. "Or are you one of *those people* who likes having someone else take charge of their life?"

Thinking it was time to fuck with this asshole, she gave the girls a conspiratorial smile as she said, "There's something to be said for having someone take control, Dwain. It makes things simpler. Maddox takes care of all those little decisions that drive me nuts. I don't have to waste time debating what I'm going to have for breakfast. I don't have to worry about what I'm going to wear. I don't have to fret over whether or not it's just plain weird to obey his order to call him Big Papa. Or whether I shouldn't like that he calls me Daddy's little swallower. Or whether my dressing up as Khaleesi, mother of dragons, for our monthly meet is really all that necessary." At this point, the girls were almost creased over with silent laughter.

There was a long moment of silence. Dwain sighed. "You're fucking with me right now, aren't you?"

A snort popped out of Harper.

"Wait, am I on *speakerphone*?" he demanded.

"What? No, of course not," Raini assured him, but she wasn't sure he heard her over the sound of the girls laughing their tits off. "So, anyway, I hope you—" And she had dead air. "He hung up on me. So rude." Shrugging, she dropped her cell into her purse.

"Daddy's little swallower?" echoed Khloë, her eyes dancing.

"It has a nice ring to it," said Raini.

"I'm assuming *he* called *you*, because I can't imagine a scenario in which you'd have called that dweeb," said Harper.

Raini nodded. "He's in the Underground with friends. He wanted me to meet up with him later."

Khloë's face scrunched up. "Why?"

"He thought it would be good for us to 'clear the air' so things aren't awkward between us anymore," replied Raini. "Apparently, he thinks Demi would want that."

Devon shook her head in disbelief. "Demi would have you two on completely separate planets if she could."

"Well, he has yet to figure that out," said Raini. "So, what are you all doing here anyway?"

"We came to get you," Harper told her. "We've got a busy day ahead of us—starting with breakfast at the cute little café down the street that has the Italian vibe."

Raini double-blinked. "Wait, what?"

"We're not opening the shop today for two reasons," said the sphinx. "One, we're all far too tense after last night's events and need some downtime. Two, news of what happened has already circulated throughout the demonic grapevine. Anyone who walked into the shop would have quizzed you like crazy. I think I can safely say that none of us are in the mood for that."

"So we're going to have a girl's day out." Beaming, Devon gave a little clap. "Yay! I love those."

"Don't bother objecting, Raini," began Khloë, "I already rescheduled all the appointments. No one seemed surprised that we weren't opening today. Now let's get moving—I'm hungry."

Raini's heart squeezed. They weren't proposing a girls' day because *they* needed one. Not really. They were doing it for her. They were trying to take her mind off things. And she adored them all for it. "What is it exactly that you have in mind?"

Harper grinned. "Oh, you'll see."

First, they had breakfast at the café, just as Harper had said. Next they went to the mall where they did some shopping, ate Thai food for lunch, and did a little more shopping. Being Harper's bodyguard, poor Tanner had to come along, and he ended up being the mule. Raini's own guard stayed out of sight most of the time.

After that, they headed to the movie theater, and Tanner was no happier with the romcom than with the shopping trip he'd been subjected to. Once the movie was over, they ate dinner at a fancy restaurant where they drank *far* too much wine . . . and so the tipsy women all ended up back at the penthouse, at which point they engaged in a very deep, serious conversation.

"Dude, that's not how you do it," Raini told Devon, standing beside her in the middle of the living area.

The hellcat frowned. "What? Course it is."

"No, it's not."

"I have this *mastered.*"

"I'm telling you, Dev, you're doing it wrong."

The hellcat looked at Harper, who was sprawled on the sofa humming a tune. "Have I, or have I not, got the Gangnam Style dance down to a tee?"

The sphinx grimaced. "Raini does it better. You keep forgetting to twirl your arm in the air."

"And you look more like a bunny bouncing than someone riding a horse," added Khloë, lying on the floor drawing patterns on her arm with a black sharpie.

Devon flushed. "Up yours, heifers."

Raini planted her feet. "Look, copy what I do." She slowly ran through each dance move, not moving onto the next until Devon had mastered the one before it. Satisfied that the hellcat no longer looked like a bouncing bunny, Raini said, "Cool. Now come on, let's Gangnam *the fuck* out of this dance."

Raini sang the chorus of the song while they danced. Harper sang along and clapped while Khloë wolf-whistled and egged them on. It was all going great until, somehow, Devon went ass over tit. Raini honestly didn't know how it happened. One second her friend was right beside her, the next she was sprawled on the floor. But she was *still* dancing. Or trying to. It seemed to take her a few moments to realize she wasn't standing anymore.

Blinking, Devon looked up at her. "What happened?"

"You sort of fell," replied Raini. "Harper, stop laughing!"

The sphinx snickered. "*You're* laughing, too!"

Yeah, Raini totally was, but at least she was doing it *silently*.

"I hate it when my dignity sails away." Devon frowned at Khloë, who'd scooted closer, a pen still in hand. "Don't you *dare* draw on me, Wallis."

"Come on, just a little pic of a baby hippo," said Khloë.

Devon's face softened. "Aw, that would be *so cute*." She held out her arm to the imp.

At that moment, Maddox's mind touched Raini's. *What have you done with yourself today?*

She inwardly snorted. *Like the guard you assigned me doesn't report back everything I do.*

I'd rather hear it from you.

She wasn't sure why that would be, but he certainly sounded sincere, so she gave him a quick rundown of her day.

So you enjoyed yourself? he asked, genuinely sounding like it was . . . important.

I did. The girls wanted to take my mind off everything, and it definitely worked.

Good. His mind slid against hers just before it was gone. Yeah, he wasn't much for goodbyes.

"Yoo-hoo," Devon called out. "Are you back with us?"

Raini sighed. "I was trying to have a conversation, feline."

"Maddox checking in again?"

"Yup."

Devon twisted her mouth. "Am I the only one who thinks Maddox didn't buy that you had help killing the angels?"

"Nope," said Raini, none-too-gracefully sinking on the sofa. "I think it, too."

Harper lifted a hand. "So do I. It's weird that he didn't call you on it."

Raini tilted her head. "How ironic is it that we struggled to find an angel not so long ago . . . and now they're all up in our shit? I mean, three appeared in my kitchen. With halos and everything. Fucking bastards deserved what they got."

"Totally. Utterly. Completely." Devon hummed. "Hey, I wonder what Maddox did to the others. I am thinking he did *not* give them a quick, painless death. He's uber scary, ain't he? I don't know where Demi got the gumption to snark at him. She probably thought he wouldn't hurt her because she's your sister. For a minute there, I thought he might."

"Same here," said Harper. "If looks could kill, she'd have been a scorch mark on the floor. Man, he did *not* like her. Nu-uh. But then, neither do I."

Devon snorted. "Dude, who does?"

"Dwain," replied Harper.

The hellcat waved a hand. "He's a dweeb, he doesn't count. I'm still miffed about the shit he said to you earlier, Raini. Want me to let my power loose on him? It might be fun to watch his bones shatter and blood pour out of his orif—orif—*orifices*."

"Or I could deal him some soul-deep pain, if you want?" Harper offered. "Or me and Devon could both tumble on his shit at the same time."

The hellcat's eyes lit up. "Yes! Yes, that would be so—*Khloë, why have you drawn a fucking penis on my arm?*"

"It's not a penis, it's a hippo," Khloë insisted. "Look, see, that's the head, this is the body—which yeah, needs some legs, but I forgot about those. I remembered to give him feet, though. Well, two."

Devon clenched her fists. "Why do his feet look like huge hairy balls? And since *when* does a hippo's head have a fucking line running down the center of it?"

Khloë lifted her shoulders. "So Fritz here is a little different from most hippos, so what?"

"Fritz?"

"That's his name."

"His name? You named—*don't write it on me, you weirdo*! God, what is *wrong* with you?"

"Do you want the whole list?"

Hearing the elevator fire up, Harper said, "I think the guys are here to take us home."

"Good," bit out Devon. "Because if someone doesn't get this imp away from me, I'm gonna kill her."

"You love me really," Khloë insisted.

"I can love you and still want to drown you."

"Why drown? There are easier ways to kill me."

"But there'd be something almost comforting about sticking your head in a toilet."

Khloë pursed her lips and shrugged one shoulder. "Seems like a lazy method of murder to me. You should really get more creative."

The elevator doors opened. Knox, Levi, Tanner, and Keenan strolled out and crossed the foyer.

Khloë smiled brightly at her mate. "Hey, Jon Duan."

Keenan's brow furrowed. "I think you mean Don Juan. Which, as I've told you a gazillion times, isn't my name."

"Can I help it if it suits you?" she asked, to which he only rolled his eyes.

Knox helped Harper stand and dropped a soft kiss on her mouth. "So, you went heavy on the wine?"

"My buzz is wearing off now." Harper frowned. "Which doesn't seem fair."

Tanner looked down at his mate, who was sulking in a cross-legged position. “Why did you draw a cock on your arm?”

“I didn’t!” Devon pointed at Khloë. “It was *her*.”

The imp rolled her eyes. “Quit with the drama, diva. It’s only a little hippo.”

Levi stifled a smile. “Yeah, hippos don’t look like that.”

Tanner pulled Devon to her feet. “You really should have known better than to trust Khloë with a pen *anywhere* near your bare skin, kitten.”

Keenan nodded. “While I was once sleeping off a hangover, she drew an arrow on the small of my back that pointed toward my asshole and wrote, ‘Exit only. Except on Saturday nights—bring lube and a friend.’”

Khloë chuckled. “Even better, I took snapshots of it and told him I’d uploaded them onto social media. He *freaked*.”

Who wouldn’t have? Raini lifted her finger. “The moral of the story? Never leave a bored imp unsupervised.”

“Amen to that,” said Keenan, draping an arm around Khloë’s shoulders. “Time to go home.”

The girls all exchanged goodbyes and love-yous.

Alone, Raini sighed and went straight to the spare bedroom she was using. There, she shed her tank top and jeans and then fell face-first on the bed. After all the walking, shopping, drinking, and dancing, she was too exhausted to do anything other than *crash*.

CHAPTER NINE

Standing at the foot of the bed in the shadowy room, Maddox watched his anchor sleep. She was sprawled on her back with her arms above her head, her body twisted at the hips so that her joined legs tipped to the side. Not a single line creased her face. She looked peaceful. Serene. And sexy as fucking hell in nothing but pink lacy underwear.

He'd known when he touched her mind that she wasn't awake, but he'd come anyway. His demon had badgered him all day to seek her out. It had wanted to check on her—the telepathic contact hadn't been enough, nor had Carmen's reports confirming that Raini was fine. The entity had needed to *see* her. And now, looking at all that flawless skin, it wanted to touch her. Taste her. Fuck her.

Maddox could relate. His cock was rock fucking hard and throbbing like a bitch. He wanted to flick open the clasp on her bra. Wanted to peel off her panties. Wanted every inch of her bare to his view.

A deep sense of possession gripped him tight. This beautiful creature was his. Not in every way, no, but he had rights to her that no other person would ever have—those rights were his alone, and no one could take them from him. No one else could be who he was to her.

He'd never felt possessive of someone before. It had taken some getting used to. In general, he wasn't particularly territorial—unusual for his kind, really. If asked, he would have said he didn't have such a depth of territorialism in him. And he would have been wrong.

Raini slowly turned her head, still sleeping, and one finger twitched slightly. He knew she'd had a hectic day. He knew he should leave and let her rest.

He also knew he wouldn't.

The truth was he hadn't come here simply to placate his demon. He'd come for her; come to take what he'd wanted since the moment he first laid eyes on her. He'd waited long enough.

He'd given her the time she needed to get comfortable around him—or as comfortable as she could ever hope to feel around him. She'd come to realize that she was safe with him. She trusted that he wouldn't harm her. She knew that his determination to have her was real and that he wasn't under some preternatural influence.

Of course, there was a chance that her demon would surface and tell him to fuck off. He would, if that was what it wanted. He wouldn't force the entity any more than he would Raini. They both belonged to him.

Moving slow and easy, Maddox righted her hips and parted her legs, watching as a little line formed between her brows. Kneeling on the bed, he ghosted his hands up her toned legs, soaking in the feel of her warm, butter-smooth skin.

She shifted slightly, turning her head on the pillow, and

her eyelids began to flicker open. Languid amber eyes glanced around then settled on him, punching him right in the gut. She double-blinked and then squinted, as if not sure she was truly seeing right. “Am I dreaming?”

“No.” He took a moment to admire the delicate vine tattoo that began on her outer thigh, curled over her hipbone, swirled diagonally across her body, and disappeared under her bra. He wondered if it ended there or continued around her back. She had some other tattoos here and there, and all were striking. But the vine was exquisite.

She swallowed. “What are you doing here?”

Maddox caught the waistband of her panties. “I would have thought that was obvious. Should I leave?”

For a long moment, she looked at him, biting her lip.

“If you want me to go, just say it, and I’ll go. I will. All you need to do is say it.”

She bit her lip harder, still staring. Finally, she said, “Stay.”

His demon grinned, triumphant. Maddox used flickers of hellfire to burn the seams of her waistband until each side tore open. That done, he tossed the scraps of lace on the floor.

He spread her thighs wider and settled himself between them on the mattress, his cock twitching at the perfect view he now had of her pussy. “So pretty and pink.” He licked the crease of her thigh and dipped his thumb between her folds just enough to whisper it over her clit.

Her hips jerked, and she sucked in a breath.

“So very responsive, too.” He parted her soft folds with his thumbs and blatantly dipped his tongue inside her core, needing a taste, loving her little gasp. *Sweetness and spice.* He hummed. “I’m going to enjoy this.” He spread her folds a little wider and all but buried his face in her pussy.

Oh, God. Raini fisted the bedsheet, shamelessly arching into his mouth as he expertly ate her out. She was not dealing with an amateur here. No, this dude was a seasoned vet.

Thank you, Jesus.

The last few men who'd gone down on her . . . well, the experiences had been somewhat disappointing. There were classic mistakes some men made, thinking women liked it—being rough with her clit, trying to get beneath her clitoral hood, spelling the alphabet down there with their tongue like, what, why did they even do that?

The worst, though, was when they didn't *listen*. Once, when a guy was *jabbing* her clit with the tip of his tongue like he was trying to drill a damn hole through it, she'd told him he was being too rough and needed to ease up the pressure. He'd said, "*Look, I know what I'm doing, so just enjoy it.*"

Um, no, Mr. Condescending. Vagina-owners knew best.

Maddox, well, she was not gonna need to give this guy any direction. Nu-uh. He was driving her fast to O-town, and he was doing it with some *serious* skill. Adding to the pleasure, his hands roamed—grazing her bra-clad breasts, stroking her belly, palming her ass, gripping her hips to hold them down.

Raini was soon a moaning, whimpering, bucking puddle of *oh God I need to come*. But Maddox didn't rush her to the finish line. No, he'd set up camp and apparently wasn't done yet. Like she'd complain.

He left no part of her pussy untouched, as if determined to find every hot spot. And oh, he did. That tongue was tireless—swiping from side to side, licking up and down, lapping and swirling around her clit, teasingly circling the entrance of her pussy. More, he varied the speed and pressure, keeping her off-balance.

She jolted as he drove a finger inside her and hooked it just right. Oh, O-town was so much closer now. Working her clit with his tongue once again, he pumped his finger in and out of her. Each thrust stroked her g-spot, ramping up the pleasure and building the friction until she thought she'd explode.

And then she did.

Her release thundered through her body and seemed to contract every muscle. Her back bowed, her head flew back, and her mouth fell open in a silent scream. She slumped onto the mattress, her breaths coming hard and fast. *Yowza.*

Maddox wiped his face on her inner thigh. "I like this tattoo," he said as he began to kiss his way along the swirly vine, stopping only when he came to her bra. His eyes shot to hers, gleaming with need.

"I gotta say, I did not foresee this happening," she said.

"You knew I'd come for you."

At some point, sure. But she hadn't thought he'd just freaking *appear* during the night. Her demon wasn't all that surprised, though. It was also strangely unbothered by his presence. There was even an element of smugness there.

"This needs to go." He unhooked the front clasp of her bra and pushed the cups aside, freeing her breasts. Her nipples went tight under the heat of his gaze. Tugging on one bra strap, he said, "Take it off."

Happy to comply, Raini quickly did so and then lay back.

Kneeling above her, Maddox swept his eyes over her, seeming somewhat satisfied by the fact that no more clothing now stood in the way of his view. "Fucking perfect."

"You're not naked. This is a problem for me. A mega one."

His mouth quirked. "A mega one?"

"And as my anchor, it's kind of your job to help me with my problems."

"That is true," he allowed.

Raini's feminine parts fairly clapped their hands with glee as he started unbuttoning his shirt, revealing more and more of his chest. She felt her mouth dry up. Hell, the dude. Was. *Built.* All hard and toned and perfectly defined.

When he shrugged off his shirt and all the muscles in his broad shoulders and arms rippled and bunched . . . yeah, wow. Just wow. She took a few mental snapshots so she could use them when badgering the clit-ness on future lonely nights.

The show then got even better; his hands dropped to his fly, he lowered his zipper, and *holy shit* that thing was not going near her ass at any point. She'd cast his groin enough subtle glances in the past to know he was packing some serious heat, but she hadn't realized he was that thick.

Not that she was complaining. She'd happily take his cock for a spin. It just wouldn't be entering through the back door.

She took some more mental snapshots while he rose from the bed to shed the rest of his clothes. In a matter of moments, he was naked and back between her thighs. She lifted her hips and ground against his cock, gasping as it bumped her clit. "In me."

He snaked his hand up her body and filled it with her breast. "Fits in my hand like it was made for me." He closed his mouth around her nipple.

Her breath catching in her throat, Raini sank her fingers into his hair. He didn't simply suckle, he *played*. Licked. Nipped. Sucked. Tugged on the bud with his teeth. He kept switching it up, so she didn't know what was coming next. He did the same to her other nipple, taking his time, like her body was his to play with.

His hands weren't whatsoever idle. Bold and sure, they cupped and squeezed and stroked her breasts. Sometimes he'd be rough. Sometimes he'd be gentle. *Too* gentle, making her so desperate for more that she could have cried. "*Maddox*."

His cock throbbing at the sheer, unadulterated want in her

voice, Maddox released her nipple and reached down to rub the head of his cock between her slick folds. "I want to take you without a condom. You on the pill?"

She licked her lips. "Yes."

"I'm clean. I've never fucked a woman bareback before."

"Why change it up now?"

Maddox lodged the broad tip of his dick in her pussy. "The others didn't belong to me. You do." He slammed home, grinding his teeth as her pussy gripped him *so fucking tight*.

A hint of pain flashed across her face as she sucked in a sharp breath, digging her nails hard into his back.

"Easy, baby." He smoothed his hand over her forehead, brushing her hair aside. "You're good." He sipped from her mouth, nibbling her lips with his own, lightly flicking the tip of his tongue against hers. She responded; the kiss was soft, slow, shallow. As her body began to relax beneath him, he hummed in approval. "That's it."

He rocked his hips, touching a spot inside her that made her gasp . . . and the kiss went from gentle to ferocious in a second flat. They ate at each other's mouths—savage, hungry, demanding. Like neither could get enough.

She sucked on his tongue, sending all sorts of explicit images sailing around his brain. He loved how bold she was. As a succubus, she was a highly sexual being, but she wasn't entirely comfortable with it—had even taken long periods of celibacy here and there. He'd worried she'd hold back from him in bed, which was something he wouldn't have tolerated. But she was right there with him, giving as good as she got. His demon loved that.

"Wrap me up tight. Good girl." Maddox drew back until only the head of his cock was inside her, loving how her pussy—blazing hot and gorgeously slick—clung to him so tight. He slowly sank back inside her. "You know demons have addictive personalities, don't you?"

She frowned, as if unsure where he was going with this.

"I could get addicted to this pussy." He had the sudden feeling he already was.

Maddox took her soft and slow, giving her the occasional hard thrust every now and then. He kissed and licked at her neck, aching to bite down and have just a *little* taste. He didn't *need* to feed. The blood of the halo-bearer he'd recently killed would keep Maddox's cravings at bay for a few months. But he longed to know how she tasted.

"Maddox," she said, her voice shaky. "Faster."

"I've waited months to have you beneath me. I have no intention of rushing this."

Raini inwardly cursed. It was okay, though. She could eat at his control with some scratches, nips, and maybe even a few none-too-heartfelt pleas.

Except . . . none of that worked.

He kept his thrusts lazy and gentle, no matter what she did or said. Growling in sheer exasperation, she dug her nails deeper into his back. "Dammit, Maddox!"

"So little patience," he mocked.

"Yeah, well, sometimes a girl likes it a little rough," she sassed.

A rush of cold air swept over her, and his eyes bled to black as the demon took the wheel. "You want rough," it began, "I'll give you rough." It slammed home hard enough to shock a curse out of her.

Fucking *Jesus*, it just . . . took her. There was no finesse, no mercy, no mindfulness of her comfort. The demon quite simply jackhammered into her like it didn't even give a shit if she liked it.

Raini half-expected her own inner demon to bristle at the

sexual aggression, but all the strength, intensity, and pitilessness pushed the entity's hot buttons in the best way.

Maddox's demon grabbed a fistful of her hair and tugged, positioning her head how it wanted it, forcing her to look up at the demon . . . as if it wanted her to know *exactly* who was fucking her right then. "You will come while I take you like this, so your body knows it is mine as well as his."

Um, actually, her body didn't belong to either of . . . oh shit, she was gonna come. The entity had shifted its hips so that it hit her clit with every thrust, and she was fast approaching O-town again.

"Eyes open," the demon ordered, pulling on her hair.

She hadn't even realized she'd closed them until then. She forced them open, looking into those predatory black eyes. The entity pinched her nipple painfully hard, and the harsh sting threw her over the edge. She came with a hoarse cry, tightening her limbs around the demon, distantly noting it hadn't found its own release.

It looked down at her, a glint of satisfaction in the cold depths of its eyes. There was also possession there, like it considered her . . . claimed. Or something. Then it retreated, and Maddox's blue gaze locked with hers.

"My turn." Maddox got to his knees, hooked her legs over the crooks of his elbows, and leaned forward to plant his forearms either side of her head—making his cock slide even deeper inside her. "I warned you that my demon wouldn't go easy on you," he reminded her. "I also warned you that I wouldn't either." And then he was powering into her. He was just as rough as his demon, but not so cold, detached, and animalistic.

Even as he brutally used her, Maddox was fully in control. Which she got off on. He wasn't fucking her this way because he'd lost it, he was doing it because it damn well *pleased* him.

She just dug that he made no bones about taking exactly what he wanted.

Unlike him, she wasn't so composed. Her control had *frayed.* She was arching and writhing and demanding more.

He gripped her jaw tight. "Look at me." He speared her with those steely eyes. "I'm going to be in this pussy often. As often as I want. And I won't be sharing it."

She thought about arguing, but there was no point. She'd want him again. One night wouldn't cut it. She snarled. "Yeah, well, you'll give this cock to me as often as I want it. And I won't be sharing it."

"Then we understand each other."

"I guess we do."

"Good." He released her jaw and fucked her harder, but not so hard that it was *too* much . . . as if he wanted her riding the edge of pleasure/pain. Oh, she was very much there. And she was goddamn loving it.

Even though she'd already come twice tonight, an orgasm was building inside her once again. How could it not, when his fat cock was pounding into her over and over? More, his chest grazed her tight nipples, his shaft stroked her clit, and his balls slapped her ass with every savage thrust. "I'm not going to last long," she said.

"I know." With one hand, he angled her hips more toward his and then began slamming his cock even deeper inside her. He groaned. "Yeah, definitely addicted to this pussy. I can feel it getting hotter and tighter. Let go, baby. I want to watch. I want my come so deep inside you, you'll never get it out."

Pure pleasure cracked through her body like a whip of lightning. Each electric wave of it made her body shake and buck almost violently. A scream tore out of her throat as her pussy clamped down on the cock that was thickening inside her.

"Yeah, baby, that's it. *Fuck.*" His spine locked as he exploded, growling through gritted teeth, filling her with everything he had.

Careful not to give her too much of his weight, Maddox tucked his face into her neck as they lay there shaking and panting. He'd known the moment he met her that he'd one day have her. He'd known it would be good, but he hadn't known it would be *this* good. Hadn't thought it would be so insanely fucking mind-blowing. Not even the electric chemistry that flared between them had prepared him for that.

Lifting his head, Maddox stared down at her. His gut clenched at the languid, sex-drunk look on her face. "My demon was right in what it predicted."

"What's that?"

"You were worth the wait."

CHAPTER TEN

"You let Maddox go paddling up Coochie Creek, didn't you?"

Devon nearly choked on her herbal tea. Sitting beside the hellcat, Tanner patted her back and shook his head at Khloë, like she was beyond help.

Harper gave the imp a pained look. "Can you stop using that phrase, please?"

Ignoring her, Khloë focused on Raini. "You have that 'I got laid' glow right now. Was it good?"

"Better than," Raini admitted, carefully lifting her hot cup; the cappuccino-scented steam rose to greet her. As per usual of a morning, they'd met up at the coffeehouse next door to Urban Ink. The place was always busy, so it was pretty noisy with the murmur of voices, hum of machines, and clatter of dishware.

Devon grinned. "Does that mean you're glad you took my advice and let it happen?"

Considering the man's tongue possessed some dark pussy-eating magic . . . "Oh, yeah." Maddox had taken her twice more before leaving in the early hours of this morning, and his demon had briefly surfaced each time.

Maddox hadn't been lying when he said that neither he nor the entity would go easy on her. She had no complaints about that, and nor did her demon. It still wasn't happy with him, but it did like that he hadn't just gotten himself off and then left. It liked that Raini's pleasure had been important to him.

"Will it be a one-time thing?" asked Harper.

"No." Raini sipped at her drink. "It'll be an anchors-with-benefits thing." Until Maddox got tired of her, that was. It probably wouldn't take long. Demons got bored easily.

She figured she might as well get her kicks while she could, because the novelty of having someone in her bed who wasn't under any preternatural influence wasn't something to sniff at. Plus, she may never experience it again.

Harper's steady gaze took her in. "You're definitely okay with that?"

Raini felt her brows draw together. "You don't think I should be?"

"I didn't say that," replied Harper. "I just want to be sure you won't be hurt when the fling comes to an end. I know you told us the other day that you didn't think he had the potential to hurt you, but that was before you slept with him. Sometimes people can feel a slight connection with someone during moments like that."

Raini felt her nose wrinkle. "I wouldn't say I felt a connection with him. You know trust and emotional intimacy go hand in hand for me. If I don't trust someone, my guard won't lower around them. It just doesn't happen." She supposed it was a self-defense mechanism. "I trust Maddox in some ways, but not in all."

"I only wanted to check you're good."

Raini smiled. "And I adore you for caring."

"But you adore me more, right?" asked Khloë, stirring her frozen latte with her straw.

Raini looked at the imp. "I love you all equally." They'd kind of been over this before.

Khloë's brow furrowed. "Why? I'm more awesome than they are. And I bought you a donut. Doesn't that count for anything?"

"Actually, you stole the donut," Raini reminded her.

"Which amazes me, since no one noticed her go behind the counter and swipe food from the glass display case," said Tanner without even looking up from the newspaper he'd taken from a nearby table.

"Imps could steal the shirt off your back before you'd even realized it," said Devon. "Or purloin, as Lachlan would say."

Khloë chuckled. "He's a blast. I love your dad, Raini."

"So do I, but I wouldn't love for him to find out that me and Maddox currently have a thing going on," said Raini. "He'd get it all twisted in his head. He'd claim Maddox is using me and all that stuff. Then he'd go into pyro mode. So we keep this information to ourselves, yes? Of course you can tell your mates, but no one else. I mean it, Khloë."

The imp's eyes widened. "Why would you think I need a double-warning?"

"Because although you're good at keeping secrets, you often choose to share them," replied Raini. "No, don't say it isn't true—we kind of know you."

Khloë sighed and set down her frozen latte. "I won't tell anyone other than Keenan."

"Not even Teague," Raini pushed, referring to Khloë's anchor.

The imp nodded. "Not even Teague."

"Thank you." Raini took another sip of her drink. "Now

maybe we could talk about something else. Like the new brand on Harper's palm that she thinks we haven't noticed."

The sphinx's lips thinned. "At this rate, it'll only be a year or so before I barely have an inch of unbranded skin."

Raini chuckled. If a person's inner demon was possessive of someone, it often branded them. The marks looked like tattoos, and they only faded when the entity's interest in the person they'd branded faded.

Devon tossed her mate an exasperated look. "Tanner's demon branded my ankles. My *ankles*. It looks like they've been shackled."

"Let me see." Raini looked down as the hellcat twisted in her seat and tugged up her jeans a little. "Damn, they really do look like shackles."

Tanner shrugged. "My demon's very possessive."

"Knox's takes the cake," said Harper. "Each time it leaves a new one, I sigh in relief that it doesn't say 'Chattel of Knox Thorne' or some shit like that. It's always . . . crap, we need to finish up here, it's time to open the studio."

They finished their drinks, put their rubbish in the trash, and headed to Urban Ink. Tanner smacked a kiss on Devon's mouth, patted her ass, and then left.

The day went like any other. The phone repeatedly rang. Clients came and went. People came in to check out the portfolios and enquire about making a booking. It was a normal, restful day. So as they were readying the studio to be closed, Raini almost jumped when Khloë burst out, "You've *got*. To be. *Kidding the shit out of me*."

Raini frowned. "What? What's wrong?"

Khloë jabbed a finger at the computer monitor. "One of our clients forwarded this email to me. Mara said she received it just now and thought we ought to know."

Raini crossed to the reception desk, along with Devon and Harper.

Reading the email, Raini felt her mouth drop open. Someone who'd signed the email "Emmett" claimed they'd heard from a friend that Mara was a regular here and thought she should be warned that Urban Ink had "gone downhill." Emmett told quite a story of a "horrendous experience" he'd allegedly had where Raini had made several passes at him throughout an unnecessarily long session during which she'd given him not only the *wrong* back tattoo but a *crooked* one that got hideously infected.

He also said that when he'd complained and asked for a refund, Harper had yelled at him and threatened to send Knox his way. Emmett also mentioned hearing from others that they'd had bad experiences at Urban Ink—dirty needles, misspellings, wonky tattoos, overpricing, shitty customer service, tattooists trying to bully them into tipping. Emmett had topped it all off by advising Mara to spend her money elsewhere in future.

"Lying bastard," Raini bit out, just as furious as her inner entity. "It's got to be our friend the fucking boycotter."

Khloë nodded, her mouth a harsh line. "What I'm wondering is . . . has he sent this email only to Mara, or has he sent it to others too? Like our entire goddamn client base. I'll make some calls and find out."

"We also need to email this asshole at some point," said Devon. "Then again, that would be awarding his bullshit with attention. I'd much rather yank out his teeth. We didn't manage to track him through the post he put on the forum, but maybe we can track him through that email address and make him see the error of his ways."

Oh, Raini and her demon were all for that plan. "This person definitely needs something thick and sharp rammed up their colon." She looked at Harper. "Do you think it could be one of Knox's jealous exes? They do like to annoy you."

Her expression pensive, Harper stared at the computer. "Khloë, remember all those canceled appointments?"

"Yeah," the imp all but grunted.

"A few of the clients were mine, but not many, right?" asked Harper.

Khloë nodded. "Right. A couple were Devon's, but most were Raini's."

"And the person who posted the bullshit review on the forum blamed Raini," said Harper. "This, again, is mostly directed at Raini. Mara is one of her regular clients. Although this email briefly mentions me, Raini seems to be the main focus here." Harper shook her head, adding, "I can't believe I didn't notice it before. I originally thought the boycotting was an indirect attack on my lair due to how many enemies Knox has. But now I'm rethinking that theory."

Raini frowned. "Wait, you think this is all personal to me?"

"I do," said Harper, folding her arms. "I think this Emmett person somehow managed to get hold of our client base and specifically targeted the majority of your clients, only including a few of mine and Devon's to muddy the water so we'd do exactly what we did—not realize this is all directed at you."

"I'd have to agree with Harper on this one," Khloë cut in. "She's right; you're the main focus, Raini. That sort of got lost among everything else at first."

"No," said Raini. "Emmett claimed I was his tattooist, yes, but he talked more about Urban Ink itself, painting a really awful and utterly false picture of it."

Devon nodded. "True, but the studio is half *your* baby. By hurting the business, he's hurting you. I didn't see it before, but I see it now—this person is trying to sabotage *you*."

Raini gave her head a shake. "I hear what you're saying and I get why you'd think that. But it doesn't make sense. I'm only little ole me. I don't have big, bad enemies."

"Emmett—or whatever the fuck their real name is—doesn't have to be a big, bad enemy," said Devon. "He just has to be someone who wants to fuck you over. Which is why you need to call Jolene. As your Prime, she needs to know about this."

Knowing her friend was right, Raini contacted Jolene, who had Ciaran teleport her to the studio.

Her face hard, Jolene said, "It would be nice if we could get through at least a month without someone targeting Raini in some way. Don't worry, it will be dealt with," she assured Raini, her tone somewhat menacing. "Now, someone read out this email to me."

Khloë quickly did so, her tone clipped.

Ciaran cursed. "Motherfucker."

"Ain't he, though?" said Devon, locking the front door.

"I say we head to the break room while we discuss this," said Raini. "I feel the need for a cup of tea coming on."

Khloë lifted the phone. "I'll join you once I've called some clients. We need to know if others have been sent this email."

A few minutes later, Raini, Harper, Devon, Jolene, and Ciaran were gathered around the break room table, drinks in hand.

"Now that it's clear the attempt to boycott the business is a stab at Raini," began Ciaran, "do we think that the person behind it could have orchestrated the whole dagger incident? That it was never meant to hit Knox?"

"I do," said Devon. "And I think it was Dwain. He has motive—that being revenge. I think he resents Raini's succubae powers, so he sent Dagger Guy to take them from her."

While Dwain most likely did resent them . . . "I don't think what happened all those years ago warrants this kind of reaction.

It's not like I broke his heart. His feelings weren't real. Yeah, okay, it would be a bitch to realize you *thought* you loved someone when, in fact, your mind had been preternaturally manipulated. But you wouldn't one day set out to ruin them, would you? Plus, it was a long time ago."

Harper lifted her finger. "Firstly, demons always get even, Raini. They'll wait years if they have to, but they'll get it. Secondly, what happened wasn't that simple. I agree that you probably didn't break Dwain's heart when you rejected him. But his pain will have been real right up until the moment he was free of the snare."

"If I realized I'd been weak enough to get caught up in one, I'd feel fucking humiliated," said Ciaran. "Even a little emasculated. It would make it worse that everyone in my lair knew about it, including my family, my Prime, and my friends. In Dwain's case, it also included his anchor."

Devon rested her hand on Raini's arm. "It isn't your fault that he left, so it isn't your fault that he gave up his job and moved out of his home, or that his relationships with Demi and his loved ones suffered due to him not being around much. But that doesn't mean he doesn't hold you accountable for it."

"He's mated now, though; he's happy," Raini pointed out.

"That doesn't necessarily mean he isn't still itching to get some revenge," said Harper. "That whole 'love heals all' phrase? It doesn't always work that way."

Raini bit her lower lip. "I'd like to think that, if for no other reason than that I'm Demi's family, he'd let the past go. But if it *is* him, it doesn't make sense that he came back to visit. Surely he'd have wanted to lay low, hoping we wouldn't think to pin anything on him. Out of sight, out of mind, right?"

Just then, Khloë barged into the break room. "Several others confirmed they'd received the same bullshit email. Most were

Raini's clients." She dragged a chair toward her, making the feet scrape along the floor, and plonked herself on it. "That motherfucker needs to pay for this shit. I typed up an email explaining the boycotting attempt—without going into too much detail, of course—and sent it to all our clients."

"Good," said Harper. "And you're right. He is a motherfucker."

Khloë folded her arms. "It's got to be Dwain, right?"

"I would say so," Jolene told her. "But we shouldn't rule out others. And I hate to say it, Raini, but Demi is someone we should be looking at."

Raini stilled, balking at that. Her demon, however, agreed with Jolene. "She's my sister. Which doesn't mean much to her a lot of the time, I know. Same as I know that she blames me for Dwain being mated and would probably like me to suffer for it. But she didn't know he was mated until he showed up with Harmony. The boycotting started *before* that, right?"

"It did," Harper confirmed. "But Demi also blames you for how she and Dwain are no longer close. I remember how she used to whine that she'd lost her anchor because of you. I know she technically didn't lose him—he stayed in contact with her over the years—but she lost the closeness they once had; lost the chance to make him love her as more than his anchor. So she probably thought it karma that your own anchor didn't appear to want you. She'll have been pissed to later hear that Maddox is in the picture. Maybe even so pissed that she decided to fuck with your life."

"She might have even hired Dagger Guy to strip you of power," Devon speculated. "Maybe because, like Dwain himself, she resented that you were able to snare him."

Raini's entire being rebelled at that theory. "She wouldn't go that far. The demon world is a brutal place. She wouldn't want me completely helpless."

Jolene hummed. “How long is she away on her cruise for?”

“Three weeks,” Raini replied.

“If need be, I can send Ciaran to retrieve her from the ship and bring her here for questioning,” said Jolene. “But right now, I’m leaning toward our culprit being Dwain. I want to question him first. Ciaran, I’ll need you to teleport to his house and dump his ass in our penal complex.”

Ciaran pushed out of his chair. “It’ll be my pleasure.” With that, he disappeared.

Jolene picked up her drink, her shrewd eyes on Raini. “Have you told Maddox about the boycotting?”

“No,” she replied. “I know he’s my anchor, but we don’t confide in each other about stuff. And I consider this to be Urban Ink business.”

“It is, but you should tell him,” said Jolene. “Maybe one of his demons doesn’t like that you let him halfway into your life—or, more to the point, that he let you halfway into his.”

Raini instantly thought of Marcella, which made her demon snarl. “Maybe.” What had Maddox said? That Marcella didn’t like to give up or back down? Perhaps she still had her sights set on being his co-Prime.

“You’ll also need to tell your parents,” Jolene went on. “They’ll be upset if they later find out you kept this from them—especially if it comes to a point where I have to question your sister.”

Raini groaned. “My dad and my uncles are going to freak. They’ll never agree that the culprit could be Demi. They’ll either blame Dwain or Maddox’s demons, and they’ll want blood. You’ll stop them from doing something stupid, right?”

Jolene arched a brow. “That would require the sort of power no demon on this Earth possesses. Once the Campbell men get something into their heads, there’s no getting it back out.”

Sighing, Raini slumped in her chair. “Yeah, I know.”

Ciaran reappeared, his face a mask of frustration. "Dwain wasn't at his home, Grams. And get this . . . I don't think Harmony even lives there."

Jolene's brow creased. "Why?"

"I noticed it had a real bachelor pad feel," replied Ciaran, retaking his seat. "It rubbed my instincts wrong, because I remember him telling me how much he loved living with Harmony, so I had a look around. There were no pictures of the two of them, no women's 'touches' to the place. And when I checked the master bedroom, I didn't find a single item of women's clothing. There was no extra toothbrush, no women's shampoo, no perfumes or cosmetics lying around—nothing. Now, sure, she would have packed some of her stuff for her visit here, but surely there would have been bits and pieces of hers still in the house."

Devon blinked. "Why would he say he lived with her if he didn't?"

"And if they *don't* live together, why would he at least not let his mate leave some of her things at his home?" asked Jolene. "It's possible that she hadn't wanted to, of course, but I don't see why that would be."

Raini narrowed her eyes at her Prime, sensing . . . "You think they aren't mates."

"I think they're not even a true couple," said Jolene. "I think he came here and lied his ass off. He had to have known we might at some point realize the boycotting is personal to you, and so he'd also known that we'd then consider him a suspect. He thought if he looked happily mated, no one would think he was behind the things that were happening."

"I'll bet that's also why he wanted you two to 'clear the air,' Raini," said Harper. "He thought if you bought that he held no grudges against you, you wouldn't consider him a suspect."

"Maybe he also came here to get a front seat to the show; to see how his actions were affecting you on a personal level; to see the damage for himself," Devon mused.

Raini frowned. "But wouldn't he have stayed longer, if that were the case?"

"Who says he hasn't?" asked Harper. "Ciaran said he wasn't home. It might not be that he's simply out grocery shopping. It might be that he never left Vegas."

"Unfortunately, Harper is right," said Jolene. "I'll station someone at his house. If he returns, they'll notify me. We need to find out more about Harmony, if that's even her name. We have questions she might be able to answer."

"Leave it with me," said Khloë. "I'll consult my sources."

Jolene nodded. "If it's not Dwain or Demi, it has to be one of Maddox's lair." She looked at Raini. "It's quite a coincidence that the boycotting started near the time you and Maddox made your deal. I don't believe in coincidences. My guess is he'll find it just as suspicious. Ensure he looks into it, Raini. If he doesn't, I will. And he won't like how I go about doing it."

CHAPTER ELEVEN

Sitting on the sofa at the penthouse a few hours later, Raini rubbed her thighs. She wasn't looking forward to this conversation at all. Jolene was right; she needed to tell Maddox about the boycotting, because there truly was a chance that one of his demons was behind it. But he wasn't going to like the implication all too much, and he might even get pissed at Jolene.

If the situation were reversed, Jolene would certainly have felt—at the very least—extremely insulted that another Prime would accuse one of her demons of such an act. She'd still have performed an internal investigation—Jolene wasn't a woman who left anything to chance. If she'd discovered that one of her lair was guilty, she'd have dealt with them swiftly. Maddox would most likely do the same.

A little voice in Raini's head, however, questioned if he really *would* act. He acknowledged her as his anchor, and he'd sneakily forged his way into her life. But she wasn't his top priority. He put his lair first. Hell, he hadn't even formally introduced her to them. She'd only met a few.

If one of them *was* the asshole boycotter, would Maddox do much more than give them a slap on the wrist? Would he admit their guilt to outsiders? She'd like to think that the answer to both questions would be yes, but she couldn't be sure.

She could, however, be sure that he'd get all snarly simply because she hadn't mentioned the boycotting before. Raini hadn't violated the conditions of their deal by not sharing the recent shitty events with him, but that wouldn't matter much to Maddox. Not when he had a strong sense of entitlement where she was concerned; not when he was so determined that she rely on him.

Blowing out a breath, Raini reached out to touch his mind. *I know you're probably mega busy, but could you please come see me when you have a few spare minutes?* she asked, cool and casual. Nothing in her telepathic voice gave away her anxiety, so she was more than a little surprised when he abruptly appeared right in front of her.

"What's wrong?" he immediately demanded, glancing around.

A little touched that he'd responded so fast and with such obvious concern, she replied, "It's nothing huge. Jolene wants me to share something with you."

He narrowed his eyes. "What is it?"

Raini cleared her throat. "So, for the past few months, someone has been trying to boycott Urban Ink. We thought it was personal to Harper and Knox, since she owns half the business. But today, well, something else happened and . . . it occurred to us that the main focus seems to be me."

His expression didn't change, but there was a slight hardening to his jawline. "Explain."

Raini gave him a quick but succinct summary of the

boycotting attempts. "I'm not entirely sure I believe this is all directed at me, but Jolene and the girls do."

"As do I," he said, his voice smooth as silk but . . . dark. Almost menacing.

"Jolene thinks my sister's anchor is most likely behind it."

"Why?"

"He tumbled head first into a snare some years ago and declared he loved me." Raini relayed the occurrence to Maddox, adding, "Jolene intends to question him once she gets her hands on him. But she believes there's also a chance—"

"That it could be a demon from my lair," he guessed.

"Yes. She wants to cover her bases, that's all. She likes to be thorough. She figures it's best not to assume anything. So she'd like you to look into it. I don't think I have to warn you that she'll do it if you don't. If it was the other way around, you'd do the same."

Maddox felt anger bubble up inside him. He knew she sensed it. He knew she'd think he was pissed that Jolene would imply that one of his demons had targeted his anchor. And yeah, the implication did fucking rankle. What really pissed him off was that he was only learning of all this *now.* "Why didn't you tell me about any of this sooner?"

Lounging on the sofa looking infuriatingly casual, Raini frowned. "It wasn't part of our deal that I tell you about every little hiccup in my life. Initially, that was all this seemed to be."

"But I would have wanted to know about it. You know that."

"Only because you're nosy as hell. That isn't my problem. I'm not going to cater to it. There was no reason to tell you. It didn't affect you."

Anger again spiked through him. Maddox took a step toward her. "*Anything* that affects you affects me."

"And if your club was having problems, you'd have told me all about it, would you? No, of course you wouldn't have. Because it simply has nothing to do with me. What goes on with Urban Ink has nothing to do with you."

"This isn't some issue about overheads or even rude clients. Someone has been shitting all over your name in an attempt to disparage you. You, *my anchor.* So it has everything to do with me." And it was an insult he'd have wanted to address, because absolutely fucking no one got to target her this way—he and his equally pissed-off demon intended to communicate that message to whoever had dared do it. "This shouldn't be the first I'm hearing about it."

The air cooled as her eyes bled to black. "You seem so surprised that she did not immediately spill all of this to you," her demon said. "Why? Because she has been so cooperative in other ways?" It gave him a look of disdain. "You have been too arrogant to see *why* she has given you so little trouble."

Maddox squinted. "What does that mean?"

"You think you understand her. Wrong. You see only what she wants you to see. You will never see more, because you have chosen to never earn that privilege. That is your choice. But never think you have, or ever will, coerce her to do anything. She is smarter and more cunning than you have given her credit for. You underestimate her, and she allows it. Just as she allows you to believe that you are running this show. Each time she made a concession, she furthered that illusion for you. But that is all it has ever been—an illusion.

"I tell you all this for one reason only: I am sick and tired of watching you sing a tune and insist that she dance to it. She deserves better. If the only way you can accept her is if she is firmly under your control, then you need to exit her life. Because you will *never* control her. Make your choice. Take her as she is or leave her be."

Once her demon subsided, Raini sighed in annoyance. Why did the entity keep warning him that there were things he didn't know? Why would it not just let him stay in the goddamn dark? Her demon only shrugged, seeing no need to justify itself. Maybe it was simply that, unlike Raini, the demon did not like that others underestimated it. Perhaps the entity had wanted its anchor to know it was stronger than he believed.

Maddox tilted his head. "I could be wrong, but I think your demon would happily dismember me."

Raini rubbed her temple. "It *did* want to do that at one point. Now it wants to incinerate you and dance around your ashes." God, she needed a drink. Preferably one that was high in alcohol. She stood, meaning to head to the kitchen, but Maddox's hand shot out and grabbed her wrist.

"Your demon was wrong to think that I underestimate you and haven't seen that you hide parts of yourself from me," he said. "I didn't miss that cunning streak either. Nor was I surprised by it—all offspring of imps are calculating whether they're imps themselves or not. And despite what your demon insists on believing, I don't wish to rule you. If I did, I'd have made you my own personal puppet."

It was honestly unnerving to know he had the ability to reduce her to that. "I know. But you do expect more of me than what you're entitled to get, and that's not going to fly with me or my demon. I've told you before, you can't be the main figure in my life when you only have one foot in it. That's not how this is going to work. And even if I did make you the center of everything—which is never gonna happen, by the way—it still wouldn't make you any less edgy. You try to take charge because you think you can control the bond's draw. You can't, Maddox. It will always call to you. It'll never ease up. It'll never go away."

He stepped closer. "If we were to form the bond, you'd need to part with your secrets eventually."

"So would you."

"And I can't. They're not just my secrets to keep."

She stilled as realization hit her. "That's why you're holding me at a distance."

His gaze followed the path of his hand as he slid his hand from her wrist up her arm, over her shoulder, and up to curl around the side of her neck. "I can't give you more than I'm already giving you. Which isn't enough, I know. But it's all I can give. So we go on as we are and make the best of it. Because I'm not letting you go."

Raini stared at him, wondering what secrets he could possibly possess that drove him to hold back from his own anchor. If they weren't just his secrets to keep, they had to involve his lair. And while she wished he'd trust her with them, she knew all about keeping secrets to protect yourself. She would have parted with hers if they had bonded, but if keeping her secrets had been necessary to also protect her girls or lair members, she wouldn't have shared them with Maddox. Not without their permission anyway. So she'd be a total hypocrite if she gave him shit—even in her own head—for doing what he'd done.

Raini swallowed. "If that's the way it has to be, then that's the way it has to be. I don't expect you to tell me things that would make others vulnerable. I can accept your reasons for making the choice you've made. But it doesn't change that if you're not in this all the way, you can't expect me to confide in and rely on you. You just can't. Or you could, but you'd only spend your life thoroughly disappointed because you won't get your way in this."

Relieved and grateful she hadn't pushed, Maddox gave her neck a little squeeze in thanks. On one level, it galled him that she wouldn't simply turn to him when she needed help or advice, even though he hadn't earned that. On another level, he respected that she stood firm and refused to allow him to bulldoze her.

Similarly, despite the entity's vexation with being held at arm's length, it was impressed by her resolve. Not that it had ever perceived her as a pushover. No, like Maddox, it had recognized straight off that Raini was no weakling.

"You know, your name suits you," he said.

"It does?"

"Yes. You're rain and lightning and thunder. A storm. Electric and intense with a will of your own. But you're not one of those people who wears their inner strength loudly and boldly, daring the world to come at them. You're content to be a quiet force of nature, but you're still very much a force." And he'd be a fool to forget it.

"Oh. Um, thanks. I think."

"Back onto the original subject, you only gave me a bullet-point version of what's been happening," said Maddox, sliding his hand from her neck into her hair, letting his fingers comb their way through the blonde, pink-highlighted curtain. "I want every little detail, no matter how big or small those details are. I can't properly look into this situation if I don't possess all of the facts."

"Okay. But I really need a drink."

Maddox followed her into the kitchen as she began to relay the full story. He didn't want to believe anyone from his lair could be responsible; that they would target the anchor of their own Prime, a woman who'd done nothing to them. But could one of them have done it? Euan and Marcella might have been tempted. He wasn't sure they had the guts to take such risks, though. Given all Raini had told him about her sister's anchor, Dwain seemed the likeliest culprit.

Watching as Raini took a sip of the wine she'd poured herself, he said, "There are a couple of people in my lair who might target you. I'll question them. If they're responsible, I'll deal with it."

Raini leaned back against the counter. "I'm guessing one of them is Marcella, but I don't expect you to confirm that. I didn't mention her to Jolene. She wouldn't have been able to resist interrogating her, and I don't want you and my Prime at each other's throats."

"The only person who'll be questioning my demons is me."

"Ooh, how very menacing you sound. But Jolene won't care how powerful you are or what gifts you're rumored to have. The woman has no fear. She's playing nice with you right now, but that can change in a heartbeat."

"I'm well aware of that."

"Then you're also aware that, just as she can't interrogate your demons, you can't go questioning Dwain or Demi."

Fuck, he'd walked right into that one. His demon chuckled, reluctantly impressed by the trap she'd neatly sprung. "You expect me not to question the most obvious suspect?"

"Yes, I absolutely do expect that. Don't let the fact that Dwain has a big motive blind you. That's not to say he's to blame."

"I agree." Maddox crossed to Raini and planted a hand on the counter either side of her. "'Big' is relative, depending on what the individual in question considers significant. But it is very suspicious that Dwain appears to have lied about being mated. And if he continues to stay off the radar, I'll be even more inclined to believe he's at fault."

"But you won't go question him without first clearing it with Jolene, right?" Raini prompted. Whatever she saw on his face made her snicker. "Not used to clearing shit with people, huh? Well, make an exception. I really don't want you two fighting."

Sensing that her anxiety was very real, Maddox assured her,

"I have no intention of making an enemy of your Prime. I would much rather she and I continue to play nice, since it makes life easier for you. Now, back to the subject of your sister's anchor. Did he have much contact with you while in Vegas?"

"Not really. He did call me yesterday, wanting to meet up for lunch. I politely turned down the invitation. But he pushed and got all pissy, so I . . . toyed with him a little."

"Toyed with him how?" Maddox felt his mouth quirk as she told him of her short phone conversation with Dwain. "I see."

"I'd imagine he wasn't feeling terribly happy with me."

"Which could have prompted him to strike again," Maddox mused. Yes, many things definitely pointed the finger squarely at Dwain. "I want to be kept in the loop about this."

"If there's anything to pass on, I'll tell you."

Satisfied, he said, "Good. I also need you to forward me the email that this 'Emmett' sent. I'm assuming you can remotely log into the studio's email account."

"You think you can find out who sent it?"

"Possibly. I won't know unless I try. Now I need to speak with some of my lair members. First . . . " Maddox took her mouth, sweeping his tongue inside, swallowing her soft gasp of surprise. She tasted as good as he remembered. He wanted to feast, savor, consume. But he had a few things to do.

He broke the kiss with a sharp nip to her lower lip. "Sleep naked."

Her brow furrowed. "Why?"

"I'd rather not have to burn any more of your panties with hellfire just to get them off you." With that, Maddox teleported to his office and then summoned both his sentinels. They materialized near the small bar.

"Something wrong?" asked Hector.

"Find Euan," Maddox ordered. "Bring him to me."

Carmen let out a tired sigh. "What did the dumb fucker do now?"

"Possibly nothing," replied Maddox. "Possibly something that will earn him a punishment. Someone is attempting to boycott Raini's business, but it's not as simple as that."

Sinking into his office chair, Maddox brought them up to speed. "Jolene has suspects within her own lair. She's right to also consider that one of my demons could be behind it, given the timing of when it all began. I doubt they are, but I have to look into it."

Carmen pursed her lips. "Slander is both Euan and Marcella's style—they've proven that recently with the shit they whispered about you. They'd never make a direct move against her for fear of what you'd do. Sly maneuvers like this, though? Yeah, they might do something like that."

"If it's one of ours, my money is on Marcella," said Hector, folding his arms. "Not just because she feels threatened by Raini, but because she resents that—as your anchor—Raini has a true place in your life. It's the one thing Marcella has always wanted."

"I intend to have a little talk with Marcella as well," said Maddox. "But I'd like to speak with Euan first. Fetch him for me."

Hector nodded and then teleported away.

Maddox looked back at Carmen. "Who's currently assigned to Raini?"

"Duncan and Hoyt," she replied. "They find it highly amusing that they're making the employees at the Underground hotel pretty nervous. Jolene's also stationed two demons to watch over Raini, as have the Thorne Primes."

"I expected that they would." While a part of Maddox reflexively balked at the thought of others taking on the duty of protecting her, since it was rightfully *his* duty, he'd prefer that she had the added surveillance. Halo-bearers would struggle to get to her while she was so well protected.

He'd briefly wondered if they could be responsible for the boycotting, but he'd dismissed the thought almost as soon as it drifted into his brain. This was too personal.

Just then, Hector reappeared with Euan, who looked appropriately put out. The mere sight of him made Maddox's demon snarl. It saw only weakness when it looked at Euan. So much bitterness, arrogance, and false bravado.

Euan frowned. "I hope this won't take long. I wasn't even halfway through my dinner."

Maddox gestured at the leather chair opposite him. "Have a seat." In the past, he'd always been glad for his own sake that there was no way to read the mind of a descendant—their mental shields moved like a labyrinth, protecting their thoughts and secrets. But right then, it was supremely irritating, because he had no way of plucking the truth out of Euan's mind.

For a moment, the other male looked like he might refuse the invitation to sit. But then he crossed to the chair and sat with a sigh. "What is this about?"

"Something was brought to my attention today." Maddox drummed his fingers on his desk, feigning a coolness he didn't feel. "It seems that someone has gotten it into their heads that it is perfectly acceptable to disparage my anchor's name and boycott her business."

Euan went very still. "Let me guess," he said, his tone dry. "You suspect me."

"Do you have a reason why I shouldn't?"

"Well, I am your cousin. Just because we don't see eye to eye doesn't mean I would make trouble for your anchor." Euan's brows drew together. "You would automatically suspect that members of your own lair are involved?"

"When one of those members has proven he's very fond of slandering people's names and has recently shown an unhealthy lack of self-preservation, yes."

Euan's eyes flickered. "If anyone from our lair is responsible, it's Marcella. It's her you should be talking to. I have nothing to do with whatever's going on around your precious succubus. You're pointing the finger at the wrong person."

Maddox pursed his lips and then shrugged. "All right."

Euan stared at him, his lips parted. "W-what?"

"Well, if you say it wasn't you, it wasn't you."

"You . . . you believe me?"

"Should I doubt your word?"

"No, I just . . . well, it's . . . You don't trust me."

"True," allowed Maddox. "But I don't trust most people. Your dinner will get cold if you don't return to it."

For a long moment, Euan watched him closely, clearly not so convinced that Maddox believed him. But then he teleported away.

His brow creased, Hector turned to Maddox, "You didn't interrogate him, just lightly questioned him. Why?"

"If I was to leave a single mark on him, he'd run around the lair telling everyone I'd hurt him—one of his demons, a member of my family—merely because I suspected he might be trying to stain my anchor's name."

"And you think that's why he might have done it, if he is guilty," Carmen guessed. "So he could argue that we couldn't trust you to put us before her."

"If Euan's behind it, yes, I think he'd hope for that," Maddox confirmed. "But if I truly believed he was the culprit, I'd have interrogated him in any case. For me, the likeliest person to be at fault is the anchor of Raini's sister."

Carmen worried her lower lip. "Would you put Raini before our lair?"

"Would you put Hector before it?" Maddox shot back, already knowing the answer. "I've forsaken the anchor bond, Carmen. That's as much as I'm willing to do."

"I get it,' she said. "And for what it's worth, I wish you weren't in a position where you have to forsake it."

So did Maddox. Raini was right in what she'd said—the bond would always call to him. He'd never be free of that. His demon would never be free of it, which increased its anger with each day that passed. Honestly, Maddox sometimes worried that the entity might take the matter into its own hands. Because although it understood the need to protect their kind, it would never put others before its own wants.

He cut his gaze back to Hector. "Bring Marcella to me."

She must have put up a minimal amount of fuss, because the sentinel returned with her mere moments after he'd left the office.

Marcella gave Maddox a sultry smile that held a mocking tint. "Changed your mind about wanting some private time with me? You only had to call and say so."

He gestured to the chair that Euan had vacated. "Sit down."

She glanced from one sentinel to the other, taking in their sober expressions, and her sass fell away. "What is this?"

Maddox tipped his chin toward the chair, not speaking until she'd finally sat down. "I have a question. If you were me, and you heard that someone was trying to boycott your anchor's business and shit on their name, who would you suspect could be involved?"

Marcella's eyes widened. "You believe *I* did that?"

Maddox flicked up a brow. "Is that what I said?"

Her mouth tightened. "We wouldn't be having this conversation if you didn't believe it was me."

"Now that's where you're wrong, Marcella. If I wholeheartedly believed it was you who was playing these games with my anchor, you'd be in the cellar right now begging for mercy you'd never get." Her pleas would mean nothing to him or his demon.

She swallowed hard. "But you suspect me."

"Do you think I shouldn't?"

Her mouth bopped open and closed. "I can see why you would. It's no secret that I don't like that she's around. But it's also no secret that I don't like pain. I have nothing to gain from playing with her. The only thing it would get me is hours of torture. She's not worth that for me."

"Hmm. Any theories on who in our lair might be tempted to toy with her?"

"If I did have any, I wouldn't name names."

"Noble. Euan wasn't so noble. He pointed the finger right at you."

She. "Of course he did. It's just like him to throw someone under the bus to divert suspicion from himself." She paused. "I didn't do it, Maddox. I swear to you, I didn't."

"Glad to hear it," he said. "Enjoy the rest of your evening."

Surprise rippled across her face. That surprise quickly gave way to wariness. Just as Euan had done, she waited a few moments before teleporting out of the office.

"Think she was telling the truth?" Hector asked him.

Maddox rubbed at his jaw. "She meant it when she said Raini wasn't, in her mind, worth going through hours of pain. But she'd play such games if she thought she could get away with it. As for having nothing to gain by it? That's both true and false. Hurting Raini wouldn't gain her what she wanted."

"Which is to be your co-Prime," said Carmen.

Maddox nodded. "But it would gain Marcella the mere

satisfaction of pissing off both me and Raini. She's spiteful enough to do that." Nevertheless, he wasn't convinced she was to blame.

"It could be Euan *and* Marcella working together, though I doubt it," said Hector. "Neither would trust the other not to be setting them up to take the fall. What now?"

"Now I try tracking the sender of the email," replied Maddox. "I've had Raini forward it to me. And if it does lead me anywhere, I would say it will lead me to Dwain."

"At least you don't have to worry that she'll be physically harmed by whoever's doing this," said Carmen. "They appear to be content with simply fucking with her."

"Not if they're the one who sent the astral projector her way," Maddox pointed out.

Hector frowned. "But I thought he was aiming for . . . You think he *meant* to hit Raini?"

Maddox shrugged, feeling his jaw harden. "What I know for sure is that my demon wouldn't have been able to handle knowing she was so vulnerable. It would have worried about her day and night. I'd have been no better. My attention would have been divided, which isn't good when you have halo-bearers on your ass.

"Also, I'd have spent more time with her than usual, trusting that she was safe while with me, so someone could have then made a case that I was too distracted by my anchor to lead the lair properly anymore. That would have caused a massive wave of unease among the lair, considering our demons are relying on me to keep them safe from the halo-bearers."

"Making her vulnerable would have, in a roundabout way, made you vulnerable—not just to attack from halo-bearers, but as a Prime," Carmen realized.

"Which would have suited both Euan and Marcella," said

Maddox. "Euan, because he wants to be Prime. And Marcella, because her only hope of mating the ruler of this lair is if said ruler isn't me. So, yes, there's a very real possibility that one of our own betrayed me this way. I don't think they did, but we can't rule them out."

Carmen sighed. "Hell."

CHAPTER TWELVE

"I was actually a little disappointed."

Pausing in typing an email on his phone, Maddox frowned at the bartender. "You were disappointed that no brawls occurred? You spent most of yesterday complaining to me that there were *bound* to be brawls between them and our lair and that you didn't want to have to deal with the fallout."

"Yeah, but a part of me was hoping we'd get to kick some angel ass," said Alonso, hanging a glass above the bar. "I know they chose to fall, but they're still angels for the most part. Viper must have warned them all to curb their behavior, though, because they were polite as my Grandma Edna."

"Your grandmother's name was Ophelia, not Edna. And she was never polite."

"You know what I mean." Alonso held up a bottle of bourbon. "Want a refill?"

Maddox nodded. "Sure."

Alonso topped up Maddox's glass and then went back to

cleaning the long bar. The club would open in a few hours, and the space would be filled with people, music, and flashing strobe lights. For now, with only him and Alonso around, it was quiet.

Maddox took a swig of his drink and turned his attention back to the email he'd been typing. He'd no sooner pressed "send" than two things happened. One, he sensed that he and Alonso had company. Two, Alonso cleared his throat hard.

Maddox twisted on the barstool. Ten hooded figures stood around, still as statues, their jewel-like eyes focused on him. If they thought concealing their halos would disguise them somehow, they were wrong.

His inner demon stretched with a grin, looking forward to what would come next. It had been itching for a fight since learning that Raini was on someone's shit list. Which was why Maddox had left a "hole" in his security measures to allow any angels to enter the club—a hole he'd now closed, trapping the halo-bearers inside.

"Ah, more of Castiel's boys," said Maddox, sounding as calm as he did bored. "How is your puppet master?"

Stiffening, they exchanged glances.

Maddox gave Hector a telepathic heads-up and instructed him to round up the others. The entire lair was already prepared for such a situation; they knew what to do.

The angel who appeared to be leading the mob dropped his hood, and the others followed suit. "We are not here to fight," he said. "We only want to talk."

"She wouldn't do this, Raini. No way," Evangeline insisted. "You and Demi might not see eye to eye, but she's your sister. She loves you. She wants what's best for you."

Leaning back against Harper's office desk, Raini was glad that she and her mother were having this conversation over the phone, because Evangeline would have noticed the "yeah, right" look on her face. Maybe Demi did feel *some* sort of sisterly affection for Raini, but she'd never wanted good things for her.

"She wouldn't boycott your business," Evangeline went on. "She knows how much the tattoo studio means to you."

Which was why some people believed Demi might be responsible. Well *that* and she was mysteriously missing.

It had been a few days since it first became apparent that the boycotting was focused on Raini. Dwain was still in the wind, and no one could locate Harmony either. Just as irritating, no one had been able to trace the origin of Emmett's email because he'd used a proxy server to mask his IP address.

Thinking that Demi might know where Dwain would hide, Jolene had sent Ciaran to retrieve her from the cruise ship. But after speaking with the friends she'd booked the trip with, Ciaran had discovered that she'd never boarded. Also, she'd apparently texted one of said friends to explain that she'd had to cancel due to an emergency.

People had tried calling Demi ever since, but her phone was switched off. Their attempts to telepath her had been equally unsuccessful—they'd hit a "wall" each time. She possessed the ability to block telepathic contact, and it appeared that she was currently utilizing said ability.

Evangeline believed that Demi, heartsore about Dwain being "mated," must simply want some alone time. It was possible. Raini wasn't sure what to believe. People did many cruel things while hurting, even to their own family, so she couldn't make herself dismiss the idea that Demi wouldn't slyly attempt to boycott Urban Ink.

"Your dad and uncles are hunting Dwain like bloodhounds."

Raini had suspected they would. "There are a lot of

people looking for Dwain. He'll be found sooner or later." Hopefully sooner.

"His parents swear they have no idea where he could be, but I'm not sure I believe them. He's their son. They wouldn't give him up. I wouldn't give you or Demi up. I wouldn't want to believe either of you were . . . " Evangeline let the sentence trail off, realizing she'd all but admitted that her love for her daughters could be muddying her thoughts.

"Guilty," Raini softly finished.

"That doesn't mean I'm being willfully blind here. I'm not only believing what I want to believe. I *know* my daughters. I know what they're capable of. Demi isn't capable of any of this," Evangeline insisted, her voice breaking. And then she was sobbing.

Her stomach sinking, Raini closed her eyes. "Don't cry, Mom."

"I'll speak to you again later, sweetheart," Evangeline croaked, and then the line went dead.

Raini put a hand to her forehead. Her mother never cried. Ever. She always kept it together, no matter what was happening. Hearing her sobbing like that . . . God, Raini hated all this.

The door creaked open, and Khloë popped her head inside the office. "You okay?"

"Eavesdropping again?"

"I don't have a truthful answer to that question that won't irritate you." Khloë crossed to her. "Your mom's struggling to accept that Demi could be Emmett, huh?"

Raini nodded. "I'm struggling to accept it myself." Her demon didn't find it so unlikely. "My mom thinks 'Emmett' can only be Dwain. He's Maddox's main suspect, too."

"He doesn't suspect any of his own lair?"

"He admitted that one or two might feel inclined to pull this crap, and he swore he'd question them. When I later asked how it went, he said there was no evidence linking them to the crimes."

Raini had pushed for more info, but he'd been delightfully vague. If he did truly suspect any of them, he wasn't prepared to admit it to her. Probably because he worried she'd tell Jolene, who might then be *way* too tempted to question them herself.

Since learning of the boycotting extravaganza, Maddox had begun telepathically checking in more than usual. He also came to Raini each night, and he always took her at least twice before leaving. He never stayed over, but she hadn't expected that he would. They weren't a couple, they weren't building anything. Plus, Maddox seemed the type who liked to sleep alone; who liked his space.

His demon always surfaced during sex, even if only briefly. It had developed a habit of biting her—usually on her neck, but any part of her seemed to be fair game. The bites were never hard enough to draw blood, but they weren't light little nips either. She'd once mentioned it to Maddox with a raised eyebrow. He'd only shrugged, blasé.

Just then, the studio's phone began to ring. Khloë sighed. "I need to get that before Harper starts barking at me."

"*Khloë, you need to get that!*" Harper yelled from the shop floor.

The imp rolled her eyes. "Too late. Come on, let's go."

Raini followed her out of the office, closing the door behind them.

"Khloë, phone!" Harper again shouted.

Crossing the shop floor, the imp raised placatory hands. "Untwist your panties, sphinxy."

Harper frowned, pausing in tattooing a woman's foot. "Sphinxy?"

"It's a word," said Khloë. "Aunt Mildred used to—"

"Oh no," Devon cut in, turning from her client to the imp. "Do *not* mention that fictional woman in my presence."

Reaching the desk, Khloë shook her head. "I can't *believe* you don't remember her." She lifted the phone and answered the call with her receptionist voice.

Needing to grab some supplies to get her station ready before her next client arrived, Raini headed into the stock room at the rear of the studio. She made a beeline for the shelf that—

Hands clamped around her arms from behind, her surroundings flashed white, and then she was dumped on the ground. A cold, hard, damp ground. Before she could even *think* to react, hot pain blazed along her upper arm.

Hissing, she twisted, a ball of hellfire in hand . . . but she was alone. Whoever had brought her here had swiftly left. Where *was* here? And why did it smell of must, mildew, decay, and dirt?

Her inner demon rose to full alertness, absolutely furious. The power within Raini slinked to her fingertips, ready to protect and defend.

Raini touched the throbbing spot on her arm. Her fingers came away with blood. The bastard who'd brought her here had sliced her arm, probably with a blade. Oh, she was gonna dropkick a fucker.

She rubbed at the floor to wipe the blood from her fingers and glanced around. Taking in the gray stone walls, stacked crypts, plaques, urns, religious statues, and burned-out candles, she felt her stomach bottom out.

A mausoleum. She was in a fucking mausoleum.

One that wasn't well tended to, given the spiderwebs, dead leaves, layers of dust, scabby mold, and the miserable look about the place. Why the hell would someone bring her *here*?

Struggling to her feet, she noticed that the stone walls were carved with . . . was that Latin wording? It was hard to tell. With only one window, the place was pretty damn dark.

The air was stale, clammy, and so bitterly cold she shivered. She could hear water dripping and scuttling sounds that had better *not* be rats. But there were no voices, no footsteps, no indication of people inside or outside.

Not feeling inclined to stick around, she reached out to touch Maddox's mind. But failed. Like something was blocking the mental pathway. She tried reaching for Harper. Again, it didn't work. *The fuck?* She tried contacting several other people—Jolene, Khloë, Devon, Ciaran. Not once did her psyche manage to touch that of another.

Her pulse began to speed up, and her demon became even more tense. Cursing beneath her breath, Raini made a beeline for the stone door a few feet away, shuddering when a stray spiderweb ghosted over her shoulder. *Ew.*

She shoved, pushed, and kicked the door. It didn't open. *Fuck.*

She tossed a ball of hellfire at it, hoping the flames would consume the stone. They didn't. They merely licked at the door before shimmering away. Some kind of power or magick acted as a barrier. Hurrying over to the small window, she saw that it was welded shut. She blasted the glass with hellfire, but the flames did nothing. Her breathing turned quick and shallow, and she swallowed hard.

Trapped. She was trapped.

A deep growl sounded, echoing in the large space, raising the hairs on the back of her neck. She spun on her heel and tracked the sound. Her heart jumped as she saw a pair of red eyes watching her from the shadows. Understanding rapidly dawned on her. The preternatural measures in place weren't there to keep *her* inside, they were meant for something else. And she'd just been dumped in here with it. *Oh, shit.*

*

"You only want to talk?" Maddox lifted a brow. "And that requires ten of you, does it?"

The angel's mouth tightened. "We would like you to hear us out."

"Would you now? Well, I'm only interested in talking with Castiel. Perhaps one of you can call him here."

"We don't know of any Castiel."

Barely refraining from rolling his eyes, Maddox took another swig of bourbon. "Of course you don't."

"We are only here for our brothers. We want you to free them."

Maddox frowned. "Brothers? Are you referring to the last halo-bearers that came for my lair? Or do you mean the ones who went after my anchor?"

"All of them. Set them free, and we will ensure that no other halo-bearers bother you or your lair."

Maddox twisted his mouth. "Hmm, interesting proposition."

"Will you agree to release them?"

Sighing, Maddox set both his phone and glass on the bar. "Let's not play games. You know they're dead. You're not here to enquire about them. You're here to launch an attack, and you're stalling. The question is . . . *why* would you stall?"

The angel's eyelids flickered. "You can't possibly have killed all of them," he insisted, apparently deciding to ignore Maddox's assertion.

Uneasy, Maddox narrowed his eyes. "What is it you're waiting for?"

"I've already told you why we're here."

"And you lied. You're waiting for something."

Several descendants teleported into the large space, ready to battle. Instead of tensing, the halo-bearers smiled. And then it happened. The sound of a large blast thundered through the air outside the club, like a bomb had detonated. The forms of the halo-bearers began to shimmer as they prepared to waver away, but then they all stilled with a frown.

"I'm guessing you just bombed the club with holy fire," said Maddox. "I'm guessing you're also now wondering why the building isn't falling apart, *and* why it is you can't seem to leave. The truth is . . . you walked right into a trap. And if I hadn't killed your other 'brothers,' they would have told you that using holy fire would be pointless. So sad. But hey, I can lighten things up. A joke would work, right? You'll like this one. Ten angels walk into a bar." Maddox launched an arctic energy ball at the halo-bearer in front of him, striking the bastard right in the gut.

"I want at least one of them alive," Maddox told his demons. Then pandemonium broke out. It was ugly. Chaotic. Turbulent.

People dodged, ducked, and weaved to evade the barrage of hellfire, holy fire, telekinetic force, and Maddox's ice-cold energy. Some teleported or wavered from spot to spot, trying to get the drop on their enemies.

The glasses hanging above the bar smashed. Tables and chairs cracked or tipped over. A speaker collapsed to the floor, almost falling on an unsuspecting descendant.

It quickly became clear that the halo-bearers were no strangers to battle. They fought hard, shelved their pain, kept up the pressure. But they were fighting beings that had a real hatred for them; beings who wanted to avenge the many descendants that had recently been killed just because of an overly ambitious archangel.

Even as their flesh blistered from holy fire burns, Maddox's demons relentlessly attacked the intruders. That relentlessness soon paid off. The angels gradually weakened under the assault, bleeding, burning, and bruised.

Nonetheless, two tag-teamed Maddox. Once they realized the holy fire had no effect on him, they changed tactics. Maddox soon became their fucking punch bag. Telekinetic strike after telekinetic strike assailed his body—a fist to the jaw, a kick to the kneecap, a blow to the temple, a punch to the throat.

Maddox retaliated hard, hurling beams of cold, crackling energy their way. But the duo had taken cover behind the bar, so it bore the brunt of his attack.

He hissed as telekinetic fists pounded his ribs, stealing his breath, sending pain rippling through his body. He was done with his shit. Maddox teleported behind the duo—a risky move, but it paid off, because they didn't anticipate it. As such, they didn't even feel the scatter shots of cold energy until it was too late and the power was ravaging their insides.

Leaving them to die, Maddox teleported back to his original spot. A halo-bearer materialized a few feet away, smirking. A hard, dazing impact slammed into Maddox's psyche, making his vision go black for a second. Recovering fast from the blow, he telekinetically gripped the little fucker's throat and raised him high in the air.

He's the last one alive, so you might not want to choke him to death, Hector warned.

Inwardly cursing, Maddox dropped the angel on the floor and popped a containment forcefield around him.

An unfamiliar mind touched Maddox's. *Please tell me Raini's with you*, said Harper.

Tension filled his muscles, and his hackles rose. *What's wrong?*

She was here, and now she's just . . . not. We don't know where she is, and she isn't answering our telepathic calls.

Fuck.

Moving very slowly, Raini began to back up, not once looking away from that red gaze. Her heart was pounding so hard she was surprised it didn't hurt. *Maddox! Harper! Jolene!*

No one answered. How could they, when she couldn't even touch their minds?

Another rumbly growl echoed in the air, almost making her flinch. She wasn't defenseless. She could kill whatever it was. Nothing with a brain stood a chance against psychic hellfire. But there was no saying what powers it had; no knowing if it could disable her before she had a chance to—

It crept out of the shadows, and she came to a surprised halt. A person, she realized. It was a person. A man.

She squinted. She knew that face. She knew those eyes—she'd seen them glazed with lust as the succubae allure hit him hard in the parking lot outside the Damned . . . only there'd been no red glow to his irises then. He'd been utterly normal. Well, he wasn't now.

His eyes weren't glazed with lust now either. No, there was something else there. A madness. A predatory hunger. A bestial awareness, as if the man was buried beneath whatever had taken him over. Or maybe that man was gone altogether. No, surely if the guy couldn't come back from this messed-up state, Maddox would have destroyed him.

"Stay back," she warned, but the demon didn't. He kept coming, *stalking* her, watching her like a cobra.

Shit, she did *not* want to kill one of her anchor's demons. Especially when the guy didn't seem to be in his right mind. Something was very wrong with him.

If she hit him with a low blast of psychic hellfire, it would be a shockwave of scorching heat as opposed to a blaze of fire. As such, it would knock him out, not kill him. Probably. She'd never tried it before. She'd only been trained to keep control of the power, not to wield it in different ways.

Not moving her eyes from him, she kept backing up. He kept moving forward.

Raini thought about tossing a ball of hellfire at him, but that might merely prompt him to attack. It seemed best to stay calm, to make no sudden movements, to do nothing that could be misconstrued as a challenge.

He paused, his nostrils flaring, and then squatted on the floor. He bent over sniffing, and then—*ew*—licked at the ground. No, at the blood staining it. *Her* blood. His eyes snapped back to her, almost whirling with madness.

Her heart slammed against her ribs. "Stay. Back."

He lunged.

CHAPTER THIRTEEN

She darted out of reach and hurled an orb of hellfire at him. It struck his chest, burning through his tee and blistering the skin beneath. He didn't even *wince*. He just pinned her with that cobra stare again. Raini conjured another orb. "*Stay the fuck back.*"

He pounced again.

She tossed the orb at his head and moved out of range, almost colliding with a statue. Slipping behind it, she shoved it hard. It fell to the ground, missing him by mere *inches*. He hadn't jerked back to avoid it, as if his attention was focused so wholly on her that he saw nothing else. If he was aware of the hellfire eating at his face and scalp, he didn't show it; didn't exhibit any sign of being in pain.

"Snap out of it!" she yelled.

He snarled, exposing his teeth, and then charged her like a goddamn bull.

Raini backpedaled fast, slowing him down by hitting him with hellfire orb after hellfire orb and—

She tripped over something and fell back, landing hard on her butt. The fucker leapt at her. She skidded back fast on her elbows. She wasn't fast enough. He landed between her legs and savagely sank his teeth into her thigh.

Crying out, she struck with a low blast of psychic hellfire. Power shimmered through the air like waves of heat and rushed up his nostrils and down his ears. He sat up with a gurgling sound, his eyes rolled back into his head, and he toppled to the side. She again used her elbows and heels to swiftly shuffle backwards. Breathing hard, she almost jumped out of her damn skin when Maddox appeared beside her.

He took in the scene and cursed a blue streak. Some sort of forcefield popped up around the other demon, surrounding him like a bubble.

Maddox crouched at her side. "Raini? *Raini*, look at me."

Blinking hard, she gave him a cursory glance, not yet comfortable with taking her eyes off her attacker, who didn't appear to be moving. "I'm okay."

"No, you're not." Maddox put his palm flat against hers.

She winced as his power crackled through her system, heading straight to the cut on her upper arm and then down to the bite on her thigh. "Is he dead? I tried not to kill him."

"He's alive, just unconscious." Maddox helped her stand. "How did you get here?"

She licked her lips, still watching his demon. "Someone dumped me here—I didn't see them, they grabbed me from behind, dropped me on the floor, sliced my arm, and then disappeared. It happened so damn fast. I called out to you and several other people over and over."

"I'd have come if I'd heard you. This place is shielded; it prevents telepathic contact."

She frowned. "Why? And what is this place?"

A place Maddox had never meant for her to ever know existed. *Fuck.* There was no way he could easily explain any of this away. No way he could convince her that nothing was wrong with the demon who'd attacked her. Which left him only one choice. He'd need to take it all from her mind.

Regret churned in his belly. The thought of stealing her memories made him feel ill. It seemed wrong. A betrayal. And he hated that he had no other option. "A mausoleum near my home."

Raini slid her gaze back to the demon on the floor. "He used to walk me from my car to your club. He's one of yours."

"Yes," Maddox confirmed, his voice sounding flat even to him. "His name is Gunther."

"Something's wrong with him. He licked my blood from the floor. He bit me. He . . . It was like he was crazy. There was a kind of . . . bloodlust in his eyes."

Since she'd very soon forget it all, Maddox admitted, "That's because he's going through a haze."

She blinked. "A haze?"

"That's what we call it. It's like a fog in your brain. A red mist. It takes hold of you. Buries everything that makes you *you.* Takes away your reason, rationality, and control." He paused. "It happens to descendants sometimes, even if we answer our cravings."

"Cravings?"

"The madness, bloodlust, is usually short-term. It tends to last about a week. Then it passes. But during that time, we will feed from anyone. We will gorge and gorge until we make ourselves ill. That's why a descendant in a haze is isolated. We shield the building because otherwise they'd telepathically scream at us day and night."

Raini stared at him. "When you say 'feed,' you mean . . ."

"I mean descendants drink blood, Raini," he said, his voice

toneless. "We need it. It's the curse of every fallen angel, and that curse was passed on to us. We don't need to feed every day. Most of us can go at least a month without feeding. I can go approximately three months without it. But no matter how consistent the feeds are, a haze can still take us. I didn't name the club 'the Damned' because I liked it. *We* are damned. Every one of my kind."

Raini felt her pulse kick up. Blood. They drank blood. Went through fucking *hazes*. She slid Gunther a quick look. "Has that ever happened to you?"

Maddox gave a slow shake of the head.

"But it could?"

He only nodded.

"Okay." Reeling from all he'd told her, she pulled in a long breath through her nose. Jesus, it was no wonder descendants kept to themselves; they had a lot to hide.

As he watched her closely with a cold distance in his eyes, she could tell that he was expecting judgment, revulsion, and fear. He thought she'd turn away from him; that she'd be repulsed. And that was plain insulting. He couldn't *help* what he was. None of them could. They were making the best out of a bad situation.

"If you'd asked me to guess what you were keeping from me," began Raini, "I wouldn't have said this. I suppose it could be worse."

His brows dropped. "Could it?"

"Things can always be worse." She bit her lip. "You're going to take these memories from me, aren't you?" There was only one reason he'd be so forthcoming—he intended to make her forget it all.

He didn't respond, he just watched her steadily. Yeah, he was going to wipe away the memories. The thought made her stomach roll, but it was hard to judge him for it. Hard to judge him for protecting himself and his kind as a whole, even as it hurt that he didn't trust her.

"Someone put me in here with him," she said. "They wounded me so he'd smell the blood. They left me here to die. Who would do that?"

"Probably the halo-bearers that attacked my club around the same time," replied Maddox, flitting his gaze over her face, seeing none of the disgust he'd expected. His demon was surprised by her easy acceptance but had no problem trusting it was real. Maddox, however, wondered if maybe she was in shock after her ordeal with Gunther.

"The angels know about this place, about your curse, as you call it?"

"They definitely know about the latter, and they've probably watched us while waiting for an opportunity to strike, so they'll have noticed we isolate those in a haze. They tried taking out the club with holy fire; they intended to kill me. I think they thought that if you were brought here, you'd telepathically call one of your lair for help when I didn't come. They would then find Gunther, and my kind's secrets would be exposed."

"In which case, my lair would forget about siding with yours against halo-bearers, especially if Gunther managed to harm me."

"It's a guess but, yes, that's what I believe. The halo-bearers need a way to get Jolene off their ass so no wars break out. They couldn't have known that this place was shielded to prevent telepathic contact, so they had no reason to think you wouldn't be able to call out for help."

She only nodded, her expression pensive.

"I don't like how well you're taking all this."

Her brows lowered. "Why not?"

He towered over her. "Raini, I'm telling you I drink blood. Crave it. Need it. I'm telling you I could be taken over by a haze that would make me all but insane."

"I know. It's a doozy. But I grew up around imps. I've heard weirder shit than this."

He could actually believe that. Still . . . "You're missing the bigger picture. Remember all those bites my demon gave you? The only thing that stopped it from breaking the skin and drinking your blood was that the entity thought you'd loathe it for doing so—that's all. So show a little loathing, Raini, or I can't guarantee it won't bite you for real one day. It wants to taste you. So do I."

She sniffed, haughty. "I'd be a little offended if you didn't. I don't see why my blood would be less appealing than anyone else's."

His demon chuckled, delighted and making all sorts of erotic plans. Maddox? He did not understand her. He just didn't.

A groan came from Gunther. He lifted his head and looked at them through eyes that—*what the fuck?*—no longer held a red glow. "Maddox?" he croaked. He squinted at Raini and then closed his eyes. "Shit, I think I bit her. Is she okay?"

For a long moment, Maddox could only stare at him. "Yes," he slowly replied. "As are you, apparently." Which made absolutely no fucking sense.

Gunther blinked at Raini. "What did you do?" he asked, curious and confused. "It felt like my head was on fire. Like an insane amount of heat blew through my mind, and then the haze suddenly . . . cleared, but then I passed out. Seriously, what did you do?"

Gaping at him, Raini paled. "I didn't try to kill you," she answered vaguely.

Insane amount of heat? Only one thing could truly heat a

person's psyche in any way. Maddox looked down at her, his eyes narrowed. "But you could have killed him, couldn't you?" He hummed. "It's little wonder your demon is so confident you could take me on and win. Psychic hellfire is a very potent weapon. A full-on blast of it can consume the mind completely."

She swallowed and looked away.

His demon, warped as it was, found it a turn-on that she could so easily destroy it. Maddox didn't understand the entity any more than he understood his anchor.

Gunther frowned, struggling to his feet. "That's what it was? Jesus, no wonder it felt like it was going to blow off the top of my head."

"Instead, it literally consumed the haze," Maddox mused, dropping the containment forcefield. "Interesting."

Gunther cricked his neck. "Celia okay?" he asked, referring to his mate.

"She will be now that you're back with us. She's been worried. Go to her. I want you both in the cathedral in twenty minutes, though. I'll be calling everyone there for a meeting. Tell no one other than Celia what happened here until afterward." Maddox had a little something to deal with before beginning the meeting, but he wasn't about to leave Raini in the cathedral or anywhere else alone. He wanted her where he could see her, which meant taking her with him. His demon, still wound tight on discovering she'd been taken *again*, would accept nothing else.

"Understood." Gunther nodded at Raini and then teleported away.

She frowned. "Wait, why didn't he teleport out of here earlier? And what do you mean by cathedral?"

"We can't call on our abilities when in a haze. We can still use telepathy, but I suspect that's because it's such a basic gift. Very few don't possess it. Plus, it doesn't require the same level of concentration that it does to access other abilities. Even babies can do it." People were trained to call on and control their gifts, but no one really needed help to use telepathy—it was too instinctive for demons, perhaps because they were predominantly psychic creatures. "And by cathedral, I meant cathedral."

Maddox closed his hand around her wrist and teleported back to the club. The descendants who'd fought alongside him earlier were still there, doing their best to put the place to rights. The club was in no state to open for business tonight, though.

The traces of ashes on the floor told him that the dead halo-bearers had been incinerated. The only angel left was still trapped in the forcefield, shivering, his lips blue, his cheeks red.

Um, Maddox, Raini began, *I've got a lot of people telepathically calling out to me. They noticed I was missing. I've assured them that I'm okay, but they're wanting answers, and I'm guessing I can't give them the full truth.*

No, she definitely couldn't. *Tell them you couldn't respond to their calls because you've been unconscious until now. Say we'll meet them at the penthouse in an hour, where we'll then explain the rest. There are a few things we need to do first.*

They won't be happy about the wait, but okay.

Releasing her wrist, Maddox stalked toward the angel. "So, the plan was to set my lair against my anchor's. Another divide-and-conquer strategy. Your archangel is sort of a one-trick pony, isn't he?"

The halo-bearer averted his gaze, tense as a bow, braced for impact.

What happened? Hector asked. *Duncan just called saying the women Raini works with seem to be a little frantic right now. He and Hoyt are barreling into the studio as we speak.*

His gaze still on the angel, Maddox replied, *Someone took*

her, but she didn't see who. It could even be our guest here. Maddox narrowed his eyes on their captive. "I need you to pass on a message to your precious archangel. Can I trust you to relay it, word for word?"

The halo-bearer's upper lip curled. "I will do *nothing* for you."

"Thought as much." Maddox telekinetically flipped him over and split open his robe to bare the skin of his back. Pinning the angel still with power alone, Maddox lowered the forcefield. "Now let's see . . . I'd like to say a great many things to your leader, but I only have a small canvas, so I'll have to keep it short and succinct."

Maddox raised his hand and released a stream of icy energy from the tip of his index finger, focusing it on the flesh of the angel's back, and then he began to write. The halo-bearer screamed through his teeth, and those screams soon turned into pitiful whimpers—every sound was like music to his demon's ears.

Hector whistled once Maddox was done and read it aloud. "*You really think you're worthy of being one of the Seven, Castiel? Then stop sending minions and face me yourself—I dare you.*" Hector chuckled.

Maddox reopened the hole in their preternatural security and released his telekinetic hold on the halo-bearer. "Go." The angel instantly wavered away. Maddox then once again closed the hole.

"That taunt will make good bait," said Hector. "Do you think Castiel will rise to it?"

"I think his ego will. Whether or not he'll come face me is another thing altogether." Maddox swept his gaze over every descendant in the room as he said, "I'm holding a lair meeting in the cathedral in ten minutes. Everyone is to attend. Spread the word."

Hector flicked a look at Raini. "What did the halo-bearers do to her this time?"

"I'll explain at the meeting."

Just then, Jolene's mind touched his. *Maddox, I do not know what you deem more important than bringing Raini to me, but making me wait isn't acceptable.*

He inwardly sighed. He understood that Jolene needed to see Raini with her own eyes, but he couldn't delay this meeting, and he certainly couldn't invite Jolene to it. *You'll see her soon. You've spoken to her telepathically. You know that she's fine.*

Not good enough.

It'll have to be, because we have business to take care of before we can meet with you and the others.

I am her Prime, *Maddox.*

And I'm her anchor. I need her at my side right now—I refuse to justify why or to argue with you about it. Maddox broke the connection and turned to Raini, who was glancing around the club, taking in the damage. If she was at all bothered by what he'd done to the halo-bearer, she gave no indication of it. Then again, she was probably as pissed at those fuckers as he was.

Maddox stalked to her. "Time to go."

"Where?" she asked.

In answer, he teleported her to the raised altar within the cathedral.

Raini felt her mouth drop open as she gazed around. The cathedral had an old world medieval feel. Vaulted ceilings. Mosaic floors. Exquisite artwork. Broad beams. Stone arches. It was like something out of a gothic fairytale. "Wow. Why are we here?"

"It's where we often hold our meetings." Turning toward one of the stained-glass windows, Maddox pointed to the nearby building. "That's where we live."

She blinked. "You . . . you all live in a monastery?"

He shrugged. "Private joke." Tilting his head, he added, "I wouldn't have thought that psychic hellfire could obliterate a haze. It's always been portrayed as a negative ability. I wonder if there are other constructive things you could do with it."

She was equally surprised by what had happened, but it made sense that the hellfire's heat could consume the fog clogging their brain—like hellfire itself, the heat was potent. "I wouldn't know. I use it very rarely."

"That's how you killed the halo-bearers in your kitchen."

"Yes." Feeling a little exposed now that he knew her secrets, Raini folded her arms. At least he wasn't exhibiting any of the wariness that her lair members would for sure feel if they knew. "So, what false memory are you going to plant in my brain? What am I going to believe actually happened tonight? For the record, it doesn't seem fair that I'll forget the skeletons in *your* closet but you and your friend will remember *mine*."

Hinges creaked as one of the heavy wooden doors were heaved open. A cluster of descendants strode inside, their steps faltering when they noticed Raini.

"What is she doing here?" one asked Maddox, though not unkindly.

"All will be revealed shortly," Maddox told them. "Take a seat." Turning back to Raini, he guided her to a stool near the wall on her left. "You should sit and conserve your energy. We'll be meeting with your people next."

Yeah, and that might not go so well. Jolene was particularly furious with him for not taking Raini straight to her. Jolene wasn't happy with her either, since Raini—knowing the Prime would send Ciaran to retrieve her—refused to say where she was.

As the minutes went by, more and more people filed inside the cathedral. Some asked why Raini was present. Others simply cast her confused looks. All appeared uncomfortable with having an outsider there. Now that she knew the secrets they protected, she could completely understand.

Gunther and a slender brunette who had to be Celia entered last. She gave Raini a tentative smile, so Gunther must have given her the full story. Hector then closed the door and took up a position near Raini. The woman who often guarded her—who Raini heard another demon refer to as Carmen—stood opposite them.

Facing the people seated in the pews, Maddox planted his feet. "I'm sure you've all already heard by now that halo-bearers launched an attack at the club. I'm sure you're also wondering why my anchor is here. I found her in the mausoleum about twenty minutes ago. Seems like a halo-bearer dumped her there, leaving her with Gunther, no doubt counting on her reaching out for help."

"And, out of my mind with bloodlust, I tried to kill her," admitted Gunther. Wincing, he shot Raini an apologetic look. "Sorry about that."

"Will you be careful of the terminology you use around her?" one descendant complained at Gunther, scowling. He then turned to Maddox. "You cannot let her remember any of it."

"On the contrary, Euan, I think it's to our benefit that we allow her to remember," said Maddox.

Surprise gripped Raini's gut. The same emotion flashed on many faces.

Euan's head jerked back. "What? How the hell could that be to our benefit?"

"You heard what Gunther said. He was out of his mind with bloodlust. Now he's not." Maddox's brow inched up. "You haven't wondered why that is?"

Silence fell, and people exchanged confused glances.

"Raini did something to him?" asked Hector, sparing her a quick look.

"She hit him with a low blast of psychic hellfire to knock him unconscious," Maddox explained. "The blazing heat burned away the haze of bloodlust."

"*Burned* it away?" asked the female sentinel.

Maddox nodded. "I don't have to tell any of you just how deadly psychic hellfire is. Raini could have killed Gunther. She didn't, despite his intention to kill her, because she knew he was one of us, and she knew something was wrong with him. You want me to repay her for that by removing the memories from her brain?"

Celia cleared her throat and offered Raini another tentative smile. "Thank you for not killing him. He told me he bit you. It would have been easy for you to take him out there and then, but you didn't."

"And while I'm sure we all appreciate that," began Marcella, "it's not a good reason to let her remember. Our secret—"

"I'll keep yours if you keep mine," Raini cut in, sweeping her gaze along the pews. "No one is all that fond of psychic hellfire for obvious reasons, so you can understand why I don't advertise that I can use it. Very few people knew until tonight. If you agree to say nothing about it, I'll agree to say nothing of your own secrets."

Marcella's expression was a pure challenge. "How do we know you'll keep your word?"

"How do I know you'll keep yours?" Raini shot back. "Let me ask another question. You're all eager for me to have these memories yanked from my brain. Would any of you be so easy about having *yours* taken from *you*, especially if you'd given your word that you wouldn't share what you didn't ask to discover?"

"I say we take a vote," Euan piped up, standing. "Those in

favor of her having her mind wiped raise your hand." He lifted his own, far too fucking pompous to live in her demon's opinion.

"This isn't a democracy," stated Maddox, his voice hard and deep. "Sit the fuck down or get the fuck out."

Euan's face flushed, but he stiffly sat. Raini's inner entity snickered.

A descendant in the front row sighed at Raini. "I get that you didn't ask to be put in this situation; that it isn't your fault that you know too much. But the fact is that you *do* know too much."

"I do," Raini allowed. "I get why you'd fear an outsider possessing your secrets. I don't much like the feeling either. But you'd be fools to ask that Maddox erase my memories, and you know it. Because you also know you could use me; that no more of your lair would have to suffer through another haze if I was on hand."

"And you'd be fine with us using you?" challenged Marcella.

Raini wouldn't piss on the woman if she was on fire, but . . . "I'd be fine with doing my anchor a favor. I don't really much care about any of you, purely because I don't know you. But if Maddox asked me to spare someone the torment of a haze, I'd do it."

A pretty redhead spoke up. "How can we trust that you won't . . ."

"Destroy your anchor bonds? I guess you can't." And that was why no one liked being around someone with Raini's ability. Not only could a huge blast of psychic hellfire liquefy a person's brain, a simple well-aimed zap of it could do the very thing that no other demonic power could do. It could incinerate an anchor bond.

CHAPTER FOURTEEN

When it became apparent that Raini could wield psychic hellfire, the first thing she'd been taught to do was strangle the ability. Her parents had explained how important it was that she never use it. It wasn't until she was much older that Jolene decided it would be best if Raini learned how to control it rather than simply suppress it.

Perhaps the Prime hadn't liked that she'd asked Raini to effectively cut off a small piece of herself, but Raini hadn't minded. It was better to have spent years suppressing it than to have accidentally destroyed an anchor bond. Once destroyed, there was no way to restore it. Worse, the unnatural severing of the bond could trigger the affected demons to turn rogue.

The entity that lived within every demon was a heartless psychopathic predator. The only thing that gave it a sense of balance was that it shared its soul with a person. If it no longer had that person's sense of goodness touching its soul, it would be a being of pure darkness. The ultimate evil.

Rogues weren't insane, but they cared nothing for logic. They felt no need to curb their desires, no matter how cruel those desires were. They'd kill indiscriminately for no other reason than that they felt like doing so—and they wouldn't care if their actions caught the attention of humans.

The dark satisfaction they attained from inflicting pain and misery was like a drug to them. So, yes, it was never good to have a rogue on the loose. The death toll would always be high.

Only one other person in the history of Raini's lair had ever possessed the ability to wield psychic hellfire, and that person had left behind awful scars that taunted the lair even a century later. On losing his own anchor in a tragic accident, Doyle had been so utterly devastated that he'd withdrawn from life, leaving his demon in charge.

The entity had wreaked havoc— cremating anchor bonds here, there, and everywhere. The result? Their Prime and a high number of others turned rogue.

Just one rogue could cause utter chaos. A whole horde of them were practically impossible to defeat. They had not only attacked the others within their lair, they targeted outsiders and humans—causing an epic clusterfuck.

Several of the other Primes had united to destroy the rogues, leaving the lair so small and vulnerable that some of the larger lairs had taken advantage—bullying them and trying to steal away the more powerful members, even if those members were children.

Jolene worried that if the rest of the lair knew of Raini's ability, they'd demand that she leave for fear that history would repeat itself. And so they'd kept it quiet, hoping there never came a time when the information fell into the wrong hands. That time might now have arrived. The fact that she possessed the descendants' secrets should still the tongue of anyone who felt like causing trouble for her. *Should.*

"I say we trust her," said Celia, to which Gunther nodded.

Euan bristled. "And what if she breaks her word?"

"She hasn't done it so far, has she?" Maddox pointed out. "If she was a person whose word meant nothing, she wouldn't have come to me the day after I healed her friend. She wouldn't have allowed me to place the psychic tag in her mind. She wouldn't have stuck to our deal every step of the way."

An elderly descendant sighed. "I can't say I trust that she won't betray us—like she said, she doesn't know us—but I trust she won't betray you, Maddox, so . . ."

The redhead again spoke. "I don't feel comfortable with this. I know that she's your anchor, Maddox. I have nothing against her on a personal level, but I . . ."

"Let's say a haze took Jordan tomorrow, Pen," Maddox said to her. "Would you be happy to isolate him in the mausoleum where he'd scream and scream but no one would hear him? Or would you want Raini to help him?"

Pen snapped her mouth shut. A deep sigh left her. "All right, if you honestly believe she won't betray us, I'll agree to trust her. I'm still not comfortable with it, but I'll do it."

Others said pretty much the same thing, even Marcella.

Euan shot to his feet, glowering. "Letting an outsider possess this knowledge goes against *everything* our kind is taught." He sliced his gaze to Raini. "If you betray our secret—" He cut off at the growl that rumbled out of his Prime.

Maddox glared at the piece of shit. "Don't. Fucking. Dare. You do not threaten her. Ever. Is that understood? Bear in mind that I've killed people for less."

Clenching his fists, Euan opened his mouth . . . but he said nothing. He teleported away instead. Which Raini's demon found seriously disappointing, because it had wanted a chance to pummel the little shit.

"The meeting is over," Maddox declared.

Descendants began to leave until, finally, there was only him, Raini, and his two sentinels.

Carmen blew out a breath. "That actually went pretty well."

"I thought so," said Hector. "But then, they probably only behaved so cooperatively for selfish reasons."

Maddox nodded. Yes, his demons would want Raini to step in if they or someone they cared for were taken by a haze. They'd spent too long watching each other suffer in such a way, never believing anything or anyone could help them.

Maddox held his hand out to Raini. "Now for our next meeting. There's still some time left before it should begin, but I have a feeling that Jolene and whoever else is concerned for you will already be waiting, anxious to see you."

"This won't go so well. They're pretty mad at us both." Standing, she placed her hand in his. "Before we go, we need to get our story straight. What am I supposed to tell them happened?"

Maddox thought on it for a moment. "As I know you'll want to tell as few lies as possible, we'll simply say that you were knocked out by a psychic blow and then wavered to my club by a halo-bearer who hoped to use you to distract me; that you didn't come around until after the fight was over." It meant she'd have to say very little, since she could claim she was unconscious for most of what happened.

"Okay," she said simply.

"I know you don't like the idea of deceiving them—"

"Really, it's okay. If they knew, they'd understand. It helps to know that."

He studied her face and then, satisfied she truly understood the lies were necessary, he nodded.

"Want Carmen and me to come along?" Hector asked him.

Maddox shook his head. "Keep an eye on things here. It's doubtful that Castiel will make another move tonight, but there's always a chance." With that, he teleported himself and Raini to the living area of the penthouse.

He wasn't in the least bit surprised to find the room full of people, including her parents, her colleagues, and Jolene. Things went exactly as he'd expected they would. People descended on Raini, checked she was fine, and demanded to know what happened.

He told them that she'd been dumped at the club during the halo-bearer attack as an intended distraction, and that Maddox had killed the angel responsible and placed her out of harm's way.

While her friends, family, and lair members were grateful that he had "saved" her, they were still furious about being prevented from seeing her straight away, and so they spent a little time ranting about it.

Maddox didn't attempt to explain or justify it, seeing no reason to do so. He'd made the right decision by Raini . . . who was now rubbing her temples, he then noticed. Maddox felt his jaw tighten. "You've all seen that Raini's fine," he said, cutting them off. "You've heard what happened. So perhaps you could stop yelling—she's had a tough time of it, she doesn't need to be dealing with your anger on top of everything else."

Many sighed and lost their confrontational postures.

"He's right," Devon said to no one in particular. "We all need to calm ourselves down."

"It's not that easy," said Evangeline. "I'm still an internal mess after hearing that *both* my daughters were missing."

"But surely you all now understand why Maddox couldn't just drop everything to bring me here," said Raini.

"I do, yeah, but surely *you* can understand why we might have wanted answers like *yesterday*," Harper said to her. "I absolutely shit myself when I realized you were missing. Devon was in a blind panic. And Khloë went quiet, which is *never* good."

"I answered your telepathic yells as soon as I regained consciousness," said Raini.

"But you didn't tell us what happened, which meant our imagination pretty much went *wild*," said Khloë, whirling her fingers near the sides of her head.

Raini lifted her shoulders. "I was a little out of it when I first came around from the psychic blow," she lied so smoothly and convincingly that his demon was rather impressed. "Maddox thought it'd be better if I conserved my energy—using telepathy wasn't gonna do that."

Harper snapped her mouth shut, unable to argue that.

Jolene went toe-to-toe with him. "I appreciate that your attention was somewhat divided earlier, considering you had halo-bearers to deal with and one hell of a mess to clean up," she said, not *sounding* as though she truly appreciated it. "But you could have brought her to us after the battle was over."

"I could have," he granted, which appeared to take her off-guard.

"And yet, you didn't."

Maddox gave a lazy shrug. "I don't particularly see why I should have."

Jolene's brow hiked up. "You don't see why?"

"No. I see why you would have wanted me to do it, but this isn't about you." Maddox looked around the room. "It's not about any of you except Raini. That seems to have gotten lost among your own anger and anxiety, which I don't find an excuse."

"Is that a fact?" asked Jolene.

"Yes, it is. Raini was plucked out of her place of

work—somewhere very special to her, somewhere she's always considered a haven—and tossed into a dangerous situation. I cared more about her state of mind and well-being than I did yours. I wanted her where I could see her; where I knew she was safe. And if she and I find ourselves in a situation like that again, I will do exactly the same thing. You're her Prime, I understand that. But never expect me to put you or your rights before her, Jolene. It won't ever happen."

There was a long moment of silence, and then Jolene's mouth curved into a smug smirk. "Good. It's about time you stepped up."

Letting out a relieved breath, Raini raked a hand through her hair. "Please tell me this means you two aren't going to get into a—*Dad, put the knife away*."

Lachlan turned wide innocent eyes on her. "Do I tell you what to do with *your* things? No."

She inhaled through her nose, her fingers flexing. "*Dad*."

He frowned and waved a dismissive hand. "Stop making a fuss over nothing."

Sliding an arm around Raini's shoulders, Evangeline gave her a little squeeze. "Relax, sweetheart, he's not going to throw it."

Raini looked at her. "You said that at Aunt Rissa's birthday party. Twenty seconds later, my ex had a blade buried in his shoulder."

"That was an accident," said Lachlan. "I was aiming for the pinata."

Raini let her head fall forward. "I'm done."

It was another hour before people began to leave the penthouse. Eventually, only she and Maddox—who her father had apparently decided not to stab—were left.

"Jolene sensed there was more to the story, but she let it be," he said.

Raini nodded, rubbing at her nape. "I was surprised she didn't push."

Maddox crossed to her. "She probably sensed it would do her no good." He took her hand. "Come on."

"Where are we going now?" Raini blinked as the world flashed white, and then they stood in a massive swanky hotel suite. Like the cathedral, it had a vaulted ceiling, broad beams, stained arched windows, and rough stone walls. The monastery, she thought. "Is this your room? Suite? Whatever?"

"Yes," he replied, settling his hands on her hips.

The studious look on his face made her frown. "What?"

"I kept wondering why fate gave you to me. Now I know."

Anchors were supposed to keep each other strong. Given that she could free him and his lair members from a haze . . . "Mystery solved."

Cupping her chin, he swept the pad of his thumb over her lower lip. "Now that you know my secrets and I know yours, there's no reason to hold back from the bond."

Her heart jumped, and her demon went on full alert. The entity still wasn't terribly pleased with him, but it did understand why he'd so far failed to officially claim Raini as his anchor. It would give him a chance to make it right *if* he was prepared to be the psi-mate they needed, not a half-assed one.

Raini bit her lip. "Are you sure you want to form the bond?"

"Why wouldn't I?"

"If we were to do this, you wouldn't be able to keep me compartmentalized from the other aspects of your life anymore. That's not what it means to have an anchor."

"Which is why I held back before. As I said, there's no need to do so now."

"You also wouldn't be able to hold me to the terms of our deal. We'd be starting afresh as psi-mates, and we'd each deserve the respect that should come with that. You'd need to *trust* me to rely on you, not wangle my compliance out of me."

He twisted his mouth. "All right. But I want you to keep the psychic tag for now. If it hadn't been for that tag, I wouldn't have known where you were earlier. Until the halo-bearers have backed off, I'd like to have that peace of mind that I can always find you."

Yeah, she'd figured he'd say that. "I can agree to that." It cost her nothing to permit him to leave it there a little longer, and she'd rather have the reassurance that she wouldn't be plain fucked if the angels came back and pulled more crap. It was clear those guys meant business. "You'd also need to—"

"Raini, you don't have to tell me everything that comes with having an anchor. I already know, just like I know this is what I want. Everything is out in the open now. You're trusting me with your skeletons, and I'm trusting you with mine. That's how it's supposed to be. So, yes, I want to form the bond." He raked his teeth over her lower lip. "And I want to be inside you when I do it."

Maddox closed his mouth over hers and sank his tongue inside. He kissed her exactly how he wanted to fuck her; how he *would* fuck her. Hard and deep and rough.

She clung to his shoulders, kissing him back, letting him feel the bite of her nails through his shirt. Maddox slipped his hand around that pretty throat he wanted to bite. He'd held her like that when he fucked her the previous night.

His demon wanted to take her now. Knowing they were about to claim her as their anchor, the entity was too worked up to care that she might not be wet enough to take it without pain yet. It just wanted in her. So did Maddox, but not until she was slick and ready.

Still devouring her mouth, he backed her into the small

dining table, lifted her, and set her on the wooden surface. "I want you naked." He whipped off her tee and bra. "Elbows."

She double-blinked, as if striving to process his order. Finally, she lay back, keeping herself propped up on her elbows.

"That's it, exactly like that," Maddox praised, ragging off her jeans and panties. "Now don't move." He slid his hands under her ass, raised her hips, and clamped his mouth around her pussy. The sharp breath she sucked in went straight to his cock.

He loved going down on her. Loved her taste, her scent, how shamelessly she demanded more. Usually, he'd take his time; play and tease and savor. Not tonight. His demon didn't have the patience to wait, and Maddox couldn't chance that the entity wouldn't simply surface and take her before she was ready. So he drove her up hard and fast, squeezing her ass tight as she came, knowing he'd leave bruises.

Maddox lowered her hips, snatched her hand, and pulled her upright. "Taste yourself." He fisted her hair and took her mouth again, growling in approval as she tore open his fly and freed his cock. "Hungry for it?"

Oh, Raini was. She absolutely was, and she saw no need to pretend otherwise. Playing it cool wouldn't get her royally fucked, and she was *all* about those royal fucks.

She curled her hand tight around his rock-hard shaft and pumped, keeping her grip just right. During their other nights together, she'd learned what he liked and how he liked it.

Raini frowned when he removed her hand. "Hey, I was in the middle of something."

"You can make me come with that talented little hand of yours later," he said, yanking her closer. He inched the thick head of his dick into her pussy. "Quick warning: my demon is probably going to bite you. You got a problem with that?"

Nu-uh. Call her weird, but she kind of got off on the idea. Curling her limbs around him, she lifted a brow. "Would it matter if I did?"

One corner of Maddox's mouth kicked up. "No." He grabbed a fistful of her hair and rammed his cock inside her.

She winced at the flash of pain, but then the discomfort was washed away by pure pleasure as he began to move. He rode her hard, using his grip on her hair to keep her mouth pressed lightly to his, as if he wanted to drink down her every breath and gasp and moan.

"After three, we both let go," he said, and she knew what he meant—they would both ease the hold they'd kept on their psyches to stop them from connecting. "One, two, three."

Their minds collided with such force she'd have staggered if she'd been standing, and she came hard even as their psyches fused together—two spheres intersecting rather than becoming one mind. And then, that easily, Maddox's psychic presence pulsed inside her, alive with his dominance and power and strength, bolstering her in a way she couldn't explain. It even had a "taste." *Bourbon and rich chocolate dessert.* All of it enlivened and stabilized her demon.

Realizing his cock was still hard inside her, that he hadn't yet come, she opened her eyes. His entity stared back at her, its black gaze glinting with intent, and she sensed another royal fuck coming on. Awesome.

"Feeling pretty smug now that you've got what you want?" she asked, because her own demon sure was.

"I already had what I wanted; you were already mine," it replied, squeezing her breast. "Now it is merely official."

She winced as it roughly twisted her nipple. "You like to hurt me, don't you?"

The demon's mouth curved. "Only in a good way." And oh,

then it started fucking her like it hated her. Which *did* hurt in a good way. Every thrust was a little too rough and went a little too deep, but she didn't want it to stop.

She jumped as it snapped a hand around her upper throat and pressed its thumb at the hollow of her right ear. She ground her teeth as the flesh there began to burn, and she realized it was leaving the anchor mark on her.

Sheer satisfaction glittered in that black gaze. "Do it."

Knowing what it wanted, she returned the favor and left her own mark on the hollow beneath its right ear—an infinity symbol that she knew would have a slight personal difference but, right then, she couldn't properly see what it was. And while her orgasm was creeping closer and closer, it was kind of hard to care about anything else.

Still brutally jackhammering into her, the demon slipped a hand between them. "Tonight, *I* will be the one who comes inside you." It parted her folds, exposing her clit to its thrusts, and oh God oh God oh God she was gonna—

It sank its teeth into her neck. The hot stab of fire shot straight to her core and sent her tumbling into the mother of all orgasms. The demon drank and drank as her release all but destroyed her. She felt its teeth unlock from her neck just as it powered harder and harder into her pussy before, finally, it jammed its cock deep. She felt its hot come splash her inner walls.

She sagged against its chest, gasping for air, limp as a damn noodle.

A hand stroked her hair with a gentleness that told her Maddox was back in control. "You okay?" he asked.

She hummed, too fucking out of it to talk. Hell, she didn't even have the energy to lift her eyelids. She felt him press his palm to hers, and then his power rushed to her neck, healing the bite.

"You taste far too good." He pulled out of her and then carried her to the bed, where he carefully set her down on the mattress. "You'll sleep here."

She only hummed again. It was mere seconds later that sleep dragged her under.

CHAPTER FIFTEEN

His anchor sighed and stared up at the ceiling. "I guess I should have seen this coming."

Lying on his side next to her, Maddox doodled circles around her navel piercing with his finger. "You would be safer here, Raini."

"I'm perfectly safe at the penthouse. No halo-bearer could bypass Knox's security measures."

Probably not. It was the "probably" part that bothered Maddox and his demon. They needed to be as certain as possible that she was perfectly safe. His entity would prefer to therefore keep her at its side at all times, but that wasn't feasible.

"The security measures only surround the penthouse floor," he reminded her. "They could snatch you right out of the reception area before anyone had a moment to react, just as they took you from the studio. That was ballsy, but it was also effective. They may think to try it again."

She must have sensed where he was going with this, because her eyes narrowed. "Don't ask me to take time off work."

"Your girls will ask the same of you. They're as concerned as I am. They will need the same peace of mind that I need."

"I don't think the angels will try to take me again. Their plan didn't work out so well last time, and they'll expect me to be on my guard. Besides, you pretty much laid down a gauntlet. The archangel won't send more minions, he'll come for you himself."

"Maybe. But it's very rare that archangels leave their realm. It usually only happens if they choose to fall. If an ant challenged me, I'd laugh and go on about my day. That's all we are to them. Insects. Creatures beneath their notice. The only reason he's concerning himself with me and my kind is that he believes it'll please the higher-ups, who absolutely despise that a breed of demon possesses holy blood."

"So Castiel might just find your challenge ridiculous."

Maddox gently tapped her piercing. "Yes."

Frowning, she absentmindedly traced the grim reaper tattoo on his shoulder. "But aside from the one you released yesterday, you've killed every other halo-bearer he sent after you and your lair, right?"

"He could view that as weakness on their part rather than strength on mine." Archangels could be incredibly arrogant and underestimated demons a great deal. That was their mistake.

"If he *does* consider you easy to kill, he might decide to take the matter into his own hands."

"Oh, he will eventually if he hopes to make a statement to the higher-ups. But whether he'll do it sooner rather than later is something I can't be certain of. So, in the meantime, I want you close. You may be right; he may not choose to target you again. But do you really think I'll ever take chances with your life?"

"Maddox—"

"If you couldn't wield psychic hellfire, you might have died at Gunther's hands last night." The sight Maddox had found when he'd teleported into the mausoleum—her pale and injured and *bitten*—was one he'd never forget. "I noticed the amount of burns he had. You'd hit him with plenty of orbs of regular hellfire. I'll bet none made him hesitate, did they? You could have retaliated with everything in you, but he wouldn't have felt the pain. He wouldn't have been able to think about anything other than draining you dry."

She swallowed. "I know that. But I *can* wield psychic hellfire, so it *didn't* happen. I'm not helpless."

"No, you're not. But the more often you use that ability, the more you risk others finding out about it."

"So, what, you want me to not only temporarily quit my job but relocate *here*?"

He smoothed his hand up her stomach to loosely palm her breast. "Yes, that's about it."

"I might consider the first, purely because if the halo-bearers *do* return to the studio, my girls could get hurt—not to mention any innocent clients. But I won't move here. I wouldn't be safe."

"I told you, halo-bearers can't penetrate this building. Do you think I'd lie to you about that?"

"No, I don't. But I do think you're forgetting the none too small issue that your lair hasn't accepted me all the way. I don't know what that guy Euan's problem is, but he *definitely* doesn't want me here. Marcella would happily string me up by my own intestines."

"Only in her head. She knows such a move would get her killed in real life." And it would not be a quick death—Marcella would know that.

"And what if you're wrong? What if she or Euan or someone else attacked me? You going to get pissed if I'm forced to use psychic hellfire to defend myself?"

"Yes, because it would rob me of the chance to punish them

for hurting you." His demon would want to get its licks in just the same.

"I wouldn't feel safe here, Maddox. Or welcome, for that matter. I wouldn't be able to settle. I'd be on edge all the time."

"You're so certain my lair doesn't approve of you?"

"Uh, *yeah*."

He shook his head. "That's never been the issue, Raini. They were nervous about having an outsider around. Their reservations were never personal to you."

"They were in the case of Marcella, because she wants to be in this bed, doesn't she?" Raini squinted, a dangerous glint in her eyes. "*Has* she ever been in here?"

"No. I don't shit where I eat."

"In other words, you don't sleep with your lair members?"

He thumbed her nipple. "It can bring complications."

"And sleeping with your anchor can't?"

"Nothing was going to keep me from having you. I knew that. I knew better than to fight it, so I didn't try. I don't see why it has to complicate things. Do they feel complicated?"

"Not right now, no."

"Good." He sucked her nipple into his mouth, liking her little gasp. He'd woken her not long after he put her to bed, needing her again. Needing to come inside her, since his demon had robbed him of that the first time round.

The feel of her psychic presence in his mind was more intimate than he would have expected. Perhaps because it *felt* like her; because it hummed with her strength, her sweetness, her spunk, her innate sensuality. And then there was her psychic taste. *Vanilla, peaches, and cream.*

At first, it had felt strange to be so connected with her, to feel their minds occasionally brush against each other on instinct, but he was becoming accustomed to it now. And he knew that, for all his power, he could never have stabilized his demon the way this bond did.

She flinched when he raked his teeth over her nipple. "Your demon didn't take much of my blood last night. Is that normal?"

He lathed the taut bud with his tongue to soothe the sting. "Unless we're taken by a haze, we don't need to drink much."

"Do you guys only feed from each other? I mean . . . I don't see how else you can hide what you do."

"It's not difficult, because descendants can heal minor injuries. Then we remove the memory afterward."

"Wait, *all* descendants can go patrolling around people's heads the way you do?"

"No. They can only remove a very recent memory—nothing more."

She trailed a finger down his chest. "But *you* can do more than remove a recent memory. Much more."

"My psychic abilities are stronger than that of the other descendants. Probably due to my archangelic blood." It was strange speaking of all these things he usually held inside, but it didn't feel uncomfortable. He knew he could trust her. No one had ever been solely *his* before, but Raini was.

"So archangels are super strong in a psychic sense?"

"That is what I've heard. I've only ever met one. He recently fell, and he isn't very forthcoming about what he is. I do know he has to drink blood, so it's not just fallen angels that are cursed with it."

Sighing, she shook her head. "I had no idea that happened to the Fallen."

"Most don't." Maddox brushed his thumb over the small, glistening mark his demon had left beneath the hollow of her ear. The line at the center of the infinity symbol had very small wings. He'd gotten a good look at his own mark, so he knew an R sat within the first loop of the symbol.

"The masters of the upper realm don't like it when angels fall," he went on. "This is their punishment. Personally, I think it's mostly supposed to serve as a deterrent to those who might consider falling. It probably works in most cases—who wants to survive on blood? Others, for whatever reason, are prepared to live that way."

"How often do they have to feed?"

"Weekly. My kind doesn't. We don't have the same appetite. It's *in* us, but it doesn't rule us. It's more like a . . . side-effect of whatever angelic genes are locked into descendant DNA."

She shook her head as she said, "I can't believe it didn't occur to me that the reason your kind is so insular is that you have things to hide. I, like others, just assumed you didn't hold other breeds in high esteem."

"We don't, because the majority of them treat us as less. We're not *all* so inclusive, though. There are even some descendants who choose other breeds as mates. In those instances, they either stick to the common practice of hiding their curse from their partners, or they make the decision to trust said partners with their secret. But they know their lair will kill their mate should that person betray their confidence, so they don't trust lightly."

"And since no one really wants to take a mate who they'll need to either lie to or be prepared to one day let their lair kill, they commonly choose to mate with another descendant." Raini understood, hiding the compassion she couldn't help but feel—no alpha male reacted well to someone feeling bad for them, which she thought was plain dumb, but whatever. "I guess it helps that your anchors, until now, were only ever descendants. Why do you think that is?"

"We've always assumed it's because the other breeds of demon don't possess angelic blood like we do."

"Makes sense. Do you wonder if more of your kind will soon have other breeds of demon as their anchors?"

"We've all wondered that ever since I found you. In most cases, having a psi-mate stabilizes us enough to stop a haze from taking us."

Raini blinked. "Really?"

"Yes. It's why each of us long to find our anchor. It's our one hope of being spared that nightmare. But as fate gave me you, my demons are now fearing that if their anchor turns out to be another breed, they may have to forsake them."

Her heart squeezed. "God, no wonder they're having such trouble accepting me. It's not just about an outsider knowing their secrets. Accepting me means accepting that their futures regarding their psi-mates are in flux, and many of them may actually never have the one thing that could spare them the hazes." *Hell.*

"Some, like me, have never had to endure one, but that doesn't mean they never will." Maddox ghosted his fingertips along her collarbone. "How many of your lair know of your ability to wield psychic hellfire?"

Rolling with the abrupt change of subject, she replied, "Not many. My parents, my sister, my girls, my dad's brothers, Jolene, and Khloë's brother."

"Why do you feel you can't trust more of them with your secret? They're your lair members. Surely it wouldn't make them hesitate to accept you."

"It's because of what happened with one of our old lair members, Doyle." Raini gave Maddox the entire story, finding it surprisingly easy to confide in him. The bond was much more intense than she'd thought it would be, but not invasive to the point where they could feel each other's emotions; she liked that. "Maybe people wouldn't react badly to hearing what I can do. But if they did, they'd want me gone." Her family would leave with her, but not before her father and uncle leveled a few blocks with their idea of "household chemical warfare."

His eyes narrowed, sharp. "So your sister knows how deadly you are. She'd know you'd have to be drained of power in order to be defeated by her."

Raini stilled, sensing what he was hinting at. "She didn't send the astral projector after me. She wouldn't do that." Or so Raini told herself. Her demon didn't have such faith in Demi.

"Just because someone is family doesn't mean they're loyal. Take Euan, for example. He's my cousin, but he'd like nothing more than to usurp me. He's tried a few underhanded methods in order to do so."

Her entity's upper lip quivered in distaste. "I knew he was an asshole. My demon branded him as weak the moment he first opened his mouth."

"He is weak. Too weak to even see that the high opinion he has of himself is a fantasy."

Raini played her fingers through his short hair, lightly kneading his scalp. "Do you have any other family members in your lair?"

He shook his head. "I used to. But then our lair once went head-to-head with another—and much larger—lair of descendants. Many died, including my parents."

Her fingers stilled in his hair. "I'm sorry to hear that," she said, her chest tightening. "What caused the battle?"

"The attack on us wasn't personal. The other lair simply wanted more power, wanted to increase their numbers."

She felt her face harden. "So they went around challenging lairs, killing some members, taking others." Fucking assholes.

"Yes. It's a practice as old as time for demons."

Sadly, he wasn't wrong. "Are any of the shitheads alive now?"

"Not since I became Prime."

"You killed them all? Good."

"I didn't do it alone." He dipped his head and licked at the vein in her throat. "Every one of my demons participated in avenging those we lost. They're not all fighters by nature, but not a single one of them was prepared to hang back. They all wanted blood."

"Quite a few lairs targeted ours in the past. They generally don't bother so much nowadays."

"Because Jolene has enough plants in various places to know when a lair might think to attack her own. If she hears such a thing, she launches a pre-emptive strike, and she's never subtle about it."

Raini nodded, smiling. "Nor does she stop at just that one move. She makes them pay in many ways for a very long time—none of those ways can be traced back to her. Other Primes seem to believe it's not worth pissing her off. I think even Knox would hesitate to mess with her. It's not about her level of power, it's about her level of crazy. I adore her." She blushed as her stomach rumbled.

His mouth quirked. "Hungry?"

"Kind of."

He draped his body over hers. "So am I." He fucked her hard and fast to her utter goddamn delight, making her come so hard she'd swear she felt it in her gums.

A short time later, they were striding into the massive hall of the monastery that featured long-ass tables on which many descendants sat, eating breakfast. A hush fell over the large space as they entered, and some stiffened at the sight of her. Others merely went back to their food, paying her no mind.

Maddox guided her to the table around which his sentinels, Gunther, and Celia were gathered. Too hungry to care about looking polite, Raini didn't hesitate to help herself to the various foods that were piled on platters in the center of the table. She let the mindless chatter go on around her, concentrating on enjoying her breakfast. Until Hector spoke to her.

"So, Raini, is it true that some succubae can kill with sex? I've always wanted to know."

"I'm pretty sure that's a myth," she said before sticking a forkful of food into her mouth.

"What about the whole kiss-enslavement thing? Are there really succubae who can make a person subservient to them just by kissing them?"

Raini pursed her lips. "Some say there are. Some say there aren't."

"I wouldn't have thought a succubus could wield psychic hellfire. I was under the impression that their powers are always sex-based."

"Most make that mistake. We're often dismissed as real threats."

He set down his cutlery. "Can you only strike one person at a time with the psychic hellfire?"

She took a swig of her coffee. "The truth?"

"Yeah," he replied.

Voices quietened again, and she knew people would be having a good eavesdrop on this conversation. All right, maybe it would be better to let them know how sharp her claws were. It would be the best way to ensure anyone thought twice about targeting her.

She shrugged one shoulder and spoke matter-of-factly. "I could send out a blast of it that would liquefy and consume every brain in this room aside from my own. Your skulls would cave in, which is a dead giveaway that the cause of death is psychic hellfire, so I'd have to burn every corpse to get rid of the evidence. It really wouldn't take long, though. Then I'd go home, shower, dispose of my clothes. People would eventually find your ashes, but your deaths would never be traced back to me—I'd be very careful not to leave anything of myself behind." She frowned. "Why does that make you smile?"

"It's so . . . vicious," said Hector. "Lacks any mercy. I like that." His eyes narrowed. "You're not quite as sweet as you come across, are you?"

"Sure I am. Someone can be lethal and still be a relatively nice person. People just tend to assume that the most dangerous beings wear that danger on the outside."

"And you're careful not to," mused Carmen.

Raini lifted a brow at her. "Wouldn't you be, in my position?"

Carmen nodded. "Yeah, for sure."

"Does it bother you that we drink blood?" asked Celia.

"It's not like you do it for shits and giggles," said Raini. "You can't help what you are. And Maddox told me you don't kill your 'food,' so no."

They asked her more questions—some about her gift, some about her lair, some about her job, but nothing too invasive. She wasn't sure if they were trying to get to know her or just being nosy.

Once she was finally done eating, she leaned into Maddox and said, "I need to go to the penthouse now."

He looked down at her for a long moment and then sighed. "If you go to work, Carmen goes with you. She'll stay in the studio. If you need to enter another room, she will go with you. If you need to leave the building for any reason, she will go with you."

"I'm sensing you think I'm going to argue. Why would I? She's a badass."

Carmen snorted a laugh. "Thanks, I guess."

"Plus, when Harper, Devon, and Khloë were dealing with shit

of their own, I asked them to be smart and accept whatever level of protection they needed," Raini added. "I'd be a hypocrite to fight you on this."

Once they'd both finished breakfast, he teleported her straight to her bedroom within the penthouse. "Carmen will wait in the reception area for you," he said, cupping her hips. "You should still consider staying with me until all this is over."

Raini sighed. The man was nothing if not persistent. "I told you, I wouldn't feel safe there."

"That will change once you get to know my demons and they get to know you. Which is good, because then you'll have no problem switching to my lair either."

Her head jerked back. "Switching to—" She cut off as his mouth landed on hers and kissed her hard. Then he teleported away without a word. Raini shook her head. "Unreal."

"I thought I heard voices," said Harper, entering the room with Devon and Khloë. "What's unreal?"

Raini smiled. "Hey, I didn't realize you guys were here." Taking in their somber expressions, she folded her arms. "You've come to ask me to take some time off work, haven't you?" Exactly as Maddox had predicted.

Devon gave her a sheepish look. "We just want to make it hard for anyone to get to you."

Raini lifted a hand before the three of them could begin a lecture. "I've been through all this with Maddox. I don't want to have this conversation again."

"He doesn't want you going to Urban Ink either?" asked Harper.

"No," replied Raini. "More, he wants me to move in with him for a while. *And* eventually transfer to his lair, now that he and I are bonded." None of the girls looked surprised by her news.

"After the way he acted here yesterday, I expected him to

shrug past whatever was holding him back," said Harper. "I also figured he'd ask you to join his lair. Anchors typically like being close—it helps ease the protectiveness a little. Knox asked the same of me when we first found each other."

Devon sidled up to Raini. "How would you feel about joining Maddox's lair?"

Raini felt her nose wrinkle. "Not so good. I *love* my lair. Plus, his demons aren't sold on me. Two in particular are *not* Raini-fans."

Khloë frowned. "How can someone not be a Raini-fan? That's like someone not being a Khloë-fan—it makes no sense."

Harper looked at her cousin. "I can think of a few people who aren't Khloë-fans, and you've given them undeniably valid reasons for that."

The imp flicked a dismissive hand. "Those incidences don't count."

"Why not?" asked Harper.

"Because I don't want them to." Khloë turned back to Raini. "On another note, want to tell us what *really* happened yesterday? Maddox is a super good liar—I was very impressed—but I sensed there was more to the story."

Raini let out a long breath. She didn't want to lie to them, but there was no way she'd break her word to Maddox. "I would tell you if I could."

Khloë twisted her mouth and then shrugged. "Fair enough."

Raini felt her brow crease. "You're not going to push?"

"Some things just can't be shared," said Khloë. "At least not without betraying a confidence or putting someone's safety at risk. I wouldn't ask that of you, even if I am nosy as hell. Keenan has things he can't tell me—sentinel stuff. I get it. There are things I haven't told him, like that you can use psychic hellfire. It's not my secret to tell. Have you told Maddox about it?"

"Yes. He's not fazed." Which didn't entirely surprise Raini. He didn't seem the type to be easily daunted. "Maybe if he had the kind of history our lair has, it would be different."

"And you trust that he won't go blabbing about it?" asked Harper.

Raini nodded. "I do."

"So do I," said Khloë. "Hearing the way he shot Jolene's butt down yesterday . . . yeah, I don't worry so much about you now. He'd never put you in danger."

Devon gently elbowed Raini. "Your dad saw it, too. It's the only reason he didn't toss that knife."

Raini snorted. "He's so worked up about Demi's disappearance and the boycotting thing that I thought he might just stab Maddox in lieu of Dwain."

"That dweeb is doing a better job of hiding than I'd thought he would," said Devon, her jaw tight. "Not a single person has reported seeing him."

"My source should get back to me sometime today about our dear Harmony," said Khloë.

Raini put her hands together. "Will you call me as soon as you hear from them?"

"Of course," Khloë assured her. "And you'll agree to take some time off work, right?"

Raini groaned. It would be for the best, she knew that, but . . . "I'll be bored out of my mind."

"Why not hang out at my place with Keenan and Asher, then?" suggested Harper. "You'll be safe there."

"I want to," said Raini. "I really do. I miss my little dude. But what if I bring danger to your doorstep? To *him*?"

Harper made a *pfft* sound. "*No* halo-bearer would get through the security measures, and they probably wouldn't think to look for you there anyway."

"I told Maddox I'd take Carmen with me wherever I went," said Raini.

Devon frowned. "Carmen?"

"His sentinel," Raini elaborated. "Knox is *not* gonna be down with a woman he doesn't know being around his son while he's not there to watch over him. Neither would you, Harper."

The sphinx bit the inside of her cheek. "I could ask Ciaran to teleport Keenan and Asher here so that you'll have some company. Asher loves the penthouse, and he'd be thrilled to see you."

"That would be awesome," said Raini. "You really wouldn't mind?"

"Of course not," Harper told her.

Raini blew her a kiss. "Thank you."

Harper snorted. "You might not be so grateful after a few hours of babysitting a thieving, hyper, pyroporting menace—and I say that with all the love in my heart."

"Your son has Wallis blood in his veins," said Devon. "Did you really expect him to be anything *but* a menace?"

Harper sighed. "No, not really."

CHAPTER SIXTEEN

Later that day after Urban Ink closed, Harper came to join Raini, Keenan, and Asher at the penthouse. Sitting beside the sphinx on the sofa, Raini asked, "Does he do that at home a lot?"

Watching Asher pyroport from spot to spot with Keenan's wallet hanging from his mouth while the poor sentinel tried uselessly to catch him, Harper sighed. "Oh, yeah. Like I said earlier, my boy is a menace. But in the best way, of course."

"Of course."

"He naturally always wins at hide and seek, because he disappears to another spot if we ever get too close."

"Oh, I know. He and Keenan played it earlier. Asher kept giggling to himself, giving away his location. At first, I thought the giggles were popping out of him because he was so excited. I eventually realized he was doing it to lead Keenan on a merry chase. As soon as the sentinel started creeping toward him, he'd head to another hiding spot."

Considering he was so young, he really did have a good

handle on his pyroporting ability. There had been times when Raini wondered if Asher was in fact a sphinx as his parents claimed. He just seemed so . . . other. A kind of "other" she hadn't come across before—her demon agreed.

Raini hadn't ever said as much to Harper, though. If it wasn't something the sphinx could be up front about, Raini would respect that. Besides, wasn't that what she herself had been doing for most of her life?

Just then, Keenan made a dive for the kid but instead fell flat on his face. Asher laughed so hard he dropped to his little butt.

A ding followed the opening of the penthouse's elevator door. Soon after, Knox came striding into the room.

Asher's face lit up. "Daddy!" He rushed to Knox, who instantly lifted him and blew a raspberry on his cheek. The Prime frowned at Keenan. "Why are you lying on the floor? Your job is to guard my son, not laze around."

The sentinel's mouth tightened. "*Your son* is the reason I fell."

"You fell? A powerful demon with your training and experience *fell*?"

Asher tugged on his father's tie, and his eyes bled to black. Knox's own eyes then did the same, and they quite simply just stared at each other.

Harper huffed. "I hate it when their inner demons do that."

Raini felt her brows draw together. "What?"

"Have a private chat. They never include me, and I never quite trust that they're not plotting world domination." Seeing that Knox's entity had subsided, Harper asked, "What were your and Asher's demons talking about?"

"The weather," Knox replied with all the seriousness of a courtroom judge.

Harper turned to Raini, her face hard. "They never tell me what they're chatting about. Ever."

"Probably because it winds you up so much," said Raini.

"Probably," agreed the sphinx.

At that moment, Jolene, Ciaran, Khloë, and Jolene's two sentinels appeared in the center of the room. The female Prime frowned at Keenan. "Why are you lying on the floor? You're supposed to be guarding my grandson, not lazing around like you're on a beach."

Keenan jumped to his feet. "Like I told Knox, *I fell.* It was Asher's fault."

"Now you're going to blame an innocent child for your failings?"

Keenan snorted. "There is *nothing* innocent about him; he lives to drive people insane. Kind of like you." He looked at his mate, and his face softened. "And you, for that matter. What brings you here anyway?"

"Big news," replied Khloë.

Studying her Prime's expression, Raini said, "I can't tell whether this is going to be good news or bad news." Either way, she wanted to hear it.

"That all depends on what Harmony has to say," Jolene told her.

"My source came through," Khloë explained. "It turns out that Harmony's surname isn't Wells, it's Jenkins. And unlike what she claimed, she's a waitress, not a receptionist. She lives in an apartment local to the diner where she works, and she shares said apartment with another waitress."

"We plan to go question Harmony now," Jolene added. "Are you interested in joining us, Raini?"

Blinking, Raini straightened in her seat. "You're inviting me to come along?"

"You've had a bitch of a time lately," said Jolene. "In your shoes, I wouldn't be feeling too good about the fact that so much is out of my hands. I'd want some part in getting answers and seeking justice." *If you were helpless, it would be another matter,* she telepathically added. *But you can take care of yourself just fine, if need be.*

Raini smiled and stood. "Thanks, Jolene. I appreciate it."

"Knox and I could—" Harper cut off as none other than Maddox materialized a few feet away.

Raini's hormones began to fan themselves like crazy. They were so easy for him it was almost laughable.

Jolene gave him a courteous smile. "Ah, Maddox. Always a pleasure. You've caught us at a bad time. I'm afraid there's somewhere Raini and I need to be."

Maddox looked from her to Raini. "And where is that?"

"I would say this is lair business," began Jolene, "but you are her anchor, so I will tell you. We know where Dwain's supposed 'mate' lives. Whether she is there or not is something we don't yet know. If not, we'll head to the diner where she works and see if we can catch her there."

"I'm coming with you," Maddox declared, his tone non-negotiable.

Jolene sighed. "Maddox—"

"You're Raini's Prime; it's your right to settle these matters," he allowed. "You would look weak to others if you weren't seen to deal with your own issues—I appreciate that. But no one would be surprised to hear that you and I handled this together, given that I'm Raini's anchor. Also, Harmony may not be so cooperative. That's where I can step in."

"You can pull the information from her mind, you mean," said Jolene.

He shrugged. "If necessary, yes."

"So can Knox," Harper cut in.

Maddox slid his gaze to the sphinx. "But he isn't Raini's

anchor, he's yours." He looked at Knox. "If this was Harper, you would demand to be part of this."

Knox inclined his head. "I would. Without a doubt."

"I don't care who comes along so long as I'm one of them," said Raini.

Khloë raised a hand. "*I* care. Grams told me I can't come because I'm not part of her lair anymore. I don't see what that has to do with anything."

"Yes, you do." Jolene narrowed her eyes on Maddox. "Would you stay behind if I refused to work with you on this?"

He met her gaze steadily. "You already know the answer to that question."

Jolene threw an exasperated sigh at Raini. "You just *had* to have an anchor who's as stubborn as I am, didn't you?"

Raini felt her mouth curve. "Decades of having you as a Prime has been helpful when it comes to dealing with him."

"Yes, I can imagine you manage to get your way far too often all while looking the epitome of cooperative. You've been doing it with me since you were a child."

"She does pull that shit with me," said Maddox.

Raini lifted her shoulders. "Whatever works, right?"

"Come on, let's talk with Harmony." Jolene looked at Harper, her expression placatory. "If we require backup of any kind, I will contact you."

The sphinx snorted. "No, you won't."

"Well, we'll pretend I will," said Jolene.

Khloë sank onto the sofa and folded her arms, sulky. "We'll wait here so you can spill all when you're done."

"Okay, see you soon," said Raini.

Asher frowned and ran to her. "Waini! I want kisses!"

Smiling, she picked him up and playfully smacked kisses all over his face and neck, loving his little giggle. Raini then set him on the floor and waved. "Bye, little dude." Her surroundings flashed white, and then she, Maddox, Jolene, Ciaran, and Jolene's two sentinels were standing outside an apartment.

"This is Harmony's address," said Ciaran, knocking on the door. When there was no answer, he tried again. Still no answer. "Want me to teleport inside and check out the apartment, Grams?"

Jolene nodded. "Check Harmony's bedroom while you're there—it shouldn't be too hard to ascertain which one is hers. See if it looks like she's been here recently."

The male imp disappeared. Returning soon after, he shook his head and said, "No one's home. Doesn't look as if Harmony's been back."

Jolene licked her front teeth. "Let's head to the diner. If Harmony isn't there, her roommate probably will be."

It turned out that Harmony wasn't there, but her roommate—a woman named Adeline Hanson, apparently—was. It also turned out that said roommate was a succubus, which was probably why her male patrons were almost literally drooling over her. Her smile froze when Raini and her companions entered the diner. Adeline had to have sensed they were demons easily enough. She certainly would have recognized a fellow succubus without a problem.

She headed their way, uneasy. "Um . . . table for six?"

"No, thank you," said Jolene. "We're here to have a short chat with Harmony Wells."

Adeline licked her lips. "She isn't here. I'm actually not sure where she is."

"I see. Well, then we'll talk with her roommate, Adeline Hanson. Which would be you, correct?"

The girl paled, her eyes darting from person to person. "Who are you?"

"My name is Jolene Wallis."

Adeline swallowed hard. "I've heard of you."

"Wonderful. I'm sure you can make time for us."

Adeline gave a slow, reluctant nod. "My break is coming up. I'll meet you in the back alley in two minutes."

"Perfect. Ciaran, be a dear and order me a coffee. Then you can escort Adeline to us when you bring me my drink." In other words, Jolene wanted him to ensure that the waitress didn't scamper.

"Sure thing," he said.

Adeline gave them a stiff smile, knowing she wouldn't be able to escape the encounter.

With the exception of Ciaran, Raini and the others went to the back alley to wait. Maddox stayed close to her side, his arm brushing hers.

Ciaran and Adeline joined them mere minutes later.

Jolene smiled and took the takeout cup from him. "Thank you. Now, Adeline, I've already introduced myself. Rudely, though, I didn't introduce the others. Ciaran here is my grandson. Over there are Orrin and Mitch, two of my sentinels. Raini is one of my lair members, and beside her is her anchor, Maddox Quentin. He also happens to be a Prime. I can see by the expression on your face that you've heard of him, too. Good. That will help. Well, now that we're all acquainted, let us get down to business, shall we?"

Adeline rubbed at her arm. "I . . . Look, I don't know why you're here but—"

"Oh, I think you do. There's no need to be nervous. Our problem is not with you. We'd just like to have a talk with Harmony."

"I can't help you, I'm sorry, I haven't seen her in weeks."

Maddox inwardly sighed. He was content with letting Jolene run the show—in her position, he wouldn't allow another

Prime to take the lead, even if they were the anchor of one of his demons. Plus, the waitress seemed to be one of those people who didn't think well when they were nervous, and he made her far too nervous. But he didn't have it in him to stay silent when she was clearly holding back from them. He'd found that giving someone a little incentive to talk could often work wonders.

Taking a step toward her, he said, "Jolene may be polite, but I'm not. You don't want me to take over here. Trust me on that. Because I won't question you, I'll just pluck the information right out of your head. If you don't want me taking a walk around your mind, answer Jolene's questions, and then we'll all be on our way."

Swallowing, Adeline gave a shaky nod. "I really don't know where Harmony is, I swear."

"She isn't in trouble with us," Raini assured her. "One of our lair members, Dwain, is missing. We believe she might be able to tell us where he is."

"Dwain's missing?" asked Adeline.

Raini raised a brow. "You've met him, I take it?"

"He's a regular at the diner, but I only talked to him once. He was pretty rude to me, he wouldn't let me serve him. Doesn't like succubae much."

Maddox exchanged a brief look with Raini.

"He liked Harmony a lot, though. He always sat in her section and made gooey eyes at her."

Raini flicked a look at the diner. "So they met here?"

"Yes," replied Adeline. "They never saw each other outside the diner. She didn't really like him. Said he was a sleazeball. But he was a good tipper. And he offered her a lot of money to play the part of his mate for a couple of weeks." She lowered her eyes. "But I'm guessing you already know that."

"We figured as much," said Raini. "I don't suppose you know why he wanted a fake mate?"

"Harmony said he wanted to visit his anchor but wasn't too keen on seeing his ex again—something he wouldn't be able to get around, because she's also his anchor's sister, apparently. He wanted his ex to think he was over her, so he wanted Harmony to pretend to be his mate."

Anger spiked through Maddox, but he forced his expression to stay blank. Going by the wary look his anchor slid him, though, she'd felt the emotion vibrating against the edges of her consciousness.

"From some of the things he said," Adeline went on, "Harmony thought he was more interested in spurring his ex into asking him for another chance; that, you know, she'd get all jealous and want him back. Whatever the case, it all sounded pretty pathetic to me. Harmony laughed about it, too. But like I said, he offered her a lot of money, so she said she'd do it. The last I saw of her was the morning she left for Vegas."

"And all he wanted her to do was pretend to be his mate?" asked Raini.

"Yep, that's it. Harmony laid down some ground rules—said there'd be no sex, and that she wasn't going to spend time around his ex to help him piss her off." Adeline shrugged. "There's really nothing more I can tell you."

Jolene sipped her coffee. "Dwain and Harmony left Vegas over a week ago. We can't get in touch with him, and he hasn't returned to his house. And you say Harmony isn't back, so that is concerning."

"Well, I don't know about Dwain, but I know there's no need to be worried about Harmony—she told me she was going to be 'wandering' for a while. She does it every now and then, once she's saved up enough money. She intended to use the cash Dwain gave her to fund another trip."

"I see," said Jolene. "Have you heard from her at all?"

"She called me a couple of weeks ago to check in. I tried calling her cell yesterday, but the number is no longer in use. That's typical of when she goes wandering, though. She does no-phone trips. She always comes back, and she's always full of stories."

"What did you two talk about when she called you a few weeks ago?" asked Raini.

"She asked about how things we're going here, and she told me a little about what was going on in Vegas. She said she'd heard that his ex *wasn't* actually his ex; that he'd wanted there to be more but she'd rejected him. Harmony found it a little creepy that he'd had this fantasy in his head, but she also felt kind of bad for him. You know . . . she could have decided to take Dwain with her on her trip."

"Despite that she doesn't like him?"

"Like I said, she felt bad for him. She said to me, 'Don't we all lie to ourselves sometimes when we're hurting?' She might have invited him to go on a trip to cheer him up. She's like that." Adeline's brows dipped. "She also mentioned that his not-really-an-ex was a succubus. Is that you?"

Raini nodded. "I never meant to hurt him. He got caught in a snare."

"Ah. Yeah, I've had someone fall head-first into one and then blame me afterward. It's shitty."

"Did Harmony say where she planned to go?"

Adeline shook her head. "She didn't have a destination in mind; never does. She's a fly-by-the-seat-of-her-pants girl."

Maddox barely refrained from grinding his teeth. He'd come here hoping to learn Dwain's location from Harmony. It seemed they couldn't even be sure where she was. "Can you think of anywhere she might have gone?"

"No, sorry. She doesn't go to the same place twice because she wants to experience new things."

Jolene downed the last of her coffee. "Does she usually contact you when traveling?"

"Only occasionally," replied Adeline.

Jolene whipped out a business card. "If she contacts you, I'd like you to give me a call. Harmony isn't in trouble with us, I promise you that. It's only Dwain we seek."

Adeline took the card. "I'll get in touch if she calls."

"Thank you, Adeline. You've been very helpful."

The succubus took Jolene's empty cup and retreated inside.

"She was telling the truth," said Maddox.

Jolene nodded. "She was too scared to lie."

"Dwain really could have decided to go traveling with Harmony," said Ciaran.

"Yes, he could have," agreed Maddox. "Not that that would mean he isn't guilty of boycotting Urban Ink. He can do that remotely. All he'd require to send emails and post fake reviews are a computer and WiFi connection."

Raini blew out a breath. "What now?"

"We continue trying to find both him and Demi," replied Jolene.

Raini tilted her head. "Do you think, if Dwain *did* decide to accompany Harmony on her trip, that Demi might have gone with them? If he told her the truth, she could have agreed to go."

Ciaran frowned. "But why would he have told her?"

"Maybe he felt bad lying to her," said Raini, shrugging. "Or maybe she guessed. She could even have overheard something that gave up the ghost."

"It's possible," Jolene cut in. "She'd have initially been angry with him, but she'd have been more relieved than anything else, because it would have meant he wasn't mated. She'd have forgiven him."

Maddox slipped his hands in his pockets. "Put in that light, it isn't a far-fetched idea that Demi might have agreed to skip the cruise and instead enjoy a vacation with Dwain. And, like with him, if she *is* boycotting Urban Ink, being on vacation wouldn't stop her from being able to continue doing so. In fact, going on a trip would have appealed to her because she'd be out of reach from anyone who'd think to question her."

Raini groaned. "We *still* have too many theories and too few answers."

"We need to identify the culprit soon, because they will eventually become unsatisfied with targeting you remotely," Jolene said to Raini. "They'll want to get up close and personal."

Raini folded her arms. "Maybe I could do something that would spur them into making a mistake."

Not liking the sound of that, Maddox narrowed his eyes. "Like what?"

"Nothing too dramatic," said Raini. "Nothing that would put me in physical danger. But just consider that whoever's doing this wants me to be, at the very least, utterly miserable. So let's make it apparent that I'm not. I could throw a party or something."

"Like to celebrate that you've found and bonded with your anchor?" asked Ciaran, his eyes darting to the infinity symbol beneath the hollow of her ear.

Raini pursed her lips. "That would work. We may not *need* to throw the party. But I could be seen to be planning it, looking at venues, include all our suspects on the guest list so they'll receive an electronic invitation or whatever."

"Maybe you and Maddox could also go on a few dates," Jolene suggested. "It's not as if it isn't perfectly obvious you're currently enjoying a fling—I could tell the moment I saw you both in the same space together. Flaunt it in whatever way you can. Make our suspects believe it might be more. Dwain and Demi would both hate it. Dwain because he'd be jealous, and Demi because you'd have what she wants—a relationship with your anchor. It would bait them into acting, if either of them is indeed our boycotter."

Raini's mind touched Maddox's. *It would also bait Marcella. I don't know if it would bother Euan, but he* might *well hate that your lair will attend the party, because it would be a step toward accepting me.*

His cousin probably would hate that, because he'd hoped to use Raini's existence to get into a position of power. "We could try it. It may work."

They returned to the living area of the penthouse, where Harper, Knox, Asher, Khloë, Keenan, and Levi were gathered. Jolene relayed all that Adeline had said, sharing the theories that she, Ciaran, Maddox, and Raini had volunteered. The female Prime then told them of Raini's idea to bait the boycotter.

"That plan *does* have a lot of potential," said Harper.

Raini sat beside her on the sofa. "And organizing a party would give me something to do, since I currently can't work."

"I think Keenan will be happy to keep bringing Asher here to you. He'll appreciate the break."

"He napped today."

"Asher?"

"Keenan."

Khloë chuckled at him. "Dude, you're such a lightweight."

"No, it's that my grandson is tiring," said Jolene proudly. "And that's only natural for a Wallis."

Knox sighed. "He's a Thorne."

Jolene flicked a hand. "You know what I mean."

Khloë joined her hands together as if in prayer. "I can help with the plans for the party, right?"

Raini had seen that request coming a *mile* off. Imps *loved* a good party, and this particular imp was absolutely no exception to that rule. She was, however, a girl who did the craziest shit when "celebrating" things. "As long as you know that anything totally outrageous will be vetoed."

"Define 'outrageous,'" said Khloë.

"Remember your eighteenth birthday party? That kind of thing will be vetoed to death."

Keenan frowned at the imp. "What happened at your eighteenth?"

"I had a bonfire," replied Khloë.

Sliding his arm around her shoulders, the incubus said, "That doesn't sound bad."

"In the middle of a hotel venue room," Khloë added. "We threw chairs on the fire. Roasted marshmallows on it. Some people stripped naked and danced around it. There was also a food fight at one point, but I don't remember who started that. I do remember that quite a few guests smeared frosting on their faces so they looked like battle marks. And there was the part where the Queen tribute band got so shitfaced they tossed their guitars into the bonfire after singing 'We Will Rock You.'"

"But everyone was glad about that, because they were shit," Harper cut in. "Of course, Khloë knew in advance that they were shit. She knew everyone would think they were shit and get annoyed."

"I didn't expect them to chase the band around the room or start throwing hellfire orbs at them," said Khloë.

Harper snorted. "Yes, you did."

After a moment, Khloë nodded. "Yes, I did. Who knew those guys could run so fast?" She lifted a finger. "I *definitely* didn't think Lou would turn up and start singing Lionel Richie songs, or that he'd coax the band into being his backup dancers. They were pretty good at dancing. Just really shit vocalists. All in all, it was a good night. Right?"

Raini slanted her head. "I'd like to say no, but I actually did have a blast."

Keenan turned to fully face his mate. "The owners of the venue didn't try to throw you out?"

"No, because Grams promised we'd have an incantor undo any damage with magick," Khloë replied.

Levi looked at Jolene. "And did you?"

"Oh, yes," replied the Prime. "My word is my bond. Breaking it here, there, and everywhere would only make me look weak."

"Demons generally don't expect imps to keep their promises, though," the reaper pointed out.

"I always aim to defy expectations," said Jolene.

"I know a few professional party planners," Knox told Raini. "I'll have Harper text you their contact details later, just in case you decide you'd like some help."

"Thanks, but Belinda will be a no-no," said Raini, referring to a planner who'd been a pain in the ass when helping Harper with a past celebration.

He gave a knowing nod. "Yes, I thought as much."

They talked for a little while longer, and then Harper announced she needed to leave and give her boy a bath. Asher said his goodbyes to everyone, including Maddox, not looking whatsoever intimidated by the tall stranger. He left Raini until last, pyroporting onto her lap and using his little hands to squish her cheeks.

"Ow," she whined.

He giggled. "Want kisses!"

As she always did, Raini pressed kisses all over his face and neck, making him giggle like crazy.

"I go home now," he said, sliding off her lap.

"Okay, little dude. I'll see you tomorrow."

Scooping up Asher, Keenan nodded. "Tomorrow for sure."

Harper snickered, and then she, Knox, Asher, Khloë, and the sentinels left.

"We'll also head home now." Jolene gave Raini a one-armed hug. "You take care, sweetheart."

After Jolene and Maddox exchanged stiff farewells, Ciaran teleported his grandmother and her sentinels away.

Maddox stalked toward Raini, slow and fluid. "Are you sure you want to try goading your boycotter?"

"I was inspired by you." She arched a brow. "Isn't that what you're doing to the archangel? You want the attacks on your lair to stop, so you taunted the person behind them. I want the boycotting to stop, so I'm baiting the asshole behind it. I don't think there'll be a lot of danger involved in that. They've been too much of a coward to face me so far, so they can't be all that powerful."

"It may not be fear that's stayed their hand, it could be something else. And yes, you'll be able to deal with the situation if it comes to that. Still, I need you to promise me that you'll be careful."

"I promise. But I want the same promise of you, and I want you to mean it. Don't look at me like it's a ridiculous request. I get that you're a badass, but even badasses can be caught off-guard. You can't let a little thing like arrogance blind you."

"It's not arrogance, it's confidence in my abilities."

"I'm not hearing you promising me you'll be careful, I don't know why that is." She rolled her eyes when he hesitated. "Come on, it won't kill you."

"Fine, if it'll make you feel better, I promise to be careful."

"Good. Wasn't so hard, was it?" Raini put a hand to her stomach. "I'm hungry."

"You haven't eaten dinner yet?"

"Nope."

He took her hand and pulled her to her feet. "Then how about we eat out?"

"Go on a fake date like Jolene suggested, you mean?"

"No," he said, his brow briefly creasing. "I want to take my anchor, a person whose company I enjoy, to dinner."

"Okay, then. Do you have anywhere in particular in mind?"

"I know a place you might like."

"Where?"

"You'll see." He pulled her flush against him, aligning her body to his, and slid a hand down her back to palm her ass. "Before we go anywhere, I want a kiss."

"A kiss?" She looped her arms around his neck. "Hmm, I can make that happen."

CHAPTER SEVENTEEN

"Personally, Raini, I think it was pretty brave of you to pick a casino for the party venue," said Harper, speaking via video call. She, Devon and Khloë were having lunch at Urban Ink; they'd called Raini to check how the party preparations were going. "I mean," Harper went on, "you realize your dad, uncles, and most of my relatives will spend the evening cheating at cards and fiddling the machines?"

"Yup," replied Raini, prepping the coffee machine. "But it's worth noting that there probably won't be a reason to go ahead with the party, so I'm not stressing over it."

Khloë frowned. "Why wouldn't we go ahead with it?"

"Because this is about provoking my cowardly foe," Raini reminded her. "If it works, they might react *way* before the party date."

"You could still go through with it, though," the imp insisted. "Finding your anchor *is* something to celebrate. Why wouldn't you want to? Why wouldn't you want to share your joy—"

"Enough with the fake pout," said Raini, rolling her eyes.

"I just really want there to be a party. So much shit has gone on lately, we deserve a celebration of some kind. Tell me I'm wrong."

"Our friendly neighborhood boycotter could actually show up and cause a stink." Devon sipped some of her soda. "I would've thought that they'd have made another shitty move by now."

Raini grabbed a mug out of the cupboard. "Yeah, I don't think my plot to piss them off is working." She hadn't made it a secret that she was planning a party to celebrate finding her anchor. She'd booked a venue, catering service, music band, and all that jazz. She'd also sent out lots of electronic invitations, including to Dwain, Demi, Marcella, and Euan.

Raini had also gone on plenty of fake dates in the Underground with Maddox. He'd taken her to dinner, to a bar for drinks, to the hellhound racing stadium, to her favorite ice-cream parlor. They hadn't *felt* like fake dates at all. It hadn't felt like they were putting on a show. It was more like they were an anchored pair enjoying each other's company and learning more about each other, solidifying their bond.

She'd learned that Maddox had no problems with PDA. He touched her often in public, and that never felt fake either. The touches—whether a feather of his fingers across the back of her hand, a light massage on her nape, a hand splayed on the curve of her spine so that the heel of his palm rested on her butt—held a proprietary edge. His touches always had, but it seemed . . . more now. Or maybe that was just her. Maybe she was getting too caught up in the fantasy that he might want more than a brief bed-buddy arrangement. Because, to her utter annoyance, she did.

Coming to feel something for him beyond their anchor connection hadn't been part of her plan at all. At first, she'd wondered if it was merely the novelty of being with someone who wasn't caught up in the succubae package. But no. Maddox wasn't a "nice guy," wasn't sweet and funny and open. He didn't shower her with pretty words and compliments. She couldn't even really describe him as "good." He was a ruthless, unforgiving, calculated man who gave no fucks about anyone outside of his circle. But Raini didn't need "nice." She wasn't looking for Prince Charming—he sounded kind of boring, really. And having grown up around imps, who weren't exactly big on ethics, she wasn't sure she'd know what to do with a perfect guy.

Other traits were important to Raini. She wanted someone she could trust to always be loyal to her; someone she wouldn't have to hide parts of herself from; someone she could rely on to always be there for her and with whom she'd always be safe. Raini instinctively knew that Maddox could be that person. The problem was . . . she didn't know if he'd be that person *only* because she was his anchor. She didn't know if she mattered to him beyond that.

Sometimes, he looked at her in a way that made her think she meant more. But Raini wasn't sure if she was merely seeing what she wanted to see; wasn't sure if it had all been part of their "we're a couple" act. She so far hadn't found the guts to ask.

Just then, Ciaran teleported into the kitchen, his expression *uber* serious.

Wariness slithered up Raini's spine, and her demon went hyper alert. "Sorry, girls, I've got to go. I'll talk to you all again later." She ended the video call before they could question her and then turned to the male imp. "Something's wrong, isn't it?"

He sighed. "You could say we have a big problem."

"What?"

"You've been outed."

Her stomach rolled. "Outed how?" she asked, but she already knew the answer.

"It has circulated around the lair that you can wield psychic hellfire."

She closed her eyes, dread filling her from head to toe. "How?" Her eyes snapped open. "How the hell could this have happened?"

"Dwain's mother received a text message from him earlier saying he wanted to come back to Vegas but couldn't while everyone was hunting him like a dog. He said he needed to wait until the real culprit was found. He added, 'Don't go feeling *too* sorry for Raini. I'll bet she never told you that she can wield psychic hellfire.'"

Her demon hissed out a breath. "Mother*fucker*."

"Yeah. She mentioned the text to her mate, who mentioned it to someone else—none of whom really believed it could be true. But *then* some others received similar text messages. Demi's best friend, Risa. A mate of one of your exes. A guy you had a one-nighter with who wasn't happy when you didn't want more."

Raini folded her arms. "So, basically, these messages were sent to people who'd have no problem spreading shit about me."

He nodded. "Dwain's mom is arguing that the sender wasn't truly him because the messages were sent via a spoofing site—he'd have no need to use one. She's right that anyone could have entered Dwain's cell phone number into the 'sender' box on the website."

Raini let her head flop forward. *Fuck, fuck, fuck, fuck.*

"I think you succeeded in baiting whoever has beef with you. But I think going after Urban Ink wasn't enough for them. Like you said, they wanted you to be unhappy. Well . . . "

Lifting her head, she bit her lip. "What now?"

"Jolene's going to hold a meeting for the entire lair outside our community center. It starts in twenty minutes. You don't *need* to be there but—"

"I'll go. If I hide, it makes me look like I think I have a need to feel guilty. I've done nothing wrong. Okay, yes, I lied to them by omission. But surely they'll get *why*."

"I think they'll get why. I'm just not so sure they'll care. Doyle left so many scars on the lair."

"I know." She raked a hand through her hair. "I guess it's safe to say that my plot totally backfired."

"They were escalating little by little all along, so they probably would have done this eventually even if you hadn't provoked them."

"Yeah, I guess."

"Man, Maddox is gonna be pissed. You going to tell him yet?"

"Not until after the meeting. He's pretty protective. He'd insist on being there, and Jolene wouldn't allow that, so . . ."

"All right. Let's get to the community center. Grams is already there." Ciaran teleported them to the staff room, where Jolene, Beck, and Martina waited—all looking various degrees of furious. They softened on seeing Raini.

Martina pulled her into a hug. "I get why you didn't tell me or Beck about your ability, but we wouldn't have held it against you, honey."

"No, we wouldn't have," added Beck, giving Raini a gentle smile.

"Thanks," said Raini. "Let's hope that most of the lair feels the same as you two do."

Jolene crossed to her. "I'd be lying if I told you that some haven't gotten themselves all worked up. Try not to take anything they say to heart. They're shocked more than anything else."

The door opened. Evangeline and Lachlan entered, looking ready to burn shit down. In *his* case, that was probably literal.

They both hugged Raini and assured her that all would work out fine. She wished she could believe them.

"You three are welcome to stand with me while I speak to the lair," Jolene said to them. "But Raini, it would be best if you leave the talking to us. Not because you don't deserve to speak for yourself, but because I won't let *anyone* use this as an opportunity to argue with you and cause a scene. You have no reason to explain or justify anything. You've done nothing wrong. I won't let you be treated as if you're on trial."

Raini nodded, because she'd never intended to explain herself anyway. As Jolene said, she had no need to. "All right."

Soon enough, it was time for the meeting to begin. Jolene stood at the northern end of the huge outdoor basketball court, flanked by two of her sentinels. Raini and her parents stood at Orrin's side while Beck and Ciaran stood near Mitch.

Most of their lair were gathered there. Many appeared shocked, others appeared outraged, and a whole lot seemed afraid. Still, some offered Raini small, supportive smiles. There were actually a few who looked bored . . . or maybe stoned—she couldn't quite tell from this distance.

Once the crowd quieted, Jolene began, "As I'm sure you're all aware, a number of our lair received text messages via a spoofing site. Those messages all claimed that Raini Campbell could wield psychic hellfire. I'm sure you all have several questions—one being, is it true? Yes, it is true. Raini *can* do so."

People instantly began talking, tossing questions at the Prime.

"Quiet," Jolene ordered, her voice a whip; everyone hushed. "Raini can wield it, just as any of us could pick up a knife and stab someone. Just as any of us could run someone over with a car or shoot someone in the head. It doesn't mean we *will* do those things. Would you expect to be treated with suspicion merely because of something you have the ability to do?"

"It's not the same," one demon claimed, earning themselves a snarl from Raini's entity.

Jolene gave the man a haughty look. "How so?"

"Psychic hellfire is lethal."

"So are the abilities of many people within this lair," Jolene pointed out.

"But she could destroy our anchor bonds!" one woman yelled, who also happened to be the mate of Raini's ex.

"Very true," allowed Jolene. "But has she ever done so? Is there a single person here who can claim that Raini has destroyed their anchor bond or otherwise harmed them in any way with psychic hellfire?"

Some glanced at each other, shuffled from foot to foot, or averted their gazes.

"You lied to us!" Demi's friend, Risa, shouted at Jolene. "All of us."

The imp beside her frowned. "You have to see *why* she said nothing, Risa. Look around you. Look at how people have reacted."

"It still isn't right," Risa stated. "You could've told us about her ability, Jolene; you didn't."

"Raini was five years old when it first surfaced," said Jolene. "*Five*. An innocent child who'd done no more than send out the heat of it toward the TV in her living room. Her parents felt the power of it, knew what it was, and naturally panicked. What would you have done if you had learned she'd had the ability back then, Risa? You would have wanted her gone, yes?"

"For the right reasons," said Risa.

Oh, because there was totally a *right reason* to banish a child who'd done nothing to anyone. Raini could only shake her head.

"I see." Jolene lifted her chin. "*You* have a daughter, Risa. She's only three years old. She could just as easily develop that ability one day. What would you do if that happened? Tell the entire lair? Live as strays? Or would you ask for the chance to help her suppress the ability? As I said, simply because someone *can* do something doesn't mean they will."

Risa's mouth bopped open and closed for a moment. Finally, she looked at the floor. Raini's demon made a haughty sound.

Jolene swept her gaze over the crowd. "I'll ask the same of anyone here who has a child. Would you have done any differently than what Evangeline and Lachlan did? If any of you can honestly tell me you would've done, raise your hand now."

Not a single soul did.

Richie, Jolene's son, sighed. "Nobody here would have acted differently, and they know it. Just as the divas know they're being *entirely* too damn dramatic right now."

"It's not dramatic to be upset that this was kept from us," a friend of Evangeline insisted, which was no doubt why Raini sensed more than saw her mother stiffen. "Jolene should have told us—simple."

"Why is that, Mandy?" asked Jolene.

"Because we would have known to be more careful around Raini," Mandy replied.

"Stopped your children from playing with her, you mean," Richie's mate, Meredith, guessed. "Seriously, Mandy, do you truly believe that Jolene would have allowed Raini to mingle with other children if she wasn't certain—for Raini's sake and theirs—that she'd be no danger to them?"

Mandy's shoulders lowered. She turned back to Jolene. "She really suppressed the ability?"

"Yes," Jolene confirmed. "But when she became an adult, I helped her instead learn to control it as well as suppress it, just as I've done for every other person in this lair who had to suppress a deadly ability when a child. It is common practice."

"Everyone here knows that, so I don't know why some of them are getting so high and mighty about this," claimed Penelope, Khloë and Ciaran's mother. "It isn't right. Raini hasn't done a damn thing wrong."

"*Yet*," sniped Risa. "I still say we should have been told about this."

Evangeline *hmph*ed. "None of you really care that you didn't know of it beforehand. For all of you, this is about Doyle, not Raini. But that's the point. She *isn't* Doyle."

"But she *could* be if she lost her anchor," an elderly woman piped up. "They're bonded now. If that bond broke—"

"If, if, if." Jolene flicked her hand. "There are plenty of people here who would be extremely dangerous if they ever turned rogue—you know who you are. And the only way I will eject Raini from this lair is if every one of you other dangerous demons are prepared to leave as well." Jolene folded her arms and raised an expectant brow, but nobody announced an intention to leave.

"Have any of you stopped to think about *why* those messages were sent?" asked Lachlan. "Seriously, think of the demons who received those texts. They're all people who don't have a lot of time or affection for my Raini—which makes them idiots, on a side note—and who'd be happy to spread the word. The sender knew that. This was done to turn her own lair against her. I wouldn't have thought it'd have worked. I thought you were all far too sharp than to let some bastard use you as pawns in a game." Lachlan shrugged. "I guess I was wrong. Which is rare."

A demon in the front bristled. "We're not letting ourselves be used as pawns."

"Aren't you?" asked Lachlan. "I beg to fucking differ, because you're doing exactly what they want you to do. You're letting yourselves be moved around like pieces on a chessboard in their game to fuck with Raini's life."

"Whoever sent the texts just thought we were entitled to know the truth," claimed Dwain's cousin.

Martina let out a soft snort. "Seriously, Gabby? You're talking stupid, and you know it. If Dwain did send those messages, he did it through a spoofing site. Why? Why not use his own cell phone? Why, if he's really so very innocent, is he nowhere to be found? And why, pray tell, did he lie to the entire lair that he was *mated*? Face it, you were played. Perhaps by Dwain, perhaps by someone else. If none of you think the timing is a *little* too coincidental, if none of you think it isn't a little suspicious that the receivers of the texts are people who would spread the word, then I don't fucking get it."

"Me neither," said Penelope.

Several others nodded or voiced their agreement, most of whom were imps. Maybe it was because they considered Raini half imp that they were more accepting than others, or maybe it was because—as a breed that was used to others holding their very nature against them—they knew how it felt to have others act all disapproving toward them.

On the other hand, it could simply be that they didn't give much of a shit how powerful she was. It wouldn't surprise her if the most dominant thought in their head was that they needed to get back to whatever illegal activity they'd been up to before being called here.

Jolene spoke then: "If Raini had harmed any of you, it would be different. But she hasn't. Not even when one of you pissed her off—and yes, a number of you did that over the years. Men who didn't like that she turned them down. Women who were jealous that the men they wanted were more interested in Raini. People who resented that they or their partners couldn't help but be affected by her allure. Raini never once used psychic hellfire against any of you. So why would you use this against *her*? Are you really going to make her pay for what Doyle did?"

"We don't want to make her *pay*," an older male said. "We just worry about what could happen. I don't think she'd use the ability against us while in her right mind. I truly don't. I think Raini's a very nice young woman, and I have nothing whatsoever against her. But if she turned rogue . . ." He let the sentence trail off and shrugged.

"Let's look at this from a logical point of view," said Bram. "Raini will never turn rogue so long as she has an anchor. Doyle chose to go rogue after his own anchor died, but I don't foresee Raini ever making such a choice. Besides, Maddox Quentin is not an easy demon to kill. He's deadlier than most people here."

It was true. And it made her demon feel rather smug and proud.

"He has halo-bearers on his ass right now, though," said Dwain's father.

"And he has killed each and every one who came at him," Lachlan pointed out. "I consider that worth noting, because those rat bastards don't make easy opponents."

Again, there was a short silence.

One of Raini's neighbors exhaled heavily. "Okay, people have had their chance to moan and whine and ask questions. Can we not just all agree it ain't a big deal and go? Because I don't know about the rest of you, but I'm feeling pretty nervous that all the kids are together in the indoor gym with only the juveniles to watch over them. Last time that happened, one of the young ones started chasing the others with a lawnmower—and I still don't know where they got that lawnmower."

Scratching the back of his head, Bram nodded. "It's a good lawnmower. I've used it a time or two."

"Which really isn't relevant," Risa snapped.

"Neither is the shit that's been tumbling out of that hole in your face," said Bram, to which a lot of people snickered.

"If any of you have come here to demand that Raini be ostracized, it was a waste of your time," said Jolene. "The only way I would consider such a thing 'fair' is if every other person here with lethal abilities was prepared to leave. Of course, those who remained would need to vow that if any of their children developed a deadly gift they would declare it to the entire lair. Are you all prepared to do those things? Raise your hand if so."

A few meekly did, but when they realized that not many others had, they lowered their hands.

Jolene's mouth thinned. "I thought so. Go home and have a good, long think about just how easily you've been manipulated into coming after a woman who's done nothing at all to you. I personally wouldn't much like what it said about me."

Once the crowd had left, Ciaran heaved a sigh. "Man, that was rough."

Swallowing, Raini nodded, though "rough" was an understatement. "I suppose it could have gone worse. Some *did* speak up for me."

"Even though many fear you now, there are only a few who're unhappy with you being here," said Jolene. "But that doesn't make it any easier for you, I know."

No, it didn't make it easier. These were her lair members, for Christ's sake. Raini wouldn't have shit on them this way—not even those she didn't like all that much. "You know, it occurred to me that whoever did this knew *exactly* who in the lair would be an enemy of mine. Only an insider could truly know all that."

Jolene sighed. "Yes, out of our suspects, only Dwain and Demi would possess that knowledge. And since Dwain wasn't trusted with the knowledge of your ability—"

Evangeline stiffened. "It wasn't Demi."

Jolene turned to her, all compassion. "We have to consider that she may be behind this."

Evangeline wildly shook her head. "She could have told Dwain while drunk or something. Or maybe she trusted him with the information. He *is* her anchor."

"It's possible," Jolene conceded. "But bear in mind that the one person most likely to be angry about Raini finding and bonding with her anchor is Demi. She'd be both furious and bitter enough to do this, because Raini has what Demi herself wants."

Lachlan rubbed at his face. "I can't deny that, but the world also thinks that Raini and Maddox are a couple. Dwain would hate that, wouldn't he? He doesn't want her to be happy."

Evangeline slashed a hand through the air. "I won't believe that Demi has any part in this."

Jolene touched her arm. "I understand that. I do. I just can't afford to think as you do. I have to be objective. You know that."

Evangeline nodded. "I do. And I'm grateful, for Raini's sake, that you are. But . . ." She turned to Raini, her eyes wet and full of apology.

"It's okay, Mom. Really. I get it." Raini honestly did, because she knew that her mother would have so staunchly defended *her* in such a situation until given proof of Raini's guilt. Plus . . . "Like you, I'm still holding out hope that it isn't her." Sliding her gaze to Jolene, Raini asked, "Do you think anyone will decide to leave because you've refused to banish me?"

"It may happen," replied Jolene. "But it would be more likely that some would threaten to leave, thinking it will make me change my mind. It won't. There is no way I will punish you or anyone else for something you haven't done."

God, the woman was awesome. A lot of Primes might have acted differently just to keep the peace among their lair, but not

Jolene. She stood for what she believed in. Stood for every one of her demons.

Raini bit her lip. "Things won't be the same anymore, will they? There are some who'll never trust me ever again now that they know what I can do."

Lachlan squeezed her shoulder. "Some might be assholes toward you, but not all. What really pisses me off is that if they were in a life-or-death situation and the only way out was for you to use that ability to save them, they'd expect you to do it. Not one person would tell you not to."

Beck nodded. "I think a big reason why they reacted this way was shock. Once the knowledge has sunk in and they've been forced to look at the situation from every angle, I doubt it'll seem so terrible to them."

Raini wasn't so sure, but it was a nice thought.

Blindsided by the whole thing, Raini was in something of a daze as Ciaran teleported her back to the penthouse. At his recommendation, she telepathed Harper to report what happened before one of the sphinx's relatives beat Raini to it.

Naturally, Harper, Devon and Khloë soon turned up at the penthouse—all furious with not only the boycotter but the people in the lair who, in Harper's words, needed "to get off their high fucking horses *now*." The sphinx had also proposed that Raini simply join her lair, which Devon and Khloë thought was the best idea ever. And right then, when Raini felt so let down, it didn't seem such a bad idea to switch lairs—which Maddox would love, since he pressured her to join his on a daily basis. And the fact that the majority of his lair were now pretty nice to her was eating at her "I'm not welcome there" argument.

Not wanting Raini to be alone, Harper tried convincing her to stay at her house that night, but Raini wasn't in the mood for company. Respecting that, the girls eventually left, but not before making Raini promise to call if she changed her mind.

She traipsed into the bathroom and over to the freestanding tub, intending to have a long soak in a hot bath, but then she just stood there. Was this really happening? Had some of her lair really turned on her because of an ability she hadn't *asked* to have?

Groaning, she turned and sat on the edge of the tub. She officially hated whoever had sent those texts. Officially. Hated them.

Until she'd stood outside the center while people scowled at her and implied she had no right being part of the lair, Raini had always felt safe and at ease among the members. They were like one big family—a family that, yeah, didn't always get along and had some assholes scattered around it, but still a family.

Now, she felt like an outsider. And she had no idea if things would get better or worse. She only knew she'd never forget this feeling; never be able to look at the people who'd turned on her today without remembering the stuff they'd said. Things really wouldn't ever be the same again.

She almost jumped as Maddox abruptly appeared in front of her. "Jesus, you need to start giving me telepathic warnings before you show up."

Maddox's gaze flitted over her face. "What is it?"

She sighed and gave him a brittle smile. "You'll be pleased to hear that the boycotter isn't one of your demons."

He very slowly tipped his head to the side. "And why would you believe it isn't one of mine?"

"Because they don't know every person in my lair who'd dislike me enough to be willing to spread a destructive rumor about me."

"What sort of rumor?"

"That I can wield psychic hellfire. Yep, either Dwain or

someone posing as him texted the information through a spoofing site to several people who aren't fans of mine. He *shouldn't* know I have that ability, but my mom's right that Demi could have told him. She might have even done it hoping he *would* leak the info, since I'm not so sure it's something she could have brought herself to personally do."

"But she wouldn't have felt so bad about it if Dwain told people," Maddox mused. "She could have denied culpability in her own mind and to others."

"Exactly."

"How did the lair take it?"

"Most are in shock." Raini swallowed and rubbed her thighs. "Jolene called a meeting. I was there and—"

"You left the building?" His eyes blazed. "You left without telling Carmen?"

Raini winced. "I shouldn't have, I know. But she would have told you we were heading out, and you would have wanted to be present. Jolene would have fought you on it, and you would have refused to stay away. Then you two would have been at each other's throats, and there was enough shit going on without—"

"Breathe, Raini." He curled his hand around the side of her neck, the anger in his eyes dimming.

"But now you'll lecture me, and I don't think I can take it without gouging out your eyes—my mood is just *foul*."

"Yes, I can see you won't manage your usual cooperative act tonight. I won't lie, I'm pissed you didn't tell me what was happening or that you were leaving the penthouse."

"Carmen will be mad about the latter, too."

"Yes, she will. But she'll be more pissed at me, just as I am."

"You are?"

"Yes, because if you felt you could trust that I wouldn't go head-to-head with Jolene, you wouldn't have been so torn earlier.

I never want you to feel you have to keep things from me. It's my fault that you do."

Raini stared at him, her lips parted. "Okay, I totally didn't expect you to be so . . . reasonable."

"It's hard to be mad at you when you look so vulnerable. The meeting went badly, I take it."

"It did. There are people who're massively pissed that they weren't told about my ability and who even want me gone, but they're in the minority. Still, it sucks balls."

Hating how alone and desolate she looked, Maddox took her hands, tugged her to her feet, and pulled her close. "Tell me the rest," he coaxed, sweeping a hand down her back. Absentmindedly picking at his shirt, she told him all that was said at the meeting. With every word she spoke, his anger built and built. "Sounds to me as if the people who don't much like you have tried using this as an excuse to get rid of you or, failing that, to at least piss you off," he said.

"Maybe. God, it was horrible. I think some will probably leave the lair. They may even try to stir others into leaving with them."

"Good. You don't need people like that around you. It infuriates me that they so easily turned on you. I'm sorry that happened. It may be that everything will settle once they've had time to get used to it. It'll be old news soon."

"But things won't ever be the same. There'll be people who won't trust me, or who won't trust my control when I'm drunk so will insist I don't drink at parties, or who might even avoid me altogether or keep their kids away from me." Raini let her forehead rest on his chest. "Your demons—people who don't even know me, who didn't grow up with me—accepted my ability better and more easily than some of my own lair members did."

He palmed her nape. "I don't think it would have worked

out that way if our history had included a Doyle. They haven't seen how destructive your ability can be, or lost people to a rogue demon with said ability. We don't have the scars that your lair has."

"I know. And I know it isn't rational of me to think that everyone from my lair might have taken the news a lot better—"

"It's not irrational that you'd hoped that they would have reacted differently." It was merely an emotional hope. He squeezed her nape. "Come home with me."

She raised her head. "I was going to have a hot bath and relax and watch TV."

"If you stay here, your relatives will appear to check on you and keep you company because they love and worry about you. But I don't think you could deal with the fuss right now."

"You're right, I couldn't. I still feel too overwhelmed by everything."

"Then come with me. I have a bathtub and a TV, remember. You can stick to the plans you had. You'll just follow through with them somewhere else."

She swallowed. "I'd be really shit company. I feel so . . . lost at the moment."

She looked it, and it made both him and his demon anxious to fix everything for her. Maddox let his fingers drift through her hair. "You're not lost, baby. I have you." He gave her nape another gentle squeeze. "And I'm not looking for company or conversation. I just don't want you to be alone. So I'm not taking no for an answer. You're coming with me."

She let out a weak chuckle. "You're a bossy bitch at times."

He felt his mouth curve. "It doesn't bother you as much as you thought it would."

"You know, weirdly enough, it doesn't."

CHAPTER EIGHTEEN

As they stood at the hostess station of the Underground restaurant a week later, Raini found herself torn. Should she be the bigger person and ignore how the hostess ogled Maddox, or should she do as her demon wanted and quite simply set the woman's shoes on fire?

It wasn't like the burns and blisters would take more than an hour or so to heal. There'd be no permanent scarring or anything. It would be a not-so-friendly warning, that's all. A life lesson, even. Life lessons were important. It would stop the hostess from making the same mistake with another couple, and that could only be a positive thing, couldn't it? Raini would be doing her a favor, really.

Maddox slid his arm around Raini's waist and settled it on her hip. "You all right?"

"Just a little tired." Of people who'd bat their eyelids at a man right in front of his date.

Okay, so Raini wasn't really his date for the evening. They

were only on an anchor outing. But the hostess didn't know that, did she?

Maddox often took Raini places these days. Harper had switched from being annoyed by how he tried monopolizing Raini's time to approving of it. It was as if he'd passed some sort of test in the sphinx's estimation. Harper probably just liked that he wasn't doing a half-assed job at this anchor business.

Whenever he and Raini spent time together, they'd talk, share, learn more about each other. And, of course, he'd repeatedly hint at her joining his lair. If she couldn't even handle watching a hostess ogle him, she'd hardly handle seeing him jump from one relationship to another. It would be easier if they were part of separate lairs. She'd know of his flings and relationships, but it wouldn't be in her face all the time.

"I like a good dessert as much as the next person," said Carmen. "But a dessert restaurant? No. No, this ain't my thing."

Hector snickered. "What you mean is . . . you can't bring yourself to eat here because you know you'd stuff your face with all different kinds of cake."

"Yes, that is what I mean," Carmen admitted with no shame.

"Well, I'm gonna order something," he told her.

Carmen frowned. "We're here on *guard duty*, Hector."

"Doesn't mean we can't eat while we're here."

Raini smiled. The Underground was jampacked with cafes, diners, and restaurants. But this was a favorite of hers. And yes, it had everything to do with the fact that it served purely desserts.

Carmen leaned into Raini. "Who the fuck is that bitch, and what is her problem with you?"

Raini tracked the sentinel's gaze and sighed at the woman sitting at a table scowling. That scowl vanished in an instant when Maddox's cold gaze landed on her.

"That's Risa," said Raini. "She's my sister's friend. She's also one of the people who aren't so comfortable with the recent news that circulated around my lair," she added vaguely, not wanting to mention the psychic hellfire out loud.

Maddox didn't move his glare from Risa. "Is she now?"

"I don't get why they reacted that badly," said Hector. "Lots of abilities can be positively lethal."

"But nothing other than you-know-what can destroy a you-know-what-else without killing a person," Raini quietly pointed out. "It's natural that some would have reservations. Be honest, you're not terribly comfortable with it either."

"But I trust that you wouldn't betray Maddox by harming one of his demons," said Hector, to which his mate nodded.

Raini blinked. "Oh. Well. Thank you. You don't know me, so I wouldn't have expected that."

"We don't know you well," began Hector, "but we know that you made a deal with Maddox that couldn't have been easy for you to make. You never complained. Never went back on it. You kept your word because it means something to you. I know it couldn't have been an easy ride, because I know Maddox. He's a control freak."

"You're kidding," Raini said dryly.

Her anchor only smiled.

"Your tables are ready," the hostess announced. She guided Maddox and Raini to a cushioned booth, being sure to wiggle that ass of hers as she walked. Ugh. Flashing him a sultry grin, she said, "Here we are." Whatever she saw on Raini's face made her dial down that smile. Wise girl. She placed two menus on the table. "Your waitress will be with you shortly." With that, she guided Hector and Carmen to a nearby booth, where they could keep watch on Maddox and Raini yet also give them privacy.

Scanning the menu, Raini bit her lip. "There are too many choices. Which is not a complaint."

"Why not get the combo platter," Maddox suggested. "It has miniature desserts—Red Velvet cupcake, Pavlova, Chocolate Pudding, Mango Meringue, and Angel Food Cake."

"That does sound like a plan I can get behind." Raini snapped the menu closed. "What are you having?"

"These."

She looked at the picture of the three small glasses of beautifully presented chocolate mousses. "Good choice."

"Drink?"

"Hmm, vanilla milkshake." Raini glanced around, admiring the décor. Framed paintings of cakes, puddings, mousses, custards, and frozen desserts adorned the bright walls. So many delicious smells laced the air—dark chocolate, cinnamon, vanilla, caramel.

It was relatively busy. Waiters and waitresses weaved around the tables, serving food or collecting dirty dishware. Talking and laughter came from the couples, groups, and families that were scattered around the large space.

Catching sight of Hector scanning a menu while Carmen shook her head in disgust, Raini smiled. "I like your sentinels more than I thought I would," she told Maddox.

"And they like you," he said. "But then, you make it impossible for people to dislike you." He paused as their waitress appeared. After she'd taken their orders and left, he went on, "I'm quite sure that most of my demons were determined to dislike you so that they wouldn't have felt guilty about not being welcoming toward you. But they didn't manage it. You won them over."

"Marcella and Euan still aren't my fans, but they've stopped giving me grief." *Probably because they wouldn't hesitate to ask me to free them from a haze, and they don't want me to not feel inclined to help them*, she added telepathically.

Most likely, he agreed. "The others have accepted you. They often ask when you're going to transfer to our lair."

Raini almost rolled her eyes. "We're back to this again, huh?"

"It would seem so." He drummed his fingers on the table. "I think you've learned by now that I like to get my way."

"It's pretty easy to sense, yeah."

"So then you know I won't let this go. You'll be safer in my lair."

"Yeah, you keep saying that. But I'm not *un*safe in my current lair."

His brow hiked up. "I didn't say you were unsafe there. I said you'd be safer in mine."

"I don't see how. What I do see is that you'd feel better if I was under your rule."

"I would, yes. Because I don't believe anyone will protect you more vehemently than I would. Jolene loves you—I see that. She even seems to view you as family in a sense. But you don't come first to her the way you do me. You're my priority. Your safety and well-being matters to me on a level it can't matter to Jolene because you're not *her* anchor, you're mine. So of course I'd feel better if you were part of my lair."

He paused again as the waitress brought over their drinks and then left, clearly rushed off her feet. "I understand that you'd prefer to be part of the same lair as your family," he continued. "Especially since, with the exception of your missing sister, you're close to them. I get that you'd feel like you were leaving them behind. But they'd understand, Raini. I think they'd even prefer for you to be living among demons who accept your gift."

Raini drank some of her milkshake through her straw, silently wishing that the reason he felt so strongly about all this was that he cared about her as more than his anchor. She also silently berated herself for being so dumb as to think it could happen. Maddox wasn't a man who bonded with people.

He took responsibility for her, he enjoyed having her in his bed, but that was as far as it would ever go. If she hadn't been his psi-mate, he'd have kicked her to the curb by now and found another bed-partner. The thought made her stomach churn and her demon snarl. The entity had grown to be highly possessive of him—and not just on an anchor-level.

Raini set down her glass. "So you wouldn't only want me to switch to your lair, you'd want me to give up my home and live at the monastery?"

He gave a small shrug. "It would make sense for you to live there. Most demons live among their lair members."

"Khloë and Keenan don't."

"Probably because the sentinel knows she'd be better off having her family close so that she's not alone when he's on duty."

Probably. Khloë tended to get into all kinds of shit when lonely or bored.

Just then, "Happy Birthday" began to play and a bunch of people gathered near a corner table to clap and sing along for the birthday boy/girl.

Raini cringed. "I would be mortified if that happened to me." She smiled as the waitress returned and set their desserts in front of them. "Wow." Raini pulled out her phone and snapped a picture of the combo platter, fully intending to send it to her girls.

"Make sure you eat it all," said Maddox, spooning some mousse. "You'll need your energy for what I'm planning to do to you once we're alone."

Oh, that made her tingle in all the best places. Which wasn't fair, because he couldn't do anything about the tingling right here. "That was cruel." Scooping up some of her chocolate pudding, she sensually sucked it from the spoon and licked the utensil clean.

A muscle in his cheek jumped. "That was equally cruel."

"I know."

Why that devious smile of hers made his cock hard, Maddox didn't know. His body reacted to her far too easily. Almost as if it instinctively reached for what belonged to it.

They talked about general things as they ate. He wanted to push her on joining his lair, but he knew better. For one thing, he'd learned where his anchor's tolerance level sat, and he was close to hitting it. For another, he didn't want her to agree to his request purely because she felt pressured. He wanted her to *want* to be part of his lair. So he kept the conversation light and easy.

His demon wasn't so content to let the subject lie—it didn't see why she couldn't simply make the transfer. The entity didn't view anyone else as having any real importance to her. But it didn't urge Maddox to push her, because it liked seeing her this way. Relaxed. Happy. Open. At ease with them.

She often seemed so edgy and lost. Not many people wouldn't be, in her shoes. She had someone looking to ruin her life, her sister was not only missing but the possible culprit, and some of her lair had turned away from her. In Maddox's opinion, she was better off away from them, but he suspected she already knew that. She just needed time to accept it.

Once they were both done with their food, he dabbed his mouth with a soft napkin. "I need to use the bathroom. I'll be back soon." He signaled for Carmen to keep a close watch on Raini and then headed for the men's restroom, knowing Hector was close behind him.

As per usual, Hector waited at the exit, on guard. Inside, Maddox did his business and then washed his hands, not all too keen on the clinical scent of the soap. Crossing to the dryer, he placed his palms beneath the sensor. The loud whirring sound of the machinery filled the air.

In the mirror, he caught sight of a figure materializing behind him. *Halo-bearer.*

Two others appeared near the row of sinks. The one at his back moved fast and grabbed Maddox's arm before he'd even had the chance to properly process the situation.

Maddox felt a shift in the air and knew the angel meant to waver him out of there. *Fuck that.* He struck out, releasing a blast of cold energy that sent all three of them zooming backwards. One crashed into a urinal, breaking the porcelain, and dropped to the tiled floor. The other two slammed into the far wall and then slid to the floor.

His blood boiling with both his fury and that of his demon, Maddox conjured a ball of arctic energy just as the door to the restroom rammed into the wall. Hector rushed inside and took in the scene with a single glance. Without hesitation, he launched a series of hellfire orbs at the angel near the broken urinal and—

Pain exploded inside Maddox's skull. His vision grayed, his ears rang, and the energy ball in his hand fizzled out. One of the three halo-bearers wavered to the spot in front of him and grabbed his shoulder.

Still recovering from the psychic hit, Maddox slammed his fist into the angel's jaw and followed it up with a hellfire orb to the face. The fucker jerked back with a growled cry of pain, his skin sizzling.

A telekinetic force whipped Maddox off his feet and sent him soaring across the room and crashing into Hector, causing him to knock down his sentinel like he was a damn skittle.

Jumping to his feet, Maddox tossed a ball of cold energy. It burst in the air and hit the angels like a scatter of bullets. The slivers sank deep under their skin, too deep to be worked out.

Maddox's demon watched with grim satisfaction as the angels jerked, shuddered, and struggled to take in a breath as the arctic energy circulated through their bodies and killed them from the inside out.

Two collapsed on the tiled floor, dead, and their halos winked out, but the third was fighting to hold on. He'd only been hit by a single splinter, so his time hadn't yet run out. His form was flickering as he tried to gather enough power to waver away.

Maddox's demon wanted the piece of shit dead and urged Maddox to end him. He could've, but he instead taunted, "Yes, run back to your master like a good little puppy and tell him he failed again. I guess he's just not 'Seven' material, is he?"

The halo-bearer shot him a hateful glare, spared his dead companions a quick look, and then abruptly disappeared.

Rolling back his shoulders, Maddox turned to his sentinel and frowned. "They got you good," he said, the ringing in his ears dimming.

Sporting several holy fire burns, Hector flicked his hand. "Pain's not that bad."

Ignoring that comment, Maddox joined his palm to Hector's and sent a burst of power into him to heal the wounds.

"Thanks." Hector sighed at the rapidly decomposing corpses. "I guess Castiel wasn't yet ready to personally rise to your challenge."

"They didn't try to wound or kill me," Maddox mused. "Not really. They wanted me weak, if possible, but not dead. They kept trying to waver me out of here."

"Waver you to Castiel, maybe?"

"That would be my guess."

"Can we come inside now?" Carmen called from outside the room.

Maddox stilled. "Where's Raini?"

"Right here with me, obviously," replied Carmen. "I wasn't gonna leave her alone for even a second."

Not trusting that a halo-bearer wouldn't make a grab for her, Maddox stalked out of the restroom and crossed straight to Raini, who was biting her lip.

"What happened in there?" she asked.

Maddox looked at his sentinels. "Home." He teleported Raini to the monastery's communal seating area and then replied, "Three halo-bearers paid me a visit. Seemed like they wanted to take me somewhere."

"Say what?" asked Gunther, rising from the sofa.

The other demons in the room all straightened in their seats, and Maddox saw that most of his lair was present. Just as the sentinels appeared, Maddox began to relay what had happened. And Raini, well, she blew a fuse. He'd never actually seen her lose her temper before. But as she paced up and down, cursing and ranting and swearing she'd make Castiel suffer in several creative ways, it was a thing of beauty. Every descendant in the room watched her, seeming rather fascinated by this delightfully vicious side of her.

Maddox tagged her by looping an arm around her waist. He drew her close. "I'm fine, they didn't take me anywhere."

Her cheeks flushed, she glared up at him through eyes that sparkled with anger. "*Not the point.*"

"She's right on that," said Celia. "I don't know about anyone else, but I've had it with these fuckers and their puppet master."

"That was a suicide mission," said Gunther. "No halo-bearers were ever going to come out of a busy restaurant in the Underground *alive* unless they wavered in and out of it in the blink of an eye. They had to know it wouldn't be that simple when dealing with Maddox, given how hard it's been for them to take him out."

"What choice did they have but to try?" asked Carmen. "They tried attacking him here and at the club—neither attempt was successful. The only public places he frequents are at the Underground."

Feeling the echo of a telepathic conversation, Maddox looked down at his anchor and noted the faraway look in her eyes. He squeezed her hand. "I take it people are checking on you."

Raini nodded. "Yes. And you. They wanted to make sure we're both fine. They're all pissed as hell that halo-bearers would dare go to the Underground, let alone launch an attack there. I think pretty much every demon out there will be mad about it."

He agreed. For demons, that was *their* place. *Their* playground. *Their* territory. Angels had no business being there.

Once he'd finished talking with his lair, Maddox took Raini up to his room, where she promptly kicked off her high heels. He'd just opened the top few buttons of his shirt when his cell phone rang. He checked the screen. *Viper.* Maddox answered, "I take it you heard."

"I heard," said Viper. "The news traveled fast. It's not every day that angels take the chance those three took."

"They didn't try to kill me," Maddox told him, watching as Raini sat on the bed, her thumbs tapping crazily fast on the screen of her cell. She'd calmed down for the most part, so it seemed that her anger ran hot and fast. "They tried to take me."

"Castiel probably sent them to nab you," Viper theorized. "Your last taunt must have worked."

"But not enough to make him come to me, which is what I ultimately want."

"I'd say you'll get what you want. Now that you've killed his minions for the third time, it will reflect badly on him if he doesn't take control of the situation and deal with you directly. He can't afford to be seen as someone who won't avenge his own people—an archangel like that would never make one of the Seven. Plus, I doubt many more halo-bearers will be prepared to essentially sacrifice themselves unless he shows some decent leadership. So there's a high chance you'll be facing him soon."

His demon hummed in satisfaction. "Good."

"Don't underestimate him, Maddox. Don't mistake his failure to face you as fear on his part. Castiel is powerful and ballsy. The only reason he hasn't deigned to face you himself so far is that he's so supremely arrogant, he sees this realm and everyone in it as beneath his notice. If wiping out descendants wouldn't gain him favor, he wouldn't have even spared you a thought."

"That sort of arrogance can be a weakness." One Maddox intended to exploit.

"That it can," Viper agreed. "I'm only saying you need to be ready, because dealing with an archangel is a lot different to dealing with the halo-bearers he's been sending your way. His power far exceeds theirs. He won't make an easy opponent."

"Why would I want an easy opponent?"

Viper chuckled. "I feel like we have so much in common. You know, it surprised me that they didn't make a try for your anchor. They mustn't have gotten word that you and her are now bonded, or they'd have killed her to weaken you. Watch her closely, Maddox. Castiel doesn't fight fair. It would be just like the sly bastard to kill her as part of punishing you for eliminating so many of his minions."

Maddox had already considered that, which was why he'd brought her straight here. "She'll be watched closely." Probably more closely than she'd like.

Viper spoke to someone in the background and then sighed. "Got to go, Maddox. Don't forget to call on me if you need to."

"I won't." Maddox ended the call and stalked over to his anchor, who was now scowling at her phone. "Something wrong?"

Raini looked up at him. "It shouldn't be so hard to convince a person not to work off their anger by burning the property of random people."

"I take it you're referring to your father."

"Yes. He doesn't see why it's a big deal, because 'objects can be replaced; material things aren't what's really important in life.' Oh, and 'crime keeps the economy going.'"

Despite its anger, Maddox's demon chuckled. It liked Lachlan Campbell. So did Maddox. The imp was a man who, like Maddox, saw the beauty in revenge.

She tossed her cell on the mattress beside her. "Hopefully my mom will get through to him, because I can't." She puffed out a breath. "Sorry I got so mad and went on a rant."

"You don't need to apologize. It was actually quite entertaining to watch. And it calmed my demon down a little, because you had most of its attention."

She snorted. "Glad I could be of service, I guess. What about you? Are you okay?"

"No. I had a nice evening planned, and those angels ruined it."

"Hmm, what did your plans entail?"

"I wanted to relax you. Feed you. Fuck you."

Her pupils dilated. "You did relax me. You did feed me. And I certainly hope you still have every intention of fucking me."

"Oh, I do. After we've gotten something straight."

She groaned. "I'm not gonna like this, am I?"

"I'd like to think it won't bother you too much. You spend most of your time here with me anyway."

She poked the inside of her cheek with her tongue. "You want me to temporarily move here, don't you?"

Maddox really had no intention of it being temporary, but she didn't need to know that. For now. "There's a strong possibility that Castiel will come for me himself. There's an equally strong possibility that he'll decide to kill you to weaken me. I don't know if an archangel is powerful enough to break through the penthouse's security, but I'd prefer not—no, I refuse—to risk it. To risk you."

"He can't enter this building?"

"No, or I wouldn't ask you to stay here."

"Where exactly would I sleep?"

"In here with me, obviously."

Raini twisted her mouth. Her pride was firmly against the idea. She could take on an archangel—no matter his power, he surely couldn't combat psychic hellfire, right? But that wasn't to say he couldn't hurt her before she'd had the chance to act, much like the first halo-bearer who came after her. Hell, a full-on blast of holy fire could severely hurt her.

Raini wasn't a fan of pain. Or of holy fire. Or of letting her ego get in the way of good sense.

If Castiel did come for her, she'd stand a far better chance of surviving the encounter if she wasn't alone in a damn penthouse. Yes, Maddox could teleport to her in an instant. But then she'd have drawn him into danger. It would be far better for her to be out of the archangel's reach, so that she couldn't be used against Maddox.

"All right, since I figure this whole thing will have blown over soon," she said. "But don't expect me to stay permanently. Don't think of this as you easing me into joining your lair." She raised a hand to hold off any argument he might have made. "Yes, I know you think I'd be better off transferring here. And you make a lot of good points whenever you start jabbering on about it. But it wouldn't be a good idea."

"Why not?"

"How will you feel when I start dating someone? Or when I take a mate?"

Something dark flashed in his eyes. "Where the fuck did that come from?"

"Anchors can be possessive of each other, as I'm sure you've already noticed. It might be a little bit worse for us because we've been . . . intimate. A lot of anchored pairs live in separate lairs because then their relationships aren't shoved in each other's faces. If I was part of your lair and dating other guys, you'd have a front-row seat to the show, and vice versa. Maybe that wouldn't bother you, but . . ."

"But?" he prodded.

God, she didn't want to say it. Didn't want to admit it, because that would probably put an end to what little they had. He wouldn't want to continue a fling with a woman who wanted more than he did.

Maybe it was better to just cut her losses and walk away now, though. Dragging the whole thing out would only make her hurt worse in the long run.

She pulled up her big girl pants, rose to her feet, and confessed, "But it would bother me to see you with other women, which annoys *the absolute shit* out of me. I thought we could cross lines without things becoming complicated. I was wrong. In light of that, it isn't a good idea for us to keep sleeping together, is it?"

He took a single step closer, eating up the small space between them. "I like what we have. My demon likes it. Neither me nor the entity have any particular interest in letting it end, and it would seem that neither do you. So why should we?"

"Because the possessiveness will only intensify if we don't."

"And why is that a bad thing?"

Feeling her brow crease, Raini stared at him. "I can't tell if you're being deliberately obtuse or you're just not seeing the bigger picture."

"You're the one who's not looking at the bigger picture."

Maddox lifted some of her hair and held the blonde and pink strands up to the light streaming in through the window. "I've never had a woman in my bed before, not even in my room. Not once. I've never taken one without a condom. Never invited them to eat with my lair. Never wanted their time or attention outside of sex."

"You've only been different with me because I'm your anchor."

Maddox's eyes drifted over her face. "You fascinate my demon, you know. It loves that you're a devious, vengeful, lethal package wrapped up in sweetness and sensuality. It likes that it's one of the few who really sees you."

Pausing, he dipped his head. "*I* see you. You know that. It scares you. The men in your past only saw one dimension of you. Having someone walk away doesn't hurt as much when they never really *knew* you, does it? But if I was to walk away, I'd have walked away from the real you, and that would hurt you. The thing is, Raini . . . I have no plans to go anywhere. You should have known better than to think otherwise."

She felt her lips part. "You're serious?"

"Originally, my possessiveness stemmed from you being my anchor; I won't deny it. But the more time I spent around you and the more facets of you I saw, the more that sense of possessiveness . . . shifted. It became different. It became about *you*. It became more. This, what we have, is more. And you know it. I have no intention of losing it; of losing you."

Raini swallowed. The guy was a master at deception, but she knew he wouldn't lie about something like this. Knew he wouldn't have said such things to her unless he was certain that he meant them. Even so, it was hard to simply accept his declaration, because she would never have expected to hear it. "You once told me you had no interest in relationships."

"That was then. This is now. I felt things changing, I could have ended this at any time to put a chokehold on that. I didn't. I let it happen. So did you. There's no sense in backing out now. I don't want to, and neither do you. I doubt our demons would stand for it if we tried."

Her inner entity would put up a resistance for sure, but . . . "If we don't pull back, my demon will develop a true attachment to you." The entities couldn't love, but they occasionally formed attachments to people. They weren't sweet or romantic, no, demonic attachments were dark and obsessive and incredibly intense. Because the entities honed every bit of their laser-sharp focus and sheer intensity into those bonds. "If that happens, it'll want to keep you, Maddox. You know that."

He gently tucked her hair behind her ear. "I do know that. Just as I know that my demon is fast developing an attachment to you. I haven't got an issue with either of those things."

"There'd be no going back," she warned him.

Maddox dipped his head so that their lips brushed. "Why would I want to go back, baby?" He took her mouth. Not softly, not slowly. No, this wasn't a casual kiss. It was a statement. A claim. A demand for surrender. And her body roared to life.

Raini kissed him back, deftly tackling the buttons of his shirt. He shrugged it off, and she planted her hands on his broad shoulders, loving how solid they were. She snaked her hands down his warm, sleek chest; feeling the hard male muscle beneath; tracing the dips and lines of his abs. She dropped her hands to his fly—

He spun her around. "Not so fast, baby."

"Fast is good."

"It is," he agreed, slowly pulling down the zipper of her dress. "We'll get to that part. But not yet."

"Why not?"

Maddox felt his mouth curve at the sulky note to her voice. "Because I don't want to." He dragged the thin straps of her dress over her shoulders and let the devil's creation drop to the floor. If his cock hadn't already been full and hard, it would have thickened at the sight of her phenomenal ass clad only in lacy, barely-there panties.

Pressing his front to her back, Maddox put his mouth to her ear. "Panties off. That's it, good girl. Now open your bra for me." Once she'd flicked open the front catch, he filled his hands with her breasts. Firm and high and petal soft, they were fucking perfect.

He squeezed and kneaded, occasionally thumbing or pinching her taut nipples. "Remember when I pumped my come all over these pretty breasts? I'll be doing that again sometime soon."

Keeping her back pressed to his front, he spun them both and then sank onto the bed with her sat between his legs. "Hook your thighs over mine. Very good." He slowly parted his thighs, forcing her own to spread wide open. "Yes, that's how I want you."

"Maddox—"

"Shh," he began, snaking his hand over her breast and down her stomach, "have a little patience." He slid one finger between her folds and then sank it into her pussy as deep as it would go. Humming at the feel of all that liquid heat, he nipped her earlobe. "You know what I think?"

"No, and I don't care," she snapped. "All I want is for you to fuck me. I don't think it's too much to ask. I let you borrow my pussy, like, all the time."

He smiled. "I don't borrow it." He swirled his finger and then slid it out of her, dragging all that slickness up to her clit. "I don't need to, because I own it."

Maddox used his fingertip to work her clit—tracing circles, rubbing back and forth, sliding up and down, alternating with speed and pressure—until she was trembling, arching, and digging her nails into his arms. "You're close, aren't you? Good." He shoved two fingers inside her and pumped hard, using the heel of his palm to rub her clit; lapping up every hoarse moan, every squeeze of her inner muscles, every rush of dampness that coated his fingers. "Come on, baby, let . . . yes, that's it."

She imploded, her head thrown back over his shoulder, her pussy rippling, her thighs tremoring. And his demon surged to the surface.

CHAPTER NINETEEN

Raini's eyes snapped open as she felt a rush of cool air sweep up her back. His inner entity had taken over, she realized. Which could be positive or negative. On the one hand, it didn't tend to drag shit out—much like Raini, it was all about instant gratification. On the other hand, it was occasionally in the mood to make her wait. She was done waiting.

Scraping its teeth over her shoulder, the demon ever so slowly withdrew its fingers from her pussy. "Stand and turn to face me," it ordered.

Breathing hard, she pushed to her feet, her knees a little shaky from her orgasm. She slowly turned and met that obsidian gaze.

The entity undid its fly, fished out its dick, and then spread its thighs a little wider. "Get my cock nice and wet, or it's going to hurt you when I drop you on it."

Her pussy clenched. *Well, now.* She knelt right there, curled her hand around the base of its shaft, and closed her mouth over the broad head. She licked, sucked, lapped, and played, already knowing exactly what the entity liked—it had used her mouth before.

Unlike those other times, the demon didn't take over. Didn't fist her hair and guide her movements. Didn't instruct her, or encourage her. It left her to do all the work.

She kept the suction tight as she moved faster, bopping her head up and down, rubbing the flat of her tongue against the underside of its cock. Deciding to include a little hand action, she began to jack the demon off while suckling on the broad tip. Not slow and easy, no, she pumped fast like—

The demon snatched her from the floor and roughly dropped her on its cock. Her back bowed, and a shocked breath gusted out of her lungs. *Jesus.*

The entity didn't give her a moment to adjust. It clamped its hands on her hips and began slamming her up and down its dick. She gripped its shoulders, holding on for dear life while it pretty much used her as it pleased.

"Mine," it snarled. Then it was *ravaging* her mouth—licking, kissing, biting.

She felt her flesh beneath its hands begin to burn, and she realized what it was doing. Branding her. Her eyes widened as the burn spread, moving higher and spanning her waist. The demon dug its fingertips into her hypersensitive branded flesh, the fucking sadist, and then it subsided.

In control once more, Maddox palmed her ass and said, "Hold on." He stood, pinned her against the wall near the window, and took her hard. Harder than he ever had before, knowing she could take it; loving that she got off on it as much as he did.

He sucked on her pulse, not biting, just wanting to feel it beat in his mouth as he fucked her. Her nails dragged down his back, her thighs flexed around his hips, her inner walls fluttered and squeezed his cock. She was close. Good. So was he.

Cool air whispered over him in a telling sign that her demon had surfaced. It slapped its hands on the back of his shoulders, and the flesh there began to heat and prickle. The demon was branding him, returning his own entity's claim. Fuck, his balls tightened. His cock swelled. His release crept closer.

"Shit, shit, shit, I'm gonna come," said Raini, clearly back with him.

Lifting his head to meet that amber gaze, Maddox frantically rammed into her and parted the globes of her ass enough for it to sting just a little. She sucked in a breath, and her inner walls spasmed around him. "Come, Raini." Rumbling a low growl, he bit her lip, breaking the skin; the tiny taste of her blood shot straight to his dick.

Her breath caught in her throat, her brow creased, and then she came apart around him.

"Fuck, yeah." Maddox rode her all the way through her orgasm, drawing it out. Finally he let go and exploded deep inside her.

She melted into him, limp and trembling and panting.

He pressed a kiss to her hair. "You good?"

"I think so," Raini slurred, feeling all hollowed out. She didn't open her eyes when he carried her to the bathroom. Or when he propped her on the counter. Or when he cleaned her up with a wet cloth. Or when he carried her to his bed. Mostly because she didn't want to look at the brands his demon had left on her hips. It was a brazen, possessive, sadistic asshole, so she didn't quite trust that it hadn't marked her in some seriously inappropriate way.

Feeling Maddox's fingers play over her newly branded flesh as he lay beside her on the mattress, her curiosity got the better of her. Squeezing her eyes shut, she asked, "What do they look like?"

"Why do you ask that with dread?"

"Because I've seen some of the brands that my girls wear. They're rarely subtle, and they're sometimes over the top."

Maddox hummed, stroking her hips again. "I like them."

"That doesn't make me feel reassured."

"Take a look."

Forcing her eyes open, she raised her head and glanced down. A gasp flew out of her. A *good* kind of gasp. Because the ends of two exquisitely detailed wings curled around her hips and overlapped at her navel, as if someone had protectively enfolded her in their wings. "Wow," she breathed. "Your demon has good taste."

"I'd say so."

"Shall we get a look at what brands my entity left on you?"

In answer, he sat up straight. Her lips parted. "It seems my demon didn't want to be outdone by yours. It used both hands, so I thought it had left two brands. It didn't. It left a big one that spans your upper back. And it's . . . well, it's a thunderstorm. An *amazing* thunderstorm. Dark clouds. Whips of lightning. Heavy rain. It looks wild and badass and magical at the same time."

Maddox grabbed her cell phone from the end of the bed and handed it to her. "Snap a picture of the brand with your cell."

She quickly did so and then showed him the photo. "I think my entity must have liked that comment you once made about my being like rain, lightning, and thunder."

His mouth curved. "I think you might be right."

"You like it, then?" she asked, a little nervous of his answer.

He cupped her jaw. "I'd like it no matter what, because it's what the brand *signifies* that's important. But, yeah, I like it."

Her toes almost curled as he kissed her soft and slow, indulging in a thorough taste. The kiss might have been gentle, but it was no less possessive than the exceptionally intense fucking session they'd just had.

Finally, he pulled back. "Do you want to tell Jolene in person that you've switched lairs, or are you happy to tell her over the phone?"

Raini tensed. "Um . . . I think we should wait before I transfer."

"Wait?"

"Yes. Not because I'm not fully committed to you—"

"It's not just a simple commitment, Raini. We're mates now. Those brands on your hips are never going to fade. This is serious. Permanent."

"Agreed. I don't want to fuck it up by rushing everything else. Plus, my parents are really worried for me right now. They'll be happy for us, but—considering their other daughter is missing—they might find it too hard to see me leave the lair. So much so that they might even want to switch along with me. Do you want to be the one to tell them they can't? Because I don't."

Maddox sighed. "I can agree that another upheaval for your parents might prove to be too much. But that's not the main reason you're hesitant to transfer to my lair, is it?"

"No, I'm leery of moving too fast. We've so far let things move at their own pace. It's worked. We should just keep doing that. Why are you smiling at me like, I don't know, like you feel sorry for me or something?"

"I had a feeling you'd say that. Do you know why? I'll tell you. It's because you don't like to jump into anything. You don't like to succumb to your impulses—unusual for a demon. But I suspect it has something to do with growing up around imps, who leap without looking and often seem surprised when that backfires. You don't want things backfiring on you, so you take a more careful approach."

She couldn't help but bristle at how easily he'd read her. "There's nothing wrong with that."

"No, there isn't." He pulled her back down to the mattress and held her flush against him. "Like I said, we're mates now. Mates don't live apart or belong to separate lairs. But if it'll make you feel better to spend time ruminating and reflecting and looking at the situation from every angle before we make those changes, you do that. One day, when you're more sure of us, I'll make my claim on you deeper by slipping a ring on your finger—that's how serious about you, about us, that I am. But I'm not going to rush or pressure you. Just bear in mind that our demons will only give you so much time to play catch-up—they won't like that we're not living together or part of the same lair."

"Why aren't you annoyed that I'm struggling to move at your speed?"

"I can be patient when I know I'll eventually get what I want."

She narrowed her eyes. "In other words, you're indulging me by giving me time."

He pursed his lips. "In a nutshell, yes."

She gave him a haughty sniff. "How benevolent of you."

A smirk flirted around the edges of his mouth. "I was thinking exactly the same thing."

"God, you're an asshole."

"I wasn't thinking that."

"You should be."

He smoothed his hand down her back. "The only asshole I'm interested in is yours."

"*Pfft*. You can be as interested in it as you like, but my ass is an exit-only zone. Nothing goes up there. *Definitely* not your cock, because there ain't anything slim or small about it."

"All right."

She narrowed her eyes. "Enough with the indulgent 'I'll let her believe what makes her feel better because I'll eventually get my way' smile."

He lathed her lower lip with his tongue. "Kiss me."

Raini sniffed. "Not feeling the vibe right now."

"I'll make you feel it." He slid his hand around her hip and down to her pussy.

"I'm not in the mood to—" She gasped as he started doing some very clever things to her clit, unerringly finding every hot spot. "You know my body too well," she grumbled.

"It knows me. It knows I'll give it what it wants. As do you, so just lay back and enjoy."

Shutting the top drawer of his dresser early the next morning, Raini turned to Maddox, who stood a few feet away with his hands in his pockets. They'd collected her things from the penthouse an hour ago, and he'd shuffled some of his clothes around to make room for her own. Not liking the self-satisfied look on his face, she clipped, "There, I'm unpacked. Happy?"

He stalked toward her. "You really should stop sulking. It makes your lips pout, and that just makes me want them wrapped around my cock. I'm pretty sure you'd rather eat breakfast before you do anything else."

As if to back him up on that, her stomach rumbled.

His mouth curving, Maddox took her hand. "Come on."

He teleported her to the main hall, where most of his demons were gathered, eating, drinking, and talking. The delicious scents of toast, eggs, bacon, and breakfast potatoes laced the air.

People said their good mornings or nodded in greeting before going back to their food and conversations. There'd been a time when the descendants had seemed awkward whenever she joined them at mealtimes. Now, well, it was old news. The only people who ever gave any real sort of reaction were Marcella and Euan—usually by going stiff in their seats or offering brittle, insincere smiles. Like Raini gave a shit.

Maddox guided her to their usual table, where his sentinels were already seated.

"So, you all moved in?" asked Hector.

Piling food on her plate, Raini replied, "Temporarily, yes."

Hector snorted. "Temporarily. Sure."

Carmen elbowed him hard. "Is there anywhere you need to go today, Raini?"

"Nope," replied Raini, shaking her head. "I need to go over my plans for the upcoming party I'm throwing, but I can do that through video calls."

She wasn't in the mood to venture out, because it had become clear that the halo-bearers had no problem with striking in public places. If she went anywhere, she'd be on edge, expecting an attack. And it was possible that Castiel might be planning to launch one, so why make it easy for him?

Just then, her mother's mind touched hers. Listening to Evangeline's telepathic heads-up, Raini felt her mouth tighten. "Dammit."

"What's wrong?" asked Maddox, stilling.

"My dad almost leveled a city block last night." Raini sighed, slicing into her bacon a little harder than necessary. "No casualties, just utter mayhem. He's almost as bad as Jolene when he's pissed. The only difference is *she* uses her ability to cause that kind of destruction; he uses household fucking chemicals."

Hector grinned. "I think I could like your father."

"Hmm." Raini shoved a forkful of food into her mouth. "I love my dad. He's a freaking treasure. He also drives me insane. I guess, as an imp, it's sort of his vocation."

"I saw him a few times while guarding your house," said Carmen. "He always spotted me, no matter how well I hid, and gave me a subtle salute. Your uncle usually sensed me, too. He waggled his tongue all Hannibal Lecter like."

Raini cringed. “Bram is inappropriate in so many ways.” Deciding it was time for a change of subject, she turned to Maddox. “What are you doing with your day?”

He took a sip of his coffee. “I need to go to the club and see to a few things. You can come, or you can stay here. I’d rather you didn’t leave the monastery, but I won’t force you to remain here. You’re not a prisoner.”

Raini couldn’t help but smile. “You say that like you *could* force me to stay. You’re so cute at times.” Adorable, even.

Hector snickered.

Maddox gave her a droll look. “I’m well aware that you could take me out with psychic hellfire, but I don’t believe you’d ever use it on me.”

Raini tipped her head to the side. “Whatever makes you think that’s the only notable power I possess? See, so cute. I just wanna squish your cheeks together right now.”

Carmen snorted. “Never heard anyone describe you as cute before, Maddox. Or speak to you so very condescendingly.”

“It surprises me that you allow it,” a voice further down the table commented, its tone hard and clipped.

Carmen exhaled heavily. “It’s called banter, Euan.”

Fisting his hands around his cutlery, Euan stared at Maddox. “I can’t believe you’ve brought an outsider to stay here. This is our home. What’s next? Are you going to bring her into our lair? Are you going to welcome her family into it if they insist on following her?”

Sipping at his coffee again, Maddox leaned back in his chair. “What’s your real issue, Euan?” he asked, cool and calm. “It isn’t that Raini’s here. It isn’t that I want her to join our lair. It’s something else. Tell me what’s really eating at you.”

Euan clamped his lips shut, his nostrils flaring.

“It’s that she makes me stronger, isn’t it?” Maddox went on.

"You stopped with your whispers, but you held out hope that the lair would eventually reject me as their Prime; that they would never accept Raini; that my keeping her in my life would weaken my standing here. Instead, she can not only prevent me from turning rogue or going through a haze, she can spare the lair any more future hazes. Maybe one or two demons in this hall aren't happy that she's here," he added, flicking Marcella a brief look. "But the others have accepted her, and you don't like it."

Stiff, Euan cleared his throat. "On the contrary, I find it a positive thing that the lair has accepted your anchor, since she will be a big part of your life and—as you said—she makes you stronger. I want that for you. I simply don't like that we weren't given a say on whether or not she could stay here. It is our home. We should have been consulted as a measure of common courtesy."

"It was wrong of me to assume that my own demons would want my anchor protected?"

Euan spluttered. "I didn't say we *wouldn't* want to help protect her."

"Why do you keep using the word 'we'? Do you feel that you are a voice for the lair as a whole?"

"I wouldn't say I'm a voice for them, but I do believe I am merely saying what everybody here is thinking."

"I see. Look around you, Euan."

The demon did so. His jaw hardened when he saw that the majority of the people present were either glaring at him or shaking their heads in disgust. A few others, Marcella included, were averting their gazes.

Maddox raised a brow. "Do you still believe everyone here thinks as you do, Euan?"

The man licked the edges of his teeth. "Perhaps they simply fear speaking up."

"I don't see why they would. I don't punish people for having an opinion. Yours is clearly that I should have spoken to you before inviting my anchor to stay in the place where she'd be safest; where I could better protect her from the beings who are only targeting her *because* of me. It is my responsibility and my honor to keep her safe, so I do not see why anyone would begrudge her being here. My demons are better than that. But, for the sake of your delicate feelings, I will ask you . . . Euan, do you have an issue with Raini staying here?"

Euan opened and closed his mouth. "No."

Hector looked at his mate. "Then why *the fuck* did I spend part of my morning listening to that pointless conversation, babe?"

Carmen patted his back. "You know Euan, Hector. He needs to feel important. But he knows he's not, so he does dumb shit that he thinks make him look and sound good. It never quite works out, so I don't know why he hasn't quit acting this way."

"I don't think it's dumb to want your opinion to be noted," said Raini. "Thank you, Euan, for not asking that I leave even though you're not tremendously comfortable with my being here."

Looking somewhat lost for words, Euan curtly inclined his head and then pushed out of his chair. He muttered something to the people he'd been eating with and then left the hall.

Maddox looked down at his anchor. "You were so good, I almost bought that."

Raini frowned. "You don't think I'm truly grateful to him?"

"No."

"Okay, fine, so I would have preferred to rip the weak prick another asshole," she admitted. "But he was hoping for that. He wanted me to be a bitch to him right here in his own home so he could look like a victim of the big, bad succubus and probably make out like I think I can take liberties because I'm your anchor. I don't know if anyone would have fallen for it, but it was what he was hoping for."

Hector's brow creased. "You're right, he was. I didn't see it until you pointed it out, though."

Raini's lips curled. "A devious mind helps you see this shit coming."

"And you have a devious mind for sure," Carmen said to her. "It's just not always apparent straight off."

Raini shrugged. "Some wear it on their sleeve. Others hide it in their panties."

Maddox almost choked on his coffee. He glared at her. *You did that on purpose.*

She flashed him a bright smile that would have weakened his knees if he'd been standing. *Well of course I did.*

He looked up as three women stopped in front of their table, one of whom was Marcella. It wasn't she who spoke, though. It was her aunt, Deborah.

Smiling a little shyly at Raini, Deborah said, "I just wanted to say that the rest of us don't think like Euan. Don't let him plant any seeds of doubt in your head."

"Thank you," said Raini. "I won't, I promise."

Marcella looked about to speak, but she instead followed the other two female descendants out of the hall. It was clear she'd had something to say, though. So he wasn't surprised that she later turned up at his office inside the Damned.

Not bothering with a hello, she instantly declared, "I'd like to transfer to another lair. Not right now while there's all kinds of crap going on, but afterward."

Maddox leaned back against his desk. "All right."

She swallowed. "You really don't care that I'll be gone, do you?"

"It won't be nice to lose a member of my lair. But I'm not going to ask you to stay for a number of reasons. One, you want to be someone's co-Prime; that isn't going to happen here. Two, I fully intend to have Raini join the lair at some point; you won't like it, so you'll be unhappy here. Three—"

"*She* won't want me here, and *her* feelings matter most," Marcella sniped, bitterness coating every word.

"What were you hoping I'd say, Marcella? Did you think I'd beg you to stay? That I'd offer you the things you want?"

She balled up her hands. "No. But I thought that, as my Prime, you'd care just a *little* bit that one of your demons intends to leave. But this suits you just fine, doesn't it?"

"No, it doesn't suit me. It doesn't please me. It doesn't *anything*. You clearly have an overestimated sense of your value to me, but I'm unsure why that is. Each and every one of my demons matter. I wouldn't like to see any of them leave, but nor would I attempt to hold them here if it wasn't what they wanted. You no longer wish to be one of us. You believe you're meant for bigger and better things than to be simply *part* of a lair; you want to co-run one. Why would I try to hold you back from pursuing the things you want?"

A sour expression twisted her face. "Will you make the succubus your co-Prime? Don't try to tell me you're not serious about her. Don't deny it, there's no point. I can see it clear as day."

"I would imagine you could, since I'm making no attempt to hide it."

Her nostrils flaring, she jutted out her chin. "You're making a mistake. A mistake as old as time. So many demons have gotten swept away by the feelings that come with having an anchor, and they've mistaken them for something else. For more. For *love*, even." She rolled her eyes. "Once you adjust to the bond, Maddox, the emotional chaos inside you will settle, your feelings will dim, and you'll realize you don't really want her the way you think you do now."

Done with her bullshit, his demon surged to the surface, determined to deal with her. The bravado left her in a rush, and she held herself very still.

"This right here is why you will not make a good Prime," said the demon. "Too dramatic. Too emotional. Too wrapped up in yourself to care about the well-being of others. You have no interest in leading, only in being followed—that is your biggest downfall. No demon can stay in power for long if they do not lead."

She swallowed. "I-I'll bear that in mind."

"See that you do. There is another thing you would also do well to remember." The entity walked toward her. "If Maddox or I want your opinion on our relationship with Raini, we will ask for it. Unless that happens, you will say nothing more on the matter. You will keep your beliefs to yourself. You will not seek us out and waste our time with your petty jealousies.

"No amount of stamping your feet will earn you the attention from Maddox that you are looking for. You insist on viewing Raini as someone who is trying to take what should be yours. You would never have been made co-Prime of this lair. You are searching for what you want in all the wrong places. He could not have been clearer on that, but you have not listened to him. Perhaps you will listen to me. There are ways I can enforce that message; every one of them will hurt you. Will it come to that?"

She shook her head hard. "No. No, I-I'll mind my own business. I'll look for what I want elsewhere."

As his demon then retreated, Maddox said, "Wise of you. Now go."

In a blink, she was gone. His demon grunted, a little disappointed that she'd backed down so easily. A lot of rage had taken up residence inside its system since the recent trouble began, and the entity would have gladly worked out said rage on Marcella.

Knowing the sound of his anchor's voice would calm it, Maddox reached out and asked, *Everything okay?*

Her mind touched his. *If you mean am I drinking shots of tequila and trying to teach Carmen how to do the Gangnam Style dance, then yes.*

His demon chuckled, and Maddox felt one corner of his mouth kick up.

Teleporting to Raini's side a short time later, Maddox didn't know what bothered him more. That a good portion of his lair were in his bedroom, or that they were all—Hector included—doing the Gangnam Style dance.

Raini grinned at Maddox. "Yay, you're back! Come on, you've gotta join in."

Shaking his head, he sank into the armchair and watched. Of course, that made enough people so uncomfortable that they began to trickle out of the room. Which suited him just fine, because he had plans to fuck Raini right on the floor where there'd be no give.

The moment they were alone, that was exactly what he did.

CHAPTER TWENTY

On the screen of Raini's cell phone, Devon gave a little clap and said, "I want to see, I want to see."

Obligingly, Raini lifted the bottom of her tee to expose the brands on her hips.

Devon gasped. "Oh, wow."

"They're amazing," Khloë breathed, sitting on the hellcat's left while Harper sat on her right. "So detailed and pretty."

Devon nodded. "I know. God, I'm so jealous." She pouted. "Why can't Tanner's demon put such cool brands like that on me? Instead, I get fingerprints and shackles."

Harper snorted at the hellcat. "For the record, none of us are buying that you don't like them." She turned to Raini. "How do you feel about being branded?"

Raini righted her tee. "I always figured I wouldn't like it, since I'd be dreading the moment when the mark began to fade—I wouldn't like to have that visual confirmation that the entity had lost interest. But Maddox and I are mates, so that won't happen."

"Have you told Grams you're now part of his lair?" asked Harper.

Raini briefly glanced to the side. "Well, no, because I decided not to transfer straight away. I don't want to rush things. That's why I've only agreed to move in with him temporarily."

Harper shook her head. "That is so typical of you. When something's important, you hesitate to grab it. Yes, we're all guilty of that at times, but *you* do it like it's your job. Sometimes we need to reach for the things we want instead of hemming and hawing."

"I'm just treading carefully. I don't want to mess it up. Plus, I want to give my family *and* Maddox's demons a little time to get used to the two of us being mated. My parents are so worried about me right now that they'd find it hard to have me transfer to another lair. They might even demand to come with me, and descendants generally only like to live among their own kind. Maddox doesn't like that I'm not transferring straight away, but he understands. He's agreed to give me time. I don't think he'd be half as cooperative if I wasn't temporarily living with him, though."

"Probably not. Alphas are pushy and generally don't do 'cooperative.'"

"Amen," muttered Devon. "But once they come to realize that their bulldozing bullshit isn't going to fly with you, they find sneakier ways to get what they want. Maddox will keep you on your toes for sure, Raini."

She didn't doubt it.

"On a more fun and interesting note," Khloë cut in, "are the party plans still going well?"

Raini told them about the most recent arrangements she'd made, including the changes to the catering menu. Khloë disappeared from view when her own cell began to ring. When the imp reappeared, her expression was hard, but her eyes were bright.

"That was one of my sources," said Khloë, her mouth curving into a smirk. "I know where the astral projector is."

Apprehending the astral asshole—who it turned out was a harbinger—had been simple enough for Ciaran and Jolene's sentinels. They'd knocked him out with a psychic blow and brought him to Richie's basement, where interrogations were often held. In no time at all, the unconscious demon was sprawled on the cement floor, trapped in a containment forcefield that Maddox had popped up around him. Her demon had been glaring at their captive ever since, raring to maul his ass in a major way.

Raini had telepathed Maddox after ending her video call with the girls. He'd teleported straight to her, looking so supremely calm it was a little unnerving, and brought her to the basement. His sentinels had come along, and they now stood with him and Raini near the wall, placing them in shadow.

With only a bare lightbulb, the basement was pretty dim. It was also creepy as hell with the dank and eerie air, the old bloodstains on the floor, the thick spooky-ass shadows, and the cloying scents of must, mold, and lingering pain. Yeah, a lot of people had died down here. She doubted that any of them had died easy.

When Jolene had declared that she wanted to lead the interrogation, most of the others in the basement had tensed, waiting for an explosion from Maddox. Raini had almost snorted. They should have known better. The guy never exploded.

He'd merely stared at Jolene and asked, "*Why bother questioning him when I can pluck the answers out of his mind?*"

"*I never said that I didn't want you to read his mind,*" Jolene had replied. "*I just said I wish to lead the interrogation. I agreed that we would work together on this, and we will. Part of that includes my taking the lead.*"

In Raini's view, it was pure Prime posturing—neither wanted the other to steal the show, because they both had a responsibility to Raini.

Maddox had given Jolene a careless "fine" shrug and said, "*You won't be her Prime for much longer, so I see no harm in letting you enjoy it while you can.*" Ignoring the narrow-eyed look Jolene shot him, he'd then crossed to Raini and his sentinels, exuding a calm that she doubted he truly felt.

It was shortly after that that Lachlan and his brothers showed up. They'd gathered behind Jolene, along with Ciaran, her two sentinels, and Richie. All were facing the harbinger, who was now beginning to stir.

Groaning, he raised his head and blinked hard. He froze as he took in the scene. His astral self practically burst out of his body . . . and bounced right off the wall of the containment forcefield. He didn't let that deter him. He repeatedly threw his astral self at the walls, relentless and determined.

That determination came to nothing.

Raini's demon snickered, finding him weak and ridiculous. It was rather enjoying seeing him trapped and helpless. Raini would be lying if she said she didn't get a kick out of it, too. If his dagger had adequately done its job, Raini and her demon would have been just as powerless in the face of danger, so it seemed only fair that he suffer this way. Karma truly was a bitch, which was why Raini had a fondness for it.

Finally seeming to realize that the only thing he was achieving was tiring himself out, the harbinger stopped attacking the forcefield. His astral self then slipped back into his body, and he stood upright.

Jolene smiled ever so pleasantly at him. "My granddaughter

tells me that your name is Terrence Gibbs. I've been looking forward to meeting you. I'm Jolene Wallis. Behind me are several of my lair members and a few . . . friends. As I'm sure you can sense, we're all quite eager to talk with you." The word "talk" carried all kinds of painful implications.

Terrence flexed his fists. "You should let me go."

"Hmm, I can't say I share that opinion."

"I have a lot of friends in high places. Friends who'd be pissed about this shit."

Every imp in the basement began to chuckle. Yeah, it *was* kind of ridiculous for him to think that his warning would make a difference to them. These were creatures who'd long ago ceased caring about little things called "consequences." That wasn't exactly uncommon knowledge. Even Raini's demon rolled its eyes.

"I don't care how many friends you have or who exactly they are," said Jolene. "Not that it matters either way. I'll never have to meet them. Nobody knows you're here. No one is coming for you. There won't be a rescue or an escape. That nifty ability you have to astral project isn't going to save you either."

Snarling, he began throwing orbs of hellfire at the forcefield. But it didn't falter, didn't crack, didn't burn. It stayed strong and steady. Raini was totally loving the look of defeat on his face. *And* the way he kept shivering, as if it was mighty cold in there.

When he finally gave up trying to escape, Jolene took a regal step forward, her heels scraping over the cement floor. "I'd tell you that you have two choices—talk or endure a tremendous amount of pain—but that would be a lie. You only really have one choice and that is to answer my questions, because I won't stand for *anything* less."

He glared at her, each puff of breath fogging the air within the forcefield.

"You went after one of my demons, Raini Campbell. You'll remember hurling a dagger at her. You'll remember why you targeted her. It's the latter we're interested in, because we haven't yet figured out what sparked you to target her."

"I ain't telling you nothing," he said.

Deciding he'd allowed Jolene enough time with the harbinger, Maddox stepped out of the shadows and sidled up to her. His inner entity smirked when Terrence went utterly still and fear flickered across his face. The harbinger would know that, if the rumors were to be believed, Maddox could invade his mind, fuck with his thoughts, snatch every secret out of his head, intensify his pain threshold, make him do any number of things—hell, Maddox could even make him *like* the pain.

Torture was one thing—people tended to believe they could hold out; that they could withdraw inside their head and shut themselves off from the pain; that they could hold onto their dignity as one last act of defiance. But having your mind fucked with as *part* of that torture? No one would want that. No one would want every part of them to be invaded.

"I'm not here to question you," Maddox said to him. "I'm here to hurt you. A lot. In whatever ways I choose. But, naturally, I want my answers first." He made a move toward the forcefield, intending to step through it—as its creator, he was the only person who could.

Terrence raised a hand and backed up. "Wait, wait, wait! I'll tell you, all right? I'll tell you about the succubus. I received a phone call through a spoofing site—someone wanted her stripped of power; they paid me to make it happen."

Anger pulsed through both Maddox and his demon. They'd expected that answer.

"Who is 'they'?" Raini asked their prisoner as she moved to stand near Jolene.

"I don't know," replied Terrence, shaking his head. "The voice was male. They didn't give me their name. They only gave me yours."

Raini narrowed her eyes. "What happened when you failed to deliver?"

"Nothing," he told her. "No one called me. No one asked me to try again." Terrence shrugged. "There's nothing else I can tell you."

"How disappointing." Maddox swiped his tongue over his front teeth. "Now, back to what I was doing before you so rudely interrupted me." He stepped through the forcefield.

Terrence's eyes widened. "I told you everything!"

"So you say. I'm not so sure I believe you." Even if Maddox had, he'd have still invaded the harbinger's mind, intent on making him feel the epitome of helpless.

"I'm telling the truth, dammit!"

"You know . . . I can rummage through a person's mind without causing them pain," Maddox told him, his tone conversational. "But I won't spare you any—my demon wouldn't allow it anyway. You didn't spare Raini. She was brought to me injured, bleeding, in pain, and weak from expending a lot of psychic energy. *You* were the cause of that. You can imagine how much I long to return the favor."

"I was only doing my job," Terrence defended. "Just like you're doing yours when you broker all kinds of shady deals. How is that different?"

"It isn't. But I don't care. You hurt someone who belongs to me. Someone I don't plan to live without. Someone I just last night claimed as my mate."

That garnered her a few looks from her relatives, but they didn't comment. None seemed surprised.

"You might have even killed her, Terrence," Maddox went on.

"The fact is . . . you were dead the moment you accepted the offer to strip her of power; you just hadn't realized that until now."

Raini winced as the harbinger's back arched and an animal-like cry of pain seemed to be *torn* out of him. He dropped to his knees, slapping his hands to his head, keening and moaning and begging for Maddox to stop.

Her anchor didn't stop. He stared down at the harbinger, his expression vacant, his eyes narrowed in concentration, completely unmoved by the cries for mercy that echoed off the walls.

Her demon was equally unmoved. Terrence hadn't had a sliver of an issue with stripping her of power. And if he'd succeeded, the halo-bearers who came to Raini's house probably would have killed her. If they hadn't, Gunther most likely would have. Her death would have, essentially, been on the head of Terrence here. So, no, neither Raini nor her demon felt any pity for him.

Finally, he slumped to the floor—maybe in relief, maybe because Maddox's mental invasion had sucked the energy out of him. And then . . . wait, was he sobbing? Oh, good Lord. If he hadn't been able to hack that, he wouldn't do well against the pain her family meant to deliver. Which made her demon clap in delight.

"You were telling the truth," Maddox said to him. "You truly know nothing that can help us. There were some other things I learned while traipsing through your mind. The location of your business, the names and addresses of your work associates, the identity of the incantor who put the runes on the daggers you keep to rob people of power."

Feeling Maddox's rage flutter against the edges of her consciousness thanks to their anchor bond, Raini knew that not one of those people would live through the night.

"Don't kill him yet, Maddox," said Jolene. "I'd like to

communicate to him just how much I don't appreciate a person coming after someone dear to me."

"We all do," announced Lachlan. "But how do we get in that energy bubble to fuck his shit up?"

"You don't need to," said Maddox, lowering the forcefield.

Jolene took a panicked step forward. "He'll astral project out of here."

"No, he won't," said Maddox. "He doesn't have the ability to astral project. He's never had it, have you, Terrence?"

Now on his hands and knees, the harbinger shook his head.

Frowning, Raini reached out to her anchor. *You made him believe he doesn't have the ability?* He could actually do that?

It wasn't difficult, Maddox replied without glancing her way. He was still focused on the harbinger. "His greatest fear . . . is being confined to a basement exactly like this while several people subject him to sheer agony. Now he'll get to live out that fear."

In other words, Maddox had planted the fear into Terrence's mind. Holy *shit*.

"You'll also find that his pain-tolerance level is at an all-time low," Maddox added.

Lachlan turned to Raini and flicked a look at her anchor. "I think I could like him. Maybe. We'll see how it goes." He slid his gaze to Jolene. "That fucker hurled a blade at my daughter. I want at him first. In the name of the sanctity of retaliation—"

"Have at him," Jolene invited, sweeping a hand toward the harbinger.

Later, when there was very little, for want of a better word, life left in Terrence, Jolene turned to her. "Raini, would you like to finish him off?"

"Sure. I'd advise everyone to get behind me." Once they'd done so, Raini sent out a wave of psychic hellfire. They all watched as he dropped, convulsed, and then went limp, his skull caving in.

"A small part of me is gonna miss him." With blood splattered on his skin and clothes, Lachlan cricked his neck. "Well, who fancies some tacos? I'm starving."

"Tacos sound good," said Bram.

Halfway to the basement staircase, Lachlan stopped and pinned Maddox with a look. "You take good care of my daughter. She wouldn't like it if I killed you, and I'd rather not have to hear her whine at me for no good reason."

Raini stared at him. "For no *good* reason? You wouldn't consider killing my anchor and mate a valid reason for me to be upset with you?"

Lachlan sighed at her. "There's never a valid reason to be upset with your own father—a loving, caring, very involved father. I raised you. Fed you. Sheltered you. Taught you how to snap a man's neck like a twig and the best place to embed a blade in the spine."

"You also tried to teach me to skin small animals, and *what is up with that?*"

"You said you were bored."

"Bored, not sociopathic."

"Well I thought it would be good father-daughter bonding time. Honestly, you're always making a fuss over nothing." Lachlan looked at his brothers. "Tacos."

After the imps had trailed up the stairs, Hector smiled at Raini. "I was right in thinking I'd like your father."

His mouth curved, Maddox took her elbow. "Let's go home."

Home. She liked the sound of that.

CHAPTER TWENTY-ONE

Damn, she was gonna come *so hard.*

Lying on her side while Maddox powered into her from behind the next morning, Raini reached back to grip his nape. He'd woken her with his finger on her clit, expertly teasing the hell out of her. It hadn't been long before he'd plunged his dick inside her, slamming home in one smooth thrust.

Now, his fingertips dug into her thigh as he fucked in and out of her, filling the room with the sound of flesh slapping flesh. His free arm was banded around her body, gripping her shoulder to hold her still for his possession. And she wasn't going to last much longer.

He put his mouth to her ear. "Mine," he bit out. "My mate. Aren't you?"

She licked her lips. "Yes."

"And you're going to wear my ring when I give it to you, aren't you?"

Knowing that by "ring" he meant a black diamond—something

demons only gifted to their mates when they were ready to make *the* ultimate commitment, she hesitated, unsure if he was ready for that or only saying it in the heat of the moment. "I—"

"It wasn't a request, baby. You'll wear it. You'll never take it off. And every time you look at it, you'll remember that I'll never let you go." He upped the pace of his thrusts, pounding harder. So fucking hard that each brutal lunge seemed to send the breath gusting out of her lungs.

Her orgasm hit her suddenly and swept her up. She came hard, arching, crying out, squeezing his cock with her inner muscles. His fingertips bit harder into her thigh as he exploded inside her.

Utterly sated, Maddox kissed the crook of her neck and began to slide his cock out of her. But then her pussy fluttered gently around him, and he smoothly sank back inside. "I think I'll stay in here a little longer."

He soothingly stroked his hand over her thigh, right where he'd gripped it tight. Her skin was already bruising. He could heal the marks, but he found he liked the sight of his fingerprints on her flesh.

"You're like a machine or something," she said, panting. "Not sure if you realized, but you woke me *four times* through the night."

"I realized," he told her. Unlike her, he hadn't been tired, so he hadn't slept. He'd sat on the chair and gotten some work done on his laptop. "You sometimes make this soft little hum when you sleep. It's the same sound you sometimes make when I'm playing with your nipples. It gets me hard every time."

She snorted. "Don't blame me for how insatiable you are."

He gently nipped the back of her shoulder. "Are you complaining about how often I take you?"

"If I didn't like it, I'd say so, not hint at it."

"Good." He slowly slid out of her. "Shower with me."

After they were clean and dressed, they headed to the main hall to eat breakfast with his lair. He was pouring a second cup of coffee when he felt a slight vibration against his mind and knew that someone had telepathically contacted her.

Dropping her fork, Raini looked up at him, her lips parted. "Demi's back."

He stilled, and his demon shot to full alertness. "Back?"

"Yes, but I don't know if she's with Dwain or alone or what. All my mom said was Demi's 'home' and that I should come see her."

They'd be definitely going to see her—Maddox had some questions for the imp. "We'll go together. Are you ready to leave now?"

Nodding, Raini pushed to her feet. "Whenever you are."

Entering Demi's living area with Maddox and Carmen, Raini glanced around the room. Her parents and uncles were gathered there, along with Jolene and Ciaran.

A false smile playing around the edges of her mouth, Evangeline pulled Raini into a hug. "Hey, sweetheart."

"Thank you for coming so quickly," said Jolene.

Raini's gaze darted from person to person, taking in their grim expressions. Her stomach rolled. "What's wrong? Where's Demi?"

"She's upstairs, sleeping. Martina is watching over her." Evangeline licked her lips and held Raini by her forearms. "We need to prepare you. She looks . . . she doesn't look good. Whoever kept her captive doesn't seemed to have *physically* hurt her, but they didn't exactly make an effort to take care of her."

Raini felt the blood drain from her face. "She was kept captive?"

Her mother swallowed. "I'm afraid so."

"By who? And where?"

"We don't yet know," said Jolene. "She hasn't woken yet. She was found unconscious this morning on the field not far from Ciaran's house. By all appearances, it looks as though she was dumped there."

"Dumped there?"

"Yes. There were tire tracks not far from where she was found, and it appeared as though she'd been dragged along the ground."

Raini winced. Guilt wrapped around her bones and made her feel like a piece of shit. Her sister had been a *prisoner.* A victim. And Raini had spent weeks thinking of her as a suspect.

Maddox's mind brushed hers. *That guilt you're feeling is senseless, baby.*

Her demon agreed, urging Raini to shake it off.

Letting her hands slide away from Raini's arms, Evangeline turned to Maddox. "I know you'll want to scan Demi's mind. But I don't think she's strong enough to endure something like that."

"It won't take any strength on her part," said Maddox. "I only require her to be awake."

Lachlan tilted his head. "When you infiltrated Terrence's mind—"

"I deliberately hurt him," Maddox finished. "I can make it so that there's no pain." Noting that neither Evangeline nor Lachlan seemed any more comfortable with it, he added, "I appreciate that you're feeling very protective of her right now and that you wish to spare her further trauma, but we need answers."

"She'll give them to us willingly," said Evangeline.

"Perhaps, but I will still scan her mind." Maddox raised a hand to stay any objections. "If it was Dwain who took her, she might still protect him and lie that he played no part in it—a demon's loyalty to their anchor runs deep."

"He's right," said Jolene. "Demi loves Dwain enough to make excuses for him in her mind, let alone protect him from what we might do to him if he's guilty. We *have* to know what happened.

I think everyone in this room can agree with that. So if Demi refuses to talk, Maddox will get the answers for us."

Evangeline and the imps nodded, though they didn't look happy about it.

A short time later, Jolene announced she'd received a telepathic heads-up from Martina that Demi was awake.

"Thank God," breathed Evangeline, making a move toward the stairs, but she paused when Jolene lifted a hand.

"Let's not all go rushing into the bedroom," said Jolene. "We have no idea what she has been through. It would be best not to crowd her."

"I'll wait down here," said Ciaran, and the uncles made the same offer.

"I think we should also not bombard Demi with questions," said Raini, giving Maddox a pointed look.

"If you want to approach this slowly and give her a chance to talk, fine," said Maddox, though it wasn't truly fine. "But if she refuses to answer, I *will* scare her into thinking I'll harm her."

Lachlan bristled. "Now wait a minute—"

"Sometimes a little fear is motivational," said Maddox. "She won't believe that any of you will follow through on a plan to push her into talking, but she'll know that my loyalty is to Raini."

Sighing, Evangeline rubbed at her forehead. "Fine, just . . . don't hurt her. I want answers the same as you, but there's no need for Demi to be hurt in the process." Evangeline then led the way up the stairs and into the master bedroom.

Demi lay there, staring at the ceiling, startingly unreactive as her lair members gathered close. Her face was pale and haggard. There were dark smudges under her lifeless eyes. She seemed tired. Weak. Undernourished.

Taking the seat beside the bed that Martina had vacated, Evangeline took Demi's hand in hers and gave it a little squeeze, but her daughter didn't even glance her way. "Demi, baby, we're so glad you're home. I've been so worried about you."

Demi still didn't react. Unsure what to make of her sister's behavior, Raini hung back and said little while her parents and Jolene sort of . . . gentled Demi—assuring her that she'd been missed, that all were relieved she was back, that she was safe now.

Evangeline brushed a lock of Demi's hair away from her face. "Tell us what happened, honey."

Silent tears began to roll down Demi's face, but she resolutely kept her gaze on the ceiling.

Raini's chest squeezed at the sight, but her demon wasn't so moved. Maddox didn't appear to be either. He stood at her side, watching Demi carefully, no pity to be seen in his eyes. On Raini's other side, Carmen stared at the female imp in much the same way.

"Demi, I know you probably don't want to talk right now or even think about what went on," Evangeline continued. "But we have to know." No response. "Who took you, sweetheart? Was it Dwain? It was, wasn't it?"

Lachlan rested a hand on Demi's leg. "It's important that you tell us everything. Surely you want to. Surely you want to see this person brought to justice, especially when they're probably also behind what's been happening to your sister."

Still, Demi said nothing, more silent tears dripping down her face.

Evangeline bit her lip. "How about we ask questions, and you just nod or shake your head? Then you don't have to admit anything aloud, but you can still tell us what we need to know."

Raini stood by as her parents and Jolene posed question after question to Demi, who never once responded. Not verbally, not with body language, nothing.

Her demon becoming increasingly pissed, Raini took a single step toward the bed. "Demi, please, tell us what happened."

Her sister's head very slowly turned her way, and her tearful eyes clashed with Raini's. There was so much despair there that it made Raini's heart hurt. Still, her sister didn't speak.

Raini took another step toward the bed. "*Please*, Demi." The plea went unanswered.

Maddox stalked forward, and Demi's eyes snapped to him. "What do you think your sister's most painful memory is, Raini?" he asked, ever so casual.

Raini blinked. "What?"

"Her most painful memory," he said, his gaze on her sister. "What do you think it is?"

Clueless as to where he could be going with this, Raini shrugged. "I-I don't know. Probably finding out that Dwain is mated. Which he actually isn't. But I don't think she knew that. At least not at first."

"Hmm." Maddox raised his hand, and it glowed red. Everyone tensed as if to act in Demi's defense, but she made no cry of pain. He looked at Raini. "You were wrong. Her most painful memory isn't hearing that Dwain is mated. It's hearing him confess to her that he loved you—it was years ago, I know, but time hasn't lessened the pain. She knew back then that he didn't truly feel that way about you—he didn't know you well enough to love you. That was why the moment devastated her so much. He *did* know *her* well enough to love her, he just didn't care for her that way."

Swallowing, Raini looked back at her sister, who was eyeing Maddox warily.

Tilting his head at Demi, he said, "You know, when I questioned one of the halo-bearers who attacked my lair, he was just as reluctant to talk as you are. He changed his mind when I told him what misery I could put him through without lifting a finger. I'm sure you're aware of what a time loop is. I can trap someone in a mental time loop, forcing them to relive something over and over. And since I now know your most painful memory . . ."

Demi's eyes went wide, and her breathing turned fast and shaky.

Putting a hand to her roiling stomach, Raini turned to him. "Maddox—"

"She's your sister, I know," he said, not moving his gaze from said sister. "But she could help you here, Raini. She could tell us all what we need to know to keep you safe. She won't, though. Not even to help herself."

Fuck if he wasn't right, which was why Raini's demon saw no issue with putting Demi through any of the torment that Maddox had planned.

"You're thinking Jolene or your parents will stop me," he said to Demi. "They won't. They can't. And you shouldn't want to see them go toe-to-toe with someone who is both the mate and anchor of your own sister."

Demi's mouth fell open. "M-mate?" she whispered brokenly.

"Yes."

Demi squeezed her eyes shut, her face lined with pain. A pain that no doubt stemmed from envy, because Raini now officially had *exactly* what Demi most wanted.

"Maybe she's unable to talk about who took her," Evangeline suggested. "Maybe she's under some kind of silencing spell or something."

Maddox pursed his lips. "Perhaps. There's only one way to find out." His eyes narrowed, and a loud gasp of surprise left Demi.

Her upper body knifing up, Demi shook her head wildly. "Get out of my head! *Get out*!" She looked at Jolene. "Make him stop."

The Prime stared down at her, unmoved. "We gave you the

chance to talk. All you had to do was answer our questions. You refused."

"Mom, make him get out of my head!" Demi appealed.

Her expression pained, Evangeline squeezed Demi's hand. "It's better this way, really. You won't have to say aloud whatever you're holding inside, but we'll still have the answers we need."

"It'll be over soon," Lachlan soothed.

Demi flung herself back on the bed and went back to staring at the ceiling, pointedly ignoring anyone's attempt to talk with her.

Finally, Maddox made a "hmm" sound and scraped his hand over his jaw.

"What did you see?" Raini asked him.

"Many things," he replied, his tone casual, his eyes cold. "She didn't know that Dwain and Harmony weren't mates. Not until a few days before she should have gone on her cruise. He confessed everything—how Harmony was only playing a part, how he'd been boycotting Urban Ink, how he wanted to get a little payback."

Lachlan swore beneath his breath. "That rat bastard," he said, taking the words right out of Raini's mouth.

"At first, Demi was angry," said Maddox, staring at the stubbornly silent imp. "She hated that you mattered enough for him to orchestrate this. On a side note, Harmony *has* gone traveling—she has no knowledge of any of this. Demi, however, knew everything. She had no plans to tell anyone what she'd learned, though. She thought it only fitting that you suffer a little."

Raini silently winced because, yeah, that hurt.

Demi rolled over to give everyone her back, and curled into the fetal position.

"Then, what?" Jolene pushed.

"She had every intention of going on her cruise as planned, but then she was drugged and taken," said Maddox. "When she woke, she was in the cellar of a cabin, and someone had put some sort of block on her mind that prevented her from receiving or sending telepathic messages. Her captor came to see her daily and leave her food. They also drugged her this morning—it's the last thing she remembers before waking here."

Her arms folded, Raini asked, "Who was her captor?"

"Dwain. Or so somebody would like us to believe. Her memories of her captor have been modified."

Stiffening, Demi peeked at him over her shoulder.

"How can you tell?" Raini asked him.

"It's much like watching a movie that has very poor special effects surrounding one character," replied Maddox. "I'm assuming that her memories were tampered with while she was drugged, because she has no recollection of it happening. It was a very professional job, but the alterations to her memories are easy to spot because they aren't holding—she doesn't want to believe that Dwain would harm her; her gut won't accept what she remembers. Her gut is right not to. It wasn't Dwain; it was someone else."

"Maybe all her memories of what happened are false," Evangeline suggested. "Maybe the whole thing was planted in her head."

Maddox shook his head. "The only thing here that is false is Dwain's presence."

Demi sat up again. "So if it wasn't Dwain, where *is* Dwain?"

"We don't know. He went missing, like you." Jolene turned to Maddox. "Can you clear away the edits that were made to her memories; can you restore them to what they were?"

"Yes," replied Maddox. "But it will take time. And it may hurt her a little." Not that the thought of that bothered him. His demon would relish it. But it was clear that Raini balked at it. She shouldn't, because . . . "Demi was overjoyed when she heard that I didn't seem to want to bond with you, Raini. She thought of it as karma; that it was only fair that you didn't have your anchor around if she couldn't have hers."

"That's a lie," claimed Demi, her voice shaky.

Ignoring that, Maddox went on, "When she started to suspect that that might change—which was sometime after I had the alarm system installed at your house—she considered coming to me and advising me not to bond with you. She even considered seducing me. She wanted to be able to look you in the eye and announce that she'd fucked your anchor. It was only Dwain's sudden appearance in Vegas that made her decide to postpone her plans—she'd intended to pick them up again after he left."

Evangeline sighed. "Oh, Demi."

Raini shook her head at her sister. "If you're intent on hating me—"

"She doesn't really hate *you*, baby," Maddox cut in. "She tells herself that she does. But the person she's really so angry with is Dwain for not feeling for her what she feels for him; for leaving her and going to live elsewhere. She blames you for that because it's too painful to accept that she doesn't matter enough to Dwain for him to stay close."

Demi's eyes welled up again. She looked at Raini. "Imagine if Maddox left Vegas. Imagine if he wouldn't let you go with him, claiming he needed 'distance' from you because you reminded him of the person he 'loved.' Do you think you'd have taken it well?"

"Not at all," replied Raini. "I understand why it hurt you so much. But I don't find it an excuse for the things you've done. You could have warned me about Dwain's plans. Or told Mom. Or Dad. Or Jolene. You could have told *someone*."

"But I didn't, and karma paid me back for that, didn't it?" Demi said, her voice hoarse. "I ended up a fucking *prisoner*. I don't know who took me. I don't know where Dwain could be. He said he was going home."

"Dwain said a *lot* of things that turned out to be bullshit," Raini pointed out. "He seriously came at me this way just because of the snare?"

"You don't see what it did to him. He felt so many things when the truth sank into his brain—hurt, embarrassed, weak, unmanned, bitter that someone had overtaken his will and fucked with his thoughts, making him believe something that wasn't real; making him obsessed with someone against his will. He didn't plan to fuck with your life until recently, though."

"What happened recently? Redeem yourself a little here, Demi, and *help us*."

Letting out a shuddering breath, Demi shrugged. "In short order, he lost his job and his girlfriend—she dumped him for his best friend, who he essentially also then lost. More, his ex said the same thing to him that you did; that he only *thought* he loved her. Feeling alone and jobless and heartsore just threw him back to what happened years ago. It was like he was mentally flailing. Feeling afloat and powerless and that he had no control over his world. I guess he . . ."

"Wanted to feel strong and in control again," Jolene finished. "He needed to work off the pain and sense of loss he felt. It's much like an abuser finding themselves a human punchbag—beating another person up is not only a way to vent, it makes them feel powerful. But why did Dwain go after Raini? I would have thought he'd have vented his anger on his ex."

"In his mind, it all came back to Raini—if she hadn't snared him, he'd never have left Vegas in the first place. The way he sees it, everything that happened is on her." Demi turned back to Raini. "When he heard from his dad that you'd found your anchor, Dwain was *so pissed*. He knew you'd always looked forward to finding your psi-mate. He wanted to ruin it for you. He wanted to mess with your head the way your preternatural allure messed with his."

Raini swallowed. "And you didn't care."

Demi closed her eyes. "I'm sorry."

"No, you're not," said Maddox, unwilling to let her play the innocent card and manipulate those around her. He was infuriated with this bitch. She could have tried talking Dwain down. She could have helped him straighten his thoughts. She could have saved her sister from further upset. But she simply hadn't bothered. "I've been in your mind. You regret what you did, but not because of how it's affected Raini. No, your true regret comes from the fact that everyone will now know what you did—and what you failed to do. It is all about you and how you feel, not Raini. At least admit that much."

Demi's eyes blazed at him. "Would you have betrayed Raini?"

"Never," Maddox answered without hesitation. "But, if she had been Dwain, I would have discouraged her from making the mess she was making. I would have pointed out that her thoughts were all tangled and twisted. I would have saved her from herself. You were happy to let Dwain make his mess because you *wanted* Raini to hurt."

Demi looked away and took another shaky breath. She opened her mouth to speak, and then suddenly her entire body went limp and she fell to the mattress, her eyes closed.

"What's wrong with her?" Evangeline burst out.

"I simply put her to sleep," said Jolene. "She needs to rest so that she can heal."

Evangeline's lips thinned. "And you don't trust her not to run."

"No, I don't," the Prime easily admitted. "Do you?"

Evangeline averted her gaze. "I'm so mad at her right now. I want to shake her and yell at her. How the hell could she do all this? God, where did I go wrong, Jolene? I thought I was a good mom, I don't know how I messed up—"

"You didn't," Jolene told her, firm. "You're her mother, so of course you would prefer to take the blame rather than think your own child could do such things. But this isn't on you, Evangeline. Nor is it on Lachlan. You're both good parents."

"She's right, Mom," Raini cut in. "You and Dad are the best. Neither of you let Demi down. She let herself down. She made super messed-up decisions—"

"That's an understatement," said Lachlan, taking the words right out of Maddox's mouth.

Having walked in Demi's mind, he'd *felt* the darkness in her. The selfishness. The spitefulness. The way she seemed unable to see Raini clearly—always looking at his mate through bitter lenses.

"Maybe you're right and we didn't let her down," Lachlan said to Raini. "But we did let you down. We saw how jealous she was of you when you were kids, but we thought she'd grow out of it. Hell, me and Bram clashed up until we reached our early twenties. Still, when your mom and I noticed the jealousy, we tried nipping it in the bud. We punished Demi, we talked to her, we treated you both equally. She did seem to snap out of it when you were teenagers, but maybe she'd just learned to hide it better. We should have been more on the ball about it or come down on her harder."

Raini shook her head. "I don't think you let me down. I think she truly did grow out of it, but that fuck-up with Dwain years ago seemed to spark the jealousy back to life. Some people let that kind of emotion eat them up. She's one of them."

Maddox blinked as Celia's mind all but thumped his own. *They're here, Maddox. Castiel and his halo-bearers are here.*

CHAPTER TWENTY-TWO

I'm supposed to call you home and straight to the courtyard, Celia went on, but don't come. *They just want to trap you like they've trapped our entire goddamn lair—Castiel surrounded the monastery with a forcefield so no one can get out. I was the only one outside, so he grabbed me before I could teleport away. Castiel's calling for you to come face him.*

Maddox clenched his teeth and, forcing himself to think through the rage that pumped through both him and his demon, asked her, *What about the cathedral? Have they apprehended it?*

No, Celia replied.

Good. Sit tight. Without hesitation, Maddox teleported himself, Raini, and Carmen to the attic of the cathedral.

"What the fuck?" Raini burst out, blinking rapidly. "Why are we here?"

"Castiel has come," Maddox told her, striding toward the small arched window, knowing that no one below would see him through the stained glass. His demon hissed at the sight of the monastery contained by a forcefield. It looked much like the ones that Maddox could form, except that it crackled with white and gold energy.

A tall, winged man stood a few feet away from the energy construct, laughing at a ranting Celia, who stood so unnaturally still that it was clear some sort of power was holding her in place. Two dozen halo-bearers were also present, glancing in every direction, clearly waiting for Maddox to appear.

Beside him, Raini gasped. "Oh, fuck. I'm guessing that's Castiel."

"Those shit-eating bitches," snarled Carmen. "He's containing everyone so that they can't teleport to safety or come out and fight him, isn't he?"

"I would say so," said Maddox, feeling his nostrils flare. "I suspect he'd be burning down the entire building as we speak if it wasn't protected from holy fire. He came in the morning because he knew it was the likeliest time to find us *all* here—other times of the day, some of us are working at or guarding the club."

"And because everyone aside from us three *is* in fact home, there are no lair members for us to call on," said Carmen.

"If it wasn't for Celia, I could have killed the bastards in one swoop with psychic hellfire," said Raini. "But if I let out a wave of it, she'd get hit, too. Do you think you could, I don't know, teleport to her and then whisk her away in a flash?"

"No," replied Maddox. "But I think Castiel is hoping I'll try it. Look at how very still she is."

"Shit, he's trapped her there somehow," Raini realized. "He's probably hoping you won't notice and that you'll go to her—placing you right in his path. Essentially, she's bait."

"Yes." A sense of urgency riding him hard, Maddox looked from Raini to Carmen. "I need you both to stay inside. I'm going to—"

"Now *hold* on a second, you cannot be thinking of going out there alone." Raini shook her head hard. "No. No way. No fucking way."

Touched by but not liking the fear in her eyes, Maddox took a step toward her. "Baby—"

"Don't you 'baby' me. You have seen how many of them are out there, right? You do realize you're totally outnumbered?"

"I've fought higher numbers—"

"At times when an archangel was included in those numbers?"

Maddox cupped her neck. "I've got this. Trust me. I wouldn't go out there if I didn't believe I could come out of the fight alive and back to you. Stay here with Carmen. I can see you're balking at that, but it's vital that Castiel doesn't get to you. That's why I brought you here instead of leaving you with your family. The cathedral is protected, the same as the monastery—those angelic bastards can't get in here or burn it down."

"I'll keep her safe," Carmen promised him.

Maddox nodded and kissed Raini hard. "I have to go. No matter what happens, you stay inside."

Raini's mouth firmed. "Fine. But if Celia somehow gets away, teleport out of sight and then I'll psychic-hellfire the shit out of those motherfuckers."

Maddox nodded. After sending a brief telepathic message to a certain someone, he teleported to the doorstep of the cathedral. "Took you long enough to turn up, Castiel."

The archangel and halo-bearers swerved to face him and braced themselves to attack. Moreover, a dozen additional angels appeared out of nowhere.

"Maddox Quentin, I presume," said Castiel in a booming voice that rang with power.

"You presume correctly. I was beginning to think you'd never work up the nerve to face me."

"You think me afraid of you?" scoffed Castiel. "How very foolish. Killing you will be easier than squashing a bug."

"Hmm, then I'd have to question why you've brought backup with you—and so very much of it."

"My angels are simply here for the pleasure of witnessing the demise of the demon who murdered their brothers."

"I wasn't alone in that. Members of my lair helped with utter delight. You're not going to drop the forcefield so they can come out and you can punish them, too? I'm thinking . . . no. I think you would rather keep them contained so that *I* don't have any backup." Maddox gave a lazy shrug. "I suppose I should be flattered that you see me as such a threat."

Castiel sneered. "You are *nothing*."

"A 'nothing' who none of your minions were able to take down—not even when they outnumbered me."

"Those fools were weak." Castiel's chin notched up. "I am not."

"And yet, you do not feel comfortable facing me unless I'm without aid."

Castiel's upper lip curled back. "Wrong again. I would not care if you had backup."

Both Maddox and his demon smirked. "It's funny you should say that . . ." He sent a brief telepathic signal, and the people he'd called on mere moments ago swiftly appeared. Viper and his brothers gathered around the halo-bearers, their eyes bright with bloodlust. "As you can see," began Maddox, still smirking at Castiel, "I'm not alone."

His gaze landing on Viper, Castiel did a double-take. "*You*."

Viper grinned. "Me."

"Traitor," Castiel hissed. He glanced at the other Black Saints, and his scowl deepened. "You're all traitors."

"And you're delusional if you think you have a chance at being made one of the Seven," said Viper. "That's never going to happen, no matter how many grand gestures you try to make. But hey, don't take my word for it."

Castiel's nostrils flared. "I will kill the descendants here," he told Viper. "Then I will kill you. And I will take your body home with me. They will all see then that I am—"

"Completely fucking delusional, like I said," Viper finished. "You won't defeat Maddox, let alone me."

"You were right, Viper," said Maddox. "He *is* incredibly arrogant. You know, Castiel, even if you were to win this battle—which you won't—you'd never get the promotion you seek," said Maddox. "Not when your higher-ups hear that you brought my anchor's lair into this. Her family now want you gone. They'll demand retribution."

His eyes red, Castiel let out a derisive snort. "They won't get it." He coughed again. "No one will ever hand me over to them."

"No, they wouldn't. But you'd be in their bad books for pissing off demons, wouldn't you? That risks starting a war. They know that. They don't want it. You really should have stuck to fucking with my lair—they won't care so much about that."

"All will be forgiven once your breed has been wiped out." The archangel conjured a high-powered ball of holy fire.

Maddox almost snickered. Oh, the halo-bearer who passed on his "message" would have also told Castiel that Maddox seemed immune to holy fire. But Castiel would no doubt believe that Maddox had no chance of withstanding an archangelic blast of holy fire—it would be so much more potent, so much more lethal.

Castiel slung the orb at Maddox, who didn't make the slightest effort to dodge it. He let it come at him; let it explode into nothing mere inches before his body.

Castiel gasped.

Maddox smiled.

Then sheer chaos erupted.

Her eyes glued to the sight outside, Raini rocked back and forth on her heels, filled with a restless energy that had nowhere to go. Anxiety nibbled at her insides, rubbed her nerves raw, and made her stomach curdle. Her mate—*her mate*—was currently fighting a fucking archangel.

When *more* halo-bearers had wavered into the courtyard, she'd almost lost her everloving mind. She might have tried to barrel her way outside if the newbies, who Carmen told her were fallen angels of some kind, hadn't appeared. They were fighting *hard*. They also seemed to be thoroughly enjoying themselves, like they either had some bad history with the halo-bearers or they were quite simply sociopathic.

The presence of one of the Black Saints, who Carmen had identified as Viper, made *all* the difference. He was so much more powerful than his "brothers," and that strength made up for the fact that they and Maddox were outnumbered—especially when the number of halo-bearers was rapidly dropping.

The battle was an ugly one. Fire hissed, power sizzled, the courtyard statues crumbled under the assault. The Black Saints bit into their foes, ripping out chunks of flesh or gulping down angelic blood. Maddox and Castiel were focused on each other, merciless and relentless.

The air was lit up with orbs of hellfire, holy fire, red crackling energy, the gold whips of lightning that shot from Castiel's fingertips, and whatever weird shit the Black Saints were throwing. The flaming balls were like holy fire in that they glowed and burned brightly, but they weren't pure white. They were ultraviolet, and they were doing *real* damage to the halo-bearers.

Poor Celia remained in the center of it all. An occasional orb of hellfire had accidentally hit her, so she was in some serious pain, but she wasn't fatally injured.

Raini's entity did not want to be up here in a musty attic, observing the battle through the small window. It wanted to be with Maddox, protecting and fighting alongside him. Raini wanted the same, but she knew better. Her presence would only distract Maddox, and the one thing he did not need when up against a goddamn archangel was to be distracted.

Behind her, Carmen placed a hand on her back. "He'll be fine, Raini."

"So will Hector, but I'll bet your head is all kinds of messed up knowing he's trapped in the monastery and, more, you can't be with him," Raini hedged.

Carmen sighed. "Yeah, it is, so I get why you're panicking. But Maddox has been through battles before, and he's survived every one of them. He'll survive this one, too."

God, Raini hoped so. She pressed both palms to her stomach—the damn thing felt heavy as fuck, like a damn rock sat in it. She moved closer to the window. "Don't take this the wrong way, but I would rather you were down there with him than up here with me."

"That's not happening. Maddox would tear my head from my shoulders if I left you."

"I'm safe here—"

"He's strong, Raini. Uber strong. And the Black Saints have totally got their shit together. Trust him to have this."

Shifting from foot to foot, Raini blew out several short, calming breaths. They didn't help. Like *at all*. "I just feel so fucking helpless. He's *right there*. I'm—"

"Exactly where he needs you to be. I know it's frustrating, but he'll fight better if he isn't wondering where you are and if you're safe."

Raini dragged a hand through her hair. "You're right. I know you're right. But I don't like it and—" She cut off at the sound of a loud thump. Pivoting on her heel, Raini sucked in a breath. Carmen was on the floor, seemingly out cold, and Euan stood over her, a gun in each hand. *Son of a bitch.*

"I wouldn't think of lunging at me, if I were you," he said, his smile pleasant.

She *would* have lunged if he wasn't pointing a gun at both her and Carmen, who now had blood leaking out of her ears. Panic gripped Raini's insides. "What did you do to her?"

Euan shrugged. "Just caused a little brain aneurism. Maddox could save her. I'm sure you're counting on him to save you both. That won't happen. And if you're thinking that you might as well charge at me if she's really a lost cause, consider this: a bullet would hit you before psychic hellfire hit me. So it might be best for you to simply behave."

Raini's surroundings flashed white, and then all three of them stood in *the fucking mausoleum*.

"I can't have you telepathing your lair members to seek help, can I?"

Raini ground her teeth, and her demon lost its mind, *demanding* retribution, intent on ripping this prick apart with its bare hands. "How the hell did you get out of the monastery?" she asked.

Euan grinned. "I wasn't inside it when Castiel and his minions arrived. I was in the vegetable garden. I teleported to the lower level of the cathedral out of sight."

Raini stared at him, her lips parted. "You didn't think to call for help? You deserted your own lair?"

He gave an unrepentant shrug. "It can be rebuilt."

"Oh, I see; you'll be its new Prime, huh?"

"Of course. Admittedly, I will not be whatsoever sorry to see the others go—they had their chance to make me their Prime; they didn't."

God, there was something so disturbing about seeing someone so satisfied at the prospect of his entire lair being wiped out. "So, you're hoping the archangel and his helpers will do your dirty work and destroy them all?"

"I do want *some* part in taking Maddox down. The easiest way to do that would be through you." Euan's finger flexed on the trigger of the gun he was pointing at her head. "If I kill you, I weaken him, and he'll then be easily defeated by Castiel. I'm not going to kill you right here, though. You see, he won't be only *physically* weakened by your death, he'll be devastated. I want to see that devastation on his face."

Her gut roiled, and a knot of fear built in her throat so thick she could almost choke on it. *No.* No, Maddox would do just as Carmen had assured her he would—he'd survive this battle the way he had survived the others. And Raini would be damned if she'd let this pathetic asshole use her to bring down her own mate. No, not happening.

Silently ordering herself to calm the fuck down, she took in a slow breath and fought the urge to lift her chin in defiance. She couldn't let Euan see her determination to fuck up his plans. She needed to do as she'd done with Maddox for months—remain cooperative, say nothing to piss Euan off, give him the illusion of complete control.

Seething, her demon wanted to peel the flesh from his bones, but it didn't urge Raini to attack. It understood the value of biding its time. They would bring Euan down. Their opportunity would come. They just had to be patient, which would be a whole lot harder than it fucking sounded.

"The Black Saints are vicious, but they'll be overpowered eventually," Euan went on. "The three of us will hang out here until the halo-bearers have decimated as many of the Black Saints as possible."

She could only pray that the battle would be over *before* Euan teleported them out of there; that he'd make his move too late.

He released a satisfied sigh. "Hearing your voice coming from the attic earlier, I knew it was a sign to act. Fate put you in my path tonight."

"Is that so?" she asked, wishing he'd give her some kind of opening so that she could lunge. Wishing he'd look away, drop his guard, sneeze, *something.* And then an idea came to her.

Raini let out the *tiniest* sliver of a sexual pheromone, so subtle he wouldn't sense it. She wasn't aiming to arouse him, just make him a little flustered. She had to move carefully, though; had to let the effects build so slowly he wouldn't notice until it was too late.

"You know, I didn't originally plan to drag you into my game," he said. "But my attempts to undermine Maddox didn't work as well as I'd hoped. Not even when he inserted himself in your life. I had to take . . . other measures." He smirked. "How is your sister, by the way?"

Raini froze. "You were the one who kidnapped her; the one who kept her captive."

"I needed people to look at others for any moves I made against you. Your sister and her anchor were the obvious choices, given that they were both possible culprits of the boycotting, so I took them. I wasn't entirely sure that either of them was guilty. I didn't particularly care. I just needed scapegoats. Taking them was necessary, since I couldn't very well have left them wandering around. Maddox would have delved into their minds and seen that neither was responsible for *all* that was happening. Then he would have looked much more closely at other suspects, such as me."

She narrowed her eyes. "What do you mean neither were responsible for 'all' that was happening? Wait . . . it was you who sent those texts to my lair members," she realized. It had to have been him, because both Dwain and Demi were already missing at that point—missing, and in Euan's custody.

"Yes," he replied, a flush beginning to stain his cheeks, which meant the pheromone was doing its job. "Dwain was kind enough to tell me who in the lair didn't like you much. He stupidly thought I'd spare him. It was a pleasure to slit the whiny bastard's throat. I would have killed your sister too, but I need her to tell others how Dwain kept her captive. I need everyone to believe that *he* was the only bad guy in this scenario."

Well, that plan hadn't worked out, because many knew that Demi's memories were edited, but Raini chose not to enlighten him on that yet awhile.

"Since people are now under the impression that he'd do something so cruel as to keep his own anchor captive, they'll find it easy to assume that he also hired the harbinger, so they won't look at someone else for it."

Raini felt her head jerk back. "*You* set him on my ass?"

"It seemed wise to ensure you were without power before I tried to kill you. I didn't know back then that you possessed a substantial ability, but it always pays to be careful. I'd intended to pin your murder on Dwain, but the dagger failed to do its job. As did Gunther, even though he was in a haze."

"It was *you* who dumped me in the mausoleum." *Motherfucker.*

"I acted as soon as I heard that halo-bearers were at the club, knowing people would naturally assume it was one of them who took you. It would have been *perfect* if Gunther had succeeded in killing you. Maddox would have been in such a rage that he'd have killed Gunther, despite the demon not being in his right mind. People would have turned against Maddox for that.

But you survived the attack, and you helped Gunther. Basically, Raini, you've been a pain in my ass."

Well, she was all about tit for tat. "And *you've* used all that's going on around you as a curtain to hide behind while you played your own sly games. All this because, what, you want to rule? Why not just go somewhere else and start your own lair?"

Euan dug his tongue into the edge of his incisor. "Did Maddox ever tell you that many of our lair died in a battle with another lair of descendants?" The question sounded so idle, yet there was a dark note to his voice. There was also a fine sheen of sweat on both his forehead and upper lip, proving that the pheromone was still at work.

"Yes." Unwilling to take her eyes off Euan for long, she briefly dropped her gaze to Carmen. The sentinel still wasn't moving. And there was fuck all Raini could do about it.

"Initially, that lair came to us in peace. The Prime, Louis, merely wanted the strongest demons from within our lair, and he offered to leave us alone if Maddox and his father, Joseph, agreed to join. The rest of us would have been spared. But Joseph and Maddox refused to go, and our own Prime refused to force them." Euan's face darkened, soured, twisted. "I lost so many people—my parents, my brother, the woman I intended to take as my mate—all because Joseph and Maddox wouldn't simply *leave*. If they hadn't been such selfish fuckers, the people I lost would be alive now."

Raini gave a slow shake of the head. "It wouldn't have happened that way, Euan. Louis wanted to take away the strongest descendants to make *your* lair easier to wipe out; he knew you'd be too powerful to defeat otherwise. It's a trick that's been used many times before. Louis would have returned to your lair another day and destroyed you all. If Maddox and his father had tried to seek vengeance, they'd have been killed, too."

"You're wrong. It was no trick. It was a genuine offer. All Joseph and Maddox had to do was transfer to another lair. It's not difficult to switch. People do it all the time. But they wouldn't, and now so many are dead. Maddox knew he had every chance of surviving. He knew it was possible he'd be made Prime if our own died. *That's* why he refused to go. And he *was* made Prime, and now he also has a mate. Why should he get to have everything when, because of him, I was left with *nothing*?" he clipped with a snarl, his eyes cold and dark as flint.

"It was never really that you wanted to rule," Raini realized. "You just wanted to see him fall."

"And he will. He has no chance against an archangel. None. Maddox will die tonight. So will you. I will take everything from him that means anything to him, just as he did me."

Bile burned the back of her throat. "Euan—"

"I will let him watch you die, just as I watched the woman I loved die. And then I will watch *him* die. But first . . . " He fired two bullets.

Maddox ground his teeth as a gold energy ball smacked into his hand; the impact reverberated up his arm. The orbs packed a real fucking punch. It was like being hit with red-hot electricity. It jarred. Zapped. Burned. It also seared cloth and skin. He was thankful that the archangel didn't seem able to scatter-shot it, because if any slivers of that energy buried themselves inside Maddox, he had the feeling they could kill him from the inside out with no trouble.

Maddox retaliated fast, firing off a series of hellfire orbs in quick succession. Three clipped Castiel's head, another struck his shoulder, and the latter hit his chest—adding to the many burns, blisters, and scorch marks he already sported.

Hissing, Castiel jutted out his chin. "You can fling as many of them at me as you like. They will not kill me."

No, they probably wouldn't. But the pain would tire him. It *was* tiring him—which was why he'd ceased flying around in an effort to both dodge the orbs and grab Maddox. It hadn't really helped Castiel much anyway, since Maddox could easily teleport from one spot to another to elude the archangel.

As Viper had warned, Castiel was far from weak. He was sharp, swift, strong. It was clear he was no stranger to battle. He could even withstand the deadly effects of the ice-cold energy Maddox conjured. Any slivers of it that buried themselves in Castiel's body seemed to hurt him, but no more than that.

The archangel's biggest weakness was that he relied too much on holy fire. He wasn't adept at fighting without it or falling back on his other abilities, so he was flailing a little here. And Maddox was fucking enjoying it.

"I *will* end you," Castiel swore. "I will end your entire lair, including your anchor."

His demon pulled back its lips, baring its teeth. Like Maddox, it was sick of listening to Castiel's repetitive threats of how he'd do this, that, and the other. Still, just hearing the archangel mention Raini made the entity want nothing more than to bludgeon the bastard to death with his own fucking leg.

"So you keep saying," said Maddox. "But I'd be surprised if you truly believe it."

A rush of adrenaline spurred him on as he attacked with a combination of hellfire, ice-cold energy, and telekinetic power. Castiel ducked, dodged, and retaliated, his reflexes admirably quick.

Around them, voices grunted, cried out, yelled warnings, or laughed. Yeah, the Black Saints laughed a lot. Like this was merely a rough-and-tumble Thanksgiving football game among relatives. They either did it to infuriate their opponents or they genuinely found some joy in battle. If it was the latter, Maddox could relate. He'd always enjoyed being in battle. There was always a feeling of . . . release when he broke into violence.

He and Castiel both stilled as a halo-bearer zoomed through the air between them and crashed into a nearby statue, sending it sprawling to the ground along with him.

"Your numbers are dwindling," said Maddox. Bodies littered the ground—bitten, broken, blistered, and bloody. *All* were halo-bearers.

Castiel scoffed at the corpses. "They were weak."

No, the Black Saints were just *that* good. Maddox was right in predicting that Viper's brothers weren't common types of angel. They were too fast, too powerful. And they were definitely seasoned fighters. A few had suffered fatal wounds, but then they'd fed on halo-bearers and, that easily, they'd healed.

Maddox wasn't sure if *all* blood healed them that fast or only holy blood. Whatever the case, it kept the Black Saints strong. He also wasn't sure what the hell those ultraviolet fiery orbs were—probably some warped version of holy fire—but they were potent enough to wrench cries of agony out of their opponents.

Castiel whipped up his arm, and the head of a statue sailed through the air. Maddox sidestepped it easily, and then they were fighting again, each striking with telekinetic power—punching, shoving, kicking, choking. Maddox knew he'd have bruises, because each hit landed like a damn mallet. One caught him in the kidneys, sending pain rippling through him.

His demon surfaced a few times, determined to get a few licks in. Maddox welcomed each surge of adrenaline. With the strain of shelving his pain and expending so much psychic power, he could feel himself tiring. It was slowing him down, which he fucking hated. The only reason the archangel hadn't been able to take advantage of it was that he too was slowing.

Just then, Castiel hurled an orb of holy fire—something he did occasionally, as if he hoped it would begin to affect Maddox at some point.

Sighing, Maddox slanted his head. "Surely your minion told you that holy fire can't harm me."

A resentful snarl twisted Castiel's face. "The holy blood in your veins is strong. It is only that that keeps you alive. If you were pure demon, I'd have killed you by now."

"If you were fit to be one of the Seven, you'd have killed me by now."

His neck corded, Castiel let out a battle cry and attacked again.

CHAPTER TWENTY-THREE

Red-hot pain exploded in Raini's kneecap as the bullet slammed into it like a hammer. The second bullet punched her other kneecap, subjecting her to another blast of unbearable agony. There was no holding back the scream—it erupted out of her throat as bones shattered and her legs went out from under her, and she landed hard on her butt.

Panting, she hovered her hands around her wounds as she stared in shock at the blooming red stains on the torn ice-blue denim jeans.

"Hurts, does it?"

Hot tears stung her eyes and, honest to God, she was surprised she hadn't passed out. She'd never felt pain like it *in her life*. It stole her breath and made nausea rise up fast.

Euan chuckled, his eyes lit with delight. "Oh, this is brilliant. Maddox will go *berserk* when he sees you like this. Hurting. Bleeding. Shot."

Raini glared up at Euan, air bursting in and out of her lungs.

Her demon surged to the surface and said, "That was very stupid. I would have killed you quickly. It would not have been painless, but it would have been swift. But now? Now I will see that you suffer for a very long time."

"And how is it you'll do that?"

The demon let a slow smirk curve its mouth and then subsided.

Euan sniffed at Raini. "If that entity of yours thinks it can call my bluff and scare me, it's wrong. You and I both know you have no way out of this situation. Perhaps you've told yourself differently and clung to some hope that Maddox would save you, but you know deep down that it won't happen."

"Sometimes hope is all we have," said Raini, her breathing still not steady. "So I can hope your plot falls apart. I can hope Maddox, his allies, and the lair survives. I can hope you'll pay for this for years to come. It's not such a far-fetched hope. All your other plans went to shit, didn't they?"

"You think you can push me into killing you here and now so that Maddox won't have to see you die?" He snorted. "Sorry to disappoint you, but I am not so easily manipulated. And there is no way that you or your demon will convince me that you are a threat." He sneered. "You can't even get up."

Not keen on being reminded of that, she clenched her teeth so hard it sent a shooting pain along her jawline. That twinge was *nothing* compared to the blinding agony lancing through her knees. It felt like they'd been showered in acid and were now blazing with fire.

There'd be no fleeing from him when he teleported them outside. Hell, there'd be no *crawling*, let alone standing or running. Not when her kneecaps were shattered and so many tendons and muscles were ruptured. Her legs were useless to her right now.

Oh, he was gonna pay for this shit. She wasn't sure how or when yet, but she'd make it happen.

Her demon sent various images flashing around Raini's brain—Euan being tossed at the stone wall; bullets being fired at his dick; a cheese grater being dragged down his face, shredding flesh. Yeah, those ideas worked for Raini.

"How sad that the person who can heal you is just outside but will soon be dead." Euan tipped his head from side to side, as if to get some cool air on his throat. Probably because the crimson flush on his face had spread down his neck.

"You really haven't thought this through," said Raini, still panting. "Not if you don't think people aren't going to find it a little fucking suspicious that you weren't battling alongside your lair."

"I intend to claim I was part of the battle; that I was left for dead but managed to survive. It's not like the angelic bastards out there will come down from their precious realm to contradict me, is it? Trust me, Raini, I have all my bases covered. People have always underestimated me. I suppose you and I have that in . . . " He paused, as if struggling to find the word he was looking for. His pupils were now dilated, and there was an almost imperceptible quake in his voice. "Common," he finished. "We have that in common."

Raini shook her head. "Doesn't matter. My lair will question what happened here. They will. Because your plan to set Dwain up failed. I don't know if you personally edited my sister's memories or you had someone else do it but, whatever the case, it wasn't the grandest job. Maddox could tell they were altered and that Dwain wasn't her captor."

He stiffened. "You lie."

"Nope. My family all know it was someone else. They want him bad. And since *you're* one of the original suspects, they'll take a nice, long look at you. And what will they find, Euan? They'll find the miraculous survivor of a battle during which *I* died. That'll be enough to make them want to have a lengthy chat with you. And here's the best part. You won't have a Prime anymore, you'll be a stray, so there'll be no one to hold off Jolene. Declaring yourself a Prime won't *make* you one—not if you have no other members. You'll still be a stray."

A vein in his temple pulsed. "Even if I believed that they know your sister's memories were edited—which I don't—it matters not. They will never find me."

"You intend to hide, huh? Some Prime you are," she taunted.

The skin around his eyes went tight. "Such big talk for someone who is facing death." More sweat dotted his forehead, and there was now a slight tremor in each of his hands—both of which she suspected were clammy at this point. While it wasn't exactly comforting to see them tremoring when he was holding two guns, it was nice to see that the pheromone was working so well.

"Now, I think it's time for us to head outside, don't you?"

Her heart jumped. "You think Castiel won't kill you?" she blurted out, hoping to keep him talking a little longer. "He wants every last descendant dead, Euan. That includes you."

"Right now, his priority is ending Maddox. Castiel won't be interested in me until after my cousin is dead—I'll have teleported away by the time he thinks to turn his attention to me."

"He'll hunt you down, no matter how long it takes. He wants to be one of the Seven. He isn't going to let *anything* get in the way of that."

"On the contrary, I think he'll be inclined to let me live as a thank-you for helping him defeat Maddox."

He couldn't be serious. If anything, the archangel would be insulted that someone thought he *needed* aid—especially the aid of a demon.

"Part of me worried that Castiel would kill him early in battle.

But as you're not enduring unimaginable psychic suffering, the anchor bond must still be alive and kicking, which means Maddox obviously is, too." He double-blinked and licked his lips. Finally seeming to notice the tremor in his hands, he frowned. "What's wrong with me? I feel . . ." He trailed off, and his eyes narrowed on her. "What have you done?"

She made sure she looked appropriately confused. "Nothing."

"Again, you lie." Snarling, he kicked at her knee. A broken scream tore out of her as a fresh wave of agony exploded inside her knee and reverberated up her leg. Spots danced in front of her vision, her stomach heaved, and she almost retched. God, she was gonna be sick. The pain was so intense she couldn't quite catch her breath.

Hating that she couldn't just wrench those guns out of his hands and liquefy his fucking brain, she took in a slow, shuddery breath. And another. And another. And another. She wasn't going to let him reduce her to this . . . creature that knew only pain and couldn't think beyond it. No. No, he wouldn't break her.

Finally feeling she could move without vomiting, she struggled back into a sitting position, biting back whimpers at how her knees throbbed and burned.

"You do look quite pathetic."

Trembling uncontrollably, Raini bared her teeth at him. She wasn't sure if she'd ever hated anyone as much as she did him at that moment. Her demon was going absolutely ape-shit, wanting him dead, buried, and then resurrected to endure torment all over again.

"I am rather looking forward to the moment when Maddox sees you're about to die," Euan went on. "He won't save you, nor will you save yourself. Cease trying to fight me—it is useless."

If he thought she would just accept her fate, he was out of

his everloving mind. But it seemed better to let him believe she was subdued. Hoping to look the image of defeated, she forced her shoulders to slump and let the tension deflate from her muscles.

He snickered, all scorn and derision. "Do feel free to scream again when we're outside."

In other words, he probably meant to kick her again.

Her surroundings flashed white, and then the three of them were a short distance away from the courtyard, where the battle still raged on around the bodies that littered the floor. Those still fighting were covered in burns, blood, and bruises. As for Maddox and Castiel, they were still engaged in a face-off, appearing evenly matched.

She instantly reached out to Maddox, *Euan means to distract you so that Castiel can end you—don't let him, be on your guard.* It was a mere second later that Euan called out her mate's name.

Castiel whipped around, an orb of gold energy in each hand, while Maddox's gaze snapped to Euan before then dipping to her. A look of such fury rippled across his face before he blanked his expression . . . as if unwilling to let his emotions get the better of him. Well, thank Christ for that.

Sensing something was happening, the Black Saints and the halo-bearers ceased fighting but remained on high alert.

Euan shot Maddox a smug smile and waited, clearly expecting him to rant or threaten him, or maybe even beg him to free her. Maddox didn't react at all. He just steadily met his cousin's stare. But she could feel his rage humming against her psyche. It was ice-cold and ran soul-deep.

Knowing his demon would be experiencing that same ire and not trusting that it wouldn't surface and reign fresh hell, Raini again reached out to Maddox. *Stay calm and think. Please don't give Euan what he wants. You won't get out of this alive if you do, and neither will I.* It wouldn't hurt to remind either Maddox or his demon what was on the line.

Euan's smile faltered when Maddox gave no reaction. "Don't think I won't hurt her. As you can no doubt see, I have no issue with doing that. I can imagine you're tempted to do something extremely stupid—your little succubus experienced that same temptation. She paid for that." It was a pure taunt. It didn't spur Maddox into exploding, though.

Raini kept flicking her gaze from him to Castiel to the other players on the battlefield. The archangel repeatedly glanced from Euan to Maddox, and she suspected Castiel hoped Euan would do something to weaken her mate. The halo-bearers kept glancing at their leader, looking for direction, while the Black Saints watched them closely.

"Before you think to order me to release Raini and Carmen, know that it won't happen," said Euan. "They'll die here. As will you and the rest of the lair. If your allies have any sense, they will leave now and save themselves." The Black Saints didn't move from where they stood. Euan snickered. "How very noble of them."

"*Some* people have honor," Raini sniped, hoping to push him into turning his attention to her. Given how agitated Euan was—courtesy of the pheromone—it hopefully wouldn't be hard to provoke him into making a mistake, which would give Maddox an opportunity to strike.

His lips flattening, Euan cast her a sideways glance. The tremors hadn't left his hands, and sweat now dripped down his temples. "You can blame yourself for this, Maddox. You failed to see the part I played in ensuring the misery of your anchor. It was *I* who hired the harbinger. *I* who betrayed her secrets to her lair. *I* who handed her to Gunther on a silver platter. I even kidnapped her sister and that Dwain fellow. You didn't see it. You failed her. And now you'll suffer the consequences. You'll suffer as I suffered."

Raini sighed. "Oh, for God's sake, will you just get the fuck on with it? No one cares how smart you think you are or what games you've been playing—they've kind of got bigger things going on right now."

Euan's nostrils flared, but he still didn't look at her. "You know what this is about, Maddox. You know how many people I lost because of you and your father. Well, now I mean to return the favor. Now you will know how I felt."

Raini made a bored sound. "Oh, dear Lord, is there no way to shut you up and hurry this along?"

A snarl contorted Euan's face. She watched his foot, knowing he meant to kick her knee again. Maybe her reaction would be a foolish move, but she didn't have any other moves to make—none that wouldn't for certain lead to either her or Carmen being shot in the head, anyway.

Time seemed to slow down as he lifted his foot and kicked out. Before it could connect with her knee, she caught his ankle, twisted it, and yanked hard. He fell on his butt, his arms flailing, and a gunshot cracked the air.

Quick as damn lightning, Maddox teleported to them . . . but not soon enough to stop Euan from once more pointing the gun at her head.

Castiel took advantage of Maddox's distraction and began attacking with a fury, hurling orbs of crackling gold energy. But her mate had obviously already anticipated that, because he'd popped up a forcefield the second he landed before her—it encompassed him, her, Carmen, and Euan. The orbs couldn't pass through it.

Sadly, due to Euan's closeness to Raini and Carmen, there'd

been no way for Maddox to exclude him from the forcefield without also excluding either her or Carmen.

Letting out a nervous chuckle, Euan kept the gun aimed at Raini's head as he got to his knees and then moved up behind her. He'd seemingly dropped the other weapon, to her utter delight. Using her as a damn shield, he jabbed the gun hard against her temple. But that was good, because she'd finally got what she wanted—he was close.

"That was very foolish, Raini," he admonished.

She turned her head slightly toward him, her mouth mere inches from his cheek, and said, "But effective."

"That depends on what way you look at it. Yes, I now only have one gun, but it's pointed *at your head*. And Maddox might be here, but that only means he gets an up-close view of the moment you die."

"Hmm, and then you'll teleport away, right?" She felt her brow crease. "Oh no, wait . . . you can't get out of this forcefield unless he lowers it, which he ain't gonna. So maybe I *will* die right here. But so will you. Actually, no, Maddox is more likely to keep you captive and torture you until the end of time."

"Drop the gun," Maddox said to him, his voice so casual and controlled that it made her nape prickle.

Euan huffed. "Oh, I think not."

A muscle in Maddox's cheek ticked. "Drop. The. Gun."

"And give you the opportunity to kill me? No. I'll make you a deal instead. If you lower the forcefield, I will teleport away without killing her."

"But then the archangel would get us," Raini pointed out, "so he ain't gonna do that either."

"Shut up," Euan hissed without looking her way. He lifted his brow at Maddox. "Do we have a deal?"

Her mate's eyes bled to black. Uh-oh. Even Euan stilled.

"This is your last chance," it told him. "*Drop the fucking gun.*"

"Or what?" challenged Euan, a tremor in his voice. "You have no moves to make here."

Raini snickered. "Not sure if you've noticed, big guy, but neither have you."

Maddox's eyes returned to normal as his demon retreated. "She's right. You have no way out of this."

"The same applies to your mate," Euan pointed out. "So it would seem we're at an empasse."

"It's *im*passe, you moron," Raini snarked.

Euan growled and, keeping his eyes on Maddox, twisted his head toward hers—that was all she needed.

She swiftly pressed her lips to Euan's and blew power into his mouth. Power that she knew would rush to his head like the sweetest, most intoxicating perfume. He blinked hard, swayed slightly, and stuttered out a breath. As his eyes then glazed over and he looked at her with utter adoration, Raini smiled.

She'd enslaved the fucker, Maddox quickly realized. His mate had the ability to enslave with a mere kiss. At any other time, it might have irritated him that she hadn't told him about it. Right then, Maddox couldn't give a fuck. Because she was *alive*, and that ability had saved her.

"Put down the gun," she whispered to Euan, who obeyed without hesitation. "Good boy. Now sleep, and do not wake until I call for you to do so."

The asshole slumped to the ground, his eyes closed—essentially out of commission.

"Baby." His pulse not yet steady, Maddox crouched down and plastered his palm to hers, his teeth grinding at the sight of her wounds. His demon was no less enraged, despite that she was now safe from Euan.

She hissed at the cold burn as his power healed her, but then the lines of pain smoothed away from her face. He grabbed her head and kissed her hard, aware that the battle had picked up again; aware that Castiel was yelling for Maddox to face him. Maddox would. But not until she was out of harm's way.

"Help Carmen," she said.

Once he'd healed his sentinel, Carmen came to with a groan. "Mother of Christ, my head hurts." She lifted said head, glanced around, and frowned. "What the hell—*Euan*. Is he dead?"

"Not yet," said Maddox, though he was highly tempted to snap the fucker's neck. But that would be too painless. No, he and his demon wanted Euan to *feel* death coming, and it eventually would. But then Maddox would heal him, and they'd do the dance over and over again.

"You missed a lot," Raini told Carmen as Maddox pulled her to her feet. "I'll fill you in later."

"It's not over yet," said Maddox. "Carmen will get you out of here. Stay with her."

Raini fisted his shirt. "No, not yet. I can end this."

He stilled, him and his demon both balking at the idea. "No, you need—"

"Listen to me. The bastards are all away from Celia now." Which told her that people had likely been wavering from one spot to another to evade strikes. "I can send out a blast of psychic hellfire without hitting her, but not without hitting *you* or—"

"I'm not leaving your side," he gritted out.

"I'm not asking you to, Maddox. As long as I'm standing in front of you, you'll be safe from the blast. But I can't let it out while I'm in here—the walls will keep it trapped. Shrink this forcefield slightly so that it only surrounds you, Carmen, and Euan—no, hear me out. I need to be exposed long enough to release the psychic hellfire. I don't know how much damage it will do to the archangel, but it will take the halo-bearers down in an instant. Then you can finish off Castiel. Unless you *want* to go through this battle all over again another day. Because none of this will be over until he's dead."

"The second you're not shielded, those orbs that bastard's throwing will hit *you*."

"But then you'll heal me. Look, I get that it goes against the grain for you to expose me while shielding yourself. It's not like that, though. I *need* you to do exactly that, or you can't encompass me in this big bubble again and then heal me once I've done my thing. Come on, Maddox, they won't expect this. It'll work."

"I'd have to agree," Carmen cut in. "If you can think past all that overprotectiveness, so will you."

Maddox pulled in a breath through his nose. Hadn't Raini already been through enough tonight? He didn't want her here, where she could be hurt again. He also didn't want her being targeted by Castiel or halo-bearers ever again, but she was right—none of this would stop until the archangel was dead. And so far, Maddox hadn't been able to take him out. This *had* to end today—even his demon could acknowledge that.

Grinding his teeth, Maddox said, "Fine. But once you're done here, you let Carmen take you off this damn battlefield and back to the cathedral's attic with Euan."

"I will, I promise. Staying here, I'd only distract you. I don't want to do that. Tell the Black Saints to scamper in exactly four seconds so that they're out of range of the blast. We'll then make our move after the count of three."

Maddox quickly gave Viper a telepathic heads-up, knowing he'd spread the word to his brothers. "Done."

Raini blew out a breath. "Three, two, one."

It all happened fast. The Black Saints disappeared. He shrunk the forcefield. An orb of crackling gold energy headed straight for her. The air rippled and shimmered as the psychic hellfire blasted outwards and smacked into Castiel and his minions. And the fucking orb hit her dead center in the chest.

Biting out a harsh curse, Maddox enlarged the forcefield and caught her before she could crash to the ground. He slammed his palm to hers and watched as her skin reknitted and the blisters disappeared. Only then did he look at the battlefield. The halo-bearers were sprawled on the ground—some unmoving, some convulsing.

Castiel was on his knees, his hands gripping his head tight.

"Wow," Carmen breathed. "They dropped like stones."

"Fucking good," muttered Raini, now steady on her feet once more.

Maddox squeezed his mate's nape, dancing his gaze from her to Carmen. "The moment I drop this forcefield, you go and take that shit-stain with you."

"We will," Raini vowed.

Maddox whirled to face Castiel and lowered the forcefield. "Go." He sensed the wave of energy in the air and knew Carmen had teleported them out of there. He took slow, deliberate steps toward the archangel just as the Black Saints reappeared. Maddox didn't look at them. He only had eyes for Castiel, who flexed his hand, clearly trying to conjure another orb of energy. He failed.

Halting in front of him, Maddox said, "I wouldn't bother trying to fight what's now inside you. You can't. It's working its way through your mind. Much more slowly than it ate through theirs," he added, briefly glancing at the dead halo-bearers, "but it'll consume yours sooner or later."

Castiel blinked up at him, the epitome of confused.

"I'd imagine you're wondering what's happening to you. Have you ever heard of psychic hellfire?"

Viper let out a low whistle. "Oh, he's dead for sure."

Castiel's eyelids flickered, his gaze lost focus, and his face drooped.

Maddox slanted his head. "You know, there's something almost . . . dishonorable about taking advantage of your weakness and killing you now. The thing is, well, I don't really give a shit. Not only did you hurt my mate and start a battle with my lair, you've done it to others. So many descendants have died because of your ambitiousness. Even one death is too many. So, on behalf of all of them . . ." Maddox fisted Castiel's hair, wrenched his head back, and forced an ice-cold energy orb down his throat.

The archangel choked, heaved, shook, swayed, arched. Then he slumped to the ground, his skull caving in.

The crackling forcefield around the monastery winked out. The crushing power that had held Celia in its grip must have released her, because she cried out and fell to the ground.

Sidling up to Maddox, Viper winced. "Archangels can heal from a lot, but he ain't coming back from that."

"Just to be sure . . ." Maddox lit up the body with hellfire, planning to ask his lair—who were now filing out of the monastery—to do the same with the other corpses. None of the dead were Black Saints, which was no surprise, given how goddamn quickly they healed and how the angelic blood seemed to strengthen them.

Viper hummed. "That psychic hellfire sure did come in handy."

Maddox turned to face him. "I appreciate you honoring our agreement and joining this fight—I won't forget it. If you ever need to call on me for backup, I'll provide it. But my mate won't. She's no weapon." His demon nodded, in full agreement.

"Not sure she's the type to sit at home while you fight. Just saying." Viper saluted him. "I guess I'll see you at the club." He disappeared, and his brothers then did the same.

Hector materialized beside Maddox, his jaw hard. "We all watched the whole thing through the windows. I've never felt so goddamn helpless. No matter how hard we attacked the forcefield, it wouldn't go down. I nearly lost my mind when I saw Carmen on the ground. I saw you heal her. She's okay?"

"She's fine," Maddox confirmed. "She's in the attic of the cathedral with Raini. They're keeping watch on Euan."

"We couldn't properly hear what he was yelling," said Hector. "What was all that about?"

"I'll tell you everything once we've both collected our mates."

CHAPTER TWENTY-FOUR

Placing the fresh cup of coffee on the nightstand, Maddox looked down at his sleeping mate. The amount of psychic energy she'd expended had taken its toll on her. She'd stayed awake long enough for him to collect her from the cathedral so that she could see for herself that he was fine, but then she'd gone out like a light. It was only during the past minute that she'd begun making slight fussing noises that said her sleep was no longer so deep.

She had no idea, but the bedroom had been jampacked with people up until half an hour ago. It was shortly after he'd cleaned the blood from her skin and put fresh clothes on her that members of his lair had trickled into the room to ask how she was doing. Sometime after that, several of Raini's circle had arrived.

They'd somehow learned of the attack before he had the chance to contact Jolene. Unsurprising, really. Imps had "ways" of finding things out.

A bunch of people—including Raini's parents, uncles,

Harper, Devon, Khloë, Knox, and Knox's sentinels—came to get a good look at Raini. Despite the amount of noise in the room, she hadn't stirred—not even when Khloë gently poked her forehead while weirdly threatening to draw a baby hippo on her face.

They eventually left, content that Raini was fine, but not before inviting themselves to dine with his lair. Maddox was quite certain that everyone was surprised by how easily they gelled with his demons. Lachlan and Hector got along like a house on fire, and Evangeline had quickly befriended Celia.

After learning of Euan's guilt, Jolene and her group had requested access to him. Courtesy of Raini's compulsion, Euan was still sleeping deeply. Maddox had known that by "access," Jolene meant she wanted to introduce his cousin to brand-new levels of pain.

Maddox had promised that the imps could have their fun with Euan once Raini woke him, *providing* Jolene didn't object to Maddox having "access" to Demi. Raini's sister might not have worked alongside Dwain, but she'd done nothing to stop him. She'd essentially given him the green light to continue hurting Raini. She'd *enjoyed* knowing that her sister was suffering. Demi had betrayed his mate on several levels.

If they had known of Dwain's guilt sooner, they would also have learned that he wasn't responsible for *all* that was happening. As such, they would have known that another person was targeting Raini; that they needed to take a closer look at the other suspects. And Maddox could have stopped Euan before his cousin went so far as to capture and shoot her.

In sum, Demi *did* have a part to play in the mess. She wasn't responsible for the actions of others, but she herself could have acted in ways that saved Raini further pain. But Demi simply hadn't wanted to.

Jolene had balked at Maddox getting near Demi, though.

The Prime didn't trust that he wouldn't trap Demi in a permanent psychic time loop. Which was perceptive of Jolene, really. She'd proposed that *he* punish Euan and that *she* punish Demi. Maddox had agreed after Carmen telepathically pointed out that Raini wouldn't like him hurting her sister. Such a thing could come between him and Raini in the long run, no matter how upset his mate presently was with Demi. Plus, Maddox would also have made enemies of her parents, which would have pained Raini—he didn't want that.

Perching himself on the edge of the bed, Maddox skimmed his fingertips down Raini's bare arm. A little line formed between her brows, and his demon smiled. He'd never known anyone to be so difficult to wake. It took over a minute of him idly stroking her skin and talking quietly to her before he was able to fully rouse her.

As her eyes fluttered open, Maddox's mouth curved. "You're finally back with me."

Groaning, she probed her temple. "My head feels all cottony. How long was I out?"

"A few hours." He helped her sit upright and then handed her the drink he'd set on the nightstand. "Your family and your girls came. They stayed for a while, but when it became clear you weren't going to wake any time soon, they left."

Cradling her cup with both hands, she took a swig of her coffee. "My dad didn't threaten you again or anything, did he?"

"No, but he did make me promise to perform certain methods of torture on Euan. Want to tell me what happened with the little bastard? I'd have questioned him already if I could wake him. You didn't tell me you could enchant with a kiss. Not even when Hector asked if there were succubae who could."

Pleased her mate didn't seem annoyed about it, Raini shrugged one shoulder. "I like to keep you on your toes. As for Euan, well, it turns out he was hiding in the cathedral." Between sips of her coffee, she relayed the entire story, watching as Maddox's face became increasingly darker. "To sum up, he needs to die a very terrible but not imminent death."

"Agreed." Maddox settled a hand on the coverlet above her knee. "He'll pay, baby." There was so much menace in those three words that her scalp prickled.

Returning the cup to the nightstand, she moved to straddle him and interlinked her fingers behind his nape. "Thank you for healing me. I knew you would."

He curled his arms around her. "I might not have been able to. If either of the bullets had hit a thigh artery, you'd have bled out long before he took you to the battlefield. I wouldn't have been able to save you."

She hadn't thought of that. "But you did save me. And Carmen. How is she?"

"Pleased to be reunited with Hector, even though he rebuked her for stupidly feeling guilty that Euan got his hands on you."

Raini felt her brow furrow. "That is stupid. It wasn't her fault."

"When I realized that Demi's memories had been edited, both Euan and Marcella became my top suspects. I wouldn't have left you in the cathedral if I'd thought either of them could get to you. It never occurred to me that either of them wouldn't be in the monastery."

"Same here." Euan had taken them all off-guard, the prick.

"Hector had noticed that Euan was missing during the battle, but he'd thought that maybe Euan had gone to the club. Hector couldn't telepath him to check because of the forcefield that surrounded the monastery. The entire lair is disappointed that they weren't able to join the battle."

"Thank God you had other backup. Your Fallen friends . . . they were full of surprises."

"I owe them."

"But I'll bet they owed you first—I know how you operate."

Maddox's mouth quirked. "That you do."

"Where's Euan now?"

"In the cellar beneath the cathedral. And he won't be getting out of it alive."

Her entity was *all* for that plan. "Both me and my demon want some time with him," she warned.

Maddox hummed. "I figured you would."

"My dad and Jolene will want to have a share of the fun, too."

"Actually, Jolene and I came to an agreement." Snaking his hands up her thighs and under her tee, Maddox explained the conditions of said agreement. "You're relieved I won't be disciplining your sister," he sensed, watching her carefully.

Well, yeah. "Jolene's harsh, but you're . . ."

"Sadistic?" he offered.

"*Your demon* is sadistic. You're brutal. Which isn't bad. It's just that she's my sister. She fucked up. Majorly. And I know, I *agree*, that she needs to be held accountable. I'm—"

"Far too compassionate for your own good."

"Not exactly. It's more that, well, it might not mean much to her that we're sisters, but it still means something to me—we did have *some* happy times when we were younger and . . . Why are you sighing at me like I'm hopeless?"

"Baby, I love you, I do, but you need to get that I won't give someone a free pass to hurt you merely because they're a relative of yours. I made an agreement with Jolene, and I'll honor it. But if Demi does anything else at all to hurt you, I *will* deal with her."

Gaping, Raini stared at him. "You love me?"

"Yeah," he replied with an "obviously" look.

She swallowed, her chest tightening. "Well, do you know that I love you, too?"

The hard set of his mouth softened. "I do now."

"Good," she said, her voice low.

He sipped from her mouth, keeping the kiss soft and shallow and lazy. Yet, every nerve ending she had woke right up, and the good ole tingles came back in full force. Because he loved her. She'd thought he might feel that way *one day* far off in the future. Not so soon.

Feeling in the mood to celebrate it, she nipped his lower lip and asked, "Want to shower with me and play doctor again?"

One corner of his mouth quirked. "Sure." Palming her ass, he lifted her. "But be warned that there's a strong chance my demon will take over at some point and brand you again—it's still wound tight after seeing you injured with a gun pointed at your head."

"Your entity has shown it has good taste where brands are concerned, so I'm okay with that."

"Well that's good, because it wouldn't have cared if you weren't."

She snickered. "Considering how possessive it is, that doesn't surprise me."

CHAPTER TWENTY-FIVE

One month later

"Adorabella?"

"No."

"Queenie?"

"No."

"Albert?"

"No."

"Barney?"

Tanner growled at his mate. "We're having a baby, not a purple fucking dinosaur."

Devon crossed her eyes. "God, pooch, you're so picky."

"And you're not drinking enough water." He pushed a bottle into her hand. "It's important for you to stay hydrated."

Raini stifled a smile. He'd been overbearing as hell since learning Devon was pregnant. It was cute, but it was also grating on the hellcat's nerves. Hence why she kept suggesting baby names that she knew would annoy Tanner.

Maddox had insisted on going ahead with the party that Raini had organized, only he'd turned it into a "welcome to my lair" party that doubled as a celebration for their mating, so here they were at the casino Raini had chosen as the venue. He'd headed to the restroom with Hector, leaving her with Carmen, of course. His protectiveness hadn't eased up, despite the danger having passed.

Built into one of the many luxury Underground hotels, the casino boasted high ceilings, mirrored walls, patterned carpets, rows of backlit gambling machines, and a small bar where patrons could sit, talk, and drink. People were scattered around the room at the various tables, or sitting on stools while playing machines. There was a lot of noise and activity. Slot machines blooped and bleeped. Dealers called out for bids. Dice tumbled along felt. Alarms dinged to announce winners. Voices muttered, cheered, or cursed.

Pretty much all the guests who Raini had invited were in attendance. The imps mixed surprisingly well with the descendants. But then, the two breeds did have one thing in common—they dealt with a fair bit of scorn from other types of demon.

The casino workers—who were no doubt usually stoic when dealing cards—appeared somewhat paranoid and anxious. Understandable. Imps were fucking brilliant at cheating, but you'd never catch them at it unless they wanted you to. It wouldn't surprise her if they made off with some of the luxury prizes that were on display. Probably not the cars or motorcycles, but definitely the jewelry.

"We should go find a seat, kitten," Tanner declared. "You shouldn't be on your feet."

Devon shot him a look of exasperation. "I've only been standing for, like, twenty minutes. Before that, we were eating our meal while watching the band play in the restaurant."

"Twenty minutes is a long time."

Devon turned to Raini, her eyelid twitching.

Raini felt her lips curve. "He's going to be hell to deal with throughout the entire pregnancy."

"Don't I know it," Devon mumbled.

"Do you think the baby will be a hellcat or hellhound?" Carmen asked her.

"Hellcat for sure." Devon sniffed, all superior. "My kind have more dominant genes."

Tanner snorted. "If you say so." He tapped her bottle. "*Now drink*."

Instead, his mate lifted a brow at Raini and asked, "So, how is being a Prime working out for you?"

Raini flicked a hand. "I leave the Prime stuff to Maddox. I'm not interested in leading."

"That doesn't mean you're not his co-Prime," Carmen pointed out.

"Well we can pretend it does." Raini had figured, what with him being so controlling, that Maddox wouldn't want to share his power. That would have suited her fine, because she wouldn't know the first thing about leading a lair. But he wanted them to be partners.

She'd officially moved in with him the day after the battle. Although she missed being part of the same lair as her parents, there was nowhere else she wanted to be.

"Has Marcella left yet?" Devon asked.

Raini nodded. "She scuttled off to her new lair last night." After which Raini had done a mental fist pump.

The hellcat sipped her water. "Did you speak to her before she left?"

"Only to say 'bon voyage.'" Raini had somehow managed to keep the sarcasm out of her voice.

Devon snickered. "I hear you'll soon be saying the same to Demi."

"Yup." Raini sighed. "I'm not all that surprised she wants to leave her lair, considering everyone kind of turned on her."

"It's no less than what she deserves," insisted Tanner.

"That's what pretty much everyone says." Dwain's parents *badly* wanted her gone—in their mind, if she'd told someone he was behind the boycotting, Jolene would have detained him . . . thus robbing Euan of the chance to capture Dwain. His parents essentially blamed Demi for his death.

"I can't help but notice that she isn't here," Tanner added.

Raini had anticipated that her sister wouldn't show. "She won't go near Maddox, which is probably for the best."

Tanner's mouth quirked. "He still wants to dole out a punishment, huh?"

"Oh yeah," Raini replied. "Knowing Jolene took care of it isn't enough for him. He works off the rage on his brand-new personal punching bag."

"As in Euan?"

"Yes. I'm getting the sense that the guy is going to be a guest of ours for a *long* time to come."

Just then, Martina approached wearing a wide smile. "See what I got from one of the boutique stores over there?" She stroked her handbag. "Isn't it fabulous?"

Raini didn't doubt for a moment that the woman had stolen it. But she didn't ask, because her attention was snatched by something else. "Do you realize someone drew on your face?"

"Oh yeah," said Martina. "Khloë drew a baby hippo on me. She called it Fritz. Is it cute? She said it was cute."

Devon choked down a laugh. "It's, um . . . something."

It was a dick was what it was. But before Raini could say as much, the imp had hurried off to the craps table. Raini might have followed her if Lachlan and Bram hadn't then appeared.

Bram elbowed her and opened the plastic bag he held. "Hey, get a look at our winnings."

Raini felt her mouth tighten. "By winnings, you mean the money you stole from whatever machine you broke into?"

Lachlan sighed. "Now don't go making a big deal out of us purloining a little bit of cash. We're not harming anyone."

"You're committing a crime," she pointed out.

"Which the economy would thank me for."

"Knox won't. The Underground is his baby, which means—in a roundabout way—you just stole from him. Could you not put the money back?"

"Returning to the scene of a crime is a surefire way to get caught. We could probably do it without him noticing, but it won't be long before the cameras switch back on. The security system wasn't easy to hack into, you know. I was impressed. Ah, that mate of yours is on his way over. I'm starting to like him. Sort of. It's a slow process."

"I hope this means you'll stop conjuring knives in his presence."

Shaking his head, Lachlan let out a heavy breath. "You get upset about the strangest things."

She frowned. "How is it strange to—you know what, I can't do this with you."

"You should be thankful I'm such a protective father. But no. You always go whining that I'm being unreasonable. I liked none of your boyfriends, but I was perfectly civil to all of them."

"You put a shock collar on my prom date."

"You said he liked surprises."

Reaching her side, Maddox slid an arm around her shoulders and looked from her to Lachlan. "Everything all right here?"

"Raini's just making a fuss about nothing again," her father said. "Come on, Bram." The two male imps stalked off.

She looked up at Maddox. "I hope you're being careful not to let any imps too close, because they don't care who it is they're stealing from. Anyone is considered fair game."

"I'm aware," her mate said, lifting her hand. His mind then touched hers. *My cock gets hard every time I see this ring on your finger.*

She smiled. *I've noticed.* As he'd promised—well, it had often come out sounding more like a threat—he'd given her a black diamond. She'd asked him to wear the matching masculine version, and he'd easily complied. Her demon *loved* looking at the ring—it was totally into bright, shiny things. Raini was more wowed by what the jewelry represented, which was that Maddox had fully committed to her—body, mind, and soul.

It won't be long before the party's over, Maddox went on. *Then I can take you home, and we'll have our own private celebration.*

Hmm, I'm up for that.

Thought you might be. Cupping his mate's elbow, Maddox led her to another cluster of guests. He wanted to get the mingling over with. For hours they walked from group to group, thanking guests for coming. Carmen and Hector stayed close at all times.

At one point, they got talking to Harper and Knox. The other male Prime was still somewhat stiff toward Maddox, but not rude or uncivil. He appeared to be reserving judgment. There was none of the typical Prime posturing, though.

As he often did, Maddox glanced down at his mate, who was somewhat tipsy at this point. So she almost stumbled when she leaned into Harper and asked, "Where's Levi? He's usually never far from Knox."

Maddox quickly steadied Raini, who didn't seem to notice.

"Either brooding or solving his problem," replied the equally tipsy sphinx, mirth in her eyes.

Raini straightened, seemingly intrigued. "Ooh, expand."

"Well . . . he found his anchor," Harper went on in a whisper that was much louder than she appeared to realize.

Raini's nose wrinkled. "And this is something he'd brood over or consider a problem?"

"I'm not yet sure how he feels about it, I just know it stunned the shit out of him." Harper put her hand on Raini's arm. "We bumped into a few of our lair members at the mall, one of whom is the sister of Levi's ex—a sister he watched like he wanted to devour her. He barely spoke a word to her, though. I don't know who initiated the psychic contact between them, but someone must have, because they both had a weird 'what the fuck?' moment and then Levi was staring at her exactly like a demon stares at their anchor—"

"Waini!" Asher shouted, dashing toward her with Keenan and Khloë hot on his heels.

"I'll tell you the rest later," Harper told Raini.

"Hey, little man." Grinning, Raini scooped him up and righted his collar. "Damn, you're rocking this outfit. It's super cool."

Harper snickered. "You would say that. You bought it."

"I like making sure my honorary nephew has style." Noticing he was holding something, Raini frowned. "Hey, what you got there? A credit card, by the looks of it. You and those sticky fingers."

Khloë chuckled. "Having the soul of an imp makes life supremely entertaining."

Carmen's lips twitched. "You think so?"

"Yup," said Khloë. "Because my life is supremely entertaining."

"Your life is mostly chaotic," Carmen pointed out. "Not so long ago, there were attempts on your aforementioned life by a

Lazarus demon who was intent on revenge after you played some part in his resurrected daughter being returned to her natural state of death."

"And you didn't find that entertaining?"

"*I* did," announced a new voice. And then none other than Lucifer—yes, the devil himself—joined their group. He smiled at Asher. "And there's my favorite nephew and future partner in crime."

Harper ground her teeth. "Okay, I *know* for sure you were not invited."

Lou smirked at her. "You missed me, right?"

"Oh, my middle finger is saluting you as we speak," said the sphinx.

Lou lightly patted Maddox on the back, like they were old friends. "Good seeing you."

Knox frowned. "You sounded like you actually meant that."

He did. Which was perplexing, yes, because Lou didn't appear to like anyone other than Asher, from what Maddox had observed.

Lou gave Knox a baffled look. "The man was involved in the demise of one of those holy farts from upstairs. More, he carries the blood of a being who did the right thing and fell to Earth long ago. Why *wouldn't* I find it good to see him?" His gaze slid to Raini. "Ah, how happy you must be to no longer have Jolene as your Prime. Switching lairs was a good call. These Wallises . . . there is no end to their evil. Not even when they marry a Thorne."

Harper rolled her eyes. "He's still sulking because Knox and I don't agree that he should be Asher's full-time carer," she explained.

"It's only right that I have quality time with my protégé," said Lou.

"Stop calling him that," Harper clipped.

"I'd make a damn good manny."

The sphinx snorted. "You have absolutely no conscience, a total lack of empathy, get stoned every day, and relish the thought of all life on Earth being eradicated."

Lou waved an encouraging hand. "Keep going, that's it, allow the hate to flow through you."

"I don't hate you. I just think you're a nutjob."

"You'll need to repeat that in my other ear. This one doesn't give a shit."

Flames abruptly burst to life around Asher. Then they were gone, along with the little boy.

"Shit, where'd he go?" Raini frantically spun around, as did the others.

Maddox pointed to the luxury car on display. "He's in there."

Harper threw up her arms. "Dammit, kid."

God, she had a pussy-eating champion right here.

Raini wasn't shy or demure in bed, so she had no problem shamelessly arching into Maddox's mouth. The man was good with his hands, but his tongue absolutely stole the show—tracing and swirling and dipping and swiping.

She fisted the bedsheets. He hadn't even stripped off her clothes. Nope. He'd tossed her onto the bed, flipped up her dress, ragged off her panties, parted her legs, and set about driving her insane with his mouth.

He was succeeding.

The man. Had. Skills. *Serious* skills. And now she needed to come *so damn bad*. But no amount of appeals, curses, pleas or threats was making him give her what she wanted.

"Maddox, don't make me come down there!"

He lifted his head and speared her with those intense eyes.

Eyes that then bled to black. His demon was now in charge. Awesome. Because it looked in the mood to slam home and fuck her raw.

It stood upright at the foot of the bed and fisted its cock. "If you want it inside you, you will have to earn it."

Oh it was a bold fucker. She went to sit upright so she could suck it off, but the demon shook its head.

"You will make yourself come. I want to watch."

It wanted a show, right.

Well, Raini proceeded to give it a show, following its instructions—pumping one finger into her pussy while using her free hand to cup her breasts, twist her nipples, and play with her clit. Sometimes the demon wanted her to thrust her finger hard, sometimes the entity wanted her to merely rub at her sweet spot. She did as the demon asked, because she knew from experience that it was the fastest way to get what *she* wanted.

"You have been a very good girl for me," it said.

Why yes, yes she had.

It withdrew her hand from her pussy and flipped her onto her stomach.

Booyah. She heard a zipper lower and did a mental happy dance. She'd just pushed to her hands and knees when the demon rammed into her pussy with such force it stole her breath. And she came—there was no stopping it. Her release tore through her body hot and fast, making her head snap back and her eyes go blind.

When her orgasm finally subsided, the demon curled over her and put its mouth to her ear. "Now, thank me for letting you come."

She gawked. Thank it? Jesus, this fucker could be *such* a pain in her ass. "Thank you," she said, a bite to her voice that earned her a gruff chuckle.

A soft kiss was pressed to the back of her shoulder—a gentle move that told her Maddox was back in control.

His hand delved into her hair and fisted tight. "Now *I* get to make you come."

Sounded good to Raini. She expected him to start powering away, but his thrusts were soft and shallow and far too freaking slow. "Maddox . . ."

"What is it, baby?"

"You damn well know what. I did everything your demon asked, and I expect—no, *demand*—to be rewarded for it."

Maddox felt a smile tug at his mouth. "You *demand* it, do you?" He loved that. Loved how she boldly sassed him. Loved how greedy she could be.

"Yes, I do. No more teasing. I'm done with the teasing. Fuck me."

He smoothly buried his cock balls-deep and swiveled his hips. "I say we make a new deal first."

"A new one?"

"Hmm. There are several conditions." He slowly reared back and then just as sluggishly drove his full length back into her pussy. "You must never leave me, you must never take off that ring, and you must never stop loving me. In return, I'll make you those same promises. Do we have a deal?"

Without hesitation, she replied, "Yeah, deal."

"That's my girl." Her hair still wrapped around his fist, Maddox pounded into her pussy. His thrusts were wild and violent and utterly unrestrained. Exactly what they both wanted and needed. "I'm going to keep fucking you so hard so often you'll never remember a time when you weren't taking my cock." She wouldn't remember how it felt to have another male inside her, only him.

He kept on slamming deep and rough, knowing it wouldn't

take long before he came—not after he'd eaten her out, watched her little show, and felt her explode around him not so long ago. Considering she'd already had an orgasm, he hadn't expected another to build so fast, but it wasn't long before her pussy began to tighten and flutter around him.

"That's it, baby, come." He snatched her head back, bit into her throat, and brought his hand down hard on her ass. Her inner muscles clamped around his dick as she came with a scream. Her blood in his mouth, he slammed into her again and again and again. Then he exploded.

When his brain switched back on, he blew out a breath. "Fuck, needed that." He released her hair and soothingly stroked her scalp. "You good?"

She slumped to the bed, resting one cheek against the mattress. "Your demon is seriously arrogant and annoying at times."

Maddox felt his mouth quirk. "I know. It gets off on messing with your pretty little head." It liked to see her nervous, unsure, and out of her comfort zone, but never in a way where it would want her to be upset or afraid.

"I've noticed. You're both dominant, control freaks."

"Agreed." He leaned down and pressed a kiss between her shoulder blades. "But you can handle us."

"Hmm."

He placed his palm to hers and pushed just enough power in her to heal the weeping bite on her throat. "You love me?"

"Of course. Always will."

He let out a low hum of satisfaction. "That's what I like to hear."

"I like to hear it, too. Why am I not?"

Feeling his lips curve, Maddox nuzzled her nape. "Demanding, snarky little minx at times, aren't you? It's a good thing I love you."

"How could you not when I'm this damn fabulous?"

"Hmm, fair point." He pulled his softening cock out of her and then cleaned them both up. Settling on the bed beside her, he drew her close. "Did you enjoy the party?"

"I did. It was nice having everyone in the one space like that, even if half of them were robbing the place blind. I was kind of surprised that so many turned up."

"By that, you mean you thought there would be several from your old lair who wouldn't attend purely because of your ability to wield psychic hellfire," he guessed.

"Yes. But aside from a few like Risa and Dwain's parents, they all came, and they were all perfectly pleasant toward me." She doodled circles on his chest with her fingertip. "Maybe they're not so much bothered by what I can do now that I'm part of your lair."

"Or maybe now that the shock has worn off and they've had time to think, they've realized they acted like assholes."

"Hmm, maybe."

"I noticed Demi didn't attend."

"Neither did Levi," Raini said quickly, clearly not wanting to remain on the subject of her sister. "Harper said he's found his anchor."

"Yes, I heard her mention it to you. The sister of his ex, right?"

"Yup. Depending on how well he gets along with his ex, that may or may not prove to be a complicated situation. Whatever the case, I can't see Levi walking away from his anchor. Not even to appease his ex."

"He'll find it a struggle if he does decide to fight the bond. I never had a prayer of holding out. Maybe I knew that. Maybe I knew that if I put you in my path often enough I'd eventually give in. Maybe that was what I wanted, despite knowing you would learn things about me and my kind that it was better you never learned."

"You know your secrets are safe with me."

He combed his fingers through her hair. "I do. Speaking of secrets . . . There's a little something I haven't yet told you. Well, it was more that I haven't had the chance to tell you until now. I only learned of it earlier today."

Raini's eyes lit with interest. "Oh? Spill."

"Celia has the occasional . . . well, I wouldn't call them premonitions. It's not a warning system—the ability is too weak to serve as one. But she sometimes sees snapshots of the future. Some are of senseless, boring things. Some are a little more significant." He paused. "Sometime after you saved Gunther, she saw a 'snapshot' of you and me near the cathedral. We weren't alone. There was a little boy and two little blonde girls with us. She couldn't give me accurate descriptions—the visual was gone too fast for her to absorb any specifics. But she thought we might like to know."

Raini's face went all soft and warm. "Why didn't she mention it before now?"

"You and I hadn't fully committed to each other at that point. She didn't want to influence whatever decisions we made. Some are uncomfortable at the thought that, beyond us having predestined psi-mates, certain things are inevitable. She worried one of us could have gotten spooked and pulled back from the relationship. I wouldn't have, though. And I don't think you would have either. I wouldn't have let you. You and I were inevitable. I took too long to see that. But now that I have, I'll never let you go."

"I don't intend to go anywhere. We made a new deal, remember?"

He nodded. "We did."

A huge smile took over her face. "A boy and two little girls, huh?"

"You're good with that?"

"Oh yeah. You?"

"In all honesty, I never gave much thought to having children until she told me of her vision. But yes, I'm good with it." He was about to comment on how great she was with Asher, but then he received a short telepathic message that made him inwardly sigh.

Her brow creased. "Something wrong?"

"That was Hector. He caught your father and his brothers trying to remove one of the stained-glass windows from the cathedral—apparently, they sell pretty well. Lachlan told him he'd give me 40 percent of the profit. Naturally, Hector sent them on their way. And he thinks one of them might have taken a shit close by."

Flushing, Raini squeezed her eyes shut. "That will have been Bram. I'm sorry. There's no excuse for them." She let out a tired sigh, and then her eyelids fluttered open. "Really, I should have guessed they'd do that. One of the first jobs my dad took me on was a cemetery heist."

"What exactly is a cemetery heist?"

"He stole—or purloined—some flower arrangements, religious statues, chapel windows, and then even went grave robbing. You'd be surprised how many people buy corpses. It's kind of disturbing."

Maddox smoothed his hand up her back. "Baby, as much as I like your father, I don't think it would be good for him to ever be around our kids without supervision."

She blew out a breath. "Yeah, that's probably a good call."

Acknowledgements

Thanks to my family for all their support, especially my son who listens when I complain how my characters won't do what I want them to do. Thanks to my assistant, Melissa, for everything she does—a lot of which goes above and beyond what a PA should do. A huge thank you to everyone at Piatkus, particularly Anna Boatman, for all the time and energy they invest in this series. Last but definitely not least, thank you to all those who have taken a chance on the *Dark in You* novels. I love you all for it.